Fae

THE REALM OF TWILIGHT

BOOK TWO OF THE RIVEN WYRDE SAGA

BY GRAHAM AUSTIN-KING

THE RIVEN WYRDE SAGA

Fae - The Wild Hunt
Fae - The Realm of Twilight
Fae - The Sins of the Wyrde

For Tristan

Savarel

Widdengate

Kavtrin

ANLAN

Celstwin

Feldane

Hesk

The Barren Isles.

The Vorstelv

CHAPTER ONE

Gavin stirred in the darkness of the cellar and opened his eyes to the gloom. It was still some time before dawn, he could tell that much by the inky blackness. The room never really became fully light, even in the day, but there were enough cracks and missing stones to let small shafts of light filter in. This, though, was the true dark of night. He shifted slightly on the straw-stuffed sacks under the blankets that served as his bed and listened to the susurration of the children in the room around him, breathing in their sleep.

He stared into the darkness as he wondered what had woken him up, and was just beginning to feel the edges of sleep reach for him again when he caught the noise - the faint sound of a bare foot and a metallic clank, followed by a whispered curse. He rolled out of his bed and picked his way to the corridor, moving more from memory than by sight. As he turned the corner to head towards the kitchen, the sight of flickering candlelight caused him to pause. Robbery among the Wretched of Hesk was rare, but not unheard of. There was little in the kitchen worth stealing - a small amount of food and perhaps some kitchen implements. The real value of the cellar lay in the shelter it offered.

Gavin shifted his weight and prepared to ease into the kitchen, but then the light went out. A patter of quick feet carried easily to him and he swore silently as he followed. Trading stealth for speed, and trusting that the intruder's own noise would mask the sound of his passage, he made his way along the corridor as quickly as he dared as he followed. He clambered out over the broken stones of the partially-collapsed building that stood above the cellar, and made his way out into the night.

The skies were clear and the half-moon lit the filthy alley enough for him to catch the shadow as it darted away. He swore again and raced after it. There was little point in stealth now.

Gavin had been raised on the streets and, though his diet hadn't always been the best, his body was well used to racing through Hesk's back alleys and spider-web lanes. He was more used to fleeing than to chasing after someone, but running was running. A life of picking pockets and stealing from market stalls had given him good reflexes and fast feet. He ran out of the alleyway, as the intruder sped away from the backstreet slums and towards the city centre.

A loose stone kicked away from his bare foot and clattered noisily across the cobblestones. He caught a flash of pale skin, as the person ahead of him glanced back and then sprinted through the night. "Shit!" Gavin lengthened his stride and strove to narrow the gap. His feet might not be as fast as the distant burglar's but his longer legs made up the difference and he began to close.

Forgotten lanterns hanging on the occasional building spilled light out onto the streets, though most were dark and cold, and Gavin could easily see the distant figure as he ran. He allowed himself to drop back slightly. Catching the intruder would only answer half of his questions, he told himself. It would be better to discover where they were going.

The streets were largely silent and, even at this distance, he could hear the slap of the thief's feet on the flagstones. They slowed and then stopped for a second before moving on. Whoever they were, they thought they had lost him. Gavin's grin was a flash of white in the dark as he ran on, silent feet carrying him after the distant footfall.

The alleys and narrow streets slowly gave way to broader avenues as they moved into the richer areas of the city. Finally, as they approached the centre of the city, the intruder slowed and then stopped to look up at the darkened stone building that was the massive cathedral of the Church of New Days. The church had moved on since its early days and the chapel in the back streets of Hesk had long since been abandoned when the grand cathedral had been constructed.

The Wretched had always been welcome in the church, and the priests had done their bit to keep them clothed and fed as best they could. A church orphanage had been open for a number of years now, but even those children that chose to remain on the streets could come there for aid. Street children from all over the city had learned to accept the place as a refuge, but there were rules. No theft would be accepted, even amongst each other, and fighting would result in a strict ban.

Gavin's smile was mirthless. The thief would find no refuge in the cathedral.

Every Wretched in Hesk knew that once the small side door closed at dusk, it would not reopen until the morning's first light. He watched as the figure moved towards a small, cobbled side street leading to the rear of the building. *Where was he going?* That route went alongside the high-walled cathedral gardens, leading to the opposite end of the building from the side door. Gavin's curiosity was aroused now, and he followed at a distance and watched.

The figure reached into a sack, and withdrew a length of rope and a three-hooked grapnel. Gavin started as he realised that this was what had been taken from the cellar. Burglary was far too risky for most of the Wretched. It took a patience and skill that had taken him years to develop. He'd mostly given it up. It was too much of gamble, even for him, these days. Although he might be able to make more in one night than in two months of begging and picking pockets, the threat of having an eye put out - or worse - was enough to put him off. He wasn't just looking out for himself anymore.

The thief kept to the shadows as he shook out the rope and made sure it was tied fast to the grapnel. As he swung it experimentally, a lock of blonde hair escaped from under his dark, hooded cloak. Gavin looked at the figure again, taking in the slight build and lack of height, and swore as realisation dawned on him. He ran towards the figure, all efforts at stealth forgotten, and closed swiftly as the grapnel swung round through the air, crashing into the figure before it was loosed. The pair of them tumbled to the ground in a tangle of arms and legs, whilst the iron hooks clanged loudly against the stone wall.

"Tessa!" Gavin gasped, as he struggled to his feet. "What in the hells are you doing?"

"This doesn't concern you, Gavin," the slight young woman said, as she dusted herself off and bent to retrieve the grapnel.

"Doesn't concern me?" he hissed. "The hell it doesn't! I haven't seen or heard a thing from you in almost a year. You vanish from the orphanage without a word. Now, months later, you sneak into my cellar in the dead of night to steal this thing." He waved at the hook she was stuffing into the bag. "And this doesn't concern me?"

"No," Tessa replied, in a cool tone. "You really ought to go home. We've made enough noise here already."

Gavin sputtered at her as she coiled the rope neatly and threw the loop of the bag over her shoulder. He looked around quickly. Dawn was still hours away, judging by the light, but she was right. His attention was drawn by a sudden flash of lantern light reflecting on the damp cobbles. He grabbed at her arm and ran for the other end of the narrow street.

"You there, stop!" The cry came up from behind them and the sound of heavy boots pounding on the cobbles echoed along the street, followed by the piercing sound of a whistle as they fled into the night.

"Constables?" Tessa shot him a filthy look as they ran. "Really, Gavin, can't you at least try to be quiet?"

He ignored her, pulling her across a broad street and into another narrow alley, its corners piled high with broken crates and refuse. The constables of Hesk were no serious match for any true member of the Wretched, but they could be annoyingly dogged. They ran through the alleyway, leaping over the rubbish that seemed intent on tripping them. A darkened doorway caught Gavin's eye and he pulled Tessa to a halt. They pressed deep into the shadows, her breath hot on his neck as they huddled back against the half-rotted door. The place had probably been a tanner's at some point. It had long since been abandoned, but the stink of ammonia and sewage still clung to the place.

He pulled up the hood of Tessa's cloak with one hand and buried his face in the rough cloth as best he could, hiding his skin from the light of the approaching lantern.

The clump of the constable's boots heralded his arrival far more than the glimmer of lantern light that carried through the rough fabric of Tessa's cloak. His steps slowed and then stopped as he turned, first this way then that. "Damned street-rat bastards," the man muttered. He hawked and then spat.

The spittle struck the stones not three feet from Gavin's huddled form and he felt Tessa shaking in his arms. In truth, they had done nothing wrong but being found in this area of the city, at this time of night, and carrying a grapnel would raise questions that Gavin was not prepared to answer.

The Wretched and the constables of Hesk had an odd working arrangement. It was an accepted fact that the thieves of the city would never really be stopped. The constables tended to turn a blind eye, so long as the Wretched kept their activities within acceptable limits. Minor acts of theft from market stalls or the disappearance of the occasional purse were largely ignored. Burglary in one of the most affluent areas of the city would not be. A beating was more likely than arrest, but neither option especially appealed to Gavin.

He squeezed his arms slightly against Tessa, trying to reassure her with the pressure. A faint squeak was followed by a metallic scrape on stone and then the puffing sound of the constable lighting a pipe. "Too old for this nonsense, anyway," the man muttered to himself in between puffs. Tessa's trembling became more pronounced. Gavin risked a peek as the light began to recede and, as he watched the constable make his way out of the alley, he realised with shock that Tessa wasn't trembling. She was laughing.

He stepped back from her and fixed her with a sour look, as she pulled her cloak straight and came out of the doorway. Her elfin face was twisted into an image of barely suppressed mirth.

"Don't you think you owe me some kind of explanation?" he said, with a scowl.

"Well, they are a bit funny," she grinned. "I haven't had this much fun in months."

"I meant an explanation for what the hell you are doing!" Gavin grated, his temper fraying.

She looked back in the direction of the cathedral. "They have Khiv," she said and the humour drained from her face like wine from an upturned glass.

"Khiv? Your brother?" Gavin asked, unnecessarily. "I thought Ylsriss put him in the church orphanage? Surely he's supposed to be in the cathedral? Hell, I thought you were there too!"

"Oh Gavin, I'm too old for that sort of thing. But Khiv..." She looked down at her feet and cleared her throat, making a rough tearing sound. "There are stories, Gavin. Children disappear from there. There are empty safeholds all over Hesk where children of the Wretched were sleeping only two nights earlier. It's even worse in the orphanage, though."

He looked around. "We shouldn't talk here. Come on." He led her back through the twisting streets and alleyways to the cellar.

The cellar was still filled with the faint sounds of sleeping children as they made their way quietly through the corridors to the kitchen. Gavin waved her into the room and closed the door tight behind her. Waking the children was the last thing he wanted to do. He pointed to a chair at the makeshift table that had managed to last through the years, despite all the odds.

"Sit," he said, and bent to get a fire going in the small wood stove. The stove was easily the most valuable item in the cellar. Small and compact, it was nonetheless made of thick cast iron and it would have taken three strong men to move it. He blew gently onto the wisp of old frayed rope he had been striking sparks onto until it started to smoke. Reaching into the stove, he blew again as he touched the faintly glowing rope against the dried leaves and slivers of wood. Within moments, he had a small fire going. Tessa watched with a faint smile as he fed first twigs, then sticks and then more substantial pieces of wood to the fire. "You were always better at that than anyone else, even Ylsriss," she said.

Gavin grunted and shrugged as he filled the heavy iron kettle and then set it onto the stove to boil. "Why don't you start at the beginning, Tessa," he said, as he sat down across from her at the table. "I thought Ylsriss had you settled in at the church orphanage before she left?"

"She settled you in there too, Gavin, as I recall."

Gavin cleared his throat and clasped his hands together on the table to stop himself fidgeting. "It wasn't the right place for me. Too long on the streets."

"Yes, well it wasn't the right place for me either," Tessa replied, a little harsher than she had intended. She reached across the table for his hand, but then thought better of it and pulled hers back awkwardly into her lap. "You're right though, about being too long on the streets." She shot him an apologetic smile. "It changes you. I don't think I could live a life like normal people do now."

Gavin nodded and glanced over his shoulder at the kettle. "So you left? What about Khiv and all the other little ones?"

"They're why I left. I couldn't fit in, couldn't accept the things they were trying to teach us. Letters and all that stuff about their Lord." She curled her lip in derision. "If their God is all powerful and loves us all so much, then why are people living in the streets? Why are there merchants getting rich from selling over-priced food to people who can barely scrape by?"

Gavin shrugged again. "I didn't make the world, Tessa. I just do what I can to get by in it."

"Well, that's why I had to leave, Gavin. The little ones deserve better than what we have. If the orphanage can give them that with their letters and learning, then that's great. I could feel them watching me though, following my lead. They'd never have had a chance so long as I was still there."

"But Khiv? You left your own brother?" Gavin's voice was hushed because of the children, but even so his tone did little to soften the accusation.

"He was better off without me, Gavin," she replied, in a flat voice. "They could give him things that I couldn't. I would just have led him back to the streets in the end."

"Which brings us to tonight," Gavin said, as he stood and turned to lift the hissing kettle from the stove with a thick, fire-scarred cloth. He went to the corner and returned with two chipped cups and a small earthenware jar, stoppered tightly with cork. As he worked the top loose and carefully poured a small measure into the cups, her eyes widened. A strong, rich smell filled the kitchen as he added the steaming water. "Is that keft?" she asked, in hushed, almost reverent, tones. "Where in the Isles did you manage to get that?"

Gavin grinned as he handed her the cup filled with the steaming dark liquid. "A Dernish scow came to trade about three weeks ago. You know how lax they can be about guarding their ships. Honestly, they're so interested in the whores and taverns, it's a wonder they ever have anything left to sell!"

Tessa laughed as she sipped at the cup, sucking the liquid through her teeth to strain out the grounds. "It's been a long time since the Dernish tried a trade. We don't have much to offer them."

Gavin sat across from her and fixed her with a serious look. "I think we've danced around this enough now, don't you?" She swallowed slowly and then gave a small nod.

"So explain." He folded his arms and sat back, waiting.

She curled her hands around the chipped cup and looked across the room into the darkened corner as she began to speak. "I used to go and visit Khiv. Not as often as I should have, but every month or so, just to check in, you know? He was doing well. You remember how thin he used to be?" Her eyes flicked at him long enough to register the nod, then her gaze drifted away again as if seeking a corner in which to hide.

"He was filling out and he was doing well in their lessons. He'd learned things I could never get my head around. Figuring and letters, not just the God stuff. Anyway, I got busy with stuff. Life got in the way, you know?" Gavin didn't nod this time. He just looked on, as impassive as stone.

"I guess a couple of months slipped past, maybe three or four. Then Elsra came to find me."

"Elsra?"

"Tiny little thing, like a waif. You must remember her, Gavin, surely?"

"It's not important. Go on."

"She'd been out on the streets for three or four days before she found me. She was soaked through and she'd obviously been sleeping in doorways. It's a miracle she wasn't snatched up by one of the perfumed ladies and put in a brothel. She's pretty enough once she's cleaned up. Anyway, she'd made so much noise asking after me that I found her myself easily enough." She looked at him, fear plain on her face. "She told me that children were disappearing from the orphanage, Gavin. They were there one day, and then gone the next."

"I expect that they leave all the time, Tessa," Gavin said, but his voice did not sound convincing, even to himself.

She gave him a frank look. "They do, but not like this." She pinched at the bridge of her nose and sighed before going on. "Some children leave. They are not locked in, they are free to leave any time they like. This wasn't like that, though. Elsra and Khiv were close, I mean really close. He was never the strongest boy and places like that breed bullies. Those two clung together and tried to stay out of the way of the others. Then, one morning, he was just gone, without a goodbye, without a word." She reached over the table and took hold of his forearm in her hand. "He wouldn't have done that, Gavin. Not without even saying goodbye."

"No one ever really knows what someone else is capable of, Tessa." He spoke the words softly, avoiding her eyes.

"Oh come on, Gavin," she said in disgust. "Use your brains. Even if everything I've said is wrong, why is the place never fills up? I've heard the thanecourts are even placing street kids in there now when they catch a pickpocket, instead of breaking their fingers. It should be crammed to the rafters, but somehow they always have room for more. That just doesn't make sense."

"Okay, I believe you." He squeezed her hand where it gripped his arm, twisting his wrist slightly to encourage her to let go. She had dug her fingers in like claws and he rubbed his wrist gently while holding her gaze. "So why were you trying to sneak in there?"

"Because it's not just the children that are vanishing, there are babies that have gone too. There in the evening and then gone the next morning. Elsra told me that the priests say they have been adopted, but why at night? She told me she's seen priests waking children in the night and leading them out of the orphanage. They don't come back. Something very strange is going on there. She's not as hard as some of the Wretched, but she's still a brave girl. Gavin, she was terrified. She was shaking when she told me."

"What have you done with her?"

"I've left her with a friend for now. She'll be fine for a few days.

He shook his head and then reached both arms up into a deep stretch. "So you thought you'd break in and then do... what?"

"To be honest, Gavin, I really hadn't thought that far through it. I was going to have a look around for starters."

He snorted in disbelief. "Sure, you were just going to scale the walls and sneak into one of the most powerful organizations in Hesk. Where did you have next on your list? The reaving schools? The thane's palace?"

She glared at him silently, drawing her legs in under the chair and crossing her ankles as she grasped her cup, her knuckles turning white.

"I'm sorry," he mumbled. "Look, I know you're worried. Have you been to speak to the priests?"

"I'm not an idiot, Gavin, of course I have," she snapped. "They told me that he'd left. I don't believe them."

"Why haven't you been to Ylsriss with this?"

She looked at him with a mixture of pity and scorn. "With what? All I have is the word of a scared child and the feelings in my gut. That's why I was going in to look. Besides," she said, with a toss of her head, "Ylsriss left over a year ago!"

"No, she's back. In a merchant's house, close to the new market square."

She stopped at that, her eyes narrowing in thought. "I don't know what she could do..."

"More than we can. She's important now. People will listen to her."

"I still need to go in and look around first," she said, clenching one fist in expectation of the response. "I'd need something solid to go to her with."

"*We* will go in and look. But tomorrow night now, and on my terms."

"I hardly-" She cut off as he raised a finger warningly.

"We're not going to discuss it. Meet me outside the Pig and Whistle tomorrow night, three bells past midnight."

"Gavin, you don't need to -"

"Yes, I do," he interrupted. "I owe your brother, if not you. You should have come to me first, instead of just stealing the grapnel. Now, you're going to have to leave. The little ones will be up soon and I don't want questions being asked that I don't want to answer."

She gave him a strange look and then left without another word. Gavin sat at the rickety table slowly drinking his keft. He knew what the look had meant. Why was he helping her? In truth, he wondered about this himself. He didn't really owe her anything, no one on the streets ever really did. You lived in isolation. Sure, you might group together for protection; you might even work together on a job. The reality of it all, though, was that they would all abandon each other without hesitation if it needed to be done. The only one he'd ever known who was different was Ylsriss. That was what the look had meant. He'd picked up the pieces Ylsriss had let fall. Maybe one day he'd be able to let them go himself.

He moved mechanically, his mind far away in thought, as he filled a large pot with water and set it on the stove to boil. The keft had left grounds in his teeth and he worried at them with his tongue as he worked. The smallest of the children were soon up and eating the watery porridge he had produced. Before long, they were filing out of the cellar, some with arms wrapped in slings, some feigning missing legs by binding them up tight inside their clothes, as they went out to work the crowds with begging bowls.

The older children would be sent to pick pockets and steal what food they could from the market. Such was the life of the street children of Hesk. There was a reason they were called the Wretched. All too soon, the cellar was silent again and Gavin made his way up the stone steps, through the ruins of the building, into the sunlight and onto the streets.

CHAPTER TWO

Gavin wandered through the city streets. He had no real destination in mind and he simply drifted, moving easily and allowing the press of the crowds to direct his travel.

Though the fleets of reavers had gone to the Farmed Lands, Hesk was still a busy place and the numbers pushing through the streets seemed undiminished by the war effort. The shops were still as busy and the market still as loud, with stall owners calling out their wares. Ahead, through the sea of bobbing heads, he caught sight of the tall helmet of a constable strolling with the crowd. Gavin smiled to himself. The constables were a blessing to any skilled lifter. Most people believed that no thief would dare to operate near a constable. They unconsciously relaxed, dropping their guard. They may as well have just handed their coin over to Gavin.

He sliced the purse of a fat merchant, his hands working almost without him thinking about it. His knife was sharp enough to cut through the strings without even the slightest tug. Only a rank amateur sliced the purse itself just to catch a coin or two. He walked casually into an alleyway and turned out of sight before breaking into a run. Three turns later and he dropped back into a walk, bouncing the purse in one hand with a grin. The sprint was just force of habit. He'd been too smooth of a lifter for years for anyone to have noticed, but it never hurt to be a few streets away by the time the mark discovered the theft. Luck was a fickle mistress and he knew better than to trust to her changing moods.

He would have loved to waste the day away, but there were things that he was going to need. A glance inside the purse revealed far more coins than he had expected, and he headed further into the maze of alleyways, deep into the slums.

A trip to a grimy back street and a knock on the right door earned him fresh greys, a shapeless mass of clothing in a strange mixture of colours, ranging from dark green to smoky grey. The outfit was loose-fitting and hung in an odd fashion, but it would serve to break up the shape of a man in the night. Gavin had never had to rely on greys himself, but he'd been told that wearing them when standing in shadows had saved the necks of more than one thief. Another two visits provided him with a newer, stronger rope than the frayed mess that Tessa had been about to use and a wickedly sharp knife, far longer than the finger-length razor he used for lifting.

The day passed too swiftly for his liking and he soon found himself back in the cellar, trying not to seem too distant as he gathered the children together for a late dinner. There were twenty children in all, ranging from fourteen, only few years younger than himself, to as young as six. As he watched them eat, he suddenly had second thoughts. *What was he doing?* He had a responsibility to these children. Only two of them had left the orphanage with him. Another eight or nine had found their way to him over the next few months. The remainder had never been inside the orphanage at all, but had found their way to him over the following months and years, drawn to him like stray dogs will form into a pack.

He looked around the cramped kitchen, letting the sounds of eating and conversation wash over him as he poked at his food, a heel of bread and something masquerading as a stew. He would be risking a lot to do this thing for Tessa. But then, he wondered, did they really need him? They had gone out onto the streets and come back with money and food. What did he provide for them that the cellar didn't provide itself? Tessa had been one of the ones he'd left behind. If he'd tried to talk her into leaving with him, then would Khiv have been sat at this table with them both now?

As the meal ended and the children began to drift away, he collared one of the older ones and explained he would be working that night. It was a while since he'd done it, but they all knew Gavin wasn't above a little burglary. Working the streets might net you a purse full of coppers, but then there were also days when it would get you nothing but a chase through the streets with an overly eager constable blowing his whistle. An occasional burglary had made the difference for them all more than once.

He sat at the table and stared at the flicker of the flames through the vents in the front of the woodstove as he sipped at another cup of keft. It wouldn't keep for much longer anyway and the bitter drink would help to keep him awake.

As midnight came and went, a gentle rain began to hiss down onto the cobbled streets. He stood in the crumbling cellar entrance, tucked into the corner of the half-collapsed building, watching the sparkle of the raindrops as they were caught in the moonlight. Eventually, the second bell sounded, mournful and subdued in the distance. He checked over his pack one last time and stepped out into the drizzle.

The streets were silent. Even those who had staggered late out of taverns and into the wet had long since found their way home. Either that or they had passed out in a gutter that had conspired with alcohol to make itself seem appealing. The night was his alone. There were certain to be other thieves out at work and the constables would still be patrolling, albeit reluctantly in this weather. They were more likely to be holed up in accommodating doorways, smoking until either the rain stopped or they forced themselves out onto the streets. Despite this reality, Gavin had always thought of the night as his own.

He moved steadily, keeping to the shadows where possible and listening carefully for telltale footfall. The constables were more or less inept, but nobody could have mistaken his intent, dressed in greys. The constables were actually the least of his worries, though. He would have to pass through the territories of two of Hesk's more vicious street gangs on his route. If he was seen, it would result in somebody bleeding and he hadn't the time. In spite of all this, his form would have seemed relaxed to any onlooker as he made his way towards the city's centre in his strange, grey clothes.

He spotted Tessa as he approached the Pig and Whistle. She was crouched on the rooftop of a building at the side of the alleyway that faced the inn, seemingly oblivious to the rain. She would have probably been overlooked by anyone else on the street. It was almost certain that she'd have been missed by anybody honest. Normal people didn't tend to look up at the rooftops, especially when it was raining. Gavin had only caught sight of her when she shifted slightly, probably to ease a cramp. He stepped out of the shadows and raised a hand in greeting, watching as she made her way to the edge of the roof and climbed down with a fluid grace.

She eyed his greys and the small pack he had slung over one shoulder, and nodded to herself as he approached. "Are you ready?" She didn't bother with a greeting.

"As I will ever be, I suppose."

Tessa led him through the streets, casting sidelong smirks at him as he hunched down deeper into his greys against the wet. The wind was picking up and the drizzle drifted in under the hood of his cloak, clinging to his hair and forming larger drips which worked their way down his neck. He swore under his breath and swatted a drip away for the third time, ignoring Tessa's quiet chuckle as they rounded the corner and stood before the cathedral.

The building was enormous. Whilst impressive in the daylight, most of its majesty was lost at night. The towers were hidden by the gloom, and the building squatted in the square as if it hadn't the strength to stand erect, brooding and forbidding as it shrugged at the darkness.

Dark windows on the second and third floors added to the image, combining with the shadows to make it look as if it was glaring out at the city. Gavin had always been able to form faces out of images. Even as a small child, he'd been able to think himself into nightmares by forming faces in the grain of the wood of his bed. He glanced up at the cathedral and gave an involuntary shudder, turning it into a shrug to mask it from Tessa.

"How were you planning on getting in?"

"The gardens are just on the other side of the wall you found me at last night." Her voice was just louder than a whisper. "From what I can remember, there are enough small trees and bushes on the other side to conceal us as we're coming over the wall. We should be under cover, even if someone is watching. From there, we'll play it by ear."

"Glad to know you've thought this all through so well," Gavin muttered, and walked into the alley. He kept to the shadows again almost without thinking about it and his soft boots made no noise as he passed over the cobbles. In the daytime, he didn't bother with boots, but tonight the pale skin of his feet would have drawn the eye. He ducked into the shelter of an overhanging roof and shook the worst of the water from his cloak as he waited for Tessa to catch up with him. She held out a hand and he pulled out the grapnel, passing it to her without comment. Noting the new rope, she nodded in approval, and then stepped away from the wall. He watched in silence as she swung the grapnel once, twice, and then flung it high over the wall. It make a gentle grating noise as she pulled the rope in slowly until the iron points dug in, then she was up and over the wall in moments.

Gavin fingered the rope for a moment and sighed. It was too late for second thoughts now. He muttered a curse under his breath and clambered up the rope and onto the top of the wall. He lay prone for a moment, the damp stone cold on his cheek as he looked down into the cathedral gardens.

The lawns were dark and silent, and the trees and bushes rustled gently in the slight breeze that drifted up and over the walls. He heard a muffled noise and glanced down to see Tessa looking up at him impatiently. He pulled the rope up and then slipped into the tree beside the wall and down into the brush.

Tessa led the way, moving out of the bushes and across the lawn on swift, silent feet, a passing shadow in the night. Gavin felt clumsy beside her, but only by virtue of his size. They went past the arched garden entrance that would have led them into the cathedral itself, and headed for the side door that would take them into the orphanage.

She stopped beside the heavy wooden door and tried the latch, then shook her head at him. He stepped around her and knelt to examine the lock with his fingertips. Dropping his pack to the floor, he rummaged around in it until he withdrew a cloth bundle, unrolling it and removing a simple metal probe. The darkness was almost absolute by the door, the high walls of the cathedral blocking what little light the moon shed in those brief moments when it peeked between the clouds. Gavin inserted the probe into the lock, using it as an extension of his own fingers, working by feel to determine its structure. Satisfied, he withdrew the probe and then selected two more thin tools. Within moments, the lock gave a quiet click and, with a nod to Tessa, he tucked the picks away in his pack. They stepped through the door, pulling it to but not fully closing it behind them.

The door led into a dimly lit corridor. A rich rug ran the length of the hallway, allowing them to move more swiftly without having to worry as much about making noise. Gavin wondered at the low-wicked oil lamps mounted on the walls. They were barely alight, but why burn them at all at this time of night? He considered the wealth of this new church as he took in the walnut wall panelling. Shaking his head, he forced himself to pay attention to what they were doing. Tessa led him through the richly appointed hallways, past heavy doors and a wide staircase, through to a more austere dining hall.

She pulled his head down and pressed her lips to his ear. "The children are all upstairs. I don't think we need to risk waking them."

Gavin was about to respond when a faint shimmer of light reflected off the polished tabletop. A glance at the entrance to the hall and the bright glow of lamplight prompted him to scan the room quickly. There was no place to hide that was worth bothering with. He pressed close to the wall beside the doorway and reached under his cloak for the knife at his belt.

"Which ones?" a voice carried in from the hallway.

"The youngest. It's always the youngest." He sounded terse compared to the questioner. He had sounded timid, nervous.

Gavin shot a look at Tessa and she nodded, pointing to her ear and then the hallway.

"I still don't understand..."

"Listen, acolyte," the voice snapped, its owner's temper clearly fraying. "You do not need to understand. These orders came from the First himself. Ours is not to question, just to obey. We are to take two of the youngest to the stones in the park tonight and meet others of our order. That is all you need to understand."

"Yes, Father." The reply was apologetic and was soon followed by footsteps, as the pair climbed the stairs to the second floor.

Gavin followed the sound with his eyes, as if he could somehow still see them through the wall.

"What now?" Tessa hissed at him.

"We wait here," he whispered. "It sounded like they were fetching them."

They crouched in the darkness, pressed against the wall beside the door. A brief search had revealed no better hiding places in the time they had. Creaks from above heralded the priests' approach as they came down the stairs. Gavin clenched his fist tight around the hilt of his knife before forcing himself to relax. Tense muscles move more slowly, he told himself.

"Lord of the New Days, this one's heavier than she looks." The creaking of the stairs made it hard for Gavin to tell which of the priests had spoken. The footsteps reached the base of the stairs and began to fade down the corridor.

Tessa pushed past him and into the corridor, stopping and looking back at him in confusion. "Come on!" She moved off without a backward glance. Gavin cursed under his breath and then followed.

He caught up with her at the doorway leading out to the gardens. She glanced back at him and nodded once, though he had no idea what that was supposed to have meant, and then eased the door open. She darted through, still crouched low, her dark cloak trailing along the ground. Gavin followed and immediately headed for the deeper shadows closer to the wall. The priests were visible in the distance, heading for the doors that went into the cathedral itself. Tessa made to follow, but Gavin reached for her and pulled her up short. "Where are you going?" he whispered.

"I'm following them, you idiot. Come on!"

"Into the cathedral? Why? We know where they're going."

"Yes, inside. Let's go."

"They said they were going to the park. Weren't you listening?"

She lowered her head. Despite the darkness, Gavin could almost feel her blush. "Come on." He led her back to the wall, secured the grapnel and clambered over. He glanced up at the sky as he waited for her. It was still dark, but dawn was fast approaching. "I don't think they're going to take their time," he said, as he heard the distant clatter of carriage wheels on cobbles. "It will be starting to get light soon."

She nodded. "Let's go."

The two ran through the streets, hoods thrown back and not bothering to keep to the shadows as they ducked into the cobweb of alleys that covered Hesk. A maze to most of the city's inhabitants, the alleyways could get you where you wanted to be far faster than many of the main roads of the city. They could also get you robbed at knife-point and left for dead in them if you weren't careful.

The park was shrouded in mist. It rose in tendrils from the river surrounding it and pushed into the park in a dense, undulating blanket. Gavin was thankful for the cover it provided them, but frustrated by the fact they couldn't see anything through the shifting grey mass. They moved quickly through the park in the direction of the stones, ears alert for any noise. This time, it was Tessa who pulled him up short, grabbing a shoulder and pointing into the murk. A yellow halo of lantern light surrounded the dark figures as they made their way through the mist. The priests wore dark robes, which would have made them almost as hard to see as if they'd been wearing greys, if it hadn't been for their lantern. They must have left their carriage at the entrance to the park and were moving over the wet grass with purpose, walking roughly parallel to the two thieves.

Gavin and Tessa froze and let the two priests overtake them before they moved again. He waited for a safe distance to form and then set off, trusting Tessa to follow. A metallic clink from behind told him that she was readying her weapons as she ran and he patted his knife through his cloak, reassuring himself of its presence.

They cut across the grass at an angle that would bring them level with the priests on the approach to the stones, yet still keep them at a safe distance. The stones lay at a natural edge to the park, bordered by thick trees and bushes on one side, and large rocks that sloped down to the rushing river on the other. As such, it would be hard to approach unseen, even with the mist cloaking them. Gavin skirted the trees, moving more slowly now in order to match the priests' pace. They were walking slowly, one of them clearly struggling with the weight of the child he carried, as the stones loomed out of the mist.

"Brothers." The soft voice cut through the mist and the silence. Not knowing quite why, Gavin stopped and dropped to the grass as he tried to see who had spoken.

"You have performed your task adequately. You may now depart." Two black-robed figures strode forward from the stones, the mist eddying and swirling around their legs like water. Their hoods were low over their faces, obscuring anything Gavin might have seen despite the lamplight. He crawled forward through the wet grass, trying to get a better view as they held their hands out for the children. One child was probably aged four or five from what Gavin could see, but the other was a babe, still wrapped in swaddling.

"The girl should sleep for another three or four hours yet, but the baby could wake at any time," the younger priest said suddenly, earning a sharp look from his companion. The taller of the two strange figures nodded in response and then repeated his earlier words. "You may depart." His accent seemed odd. It was a little thing, but it niggled at Gavin for some reason. He glanced at Tessa, who was lying next to him in the grass, but she was watching the scene intently and did not meet his gaze.

He was silent as the priests from the cathedral approached and then passed them. *Why would they bring children, and one a baby at that, here in the dead of night?* He chewed savagely at a fingernail. None of this made sense. The priests handed over the children without speaking and then left quickly. The two other priests stood by the stones as they watched their counterparts vanish into the darkness. They did not speak and held the children in a strange fashion. It wasn't a normal way to hold a child, more like the way you might hold a package. A clasp devoid of nurturing or any sense of care or protection.

For the first time, Gavin realised that they held no lamp themselves but they seemed at ease in the darkness. As the distant glow of the lamp faded away behind them, a terrible feeling of wrongness rose in him. Moonlight broke through the clouds and the light served to make the scene even more otherworldly, if that was possible. The two figures looked up at the sky in unison, their faces lifted to the light, eyes closed and lips parted. One looked around and then burst into a delighted laugh. A shimmer seemed to pass over him and then the black robe vanished, revealing a man-like figure in simple tan clothing. Gavin held back a startled gasp and felt Tessa stiffen beside him. The figure seemed normal enough, although its face was pale in the moonlight and its hair hung down past its shoulders. It turned and Gavin bit hard on the inside of his cheek to keep himself from crying out. The eyes of the creature shone in the darkness, a gentle amber glow, the colour of a candle's flame or of sunlight on water. Beside him, Tessa whimpered softly into the grass.

"This is forbidden, you fool," hissed the black-robed figure in alarm.

"Forbidden," laughed the amber-eyed creature. "Too long has it been since I felt our Lady's touch on my skin. I'll not diminish it with a glamour. Take the younglings through, if you are so eager to return."

"Te eirla su trechendar, kalien su irla!" the figure in black spat, and the argument continued in words Gavin could neither make out or understand.

Finally, the figure threw the young boy over one shoulder and then took the baby, holding it in its other hand. Gavin watched with wide eyes as it walked towards the stones, the huge blocks that formed a gateway of sorts where generations of couples had come to kiss.

He was dimly aware of Tessa moving in the grass beside him, but couldn't tear his eyes from the scene before him. The robed figure reached a hand out to one of the stones, took another step forward and half-turned to the creature. Gavin was vaguely aware of the fact they were speaking but was staring, open-mouthed, at the way the figure's leg ended in mid-air. The portion of his body that had stepped through the space between stones had simply ceased to exist. Gavin heard a hiss beside him and then a sharp metallic twang. The robed figure looked up in surprise and hissed in pain as the bolt bounced off its thigh. Its robe fell away, running like water, revealing the creature beneath it. It wore the same tan clothing as its companion and had the same burning eyes. Both creatures turned to glare at Tessa.

"Kiel serh!" the first spat. It stepped through the stones with the children and vanished.

Tessa rose to her feet and fumbled with the tiny crossbow in her hands. A smile crept across the remaining creature's face. Holding its arms wide, as if inviting the crossbow bolt, it stepped slowly towards them.

"Tessa!" Gavin said in a low, urgent voice. "Tessa, run!"

Her hand was shaking as she held out the bow and pulled the trigger. Somehow, she managed to hit the creature, but again the bolt simply bounced off, leaving a small tear in the tan cloth over its stomach. The creature laughed again, a delighted but cruel sound, and pulled a long knife from a sheath strapped to one leg. "My turn," it whispered, the sound somehow carrying clearly to them both. Gavin struggled to his feet and pulled his knife, as Tessa dropped the crossbow and drew her own blade. The thing stepped lightly through the mist towards them, and they spread apart in an attempt to force it to fight one of them or the other.

The leap was incredible. It jumped forward more than fifteen feet in a single bound. Tessa had no time to be amazed. It was on her in an instant. It landed and sank low in one fluid motion, then lashed out with one leg, pulling her off balance as it slashed at her with its knife.

It shifted backwards a step and then leapt away again, covering another ten feet. The maneuver placed it out of reach of both of them, but still close enough for it to be an immediate threat.

Tessa gasped and clamped a hand to her thigh as she fell sprawling to the grass. Her face was twisted with pain and shock. Gavin moved to help, just a simple shifting of his weight, but even as he started to move, he saw the thing tense to spring and he skittered backwards, falling onto the grass in his haste.

The creature laughed again, its pose casual as it watched Tessa pull herself to her feet. Blood was soaking through the cloth covering her leg, seeping past her hand, which she still pressed awkwardly over the slash.

"Run, Gavin," she said, in a voice tight with pain and fear.

"I can't just leave you!" he protested, though he wanted nothing more than to run.

"Just go!" she screamed, as the creature moved in again, its feet gliding smoothly over the ground.

Gavin stared at her in indecision for a long moment, his eyes watching the dark stain as it spread on her leg. She was losing a massive amount of blood at a rate which could mean only one thing. Whispering silent thanks, he turned and fled. As he sprinted across the grass towards the bridge, the sound of metal on bone was soon followed by a long and terrible scream, and then a longer, more terrible silence.

* * *

Instinct told Gavin he was being chased. It spoke to him on a primal level and whispered jagged words of terror into his ear. He couldn't spare the time to look back over his shoulder. With the speed he was running, he needed to put all of his concentration into putting one leg in front of another. He ran in a way that he hadn't since he was a small child, giving no thought to the fear of falling or the need to retain control. He fairly flew over the low stone bridge, barreling into the streets and darting into the first alleyway he came to, then twisting through as many turns as possible in as short a space of time as he could.

Finally, he stopped beside a rain barrel in a back alley. He slumped against the wall, his breath ragged and his throat burning from the effort of breathing hard in the cold morning air. The rough stones of the building scratched at his back through the thin greys as he sank to the ground but he didn't even feel it. His head was spinning as wildly as any blow could have made it.

Tessa was gone, just like that, and the thing hadn't even really been trying. He glanced around the barrel warily but saw no sign of the creature that had chased him. Perhaps it had never even been following him.

He pulled himself to his feet and dusted himself off, sheathing the knife he hadn't even been aware he was holding in a hand that ached from gripping it so tightly. He looked around the alleyway quickly and glanced up at the sky. It was still dark, but he vaguely remembered hearing the fourth bell some time ago.

Dawn was fast approaching and he couldn't be seen on the streets in his greys. Gavin went to the end of the alleyway and tried to get his bearings. His flight had been so frantic, he had taken little note of where he was going. Twin ruts in the cobbles caught his eye and his heart sank. He was in the Barrowways.

Hesk was divided into sections that were unknown to most of the population. Six major gangs operated in the city, running everything from the brothels to the pickpockets on the streets. There were smaller gangs and thieving crews, of course, but the six were the main powers in Hesk's underworld. Each had its own territory, which it protected fiercely. The Barrowways were named after the barrow routes built to service the old market. They hadn't been used in decades and the market had long since relocated to the main square, closer to the centre of the city. The area was now the territory of the Barrows, one of the two oldest gangs in the city and possibly the most brutal.

He moved unconsciously into the shadows, glancing around furtively. To be caught in their territory would be bad enough, but to be caught wearing greys would probably get him killed. He needed to get out fast or, failing that, to get rid of these clothes as quickly as possible. He made his way through the winding streets, peering into back alleys criss-crossed with washing lines, but they were all bare. It was still too early and damp for anyone to have hung clothes out to dry and none had been left out from the night before.

He moved as fast as he could while staying quiet, clenching his teeth with the effort, as he made his way through Old Market Street and past Blind Sisters, all the way to Fisher's Bells. Sweat soaked his clothes, both from the exertion of keeping watch and moving with the shadows, and also from honest fear. The night was quiet and the persistent mist still worked to dampen any noise. The silence allowed him to relax and he shifted from his low, creeping stance into a cautious walk. He had almost convinced himself he was going to make it out.

Gavin peered into another dark alley, then scurried past it and along the side of a dark inn. He stopped. The square before him was not particularly large, but there were few or no place where he could avoid being seen. He would be clearly visible as he made his way across it and skirting the edges would make little difference. He scratched at his hair under his hood as he considered his options.

A light scuff behind him told him he had waited too long and finally run out of luck. He turned, with an air of resignation, to see a small group of men, some little more than boys, emerging from the alleyway behind him. They were armed with clubs fashioned from the wood of discarded crates, and more than one of these weapons had rusty nails rammed through them. The leader carried a rust-splotched knife, and his improbably fat belly protruded from an ill-fitting shirt smeared with filth and the remnants of his meals. He thrust his stomach out even further as he eyed Gavin.

"These is Barra lands," he said, in what was clearly supposed to be a menacing tone, but was made almost comical by his streets' accent.

Gavin edged away from the wall. "I'm not working here, just passing through. I don't want any trouble."

"Passin' though?" the boy said with an incredulous leer on his pockmarked face. "On your way to the shops, are ya? Pickin' up some fish for the missus?" He looked back over his shoulder to encourage the chorus of grunts and snickers from the rest of his crew.

"Nah, I don't think so, mate." The smirk was gone as he turned back. "Not in greys."

Gavin knew they would attack soon. It might take them a few more minutes of posturing first to work themselves up to it, but it was almost a certainty. He was outnumbered. He'd have to take his advantages where he could. Without a word, he threw himself past the pot-bellied thug and into the middle of the group. He twisted and spun, lashing out with his knife, seeking not to kill but simply to injure and slow. The boys cried out in shock and pain, rearing back from his onslaught, and then the fight began in earnest.

Gavin whirled through the group, using their numbers against them. While they had to shift around him in the narrow street to try to land a blow on him, he always had a target in front of him and he slashed at anything that came within range. He dodged to the right to avoid a spiked plank and threw himself into a roll, kicking out savagely at the side of a knee as he rose to his feet. The clubs were everywhere, but he was catching only glancing blows. His knife sliced deeply into a shoulder before he shifted again. The moment he stayed in one place for more than a heartbeat was the moment they would have him. He spun tightly, a tight turn with his blade extended which somehow managed to catch a throat, and then the blood was everywhere.

He ducked and rolled again, always headed for where the gang was bunched most tightly together, slashing wildly for the inside of a thigh, but there were fewer opponents now. Three had already moved to the side of the street, clutching at wounds. The remaining gang members simply stepped backwards out of his reach when he attacked, hissing curses at him.

Gavin rose to his feet and backed away, holding his knife low and trying to ignore the throbbing aches born of half a dozen blows. Three of the thugs and the fat-bellied knife wielder still faced him. He knew they would come in a rush and running would not help him. He doubted he could outrun anything in this state anyway. He stayed low, in a fighting stance, and waited for them to move, to leave an opening, to do anything.

They came in a screaming mob of spiked clubs, sweat and murder. He shouldered his way past the first club, and the man fell screaming as he clutched at the wreckage of his eye. A club caught Gavin solidly in the side, smashing him into the alleyway and against the wall. He landed badly and then they were on him, clubs rising and falling, as they played a symphony of pain upon his muscles and bones. He felt something crack, followed by a new pressure as a rib pressed inwards, and he huddled into a ball. Then it stopped. He lay panting, fighting the urge to draw a deeper breath for fear of the pain his rib would cause him.

He felt the vibrations of the footsteps more than heard them, and forced himself to look up at the fat man as he drew closer. His face was a mask of rage and an angry wound, created by a slash that Gavin barely remembered dealing, painted a broad streak of blood across one side of his face. He grabbed Gavin, twisting and bunching the greys at his throat to provide purchase. A low moan of pain escaped Gavin's lips as Belly pulled him up, arching him over backwards and pressing the rusty blade to his lips.

"That was my brother you slashed open," he hissed into Gavin's face, his breath fetid with the stench of old ale and the food that was trapped between his teeth. Gavin barely heard the words. His eyes were focused beyond the man, on the figure that dropped lightly from the rooftops and approached silently, its strange knife held ready as it viewed the scene through its amber eyes.

The first one died without having time to scream, as the knife snaked past almost casually and parted his throat. He dropped to the ground, clutching at his throat as the bright blood flew. Belly turned at the sound, and his eyes widened in shock as he dropped Gavin and turned to face the creature. Gavin watched the fight unfold for the length of a slow breath, then pulled himself up from his hands and knees. He staggered along the alleyway, the screams chasing after him. The blood would move more slowly.

He passed almost blindly through the streets, half-bent with one hand pressed to his side. He moved like a drunk, crashing from wall to wall, as his feet strained to find the ground fast enough to prevent him from falling. A fresh pain seared through his side with every breath and he forced himself into a shallow pant. He needed to keep going. The screaming would have attracted attention and he needed to be gone.

He was three streets away before he realised it had fallen silent behind him. Fighting the impulse to look back over his shoulder, he gritted his teeth and managed a staggering run. He didn't really need to look anyway. He could almost feel the presence of the thing as it stalked him through the streets.

CHAPTER THREE

Ylsriss pulled the sleeping baby from her breast, clambered out of the bed and padded across the room. She moved slowly, stepping lightly to avoid any movement which might wake him. He'd been up four times this night already and she would have given much to get some real sleep. She lay him in the cradle and stepped back, watching as he rolled slightly and drifted deeper into sleep.

Dawn's first blush was threatening to edge over the horizon and she knew she should probably close the shutters. It would need to be dark if she was to have any chance of getting any more sleep. She also knew Rhaven would be up soon though, and she felt guilty at the prospect of lying in bed while he was struggling to get the cart ready for the shop.

Fatigue won the battle against guilt and she crawled back into the warm bed, weariness wrapping itself around her like another thick blanket. The bang came suddenly and jolted her from the edges of sleep. She sat up in the bed and looked across to the baby, but he was sleeping soundly. Another crash pulled her from the bed and down the stairs towards the door. It felt as if it was still too early for Rhaven to be up, but the noise would wake the baby at this rate. She reached for the door as the fist pounded on it again, and then wrenched it open. "Rhaven, what are you...?" She stopped herself as the man slumped down the length of the door frame and fell at her feet, his odd grey clothes dark with blood. She knelt quickly and eased him onto his back, and the deeply cowled hood fell back.

"Gavin!" she gasped, as he smiled weakly up at her.

"Thought I'd come for a visit, Ylsriss," he breathed, through bruised lips.

"What are you...? No, never mind." She helped him up into a seated position. "Let's get you inside."

It took her three attempts to get him back onto his feet, with his arm draped around her neck. She staggered with him as they lurched into the kitchen, and he all but fell into a chair. She ran back and looked out at the yard, searching the shadowy corners with her eyes, before closing the door. Nothing out there seemed amiss, but he clearly hadn't done this damage to himself.

She returned to find Gavin had pulled himself to his feet and was leaning awkwardly against the chair, one hand pressed to his side.

"Greys, Gavin?" she said, dismay mingling with the scorn in her voice. "Really?"

"It's not what it looks like, Ylsriss," he managed. "I was helping Tessa."

She held a hand up. "Don't worry about explaining anything for now. Let's get a look at you." She stripped him to his waist with a brutal efficiency, ignoring his protests. He gasped with pain as she peeled the greys from his chest, and she glanced up at his eyes with concern. He was a battered mess of red welts, cuts and scratches. His side, however, was another matter. She probed gently, tracing the line of his ribs with her fingers, and watched his face carefully.

"Can you take a deep breath?" she asked.

"Not without it hurting, but there's no blood in my breath, if that's what you're asking."

"You need to be thanking the Lords of Blood, Sea and Sky that there isn't, Gavin," she replied, shaking her head. "I've not seen a beating like this in a long time." She shot a look at the door again. "What happened to Tessa? Is she safe?"

He closed his eyes tightly before responding. "She's dead," he managed. When his eyes opened again, she saw the anguish she felt at the news mirrored in his own.

"Tell me about it later," she said, in a low voice. "We'll get you patched up and then you need to rest."

She filled a bowl with water and set about cleaning his wounds. She pounded goose fat, garlic and sage leaves together with a pestle and mortar, then smeared the foul-smelling concoction over his ribs before binding his chest tightly with strips of material. He stood in silence through it all, staring at the door as if he was waiting for it to burst open. She settled him into a spare bedroom and went to check on the baby who woke crying, as if on cue. She scooped him up and walked through the doorway, bouncing him in her arms and "shushing" absent-mindedly. Rhaven was waiting for her in the hallway, questions clear on his face. "An old friend," she said, in a weary voice, "from another life."

"We'll talk about it later. You know I don't want that life in my house, though."

She nodded, eyes downcast, and his voice softened. "You ought to get yourself back into bed, girl, once you get your guest settled. You look all done in." She smiled as she nodded again but could tell he wasn't done.

"I just don't want any trouble, Ylsriss", he said, more quietly. "He can stay until he's on his feet but then I want him gone."

"I understand," she said. She thought briefly about her bed but knew that sleep wouldn't come, so she followed him down into the kitchen. She was still sitting at the long wooden table, sipping tea that had gone cold, long after he had left the house.

It was early evening by the time that Gavin emerged from the bedroom, but it was still far sooner than she would have thought. The state he'd been in, she'd expected him to sleep right through. She was sitting in a low rocking chair that was well-padded with cushions, cradling the baby in her arms. The shadow from the door caused her to look up and she frowned at him as he stood in the doorway, wrapped in the blanket from the bed. "You shouldn't be up and about yet."

He nodded. "I know, but I can't afford to stay here. I need to get back."

"Back to where?" she asked, her tone sharp but her voice low enough to avoid waking the baby.

"The cellar. The orphanage didn't work for me, Ylsriss. Some people just aren't built that way. Over the years, I've kept the door open for any others in case they needed it."

"So you've become me?"

The corner of his mouth curled into a smile. "I suppose I have in a way."

"What happened to you, Gavin? I think you owe me an explanation, if nothing else. As for leaving, you're in no condition to go anywhere for a day or two."

He grabbed a chair and started to sink into it, before wincing and easing himself down slowly. "Yours?" He nodded at the baby.

"My son," she affirmed with a smile. "Almost a month old now."

"What did you call him?"

"He's not yet a month," she reminded him.

"You hold to that? I wouldn't have thought it of you."

"Why not?"

"You never seemed the type to be held by old traditions or superstitions."

"Sometimes the old ways have more sense in them than you'd think." She shushed the baby as he stirred slightly. "It's not just that, though. I don't want to name him before Klöss returns, unless I have to."

She shook herself visibly, risking waking the child. "Don't change the subject, anyway. What happened?"

He grimaced and then sighed. "Tessa snuck into the cellar one night and stole my grapnel. She wasn't quiet enough and I managed to catch up with her before she broke into the cathedral."

"The cathedral! Is she mad?" Ylsriss gasped.

"She's convinced there's something strange going on and that the answers are inside. Apparently, her brother Khiv vanished from the orphanage without a word to anyone."

Ylsriss fixed him with a look. "Kids do things like that, Gavin. He probably just left."

He shrugged. "Maybe he did. She was going to go in anyway. I didn't go for Khiv, I went for her."

"And so you just went along with this?" She didn't shout. She didn't have to. Her eyes spoke more loudly than her voice.

"I didn't have much of a choice, Ylsriss." He glanced at her once and then avoided her eyes. "I was the oldest of all of us in that place. They all looked to me..." He trailed off.

"I'm not seeing what that has to do with helping Tessa or doing something crazy like this."

"Don't you see? I left them. I couldn't stand it and so I left. I'm responsible for anything that happens in there. If I'd stayed, I might have been able to do something."

"You think you're responsible for whatever happened to Khiv?" Her voice was incredulous and he looked up at her sharply. "Gavin, life doesn't work like that," she continued, in a softer tone. "You're not responsible for people forever. Life is too short and too hard for that."

"Maybe, but he's still gone and I felt I owed her my help, at least."

"So what happened?"

"The priests." He paused, looking almost embarrassed for a moment. "The priests are doing something with those children, with the youngest ones."

"That's disgusting!" Ylsriss snapped, her eyes flashing.

"What? No, not that!" he said, revulsion clear on his face. "No, they were taking two of them into the park."

"What's wrong with that?" she asked.

"I need a drink," he muttered, placing one hand on the tabletop and pushing himself to his feet.

"There's some fresh water in the kettle," she said, nodding towards the stove.

"That's not what I meant." Gavin laughed.

"Oh. Well, there's some ale in the pantry, over in the corner there." She watched as he rummaged about and waved a cup at her, replacing it as she shook her head.

He poured himself a drink. "They were taking them to the park at third bell past midnight, Ylsriss. One of them was still a babe in swaddling." He nodded at her confused expression. "It's not just that. We heard them talking in the orphanage. They were acting on orders from someone high up in the church."

"What did they do with them?"

"This is where it gets weird. I don't know how much to tell you. You'll think I've gone mad." He cleared his throat and then drank deeply, looking past her and at the window as he spoke. "We followed them into the park. It was misty enough for us to move quickly and not worry about them hearing us. They were taking the children to the kissing stones, you know the ones?" He waited for her nod and plunged on. "There were two more priests waiting for them there. At least, they looked like priests to start with. As soon as the ones we'd followed handed the children over and left, they changed."

"What do you mean, they changed?"

"I don't know how to describe it. One minute they were just normal priests and then, the next, one of them was something different. Almost like the priest was just a mask he'd been wearing that he'd dropped. The other one, well, he seemed to walk through the stones. A bit like he was moving through a doorway. He was holding both the children and...Ylsriss, he...well, he just vanished."

"Did you hit your head, Gavin?"

"I know what it sounds like, Ylsriss, but I swear that's what happened. Tessa shot at one of them with a hand-bow and then it was on us. You've never seen anything move the way it did, Ylsriss. Even fighting both of us at once, it was like it was toying with us. It cut her so easily, like it wasn't even trying." He looked down and rubbed his eyes with his blanket, his breath shuddering into him.

Ylsriss looked on, her hard eyes softening as Gavin lowered his voice in confession.

"She made me leave her there." His voice was barely more than a whisper. "She knew she was already dead. The blood was pouring from her leg. I should have stayed and helped or something, but I didn't, I just ran. I didn't even look back."

Ylsriss stood carefully. "Let me get this little beast into bed and I'll be back." She paused at the doorway, looking back over her shoulder at the drink in his hand. "Get me one of those while I'm gone. I've a feeing I'm going to need it."

The journey up the stairs was a slow and cautious one, practice allowing her to avoid those steps that creaked. He was a good baby, but he was a light sleeper and she'd soon learned to avoid making noises when trying to get him down.

She placed him in the cradle and pulled the light woolen blanket over him. The sun had almost set, just a sliver remaining above the silvery horizon as it sank into the sea. The faint glitter of stars was just visible as they peered through the veil of the wisps of cloud. Ylsriss moved to the window and stared out across the city towards the harbour. She glanced at the baby for a moment, her thoughts far across the ocean.

Faint sounds from the kitchen brought her back to herself and she turned to the doorway. She didn't look at the rooftop opposite Rhaven's house. It would have taken sharp eyes indeed to have picked out the figure crouched beside the chimney. As the last light of the sun faded, the green-tinged mist rising from the creature's shoulders was just visible below its burning amber eyes. Eyes that had watched so intently as she laid the baby down.

He'd suffered by coming here so early. The hated sun was leaching the Lady's gift from him as he crouched in shadows too small to take all of his form. He had risked much by allowing the manling to escape the night before. The time was not yet right for their actions to be known. His hands burned in remembered pain as he thought back to the night before, when cold iron on the window's frame had thrown him away from it and into the light of the rising sun. These people were so unpredictable as to when and where they used the hated metal now. Things were so different from the times he remembered.

The sun finally sank below the horizon and he stood, eyes eager, then leapt across to the sloped roof. He braced his knees, ready for the impact, and wrenched the window open. Blue fire flared as he pressed his hands tightly against the protruding heads of the iron nails and, with a gasp, he ripped the entire frame away, hurling the hateful thing behind him to crash into the street.

* * *

Gavin waved a cup of ale at Ylsriss as she came back into the kitchen. The colour was coming back into his cheeks, despite his injuries. The sleep had clearly done him good.

"Here, take these," she said, handing him a pile of clothes. "They're Rhaven's and are probably too big for you, but you can't just wear that blanket all day."

"Listen, Ylsriss, I need to tell you this. I need to get it out and I'm scared you won't believe me, but just let me get through it, alright?" He blurted the words out as if scared they would refuse to pass his lips if he spoke more slowly.

"Get dressed first. I have a feeling I won't want to be interrupted."

He nodded as he slipped out with the clothes and she sipped at the dark ale while she waited.

"Okay, just let me tell you," he said, as he came back in. "That thing that we fought. It wasn't human. I ran from that park like a frightened child. I wasn't even paying attention to where I was going. That's how I ended up in the Barrowways, getting beaten to a pulp." He shook his head to stop her as she drew a breath and then he plunged on. "They would probably have killed me. I managed to take two or three of them down, but they had me on the ground in the end. If that thing hadn't waded in and attacked, I'd still be in that alley. It must have been following me, watching."

She cut him off as her face paled. "So how do you know it didn't - " She never finished the sentence and they both whipped their heads around at the crash from outside.

Ylsriss rushed to the door, ignoring Gavin as he cried out for her to wait. She slid open the peep, a wooden slat in the door behind a metal grate in the front. The yard was still visible in the twilight but there was no movement. The door fought with her as she struggled with the catches and locks, but eventually it opened smoothly. Night air reached in, caressing her as she peered out. Gavin pushed past her, bending down to study something on the ground. He crouched and lifted a piece of the mangled window frame, looking at her with confusion. A faint cry from above caused him to lift his head and Ylsriss screamed as a creature leapt from the roof, clear across the corner of the yard, to the building opposite. Her baby was clearly visible, wrapped tightly in the blanket in one of its arms, and a piece of the cloth fluttered down to them. The creature looked back at them, its burning amber eyes filled with contempt, and then it was gone.

She didn't pause but ran for the gate, tearing after the distant figure with a speed born of terror. Her son, it had stolen her son. The thought was almost too terrible to hold in her head, and she felt herself drifting into blind panic as she ran through the streets. One turn and then another led her to a square and she faltered, then stopped. There was no sign of the creature, no hint of which way it had gone. Tears flowed almost instantly and she bit her lip in grief and anger. She hadn't cried like this in almost fifteen years. Not since she'd fled her father. They came fast, hot and burning, filling her eyes as her cries tore from her throat.

She felt arms around her, lifting her from the ground that she hadn't even been aware she'd fallen to. "Effan," she whispered through her tears. "I name you Effan."

"Ylsriss!" Gavin shook her again. "Be smart. We don't need to follow it. We know it's going to the park." He grabbed her hand and lurched towards the southern end of the square, limping horribly but somehow still managing to pull her along.

The cold stones of the city cut into her bare feet. It had been years since Ylsriss had been forced to run the streets unshod, but she ignored the pain as best she could. Before long, the rough cobbles and sharp-cornered flagstones gave way to grass, wet from the evening's rains. She pulled ahead of Gavin, shaking her hand free of his grasp and ran, hearing nothing beyond her own frantic heartbeat as he fell behind.

The kissing stones emerged out of the growing murk and she could just make out the figure again. It pressed a hand to one of the supporting stones and looked upwards at the sky as if it was waiting. She threw herself at him, a whirling mass of fists and fingers curled into claws. "My baby!" she screamed, as she attacked. "Give me my baby, you bastard!"

The creature staggered back, seemingly shocked at the onslaught. Then, between one blow and the next, it reached out, casually grasped her by the throat and lifted her forwards. She choked and gagged against the pressure on her neck. The creature calmly looked her up and down with its strange burning eyes, seemingly unaware of the wailing from Effan, who lay in the crook of its other arm. The clouds parted, bathing them both in the pale glow of the newly risen moon, and the creature smiled in satisfaction as it raised its face to the light, ignoring her as she struggled in its fist.

"You too will serve then," it said softly to her, the words clear despite the odd accent.

Ylsriss had time to hear Gavin scream her name as he staggered into view, and then the creature stepped towards the stones. She felt the rough texture, as if the stone itself was passing through her very flesh and bones, and then a blast of the most bitter cold before she passed into the darkness.

CHAPTER FOUR

Klöss leaned back against the heavy beams of the thick wooden gates and watched the mud spatter from under the boots of his men as they trudged through the gates. Others were still making their way along the winding path which led through the rows of trenches and sharpened stakes. He didn't see the men. He saw the gaps. There were far too many of them for him to have known all of their names, but he recognised several faces and, more importantly, the empty spaces next to them where a friend had once walked.

The air was too still. The men were quiet, but it was more than that. It ought to be full of Verig's curses and insults, as he urged the men onwards. Klöss caught sight of Tristan moving with the men. He met the big man's eyes for a moment but his gaze slipped away, as if failing to find purchase, and continued skimming over the returning force.

A splash in the mud behind him announced the man before he spoke. "Shipmaster?" he called, respectfully.

"Yes?" Klöss turned to face the man - although he was little more than a boy, really. "Seamaster Frostbeard asks you attend him as soon as your men are settled."

Klöss grunted and gave the young man a knowing look. "That's not what he really said, is it?"

"No." The boy looked down at his muddy boots as his face reddened.

Klöss laughed, a rough coarse sound. "It's okay, lad. I can imagine what he said." He patted the boy's shoulder. "Where can I find him?"

"In his office. In the keep." He nodded towards the distant structure.

Klöss sought out Tristan in the throng again. He caught the man's eye, jabbed his thumb at his chest and then pointed into the settlement. Tristan nodded in response and turned to the men nearest him, calling out instructions.

Klöss followed the boy through the streets. The tall stone wall surrounding the fledgling city cast a deep shadow over the buildings in the early afternoon. With the exception of the wall, however, there was little stone to be seen. The buildings were mostly wooden and had a temporary feel to them, something he'd grown accustomed to when living in the camps while the fleet was being built.

The keep was the only large stone building in Rimeheld. Construction had started as soon as the walls were complete and the simple wooden building that had originally stood there had long since been replaced.

The primary focus had been on immediate defence, so the construction of the walls and ditches had been more important than the building of homes and other buildings. He nodded at the men standing guard outside the large double doors and made his way inside.

Frostbeard's study was in a small corner of the top floor and, as he approached the sturdy wooden door, he was reminded of another door, another study. His life had changed immeasurably since that day, yet here he was, fighting down a sense of dread again as he forced himself to knock.

The study was utilitarian and spartan. A simple desk groaned under the weight of various papers, and charts and maps covered the walls. Aiden looked up as Klöss entered, his face breaking into a sympathetic smile, and he motioned wordlessly to one of the chairs that faced him across the desk.

"Even if I hadn't seen how few men you have brought back, your face would have told me," he said softly. "What happened? The village wasn't that well defended."

"No, it wasn't," Klöss replied. "The village was taken easily. We were attacked later that night."

"A night attack?" Aiden wondered. "Still, even then you shouldn't have lost that many."

"They had some manner of beast with them. Tore through us like reavers in still seas. They caught us midway through the second watch. Our sentries gave no warning and they were in amongst us by the time the cry went up."

The old man narrowed his eyes. "What aren't you telling me?"

"We lost Verig."

"Men die," Frostbeard muttered, but his gaze fell to the desk and Klöss noticed his shoulders drop slightly. He knew it was all the response the man would show.

"We never expected anything like this kind of force," Klöss said. "The village had nothing like it. It was some form of elite unit."

"So why not use them to help defend the village?" Aiden looked up from the desk.

"Perhaps they didn't arrive in time? There could be any number of reasons. The point is we didn't expect these lands to have anything like these troops. This changes a few things, you realise?"

Aiden stood, scraping the chair back with his legs, and walked to one of the maps on the wall. "Not necessarily. I didn't ever plan on conquering these people. From day one, the plan was always just to drive them from their lands, to push them back." He examined the map as Klöss looked curiously over his shoulder. The map had grown in detail since the last time he had seen it, the Islander settlements now clearly marked on it along with what was known about the enemy villages. He caught himself. *When had he stopped thinking of these people as soft farmer folk and begun to think of them as the enemy?*

"Here." Frostbeard tapped the map with one thick finger. "They have a sizeable force here. According to our scouts, they've pulled most of their forces back to this point. If we strike them hard and fast, we can neutralise them and take this whole area."

"I thought the idea was to force them back and then hold, not to take more?" Klöss said in a low voice.

"Like you said, the situation has changed. We need to send a message. If we're lucky, we'll be able to eliminate those elite troops. Let's see how well they do when we're not caught with our britches down." Frostbeard turned away from the map. "Speak to the scouting parties and get a better idea of the area. I want to hear your plans in two days, before the sealord arrives."

"The sealord? He's coming here?"

"He wants a clearer picture than he's getting from our reports. This expedition puts his neck on the line too, you know?"

"I would have thought with the thane's backing..." Klöss trailed off.

"Don't be a fool, lad. The thane is out for what he can get. The council was shocked, certainly, but they won't let their power go so easily. There are those in the keepers and the merchants who are just waiting for this to fail." He moved back to the desk and sank into the chair with a sigh. "Go on now, Klöss, I've some thinking to do about how to replace Verig."

Klöss noted the tight lips and clenched hands, signs of the pain that Frostbeard was working so hard to conceal, and left without a word. He made his way through the busy streets to the high stone wall overlooking the harbour and climbed the rough wooden steps to the walkway. Like so much else, the stairs would be replaced with stone in time.

The remnants of the original watchtower could still be seen, if you knew where to look. The bay itself had changed considerably, with long wooden wharves now extending over the water and reavers at dock rocking gently. The natural curve of the land had been enhanced by a sea wall which formed the outer edge of the harbour, giving the appearance of stone arms cradling the fleet. Klöss could just make out the white sails of the fishing fleet beyond the harbour, hard at work with the great reavers as escorts, their blood-red sails clear against the pale seas.

He leaned against the battlements, the stone cold and rough under his hands, as he let his thoughts drift. Verig had been the first one to really believe in him. Though Frostbeard had sponsored him and allowed him to take the trials, Klöss knew he had mostly been humoring him. He'd never really expected him to succeed.

It was Verig who'd pushed him in training, Verig who had taken him aside after the first training raid, and schooled him in the advanced stances and sword forms. Thinking back, he could think of a dozen times when the sour-faced man had saved his life and another fifty when he'd fought beside Klöss, guarding his flank. In many ways, Verig had been the rock that he had relied on.

"Who do I lean on now, old man?" he muttered, shielding his face from the sudden gust of wind carrying spray from the waves that crashed against the harbour wall.

"I thought you would be here." Tristan's smile didn't look right on his face. It was strained and forced. "There are words for men who talk to themselves."

"You mean names."

"Names. Words. There is little difference." Tristan joined him at the wall and they watched the distant whitecaps as the wind continued to rise.

"How did he take the news?" Tristan asked finally, without taking his eyes from the water.

Klöss sighed. "It's hard to say. He's never really been one for displays of emotion."

"I forget sometimes that he is your uncle. Was he always this way?"

"Like what? Cold? I don't know how much of that is real and how much of it is his 'Frostbeard' act. He will miss Verig though, they go back a long way."

"All will. I never saw anyone fight like he could, except…"

"Except the one that killed him." Klöss finished the sentence for him.

"I didn't actually see it," Tristan admitted. "I was busy with those creatures."

There was a tone to his voice that made Klöss glance at him questioningly.

"I have never seen the like, Klöss, but there is talk among the men. Tales are being spread."

"Tales?"

"Old tales. My grandmother spoke of them to me when I was small. Of trells and keiju."

Klöss looked him up and down with a wry smile. "I find it hard to believe you were ever small, Tristan."

Tristan grunted. "You joke, Klöss, but perhaps the men are right. These things…I struck one in the face with my axe. It fell backwards but then it stood again. There was no wound. No blood."

Klöss nodded. It wasn't the first report he'd had like that about the force they'd fought barely a week before. "There was something strange about them, I'll give you that. But trells? Keiju? I think we're all a bit too old for bedtime tales."

Tristan's mouth closed with an audible click but Klöss paid it no mind. His thoughts were already on the push that Frostbeard had asked him to plan.

"This strange force aside," he said, "what do you make of their troops?"

"I think we have not yet faced them in any strength," Tristan replied, after a moment's thought. He caught Klöss's gesture and went on. "The men in the signal tower, they would have been basic guards. The villages we have attacked have been defended by poorly trained men, little more than guards themselves. If I had to wager, I would say that we have yet to face whatever true army this land has."

Klöss chewed his lip. "I think you might be right. The soldiers we fought in our first training raid were far beyond anything we have encountered so far. I think they have pulled back. Maybe they are marshalling their strength."

"A true confrontation will not be long in coming." Tristan joined him at the wall and followed his gaze out to sea.

"You're right," Klöss replied, as he leaned over the edge of the wall and looked down towards the surf. "Uncle Aiden tells me the sealord himself is on the way. I have a feeling things are changing on us, my friend." He met Tristan's eyes. "We came searching for new lands. Frostbeard never intended for us to conquer these people, just to drive them back. Something tells me this is going to go a lot further than that."

"We just go where they send us, Klöss. We always have."

* * *

The dark ship carved through the waves, the heavy prow forcing them to part as the ranks of oars drove the vessel through the leaden swells. The sails were furled, the red dyed canvas tied tight against the spars.

Klöss stood at the wharf, watching it approach. No fewer than six great reavers followed close behind and a dark smudge on the horizon hinted at more. "A bit much for a simple escort, wouldn't you say?" he muttered to his uncle.

Frostbeard favoured him with a quick grin. "The sealord needs to keep up appearances as much as anyone, lad. That's all authority really ever is in the end, what other people think of you. Besides, there's probably a fleet of haulers behind those ships. I expect they'll break off and head back out to sea as soon as they see him safely docked."

"I don't really think he's in much danger at this point," Klöss said dryly.

"Appearances, Klöss, appearances."

They waited as the huge vessel drew closer and settled at the end of the long deep-water wharf, while lines were tossed to waiting docksmen and the hawsers were made fast.

Klöss shifted and fidgeted as they waited. The sea breeze tossed his hair, irritating him. His leathers felt too constrictive, choking him. The honour guard stood too close to him, crowding him. The man was taking too long to get off the damned ship.

At last, the ramp was lowered to the wharf and men thundered down in heavy boots. They wore jet black leathers covered in bright steel plate, a ridiculous form of armour to wear on a ship. The saltwater spray would ruin it in no time. Klöss knew these were ceremonial guards. They had probably never been on a reaving in their lives. That said, they had the look of men who knew their weapons. Men whose lives were devoted to constant training, who perfected their knowledge of the sword as they guarded the sealord. These were not men he would want as his enemies.

He watched as they flanked the ramp, swords bared and held high in salute. The sealord stood at the top, gold inlaid steel plates adorning his leathers and a bearskin cloak hanging from his shoulders. He looked up at the growing city, clearly in no hurry as he surveyed the walls and harbour before joining them on the wharf.

"Aiden," he said warmly, a broad smile on his bearded face as he reached for Frostbeard's hand.

"Sealord," he said with a nod, as they shook hands firmly.

"It's quite a place you've thrown up here." The sealord waved expansively at the walls. "It's hardly a fort anymore. What are you calling it?"

Aiden winced and Klöss fought down a grin as his uncle spoke. "Rimeheld," he admitted. "It wasn't my idea," he added quickly. "Just something that came from the men."

The man's features twisted as he puzzled his way through it. "Ah, Rime, not rhyme." He laughed suddenly. "And they call *me* vain!"

"As I said, it wasn't my idea. It just sort of happened. You can't call a place this size 'The Fort' forever." Aiden's voice was gruff, as he tried and failed not to sound defensive.

"Of course not." The sealord's voice was steady but his lips quivered. "Shipmaster Klöss." He nodded a greeting and then looked up at the high stone walls again. "Shall we? I must admit, I'm curious to see what you've accomplished."

Aiden waved them on and the sealord's honour guard closed ranks around them as they left the wharf and began the climb up into the city.

Their walk through the streets was brief, punctuated with stops at the market and barracks. The city was an odd amalgam of the military and the cosmopolitan. Large portions were purely designed for use by the army, with barracks and training grounds, offices and stables. At the same time, businesses had sprung up, seemingly overnight, selling everything from foodstuffs to clothing and jewellery. It was a place in flux.

The ships had been flowing in from the Barren Isles almost constantly and lately they had contained more settlers than anything else. Rimeheld was bulging at the seams and growing in an odd, haphazard manner. The city seemed to strain against the rigid military order, like a horse that had yet to be broken. The original walls had long since failed to contain it and buildings had sprung up outside their protection, with new streets and neighbourhoods huddled up against the walls until a new outer defence could be constructed.

At the same time as the city was expanding, buildings were constantly being replaced as the temporary wooden structures were torn down to make way for their stone replacements. This gave the city the look and feel of a pot on the boil. The contents were roiling and ever-changing.

Aiden led the way, as proud as any new parent as he pointed out defence points and markets with equal enthusiasm. The tour ended in his office. The sealord raised an eyebrow as he looked around the spartan room, whilst Klöss and Aiden cleared piles of reports and plans from the chairs.

Frostbeard waved the others into seats and sank down behind the desk with a sigh. "Can I offer you any refreshments?"

"Keft, if you have it," the sealord said, with a glance out of the window. "It's a bit early for ale or wine for me."

Aiden waved vaguely at Klöss, who moved to the door to speak with the attendants outside.

"Your last report was a few weeks ago. Why don't you bring me up to speed? You mentioned you were facing some light resistance?"

"That's the problem with this level of distance, I suppose," Aiden grunted. "You're always catching up on last month's news." He stared up at the ceiling as he thought and scratched at his close-cropped beard. "The situation has changed a bit. We're holding all of the lands we've taken and there have been no real attempts to reclaim them. There was a strange, night-time counter-attack on some of our forces though, after the last village razing. Klöss here can give you more details."

Klöss swallowed and tried to force his thoughts into some semblance of order, as the sealord looked at him expectantly. "We were attacked by some form of elite unit after we'd set up camp for the night," he began. The sealord's intense stare unsettled him and he suddenly felt like a boy before his masters again. "They must have slipped past the outer sentries. They were upon us before half of us even knew they were there. They were highly trained, my lord. I'm afraid our losses were heavy."

"How heavy?" The man's voice was curt.

"Roughly a third of our force, my lord," Klöss replied. His throat felt like it was trying to close, and he fought the urge to swallow and show his nerves.

"That many?"

Klöss nodded. "They weren't routed or even driven back, my lord. They broke off the attack and quit the field by choice. It hurts me to admit it but if they hadn't, they'd probably have slaughtered us to a man."

The older man nodded and looked at the door at the knock. An attendant stepped in at Aiden's call and set down a tray filled with cups and a steaming jug. The rich smell filled the room and Klöss inhaled deeply, enjoying the aroma.

"It takes a lot to admit defeat or failure, Shipmaster. A man more vain than you might have tried to dress it differently. I appreciate that you didn't." He looked back across the desk, watching as Aiden poured the dark drink into the cups. "What are your plans then?"

"In response, my lord?" Aiden asked.

"Well, I think there needs to be something, don't you? Of course, that's just my suggestion. The theatre is still yours to command."

Klöss raised his eyebrows at that. The sentence sounded unfinished and the implied threat hung heavy at the end of it.

Aiden sipped his keft and studied the sealord's expression. Klöss found himself looking back and forth between the two of them. Frostbeard was a hard man to read, he always had been, and Klöss was finding the sealord to be cut from the same cloth.

"In one sense, the attack is irrelevant. It came after we had already razed the village." Frostbeard stood and moved to a chart on one wall, carrying his cup. "They have no towns or villages for several miles beyond this point. Any troop movements would be spotted by scouts and patrols easily before they came close to any of our territories."

"A rather passive approach, don't you think?"

Klöss watched the exchange in silence, admiring Frostbeard's self-control as the sealord jabbed at him.

"That rather depends on whether the objective is kept in sight or not, my lord." He sipped at his keft again. "The intention was to seize lands, not to enter into an outright war. I have no interest in seeking revenge for attacks. That would simply lead to an escalation of the conflict and, to be frank, we do not have a clear understanding of how large this nation might be."

The sealord absorbed this in silence, his dark eyes revealing nothing. "And what of these other attacks? This isn't the first attack you've suffered, is it?"

"How did you know about that?" Aiden burst out.

"Really, Aiden, you don't think you're my sole source of information, do you?" the sealord chided.

Frostbeard grunted, though his eyes showed his anger even if his lips kept it contained. "They were nothing. Attacks on some of the outlying villages. They didn't even bother to attack the structures. All we suffered was the loss of a few farmers."

"A touch more than 'a few', I believe." The sealord stopped him before he could go on. "We will talk more on this later, Seamaster Kurikson," he said, setting his cup of keft back on the table. "For now, I think I'd like you to have someone show me to my rooms. I have never found the journey through the Vorstelv to be a relaxing one."

Frostbeard waited as the man rose to his feet. "Of course, Sealord." He ushered him out of the study. Steam still rose from the cup on the table, the expensive keft cooling as it sat untouched.

Klöss rose and bowed, working hard to control his expression as the sealord made his exit. Frostbeard had mentioned nothing of any attacks. What else was he concealing?

* * *

Rimeheld never really grew quiet. Despite the fact that it was smaller than Hesk, it was a dense, compact city and, as the day ended, it underwent a transformation. The shops closed, the markets grew still, and the inns and taverns became busier.

The keep bustled as the servants prepared a welcoming banquet with everyone from cooks to stewards rushing to make things ready. The guards stood on the walls, slaves to convention and ritual, ever watchful in the darkness.

The moon rose, full and heavy, as it climbed out of the seas. The silvery light played down upon the still waters, dancing on the gentle swells.

Klöss stared down at the ocean as he leaned against the wall. The faint sound of the water lapping at the closest wharf carried to his ears in the breeze. They would be looking for him. The sealord's banquet would probably be a thing of pomp and ceremony. Men who hadn't held a sword in decades would be grasping wine cups and raising them high, as if it somehow mattered.

The thought was enough to make him shudder and he pulled his cloak tighter around his shoulders. The night was still enough for him to hear the footsteps and he glanced back over his shoulder at the sound before looking pointedly back out to sea.

"They will find you here, you know?" Tristan said, his face carefully blank.

"Probably, but I can't force myself to go in just yet." Klöss picked at the merlon in front of him and worried at a tiny ridge in the stone.

"There are those that would kill for a seat at the sealord's table."

"I know one they could have," Klöss muttered.

Tristan laughed and joined him at the wall. "Is it really that bad?"

"I suppose not," Klöss said, with a sigh. "It's more the fact that I don't feel I should be there. I've done nothing special. I'm there purely because I'm Frostbeard's nephew."

"I don't think many would see it that way," Tristan said, his smile gone. "You produced the fleet. You've been involved in every level of planning."

Klöss waved a hand, brushing away the words. "Those are things anyone could have done. I don't put myself as any more important than the next shipmaster."

Tristan gritted his teeth and grasped him by the shoulders. "You're being a child, Klöss. The sealord is here to inspect our progress. He is going to want first-hand reports. You owe your men more than this. You owe your fallen more than this."

Klöss flushed, growing first pale and then red as the import of the words sank in. "It's a foolish dance of flattery and pandering. I won't reduce myself to that level."

"So don't," Tristan grated, his own temper rising. "But, by the Lords of Blood, Sea and Sky, you owe Verig better than this." He bulled on, ignoring the stricken look on Klöss's face. "Get in there and get the sealord's ear. Give him a full report of that attack and make sure we get the support we need."

Klöss stared at him open-mouthed, grasping for words that slipped away like minnows in the shallows. Tristan was usually so placid. It was a shock to hear him being so blunt.

"Don't waste time talking, Klöss." Tristan steered him towards the doorway by the shoulders. "Go!"

The corridors grew steadily busier as Klöss drew close to the banquet hall. He stopped for a moment, his hand pressed to the door frame, as the rumble of conversation leaked under the door and into the hallway. The guards were exchanging odd looks at his delay and Tristan's words smarted again. Drawing a deep breath, he pushed the door open and marched in.

The press of people was enough to cover his entrance and he weaved through the crowd and outer tables, going almost unnoticed until he reached the high table. Frostbeard's expression was unreadable as he looked in his direction. His face was blank and his eyes a mystery, until a broad smile spread across his face and he waved Klöss into a chair beside him.

"I was afraid you'd got lost," Frostbeard said, as he waved a serving girl over.

"I tried to," Klöss admitted. "Tristan found me and educated me a bit." There was little point in trying to hide things from the man. A hint of steel was showing behind the grin. Insulting him with lies would only make it worse.

Aiden's face relaxed, highlighting just how false his first smile had been. "He's a good man. Remind me to thank him later." He waved a hand vaguely at the hall. "Like it or not, Klöss, you're a part of this, I'm afraid. And, as ridiculous as this is, it's every bit as important as the patrols and battles."

Klöss took the offered goblet of wine and sipped at it as he nodded. He looked curiously at the chair on the other side of Aiden, noting it was empty.

"Larren will be back in a few minutes, I expect," Frostbeard explained, catching his look. "He's under serious pressure from the keepers and the merchants to get some goods flowing. Apparently, even the First of Merchants is involved."

"The First? That seems a bit blatant."

"We have a lot tied up in this, Klöss, but if we fail we just end up dead. For them, it's their influence that's at stake. They have far more at risk." He didn't bother to hide the contempt in his voice.

"But surely…" Klöss began, but the man waved him to silence as the sealord emerged from the throng in the hall and sank back into the chair.

"You decided to join us, then?" he threw at Klöss, as he reached for his own cup.

"I apologise, Sealord. I was delayed," Klöss replied, as politely as he could manage.

The man snorted into his cup and eyed him over the rim. "Call me Larren. The title grates after a time."

"Larren, it is," Klöss nodded, leaning forward on one arm to see past his uncle.

"I take it Aiden here has let you in on the story about the keepers?" He glanced at Aiden, who was starting to protest. "He never could keep his mouth shut about things like that."

Klöss laughed and drank deeply, beginning to relax.

"So tell me then, Klöss, in your opinion, how safe are our new villages and farms going to be?"

Klöss thought for a second. "Truthfully? It's hard to say, Sealo… Larren. I don't think we've really faced any of their regular armies yet. The men they've had defending their own villages have been militia at best."

"What about the force that attacked your troops in the night raid you mentioned?"

Klöss thought quickly. "They were definitely not militia, but then I don't think they were regular troops either. If they hadn't struck us, I'd have thought they didn't have much of a standing army to speak of at all. We've certainly not faced any serious attempts to regain land that I know of. They've sent a couple of tentative sorties, but largely they seem to be falling back and consolidating."

The sealord sat back and digested that as he looked about the hall. Musicians had set up in a far corner and the faint sounds of them fine-tuning their instruments added to the growing noise. He leaned back in his chair as servers began setting platters in front of them. "We'll talk more about this later, Klöss. I must admit, not knowing the strength of their forces is grating at me. I've allowed you free reign so far, Aiden," he said, looking at Frostbeard, "but very soon, I'm going to need some hard results I can show the keepers and the damned bean counters."

"The agreement is holding then?"

"For now, Aiden, for now. I need some goods flowing though, if we're going to keep the merchants and the keepers playing nicely with us," Larren murmured, as he cut into the venison before him.

"Crops only grow so quickly, Larren," Frostbeard said.

The sealord nodded. "The chamber is a fickle beast, Aiden. The thane may have given his orders, but the chamber will twist and turn as it will."

"Surely they wouldn't go against the thane?" Klöss asked, shocked.

Larren laughed. "You're a young man, Klöss. You've had quite the career so far, but the chamber is something you clearly know nothing about." He smiled at Klöss's glower and continued. "No, the chamber won't openly defy the thane. He retains that much power, at least. It can still work around him in a thousand little ways, however. The success of this venture depends on the goodwill of the chamber and every faction there has its own agenda."

"I don't understand," Klöss confessed.

"The chamber might be bound to publicly support the thane, Klöss," Frostbeard cut in, "but if they decided to, they could end us in a matter of weeks. Slow supply of weapons, a delay in the shipments of supplies. These things could kill us just as effectively as battles and raids."

Klöss drank his wine. It gave him an excuse to keep his mouth shut for a second. "What can we do then?"

"Act quickly and decisively," Larren replied. "Find their forces and either eliminate them or drive them back. Get goods flowing and get the settlers into the new farms and villages."

"As simple as that, huh?" Aiden muttered.

Larren's smile didn't quite reach his eyes. "Well, he did ask."

* * *

Sket took a nip from the flask as he slid the peep-hatch on the gate shut. He hunched his shoulders, huddling further down into his cloak. It was starting to get colder at night already. The seasons in this place seemed skewed. It was too hot in the summer and the autumn seemed to have come too soon.

"And the rain!" he grumbled to himself, as the first drops fell. "All it does is bloody rain."

He hurried back into the guard shack beside the gate and the questionable warmth of the little wood stove. The stove wasn't much more than a small iron box, with a pipe leading through the wall to let the smoke out, but it did manage to produce at least some heat.

Rubbing his hands together over the ash-covered stove, he picked up the kettle and sloshed it experimentally before setting it on to boil. Sket squinted out through the gap in the tarpaulin that served as a door, and gazed at the stars shining brightly through the soft rain.

"Same stars, same moon." He watched as a cloud scudded across its silvery surface. "What in the hells am I doing here?"

The kettle was making a rumbling, hissing noise behind him as the bubbles rattled the misshapen container. He'd had to beg for it in the first place and he wasn't about to complain, but the thing shook worse than an oarsman's knees on his first reaving when it boiled.

He pulled it off the heat. It wasn't fully boiling yet, but the sound irritated him and he'd rather have a drink that wasn't quite hot enough than deal with the noise. He dumped a pinch or two of the ground leaves into his cup before pouring the water on. It wasn't as good as keft, but who could afford that stuff here?

"Tea," he snorted. "Stupid name for a drink anyway." It was hot though and that's all that really mattered. A distant wail caught his attention and he turned an eye to the tarpaulin as he blew on the tea. It had sounded a bit like a horn or perhaps even a flute. He stepped out into the road and looked towards the keep, rising up above the rooftops.

"They get their banquet and fine wines while Sket gets the bloody wet and this poxy, boiled leaf water. Still, it's better than soggy sheep." He'd been among the first of the keepers to respond when the call went out. They hadn't promised a glamorous life or even riches and glory. The promise of a new land and the chance to make something different of himself had been enough at the time. Now he wasn't so sure.

A flash of green caught his eye and he looked up, tracking the odd light as it swooped down towards the gate. It was hard to make out at first - just a blur of sparks and shining metal. His eyes first squinted against the raindrops, then grew wide as the spectacle became clear and the first of the horses touched down on the road leading to the gates.

The ground immediately outside the city was a maze of trenches, liberally seasoned with sharpened stakes, but the horses passed over them as if they weren't there. Their hooves touched the dirt and even threw up sods, but the trenches had no impact on their passage. It was as if gravity was a rule that could be ignored as easily as the drifting rain. They ran over the trenches without bothering to leap, the air supporting them as easily as the muddy ground had.

Sket dropped the tea as he backed away from the peep-hatch, his jaw slack as he saw the figures charging at the gate. At the last moment, he thought to check the massive crossbar was in place and snatched up the horn.

The horn blast died on his lips as the gates flew inwards. The blow didn't simply split the crossbar, it shattered it. Splinters and jagged chunks of wood shot into the city as the wooden beam, as thick as a large man's thigh, disintegrated before the blow. Sket cried out as the flying wreckage tore at his flesh and threw him backwards. He fell back to the ground, splashing in the mud as he fought to find his feet.

The creature entered the city slowly, ignoring the horns that called out from the sentries on the walls. Its hoofed feet moved slowly and proudly, claiming the ground they moved to rest upon. Sket felt the rush of warmth spread from his crotch and down his legs as the glowing eyes came to regard him. It bowed its horned head slightly, paying homage to its prey, and then waved its great hand forwards and unleashed hell.

The fae charged past the antlered being in a rush, silver swords held high as the moonlight shone on their winged helms. Sket stood awestruck, his face carrying the same expression of delighted wonder even after the blade had removed his head. As the fae tied it to its saddle by the hair, Sket smiled on, his dead eyes shining as he waited for company.

The host charged through the streets, a carnival of beauty, blood and terror as they hunted down those in their path. The alarm was raised swiftly but the Bjornmen were no more effective than a child pushing back at the waves. Twice, the fae rose back into the air, laughing amidst the screams of the fallen and the unceasing song of the flutes, only to turn in an elegant arc and swoop down upon the men running into the shadows and spaces between the buildings.

Klöss followed as the guards surged up the stairs and out onto the roof of the keep. Archers were already in position between the merlons, firing a steady stream of arrows into the attackers as they flowed through the streets.

"*This* is what you call secure?" he dimly heard the sealord demand.

He followed the voice to find its owner waving down at the streets. Frostbeard had no response as he stared, aghast, down into the chaos. His eyes found Klöss and he growled a single word that carried all of the frustration he felt as his dreams fell apart around him. "Go."

CHAPTER FIVE

Devin spooned the carrots out onto the plate and poured a small puddle of thin gravy next to the chicken. The meal was a far cry from Hannah's standards of cooking, but it was the best he could manage by himself. He carried the plate over to the table and set it in front of her, before fetching his own and taking his place opposite.

He had been up since first light and it felt like he hadn't stopped moving since his feet hit the cold floorboards beside his bed. It was nice to be able to just sit for a few minutes. He ate quickly, hunger adding a flavour to the roast chicken that he had somehow managed to leave out when he was cooking it.

It was always the same when he cooked. He could follow Hannah's recipes to the letter, but his food was never as good as hers. Perhaps the missing ingredient was the way she actually enjoyed cooking. She took a simple pleasure in the act of preparing food in a way he never had. To him, it was simply a means to an end. Meat went into the oven, a meal came out.

He speared a chunk of carrot and brought it to his lips before glancing across the table. It was a mistake and his mood sank as he saw her.

Hannah's food lay untouched on the plate before her, as she stared into space with a vacant expression. She held a fork above her plate as if she was unsure how to use it. Her hair hung loosely beside her face and draped down almost to the surface of the table.

Devin put his fork down. "You've got to eat something, Ma."

If she heard the words, she showed no sign of it. He sighed, more inwardly than out, and moved to her side, taking the fork from her unresisting fingers.

"How about a nice bit of chicken, eh?" He forced brightness into his voice and lifted the meat to her lips, taking the fork away again as she took the mouthful and chewed slowly. Her lips were slack and her mouth open as she ate. A small rivulet of the too-thin gravy ran down her chin and spotted onto the white tablecloth he'd laid out earlier. He dabbed at it quickly with a folded napkin and swallowed hard.

"Now, let's try some potatoes, shall we?" He fed her the rest of the food as if she were a small child. The meal passed in silence. He could manage to feed her but to keep his voice bright, or even level, at the same time would be one step too far. The occasional drip of gravy spattered down onto the once pristine tablecloth, mixing with the tears that fell unnoticed from his face.

The knock that came at the door sounded improbably loud in the stillness of the kitchen and he lurched backwards in shock. He stood at the door and rubbed at his face with his sleeve before lifting the latch.

"Hello, stranger!" Erinn said brightly, her face filled with a happy smile. "You've locked yourself away here for days now. No one has seen hide nor hair of you, so I thought I'd come and check…" She stopped herself mid-sentence as she took in his drawn face, the stained and dirty clothing, and the bags under his eyes. Her gaze moved beyond him into the kitchen, and flickered from Hannah at the table to the pots and pans littering the counters. "Oh, Devin," she sighed. "Why didn't you ask anyone for help?"

She pushed past him into the kitchen without waiting for an answer and set down the wicker basket she was carrying on one end of the table.

"How long has she been like this?" she asked.

"Since we got back, really," he said, in a dead voice. "She has times when she seems almost okay, but most of the time she acts like this. Like she's numb to everything around her." It felt good to say it out loud. The thoughts had been inside his head for days now, whispering to each other and feeding his worry.

"What about you? When was the last time you slept properly?" Erinn's voice had a maternal tone to it, not soft and caring, but more that of a mother scolding a child.

His silence was answer enough and she pointed a finger towards the stairs. "Go. I'll look after Hannah for a while. I don't want to see you until you've had a good eight hours."

"But what if she needs…" He cut off as her face darkened and she stabbed one finger towards the stairs again.

"Go!"

Devin fled.

* * *

It was the sunlight that woke him. A gap in the curtains let the light shine through and a narrow band burned across one eye. He groaned and rolled over, and it took long minutes before the facts managed to fully register. Sunlight meant daytime. He'd slept through the whole evening and into the next day. He lurched out of bed and reached for the clothes he'd dropped onto the chair in the corner, only to find they were gone.

Five minutes later and dressed in clean clothes for the first time in a week, he made his way down into the kitchen. The room was empty and silent, but the counters were clear and the pots that hung from their hooks in ceiling gleamed. The distant murmur of conversation drew him back through the house and out of the seldom-used front door.

A covered deck ran the length of the front of the cottage. It had been covered in leaves when he'd been ordered to his bed yesterday, but now it was freshly swept. Erinn sat in the well-worn rocker, chatting with Obair. They turned at his approach.

"I thought you were going to sleep all day," Erinn said with a smile.

"I think I could have," Devin admitted. "The sun woke me." He grimaced at the light and pinched at the flesh between his eyes.

"Headache?" Obair asked.

Devin grunted.

"You're probably just dried out. Get some water into yourself. That always works for me."

"Sit down," Erinn said, as she rose to her feet. "I'll fix you some food. Hannah's still sleeping and I know how much noise you'd make."

"You know, she seems to have turned into my mother very quickly," Devin muttered, as he sank down into the rocker.

Obair chuckled and puffed on his pipe, looking out over the fields towards the distant trees. Devin followed his gaze and then glanced at the sun for confirmation.

"Funny how fast life can change, isn't it?" Obair said, past the stem of the pipe. "You look to the sun to see how long you have until they come now."

Devin felt his eyes upon him and nodded silently, his gaze moving to the wooden walls of the cottage and the scores of iron nails now protruding from the wood.

"That wouldn't stop them if they really wanted in," Obair said. "It's more of a deterrent than anything else, making you less attractive than an alternative."

"I know, Obair. You told us all of this, remember? What do we do long-term, though? As a people, I mean? Are we just supposed to accept that this is the way the world is now?"

Erinn emerged from the kitchen with a steaming bowl of porridge and a mug of hot tea. She handed them both to Devin and met Obair's sad eyes, defiance flashing in her own as she spoke. "We fight back."

"But how?" he asked, sucking on his pipe.

"That's the problem," muttered Devin. "We know nothing about them. We saw how effective iron was at the glade. It works, sure, but we need more than that. Most of the men were next to useless."

"How do you mean?" Erinn asked. No one had said much about the terrible confrontation at the glade and, in the three days that had passed since, the focus had been upon making individual homes safe from the hunt in case it descended upon Widdengate.

"It was like the soldiers with us were half-asleep. They just stood there and smiled at the fae as they arrived. If we'd all struck at once, we might have been able to do more. As it was, only a handful of us actually fought. But that's not all of it either. We need to know what the fae actually want."

"I'm afraid that's impossible, Devin," Obair said, with a sigh. "All of the druids' records and chronicles died with them. I know little more than you do, at this point."

Devin pinched his forehead again. "Damn this headache. I can't think right with these waves of pain in my head. We need to know more about the fae, find out what they want. We need a way to talk to them."

"Talk to them!" Obair scoffed. "I can't see them coming in for a nice chat, my lad."

"That's it!" Erinn cried, as both of them turned to look at her.

"What is?" Devin asked.

She looked off into the distance as she thought. "I need to talk to Captain Rhenkin. My father too. I have an idea."

* * *

Lieutenant Larson peered into the pit as Harlen tested the bars lining the trap. "What do you think?" he called down.

"They're as strong as I can make them. The sides of the pit itself will provide

54

some more strength but…" The smith frowned up at the lieutenant and shrugged.

"I know," Larson sighed. "There's no way to test this thing, really."

The ladder shook as Harlen pulled himself out. He dusted himself down and took the mug of ale from Owen gratefully.

"Hot and heavy work," the portly innkeeper noted. "I never envied you your trade, Harlen."

The smith snorted. "Did you come up with a way to get the top on?" he asked Larson.

"Not as fast as I'd like. The only thing I can think is to just drop it on or pull it across. The captain expects a report on this shortly and I still have no real solution," Larson admitted, with a sour expression.

"That's going to be too slow, Sir. You know how quick they are," a private muttered, brushing mud from his uniform. "If we can get this right, we'll have one of the bastards like a bear in a…" He flushed as he realised who he was talking to and trailed off into silence as his sergeant gave him a furious look.

"In a trap. A bear trap!" Larson whirled around, snapping his fingers. "Why didn't you suggest that, Sergeant?" he demanded of the flustered soldier who was glowering at the private.

"My experience of bear traps is limited, Sir," he said, weakly.

"Bah!" Larson waved a dismissive hand at him. "Do you know anything about that sort of thing?" he asked Harlen, who tugged on his beard as he thought.

"It'd need to be a mightily powerful spring," he said slowly, his mind moving faster than his mouth. "Let me think on it."

"Good enough. We have a couple of days left until the full moon anyway," Larson said, looking down at the pit again. "Damned clever idea, though. You've got a bright one there in that girl."

"Don't I know it!" Harlen muttered. "She's been running rings around me for years."

Larson laughed. "One of the reasons I never had children. Daughters are the punishment for men being men. When I think back to what I was like at her age…" He stopped, glancing at the smith's rapidly darkening face "Yes, well, never mind about that. I'd best go and report on our progress."

"You do that," Harlen muttered into the tankard of ale.

Larson chuckled to himself as he walked across what had once been the village green towards the command post. The village had almost ceased to exist. The military machine that was the army encampment had absorbed it utterly.

He ran up the wooden steps into the captain's office, noting the empty chair behind the desk that groaned with papers and reports. The office was empty. Sometimes he didn't know why he bothered looking in there.

Finally, he located Rhenkin. He was walking the palisade, his uniform immaculate but his face was lined and drawn. Larson believed his primary duty was to support his commanding officer, something too many in the service neglected, in his opinion. He'd served under some piss-poor officers, men more interested in preening themselves in the mirror than doing their job, and children of nobles who'd had their commissions arranged with a handshake or a full purse.

"You've not been sleeping again, Sir," Larson noted, as the captain turned at his approach.

"Don't mother me, Larson." Rhenkin scratched at the stubble on his cheek. "Do you have the scout reports? I'd have expected them to push forward by now."

"The Bjornmen, Sir?"

"Of course the Bjornmen!" Rhenkin barked.

"Sorry, Sir, I've been working on the pit trap the blacksmith's girl thought up," Larson explained. "The scouts report they found a battle site. It seems the Bjornmen suffered massive losses, by the looks of things."

"From who?" Rhenkin wondered.

"Not us, clearly, and the king has yet to send a single man," Larson said, without thinking.

Rhenkin's eyes turned cold. "You forget yourself, soldier."

"My apologies, Sir. I spoke out of turn and thoughtlessly."

Rhenkin grunted, acknowledging the apology. "How recent is this report?"

"Two days, Sir. The next one is late but could be in any time now." Larson glanced over the wall, as if expecting to see the scouts approaching.

"Two days is too long, Larson." Rhenkin frowned at him. "They could be on our doorstep by now. Send them more often. I want a report twice daily, even if it's just to tell me nothing is happening."

Larson nodded.

"How long do we have until full moon?"

"Three days, Captain."

"If they've just suffered a defeat, now would be the perfect time to strike," Rhenkin muttered, half to himself. "Damn it, these fae are just too unpredictable. We can't risk the men in open country overnight, not until we find a way to counter these damned fiends."

"Perhaps you'd like to inspect the pit, Sir?"

"What?" Rhenkin looked up at the man, as if suddenly remembering he was still there.

"The pit, Sir. The one you ordered us to construct?"

"Oh yes, the pit. I'll take a look at it when I get a chance." Rhenkin looked down behind him towards the barracks. Off-duty soldiers lounged on the steps and lay in the grass.

"The men are looking a little shabby, Larson," he said, with a frown. "Why don't you go and sweat them for a bit? I need some space to think."

"Very good, Sir." Larson saluted and turned smartly on his heel.

Rhenkin watched him go. Larson was a good man, an excellent soldier and a damned fine officer. It seemed sometimes that the more a man rose through the ranks, the less competent he became. There was too much back-biting and jockeying for position these days.

"Listen to me," he muttered to himself. "I sound like an old man." He let out a snort at himself, "I know I feel like one!"

He stared out over the wall towards the distant trees. The land had been ravaged, raped by the needs of war. What had once been fields covered with flourishing crops was now barren earth, scarred by rows of deep trenches filled with sharpened stakes.

Hedgehogs - whole tree trunks bristling with stakes and razor-sharp blades set into the wood - lay strewn in the spaces between the trenches. Their purpose was not so much to cause injury, but to break up formations, to slow and to impede the enemy's progress. The two hundred yards immediately before the walls of the fortress that Widdengate had become were a killing field. The wooden palisade was spiked with shards of iron - nails, splinters, whatever could be driven into the wood. And yet the entire system of defences was next to useless against these fae. Rhenkin slammed his hands against the walls in frustration.

Widdengate had been spared the Wild Hunt. Where the fae had gone after they left the druid's glade was anybody's guess, but they hadn't gone near the village. That hadn't stopped satyrs and fae from attacking almost nightly since, however. The new moon had come as a blessed respite.

He turned and glanced towards the west. It was a futile motion and he knew what he would see. More trees and unspoilt fields. There was no relief column, no flag flying the king's standard. For whatever reason, Widdengate and all of his duchess's lands stood defended by his forces alone.

The sun was just reaching its highest point. He made his way down the steps and hurried through the remains of the village. The pit had been positioned close to the smithy. The idea was that the iron from the forge would cover the scent of the iron from the trap, or something like that.

A shout went up from the walls and the gates creaked open behind him. He stopped in his tracks and turned as the scout stumbled through. Even from this distance, he could see the blood staining the man's clothes. His horse was nowhere to be seen. Rhenkin set off for the gates at a run.

The man had sunk to the ground and been surrounded by a cluster of men by the time he reached him.

"Bastards shot my horse out from under me," the scout gasped, taking a skin from one of the soldiers. He drank desperate gulps between heaving breaths.

"They're on the move. Can't be more than a day and a half behind me."

Rhenkin closed his eyes against a wave of anger. It wouldn't do any good to scream at the scout.

"How many? Is it a probe?"

The man looked at him and realised who he was speaking to. He made an attempt to stand, but Rhenkin stopped him, placing a hand on his chest. "Never mind that, man, just tell me."

"No, Sir, it's got to be a full attack. I couldn't even guess at the numbers. They stretched as far as I could see."

Rhenkin swore and waved a corporal over. "Sound the bells, I want this place locked down. Bring all the patrols back in as soon as possible. And someone get me Larson!" The list ended in a shout.

The village was transformed over the next few hours. They threw the rear gates wide open to let out those villagers that chose to flee. Ballistae were wheeled into position in front of the walls next to the catapults. There hadn't been time to build sufficient platforms against the palisade to mount many of them, so the evil-looking contraptions crouched on the ground, waiting only for their prey. Teams of men scurried around the fields, covering stake-lined pits and moving more of the massive hedgehogs into position.

Rhenkin stood high in one of the watchtowers and watched the line of refugees fleeing through the gates. He'd had the civilians warned as soon as he'd heard the news.

"How many do you think?" he asked Larson.

"Sir?"

"How many have left?"

"Hard to say, Sir. We didn't have a count of them to begin with. Too many arriving and moving on."

Rhenkin nodded. "They'll have a hard time of it on the road."

"I expect we'll have a hard enough time of it here, Sir" Larson snorted. "Still, fewer mouths."

Rhenkin grunted his agreement. Fewer people meant more supplies to go round and the villagers would just have been underfoot anyway. It was ironic that he'd been sent to defend these lands and people, and the best way for him to do it was to send them off on their own.

"Harrying force, Sir?"

"Hmm?" He looked round to see Larson with a map spread out over the floor. "They'll be passing into some heavy woods before they get close. It's a good place to bleed them."

Rhenkin knelt down to get a closer look. "Send skirmishers. Three full companies on horseback if we can spare the mounts. Have them harry only, Larson."

"I'll see to it, Sir." Larson headed for the steps.

"I mean it, Larson. I don't want them to close at all. Bows only and pull back after each engagement. We can't afford to lose good men just because some idiot sergeant thinks he can fight his way to a field commission."

"Yes, Sir." Larson met his eyes and nodded again.

"Oh, and Larson?"

"Sir?"

"See if you can convince that Devin lad to go with them. He might know some likely spots for ambush closer to the village."

"Really, Sir? I don't mean to question you but…"

Rhenkin waved away the almost apology. "He accounted well for himself at that stone circle when most of the men didn't. I have a feeling he could make a good scout some day. Try him. Make sure he knows he's being asked to go, not ordered to, though. It's his choice."

"Understood, Sir."

* * *

Devin avoided the patch of dried leaves, moving to the side and setting his feet down on the bare earth and the fallen tree branch instead. The mottled green scout's cloak felt heavy, and he had to work hard to keep it from snagging and making noise. The scout ahead of him looked back, nodded in approval and then waved him forward until they all came together by a large tree.

"Alright, we're close enough now that we could see them any minute," the leader said. His voice was low, not far above a whisper, and Devin had to lean in towards him to hear properly.

"I want a skirmish line with a ten foot spacing. Do you know what that is, boy?" Jameson looked at him at the last and Devin nodded. He'd had it explained to him three times already.

"How's the lad holding up?" Jameson asked the scout next to Devin.

"Good, Sir. He's quick and quiet. Better than a lot of others I've trained." Devin's pleasure at the compliment was dampened by the way they spoke as if he wasn't there. He'd been "boy" and "lad" all day.

"You stick between Riddal and me," Jameson said, his eyes hard and serious. "If you see or hear anything, you point it out to one of us first."

Devin nodded. The man clearly thought of him as a child and he wasn't about to prove him right.

"I mean it, boy. You fire before we're ready and the Bjornmen will be the last thing you need to worry about."

"I understand, Sir," Devin hoped his irritation wasn't obvious in his voice.

"Slow and quiet now." Jameson's eyes swept the group. "I want to hear them before I see them. Don't fuck it up." His gaze landed on Devin as he swore, and then he turned without another word and was gone, into the trees.

The men spread out in a long line, keeping abreast of one another but with room between them so they could pass trees and bushes. They'd been moving since before dawn, keeping to the road for the sake of speed for the first few hours, and then heading deep into the forest. They were further from Widdengate than Devin had ever been when hunting. The woods were new to him but still had a familiar feel about them.

The line froze as a bird exploded out of the trees ahead of them, and Devin snatched an arrow from his quiver, setting it to the string but not yet pulling it back. He relaxed as he realised it was just a spooked wood pigeon and glanced to one side, catching Riddal's nod.

They moved slowly, taking the time to ensure they were silent rather than keeping to a faster pace. The skies were overcast which served to make the forest darker than usual, the thick canopy blocking out much of the light.

The woods were alive with distant birdsong and so Devin almost missed the faint crack of a twig from up ahead of them. He froze and waved at Riddal to attract his attention, gesturing to his ear and then pointing in front of them.

Riddal froze in place as he listened. He raised an eyebrow at Devin, but the woods were silent aside from the birds. His gaze passed beyond Devin for a moment. Devin looked behind him in time to see Jameson motioning them onwards with an impatient scowl.

The voices carried clearly through the trees, despite the hushed tones of those speaking. Devin crouched behind a bush and nocked an arrow. He shot a look at Riddal and received a smile in return. He'd been right about hearing something after all and the scout knew it.

He sighted along the arrow through a small gap in the leaves of the bush. The voices grew steadily louder and were accompanied by the rustle of leaves and crack of twigs. Whoever it was making all the noise knew nothing of woodscraft.

Jameson waved at him and held his hand out as if halting them, before nocking his own arrow. The voices became even louder. Their words were still indistinct, but they were clearly speaking a different language. Devin relaxed the string of his bow and waited. There was a blur of movement in the trees and then Jameson let fly. A crash of bushes and a groan of pain showed his aim had been good.

There was a shout and then men boiled out of the trees. Devin picked one at random, his arrow flying wild as his hands shook. They were coming so quickly. He snatched up another shaft and released smoothly, catching the man in the throat and dropping him cleanly. He could do this, he told himself. It wasn't that different to hunting. His trembling hands told another story, though. He quickly drew another arrow and released. His arrow joined Riddal's and they both hit the man in the chest.

The woods fell silent and Devin crouched low behind the bush, his breathing ragged and his heart pounding. He forced himself to get up and follow the others out of the bushes to reclaim the arrows. The man he'd shot lay on the ground, arms and legs straight and relaxed, almost as if he were sleeping. He looked very young, little older than Devin himself. His boyish face had blonde wispy fluff growing on his cheeks. Devin stared at him, unable to move for the moment.

"Stay there, lad," Riddal said softly. He knelt and worked the arrow out of the ruin of the man's throat. "Your other one snapped. Unlucky."

"Alright, men," Jameson called. "Let's move back and see if we can find a good place. These scouts will be missed before too long."

They had backtracked for no more than ten minutes when a shout went up. Distant screams of pain carried through the forest and Devin knew the other skirmish teams were hard at work. The fight had begun in earnest.

The day began to blur, becoming an endless succession of small ambushes. They'd shoot no more than two arrows apiece, reclaim them where they could and then run back towards Widdengate as they looked for the next ambush point.

Devin waited at the top of a steep bank. A small stream burbled as it ran through the woods below. The trees were thinner here and the ground was carpeted in ferns. They'd travelled farther away this time, giving themselves extra distance so they would have some time to rest.

Riddal flopped down next to him and handed over a small piece of dried pork. Devin nodded his thanks and began to chew.

"How are you holding up, lad?"

"I'm fine," Devin replied, lying through his teeth.

"No, you're not, but that's alright. I'd be more worried about you if you weren't scared," Riddal told him.

Devin chewed the pork and thought about that. The man reminded him of Garrit, the caravan guard. A man from a different life. Since they'd faced the fae and he'd caught a glimpse of his mother, memories had been coming back to him. They weren't all pleasant. Some were awful, like a rotten fish buoyed up by its own putrescence. Garrit was one of the more pleasant ones.

"You know, it's funny," Devin said quietly, looking over at Riddal. "I spent years playing in these woods as a child, hunting monsters and Bjornmen."

Riddal snorted. "Let's just stick with the Bjornmen, eh? They're enough trouble as it is."

Something was wrong. Devin was no strategist but even he could tell the response was not what they'd been expecting. They'd warned him that the Bjornmen would probably be confused at first, but their next likely response would be to rush at them.

"The whole point of skirmishers," Riddal had told him, "is to break up units. Armies are used to fighting in units. The men get too used to this and then they can't think on their own. You do something to force them out of their units and they just fall to pieces."

Eventually, those in command would order a rush, he'd explained. They'd charge forward to overwhelm the skirmish line, to force them either to stand and fight or to flee. The rush hadn't come though. Instead, the Bjornmen were moving much as they were, in small groups or individually.

Devin looked over at Jameson, who was crouched behind a tree, gnawing at his knuckle as he thought. "Time we were moving," the leader muttered to the rest of them. He stood, peered around the tree and then his head simply wasn't there. It exploded into pieces as the heavy crossbow bolt blasted through flesh and bone. Devin dropped to the ground in terror and looked at Riddal in a panic. Another member of their team fell to the dirt, screaming as a crossbow bolt tore through his shoulder. Trees shook as more bolts smashed into branches and trunks.

"What do we do?" Devin cried out, his voice shrill with fear.

"We get the hell out of here!" Riddal growled, and crawled on his belly down the other side of the bank, away from the incoming bolts. Devin followed close behind and sensed Tench, the last team member, crawling behind him.

They ran through the woods for what felt like hours, though Devin knew it could only have been five or ten minutes. Eventually, they slowed and then stopped.

Devin bent double, gasping as his chest heaved. Riddal pulled him down out of sight behind a stout chestnut tree and the other scout collapsed beside them.

"Alright," Riddal said between breaths. "They are a lot closer and a lot quieter than we thought. Take two lessons from that, lad. Don't ever underestimate your enemy and never ever truly relax."

"Jameson?" Devin gasped.

"Jameson's gone. Stick close to me and you'll be fine." Riddal looked through his quiver, counting quickly. He twisted Devin's, so he could see the arrows and then looked past him. "How are you for arrows, Tench?"

"Seven," the blonde man replied. "Think I might have lost some on the run."

"No, that sounds about right. We're on eight apiece." He scratched a stubbled cheek for a minute, as he looked up at the sky through the trees.

"We're not going to accomplish much more like this. I say we head back."

Tench nodded. "I'll take the rear for a while."

"Right." Riddal looked back and forth between them. "We'll try and stick together, but we're not going to be stupid here. If it comes to it, just get yourselves back to the village, together or alone."

Devin nodded. There wasn't much he could say to that.

They travelled in silence, running for as long as they could, then dropping back into a walk just long enough to catch their breath before running again. The trees and bushes became a blur, and Devin no longer had any real idea of where they were. He slowed to a walk again, his throat burning from gasping in the ragged breaths. Riddal and Tench were in similar states, both taking gulps from their waterskins.

Devin fumbled with the thing and dropped it to the dirt, where it lay amongst the footprints. For a long moment, he wasn't aware of what he was looking at. Finally, a series of disparate shapes came together to form a clear image.

"Shit."

Tench gave him a look.

"There are prints here." Devin pointed.

"Of course there are, boy. We've half a thousand men in these woods." The scout waved him off.

"No scout would leave this much of a trail. Not unless he was running." He dropped to the ground and moved forwards on his hands and knees, studying the footprints. "No, look here. These are too close together. They were made by men walking."

Riddal came over and stood behind him, looking to where Devin pointed. His eyes tracked from the deep heel impressions to the broken fern stems and through to the fresh leaves knocked free from a the bush. "The lad's right," he told Tench. "Somehow they've got ahead of us. We're behind their lines."

"How?" Tench demanded. "We've been running for the best part of an hour."

"Does it matter? Maybe it's a different group. Maybe they came in from the north of us rather than the east. Who cares? The fact is we're behind them."

"Shit." Tench sighed. "So now what?"

"Skirt around them, I suppose." Riddal shrugged.

"That won't work." Devin stood and looked back and forth between them. "What if they surround the village? We'll be cut off before the battle even starts. We need to follow them, find a weak point and get through."

"Are you mad, boy?" Tench spat into the dirt. "You might as well lie down and die here. Save them the trouble."

"Listen," Devin explained, "from what we've seen, their woodscraft is nothing special. They might have some trackers among them, but the ones who left these prints might as well be wearing bells round their necks."

Riddal gave Tench an enquiring look.

"Oh, fine!" The man dropped his shoulders. "We'll try it your way, lad, but if you get us killed..."

"You'll never speak to him again," Riddal finished for him. "It wasn't funny the first time, Tench."

Tench shrugged and shot Devin a lopsided smile.

"Come on then, let's get this started," Riddal said and led them off into the pines.

CHAPTER SIX

The Bjornman army worked its way through the forest and out into the fields. Any attempt at concealment would have been futile, it was simply too big a force to try and hide it. The skirmishers bled them slowly, but it was a small wound on a beast almost too large to notice it. The Bjornmen's response had been swift and brutal, lacking the confusion from the breaks in formation that the skirmishers had depended upon.

The skirmishers themselves had been beaten back by pure brute force, though the toll they'd inflicted had been considerable. The Bjornmen had pushed through to the edges of the forest that stood before the fields of Widdengate and there they had stopped.

Rhenkin watched the distant shadow slowly darken the wheat field as the enemy emerged from the trees. After three days of no movement, it was almost a relief to see them push forward.

He and his men had taken up position some distance in front of the village itself. He'd decided there was little point in trying to conduct a defence by limiting himself to the walls alone.

"Larson!" he shouted.

"I'm next to you, Sir."

Rhenkin looked at him without a trace of embarrassment. "Order the distance markers to be lit. Tell Whitelock to prepare his cavalry for an attack. I want him to bleed the enemy, but not to take any undue risks. We're going to need those horses."

Larson nodded. "Yes, Sir. When shall I say he is to attack, Sir?"

"I don't see much point in letting them get settled in, do you?" Rhenkin said, his gaze shifting back to the Bjornmen.

"No, Sir. We might as well do some good whilst they're still milling about."

"Get to it, then. Tell him to go as soon as he's ready."

Rhenkin waited calmly, as the men around him fidgeted. It was something that took years to move past. He'd only managed it once he had received his first command. Soldiers watched their commanders. As an officer, you didn't have the luxury of letting your nerves show.

Plumes of smoke rose in the distance, indicating the position of the newly lit signal fires. Fully fifteen foot high and packed with slow-burning wood, the bonfires would last far longer than they were needed.

The sound of hooves drew his attention to the east, where the cavalry pounded towards the still-emerging Bjornmen. He'd listened carefully to the reports from those who had survived clashes with the invaders. The enemy seemed to have no horses of their own, but their methods of defending against them were very effective.

The cavalry was lightly armoured, wearing leather and carrying only swords along with their odd-looking horse bows. The bows were similar to a standard longbow but they extended down past the horse archers' feet, with the arrow being set closer to the top of the bow rather than in the central position that was usually used. The tightly-packed horses ran towards the Bjornmen, but pulled up short two hundred yards or more from the enemy ranks.

In one motion, they launched a volley into the massed raiders. The response was instant, as the invaders dropped to one knee and raised large wooden shields. Rhenkin was impressed, despite himself. It was hard to tell from this distance what casualties they might have suffered, but the discipline of the Bjornmen was notable.

A unit emerged from the Bjornmen ranks, shields interlocked both in front and above them, as they shuffled towards the horsemen. Rhenkin watched on, bemused. The horse archers were still firing volleys into the Bjornmen. The distant thunks of arrows into the wooden shields were interspersed with occasional faint screams.

"What are they thinking?" Larson said. "Those horsemen will be long gone before they even get close."

Rhenkin shot him a sideways look. The man was right. The tortoiseshell formation was an impressive display, but it would be useless against an enemy as mobile as the horse archers.

"Unless they don't need to be that close," Rhenkin gasped, speaking slowly as the thought occurred to him. "Sound the withdrawal!" he snapped, but it was too late.

The archers had already begun to fire at the approaching Bjornmen, their arrows as ineffectual at close range as they were in volleys.

The tortoise was less than fifty yards away from them now and, as the horses wheeled, ready to withdraw, the Bjornmen struck, parting their heavy shields and revealing the crossbows they carried. The heavy bolts tore through the cavalry, ripping into riders and horses alike. As the chaos unfolded, the raiders dropped their bows and charged, crashing into the archers with swords and axes. Rhenkin swore loudly as he watched his men overwhelmed in moments, and the Bjornmen began to move forward.

"Tell Capston to prepare the archers, Larson." He didn't bother checking to make sure the man had heard him. Using the horse archers had been a costly gamble and one he couldn't afford to repeat.

He glanced back at the village. The wooden palisade had been improved upon and was heavily braced, but it was still just wood. It wouldn't hold against the invaders for long.

He would have given much to have some stone in the region, but the area was almost all farmland and forest. What little stone there was had been taken from the fieldstone walls, but it wouldn't be close to enough. On the plus side, he had more timber than he could ever need.

He watched as the archers moved into position. Almost everyone in the village who could draw a bow had been pressed into service. The first volley was sporadic, arrows flying wild or falling short. After five or six volleys, the flights were more uniform and most reached the enemy force.

The archers worked in three ranks, each firing and then moving back to the next position while the next loosed their volley, creating an almost constant rain of arrows falling onto the enemy. It also kept the villagers busy and under control. If Rhenkin was lucky, they might even kill some of the raiders.

He knew it wouldn't be enough, though. The Bjornmen had slowed to a crawl, shields held high. They were moving slowly but they were still moving forward. He looked to the trees at the rear of their lines. More Bjornmen troops were still emerging from the woods. Their numbers seemed without end.

"Tough bastards," Larson muttered.

"Let's see how they fair when they reach the first range marker," Rhenkin said, looking through the hail of arrows to the farthest bonfire.

The archers reached the fire and ran back towards the village, stopping and moving back into formation only when they reached their next marker.

"Signal the catapults," Rhenkin said, his voice calm despite the stress building inside him. The Bjornmen were surging forward, taking advantage of the archers' retreat.

The horn sounded again and, in response, the rows of catapults lurched, lofting their deadly missiles into the sky. Rhenkin watched Larson's expression as the logs struck the Bjornmen. The absence of rock and stones had almost been enough to make Rhenkin give up on the idea of catapults. That was until Larson suggested using logs. A foot-long chunk of wood might not do the same amount of damage as a head-sized rock, but it would definitely hurt. More importantly, it would not be thwarted by something as simple as a raised shield.

He watched as the Bjornmen broke into a run, large ragged holes appearing in their numbers as the logs took their toll.

"Looks like it worked," Rhenkin admitted. Larson didn't respond, his eyes still on the distant force. Forced on by the press of men behind them trying to escape the barrage, the first rows of Bjornmen had no chance to stop as the ground ahead of them suddenly fell away, revealing great pits lined with sharpened stakes. Hundreds died in an instant and the rush slowed as the Bjornmen worked their way past the traps.

The sea of Bjornmen flowed onwards, washing over the rows of trenches, splitting around the hedgehogs and passing through the endless hail of arrows. Ballistae entered the fray, as the enemy came within range, hurling bolts as long as spears into the Bjornmen ranks, but still they came on.

The archers continued to send volley after volley into the Bjornmen. The catapults were lofting huge cradles of logs into their ranks, but all too soon they had to be abandoned as the archers pulled back towards the village. The catapults, too heavy to be moved with any speed, were doused in oil and set alight in order to prevent the Bjornmen capturing and making use of them.

It was over so soon, it hardly seemed real. For all Rhenkin's efforts and planning, the first stage of defences had fallen quickly. At the same time, it felt like the day had lasted for a week or more. The blood and screaming, and the sounds of men clawing at the dirt, their last moments filled with pain and hate, seemed to go on for an eternity.

As the retreating forces approached the last of the field defences, Rhenkin began the withdrawal into the fort. The archers went first, the conscripted villagers sprinting for what Rhenkin knew was the illusion of the safety of the walls. The slow retreat across the killing field had cost the Bjornmen dearly but now, as they advanced, they were able to bring their own weapons to bear. Denied further retreat, Rhenkin's forces came within range, and the Bjornmen crossbows sang their murderous song, hurling the heavy bolts across the field.

"Send the heavy cavalry," Rhenkin ordered.

"Sir, it's time we moved the command to within the walls," Larson said, hesitantly.

"Yes, yes. I realise that, Larson. Now send the damned cavalry!"

A horn sounded, and the ranks of pikemen and swordsmen opened to allow the cavalry through. There were only five hundred of them - five hundred about to charge into an army numbering in the tens of thousands - but they were a force unmatched in Rhenkin's arsenal. In all of Anlan, there was nothing that could compete with the military might of the heavy cavalry.

"Begin a full retreat as soon as they charge," Rhenkin added.

Larson glanced at him quickly, meeting Rhenkin's eyes and wishing his own hadn't made the journey. There was nothing of humanity in them. They held only ice and duty. Cold and inexorable.

"They're almost certain to be surrounded, Sir." His words weren't quite a question.

"I'm aware of that, Larson." Rhenkin looked away, his eyes passing over the field.

The cavalry thundered across the field in three tight wedge formations. Chargers carried men in heavy plate armour and Rhenkin could feel the sound of their passage in his chest, the sound vibrating his very flesh, even from this distance.

He looked on as they lowered their lances and punched through the enemy line, carving a channel deep into the army. The lances devastated the front ranks but soon became useless. Then the true butchery began. The cavalry hacked savagely at the men they charged past, forming a wake of the dead and dying behind them. They seemed unstoppable at first, a force of nature unleashed upon the invader, but then the channels closed behind them and they were surrounded.

Arrows began to fly from the walls, the elevation of their new position providing the archers with greater range. Catapults and ballistae hurled their payloads into the fray, away from the cavalry but close enough to add to the shock and fear. It was almost visible, a ripple that spread throughout those closest to the combat, slowing their reactions, their training falling away as the fear took hold.

Rhenkin hurried through the gates and rushed up onto the walls. The cavalry had wheeled and were fighting their way back towards the village. Their number seemed undiminished and they left a swathe of destruction behind them. He glanced down at the gates to see the last of his own units sprinting inside the walls. The ballistae launched their last spears and then their operators took axes to the twisted skeins of rope, rendering the weapons useless before fleeing into the village.

He watched as the cavalry charge faltered and slowed. So much of their power was built on speed and momentum. They were torn from their saddles and, once on the ground, they were as helpless as baby birds fallen from the nest.

He watched, unable to turn his face away, or perhaps he forced himself to bear witness as their numbers fell. Two hundred. Fifty. When only twenty remained, he turned to Larson. The man's face was as impassive as his own, but his eyes spoke loudly of things he would never put into words.

"Shut the gates," Rhenkin said softly. Larson walked away, leaving him to his doubts. The gates slammed shut, the heavy crossbar dropping into place in what seemed to be a final accusation of failure.

There were no further attacks that day. The raiders pulled back beyond bowshot almost as soon as the gates had been closed. Rhenkin stood on the walls as the sun sank slowly, the colours of the sunset mirroring the blood on the fields below him. He could pick out the Bjornmen pulling siege engines into position at the rear of their lines. Trebuchets, by the looks of things. He wondered idly what ammunition they were planning to use. Smoke rose through the trees. Despite the large number of Bjornmen on the field, still more remained in the woods.

* * *

Devin moved with as much stealth as he could manage in the fading light. The sun was just above the horizon and the light would soon be gone. The woods were quiet, except for the occasional burst of birdsong, and the distant sounds of the battle carried easily to them. It was little more than the faint clash of metal, but even at this distance he fancied he could hear the screams.

He paused beside a stand of beech and rubbed at his calves. The cramp had been coming and going for the last few hours. It was a pain he could have done without, but it was nothing to the throbbing ache in his head.

He looked along the trail and waved the others forward. They were spaced out into two groups, with Devin scouting ahead, and Tench and Riddal following. Though they'd not wanted to admit it initially, Devin knew the woods better than either of them and, with the light going, it made more sense for him to lead.

It was dark enough under the trees at the best of times. The canopy was dense and, when the sun had gone down, they would have an hour at most before they were blundering along in the pitch-black.

"There's a couple of them about two or three minutes further on," Devin whispered to the others, as they drew close.

"Just two?" Riddal raised his eyebrows. The smallest group they'd encountered so far had been fifteen, but that had been hours ago.

"I saw three," Devin admitted. "One keeps going and coming back. I think he might be on watch on the other side of their camp. The other two are lying near a firepit. They've not lit it yet, though."

"Deserters?" Tench wondered.

"They could be, I suppose. Or they could be just avoiding the fight," Riddal whispered back. "Though you'd think they'd run further away than this." He shrugged, looking back to Devin. "It doesn't matter what they are really. Can we get round them?"

"Not without losing another half an hour. The woods are pretty open around here. We'd have to really put some space between us and them or risk being seen."

"It's going to be getting dark soon." Riddal glanced at the sky and scratched at his cheek. "How far do you think we are from the village?"

"Not far at all. If we could get out of the trees and just walk, we'd be able to see it in half an hour." Devin spread his hands helplessly.

"I don't want to be out here if the village is that close," Tench whispered. "If we can't go past them without wasting light, let's do it the other way."

"Fine," Riddal gave in. "We do it together and silent. I take one and you take the other." He gave Devin a look as he started to protest. "I want you to have an arrow ready. If either doesn't fall straight away, you take him. I don't want any screams. If the third man is there, you take him instead. Questions?" They shook their heads.

"How's the head?" he asked Devin, as the young man rubbed at his eyes with the heels of his hands.

"The same. It's throbbing like mad."

"Tried willow bark?"

Devin shook his head. "I think I just need water. Eating willow would just make me thirstier."

Riddal winced in sympathy. They'd run out of water hours ago and hadn't had the opportunity to refill their skins. "We'll take it slow and easy. Lead us in."

Devin nodded and set off. The three of them spread out, moving in a loose wedge with Devin at the point. The Bjornmen had made a rough camp at the base of a broad oak tree, the thick leaves offering shelter from any rain that might fall in the night. Devin led the others close to a collection of dense bushes which spread out from a stand of holly, directing them with silent gestures.

The two Bjornmen were chatting quietly in their harsh tongue. The language sounded alien to Devin, full of guttural sounds that made it sound like they were arguing, although the tone of their voices made it clear they were not. They lay at ease on the ground, heads resting on their packs. The third man was nowhere to be seen.

Devin drew an arrow and set it to the string, looking over at Riddal and Tench as they picked their targets. It wouldn't be a difficult shot. The Bjornmen were only fifty feet away, at most.

Riddal let fly and the arrow buried itself neatly in his target's throat. The man clutched at the shaft as he rolled sideways, gurgled and was still. Tench's shot, however, went wide, his arrow heading off into the trees at the other side of the clearing. The Bjornman sprang to his feet, clearly about to sprint into the trees. Devin pulled back and released in one motion, his actions automatic. His arrow slammed into the base of the man's skull and dropped him like a stone.

"Good shot," Riddal muttered, as he pushed his way through the bush to collect his arrow. "What happened to you?" he called over to Tench, as he worked his arrow free of the Bjornman.

"Bloody bird flew out of the bush as I shot," the man explained. "The arrow must have tapped a twig as it went."

Devin knelt and grasped hold of the arrow shaft where it protruded from the man's neck. It seemed like this should bother him, but he was past that. Perhaps it was fatigue. Maybe he'd just turned hard in the past few weeks. He worked the arrow back and forth, but the head seemed stuck tight.

Later, he would never be able to say what it was that had made him look up. He couldn't remember hearing anything. The Bjornman stood at the other side of the camp, shock plain on his face as he caught sight of the trio.

Faster than he would have thought it possible, Devin dropped the arrow and his fingers flew to his quiver. The arrow barely seemed to touch the string, as he drew and released quicker than he could take a breath. The shaft flew true and took the Bjornman in the eye, dropping him without a whisper.

He turned to see Riddal and Tench staring at him, awestruck. "How the hell did you do that?" Tench gasped. "I've never seen anyone move so fast!"

"In the eye too," Riddal said and whistled. "That's a shot I'd be lucky to make even if I stood still and aimed it."

"Just a lucky shot," Devin said, embarrassed. His hands were shaking. The first shot hadn't bothered him, but to kill a man without even thinking? To just act on instinct and to kill as easily as breathing? That was different, and he was both amazed and horrified by it. He waved Riddal into the lead and followed him, his mind full of thoughts he didn't have time to process.

The woods grew steadily darker until the moon began to rise. Their progress slowed to a crawl and Devin took the lead again. They would need to rely on his knowledge of the woods. The sounds of the battle had been filtering through the trees for the last few hours, but they had faded with the light. He wished they were closer, so he could see what was going on.

The forest was still except for the occasional rustle of leaves as small animals hunted in the night. They moved as fast as they dared. None of them had mentioned the fae, but they all cast frequent glances up at the full moon.

Finally, they seemed to be on familiar ground and Devin began to move more swiftly. Being so close to home made the danger seem less real. Tench and Riddal hurried to keep up with him, as he passed along the game trail and through the woods, to the edge of the clearing where he'd heard Erinn scream all those months ago, when Artor had pressed his luck with her. He pushed back a branch and froze.

The massive creature he had seen in Obair's glade stood in silence, close to where Erinn had once sat, its bearded face raised to the moon. Tiny green sparks were just visible, dancing on the skin of its shoulders and chest, as it drank the light in.

Devin waved at the others to stop as he fought the wave of terror that threatened to overwhelm him. Should he attack the creature? No, that was ridiculous. He had no iron on him and he'd seen what the thing could do when threatened with arrows.

"There is no need to hide low in your bush, manling," the thing said, in an amused tone. "I could end you in an instant, should I so choose."

Devin stepped out of the trees. "What are you doing?" hissed Riddal, grabbing for his arm.

"He already knows we're here, Riddal," Devin replied calmly.

It turned its antlered head to regard him, amber eyes shining bright in the moonlight. "I have no interest in three of your kind this night, manling. Know, however, that my children are already out at play. I expect they would think differently." He closed his eyes and raised his face to the skies again, absorbing the silvery light.

Devin was struck by the beauty of the creature. Majestic was simply too coarse a word to describe it. He felt inferior just being near it, as if even by breathing the same air as it, he was somehow an affront to its perfection.

A smile spread across the thing's face and its bright white teeth shone against the dark green of its beard. Devin wondered if it somehow knew what he was thinking.

He took a step and then another around the edge of the clearing, watching the creature all the while to see if it would react. His eyes sought out and met Riddal's, who seemed frozen to the spot. Devin waved him on and they worked their way around the creature and into the trees. It was only once the leaves of the trees had obscured the scene that they broke into a run.

Devin sprinted, fear lending a strength to his legs that he would have denied was there before the encounter. They ran wildly, the kind of running that can only be born of terror, with no thought given to stealth or of tripping over roots or fallen branches. They thought only of the need to put space between themselves and the thing that stood in the clearing, drinking in the moonlight as if it were summer's mead.

He became aware of Tench calling his name in a weak gasp and he forced himself to stop until the others had caught up with him. There were no words. Nothing could be said about it that would make it any less insane, less surreal. Instead, they met each others' eyes briefly, each seeming to recoil from the horror that shone there.

They walked on. What else was there to do?

* * *

Devin crouched low in the long grass beside the trees. It was fully dark now, but the field was illuminated by the bright moonlight and the fires that burned on the fields before Widdengate. The smoke hung low, hugging the ground, heavy with the stench of burning pitch.

He felt a moment's pang of loss. Widdengate was gone, at least the Widdengate that he had known was. Even if they managed to drive the Bjornmen back, the village would never be the same. The fields had been ruined by the long lines of trenches and littered with stakes. Grief fuelled the growing anger he felt towards these men from across the seas.

The village still stood, however. The Bjornmen seemed to have pulled back to stay out of range of anything that might be launched from the walls. Their army seemed to stretch forever in the darkness, a thousand campfires belching smoke out into the tainted night.

Devin was glad they hadn't surrounded the village. There was probably a strategic reason as to why they hadn't, but he was content just to know that there was a clear route to the walls.

"Ready?" Riddal called over to them both, in a hoarse whisper.

"Yes," he managed, hearing Tench's voice from the other side of Riddal.

"Go!" Riddal sprinted for the walls. There might have been no need to run, but even though an hour had past since their encounter with the creature in the woods, they were still jumpy. The fae were loose somewhere, the creature had made that clear. As they drew close to the limits of a bow's range from the walls, Riddal pulled out a horn and gave three long blasts. Movement on the walls showed they'd been spotted and a bell rang out loud.

"Scouts returning!" Tench bellowed, as they ran. The horn ought to have been enough, but it never hurt to be careful.

Torches bobbed as men ran along the walls and let down ropes over the side. Devin hauled himself up the rope as best he could, though in truth he did little more than cling to it as the soldiers pulled him to the top.

He collapsed on the walkway on the other side of the spiked parapet. He was home. Maybe not safe, but to be home was enough for now. Strong arms pulled him to his feet and helped him down the steps to the ground.

Everyone seemed to be speaking to him at once, asking questions and patting him on the back. The fatigue he'd been fighting seemed to have hit him all at once and his head swam.

A blur of red streaked through the growing crowd and Erinn hurled herself at him, wrapping her arms around him. She held him close and buried her head in his chest.

"Devin! I thought you were…" She pushed him away and sniffed. "You… You!" She wiped her tears away with a sleeve and slapped hard at his chest. "You scared me half to death!"

"Erinn, I…"

"You nothing, Devin. You had me scared witless when you didn't come back with the others! Don't you ever do anything so stupid again!" She flung her arms around him again as the soldiers chuckled at his helpless expression.

"Alright, that's enough, girl. Let him up to breathe," Harlen said, peeling his daughter off Devin gently.

Devin was dimly aware of a man speaking to Riddal. "Are you injured? Do you feel able to report?" Riddal nodded and the weary-looking man turned to Devin. "If you are able, son, Captain Rhenkin would like to speak to you as well." Devin nodded dumbly.

"Good lad. I'm Lieutenant Larson. I'll walk you over." He led them towards the command centre, one of the new buildings close to the barracks. One glance at the darkened windows was enough to show Larson that Rhenkin was not inside, however. He muttered something under his breath that Devin was reasonably sure was impolite at best, and led them back towards the walls.

Rhenkin stood in the watchtower staring out at the Bjornmen's fires. He nodded at Larson as they filed in and turned back to the view.

"You're late." He glanced back at Riddal with a wry smile.

"We were cut off," Riddal said. "Sir," he added, as Larson raised an eyebrow at him.

"Were you now? Go ahead and report then."

Devin was only half listening as Riddal recounted the story of their mission. He looked past Rhenkin's shoulder at the army camped out on the fields. He could see little except their fires but, despite the distance, he heard the scream clearly.

He stepped past Rhenkin, ignoring the startled look on Larson's face, to the edge of the watchtower and leant on the railing as he stared out. Shadows passed in front of the fires and the faint clash of steel carried to him.

"What's happening?" Rhenkin asked, joining him at the rail.

Devin flushed, suddenly realising what he was doing. "I'm sorry, Captain, I…"

"Never mind that, lad. You've seen something. What is it?"

"There's something going on in the Bjornman camp. I thought I heard fighting."

"What?" Rhenkin stared out into the moonlit fields.

"The fae!" Devin cried, as it hit him.

"What?"

Devin ignored him and spun round to look at Riddal. "He said his children were at play. Do you remember?"

"What's this?" Rhenkin's tone lowered as he fixed Riddal with a glare.

"I'm sorry I didn't mention it, Sir. I didn't think anyone would believe us."

"I will decide what to believe and not to believe! From now on, you will report everything." Rhenkin's voice was low and angry.

"Yes, Sir," Riddal managed, but Rhenkin had already turned away.

"Larson, give the order to clear the streets. I want everyone on the walls or in their homes unless they are in one of the street squads. Pass the word to ready iron as well."

Larson was down the steps in a moment and, minutes later, a bell began to ring.

"You'd best get yourself home, my lad," Rhenkin told Devin. "You look all done in."

"I'd rather stay on the walls if that's okay, Sir," Devin replied. Somehow the fatigue had fallen away from him.

Rhenkin considered him for a moment. He nodded. "Get yourself some iron then, lad."

* * *

Erinn sat up in her bed as the bells began to ring out across the village. She shook her head to clear away the cobwebs of sleep and swung her feet out onto the floor. If nothing else worked, stepping barefoot onto the stone floor was always guaranteed to wake her up.

Bells, not the attack horn. It was bells and that meant the fae. She felt the excitement rise in her. She'd long since stopped being scared of the creatures. Her small home adjoined the forge anyway, and there was no building in Widdengate more steeped in iron.

She made her way out into the hallway and padded along to the kitchen. Her ears easily picked out the snores of her father and she smiled to herself. The barrel-chested man had always slept the sleep of the dead. She was unlikely to wake him, no matter what she did. She went to the stove, and bent to stir up the coals and coax some fire out of them before lighting the lamp. A cup of tea would be just the thing while she waited.

The pump creaked as she filled the kettle with just enough water for a cup and set it on to boil. She moved across to the window seat and settled down to watch. The pit was invisible in the darkness. It was almost invisible in the day too. The sheet covering the iron doors had been covered in a thin layer of dirt and fallen leaves.

They said that the fae could see as well in the night as people could in broad daylight. Even if that were the case, though, they'd be unlikely to spot the trap unless they could smell the iron, and that was why she'd insisted they put it so close to the forge.

The kettle bubbled and hissed, and she pulled herself away from the window to make her drink. The village had fallen silent after the bells and she sat at the window, sipping tea that was so hot it almost scalded her, as she fought to stay alert.

Devin would have understood. He wouldn't have agreed with her, but he would have understood. You can't set a trap and just expect the prey to walk into it. It has to have a reason. There has to be bait.

She set the cup down and grabbed up the flute as she heard the distant sounds of shouting and running. Throwing the blanket from the window seat around her shoulders, she hurried outside, trying to be quiet for now and keeping close to the wall. The gap between it and the edge of the pit measured less than two feet, but she felt confident she had enough room. It would just take a little jump to get past the corner. As long as she didn't jump too far and hit the wall on the other side, she'd be fine. Erinn didn't stop to think. If she thought about it, she'd never do it. With three quick steps, she hopped over the edge of the concealed pit and into the wall.

Her arms flew wide as she tried to hold onto the vertical surface and she forced herself up on her tiptoes to try and push her weight forward. There was a moment of pure terror as she felt herself tipping backwards and then she was set. She worked her way around the pit until she was facing the street and set herself.

The nightgown was scandalous. Her father would have thrown a merry fit if he'd seen how she'd altered it. A slit ran almost to her hip on one side and she'd adjusted the bodice to make the most of her small breasts. She looked like a common harlot.

On the whole, she was rather proud of it.

It was less an item of clothing than it was decoration at this point. The night was cool and, despite the warmth of the blanket, she soon found herself shivering. Her teeth chattered, almost blocking out the sound of the hooves as they clattered around the corner.

It didn't see her at first and she froze, abruptly struck by the insanity of what she was trying to do. This was the only chance she'd get though, so she dropped the blanket and pushed her leg out through the slit in the nightgown, adopting a pose she hoped might be seductive as she lifted the flute to her lips.

The satyr's head shot round as the first note sounded. Its eyes flared bright as it walked slowly towards her. For a moment, her breath faltered and she nearly dropped the flute. She smiled at the satyr, a wicked smile as flirtatious as she could manage, and put the flute back to her lips.

It was suspicious, that much was obvious, but for all its alien nature it had the same instincts as any boy she'd ever met. The right smile and a wink, and they were all flustered and tripping over themselves trying to impress.

Erinn watched as the satyr sniffed at the air, wrinkling its nose, probably at the smell of iron. It looked around, glared at the entrance to the forge and flicked its tongue out, almost seeming to taste the air itself. A lick of its lips and then it took another step towards her, its eyes eager. Erinn lowered the flute and waited, hoping her terror didn't show. She could feel the edges of something. It was almost as if the shape of the satyr didn't fit. It was nebulous at best, but she got the impression of a strong physique and dark eyes.

She barely had the time to wonder at the odd sensation before the satyr took its final step towards her. The ground beneath it gave way and it fell into the thin section of wood holding the doors open, crashing through it and tumbling down into the pit, the sheet tangled around it.

Pulled down by the strong springs, the iron grates slammed shut behind the creature as it hit the bottom of the pit and landed on the base of the cage. Blue fire flared and it screamed, a wild and terrible sound. Erinn felt a surge of triumph but it was short-lived, as the satyr threw itself upwards, crashing into the doors to the cage.

She stood, shocked, as it smashed into the grates again and again, each impact resulting in another flare of blue fire as it leapt upwards or landed again. The fire was growing dimmer, she noticed, but the grates were also shaking violently.

The bolts! With a panic, she realised that the heavy locking bolts on top of the grates weren't yet in place. Without them, the only things holding the doors shut were their own weight and the strength of the springs.

The satyr threw itself upwards again and the left-hand grate actually lifted an inch or two before slamming closed again. She looked on in horror as the creature leapt again and grabbed hold of the right-hand grate, close to the join in the middle. Heedless of the fire that spurted around its fingers, it reached out with its other hand and began to force the left side of the cage doors upwards. Without even stopping to think how dangerous or stupid it might be, Erinn jumped down into the pit.

She landed badly. The metal squares were too small for her feet to pass through easily, but she stumbled and fell hard. Her head slammed against the iron and her vision blurred for a moment. The satyr fell as she landed, jarred off the grate by the impact. It hit the base of the cage, spitting and hissing words she couldn't understand, although venom and fury were clear in its tone. It threw itself upwards again and, this time, there was no flare of blue fire. It didn't fall either. Instead, it hung from the grate with one hand, reaching the other through one of the squares and grabbing for her.

Erinn screamed and rolled away from its flailing hand. She scrambled onto her hands and knees. Where were the bolts? It was so hard to see in the darkness. Looking down at the grate, all she could really make out were the furious eyes of the monster she'd caged.

She clambered over the grate, searching for the bolts, and shrieked as the satyr smashed into the iron doors again. They didn't move nearly as much as they had before, as if the strength had been drained out of the creature. The whole grate still shook, however, and she fell onto her chest, her hand slipping into the cage through the gaps between the metal bars.

The creature fell on her in a rage, pouncing like a terrier on a rat as it grasped her hand. Its claw-like nails scratched at her wrist and she screamed, long and hard.

The satyr pulled down on her arm, dragging her down hard against the grate, then reached for the knife it had dropped as it fell into the pit. It was the realisation of what it could do if it reached the knife that spurred her on. She forced her free hand under her for leverage and wrenched herself upwards, gasping against the pain as she dragged her knee across the bars of the cage and drew it into her chest.

Erinn forced herself up and yanked the satyr's arm through the grate, before leaning to the left and bending the limb the wrong way. It howled in rage and then finally fell, clawing at her chest and thighs as it went.

She didn't have much time to find the bolts. She'd come up with the idea for the trap, but hadn't had anything to do with the design or construction. Harlen had handled that, with the help of his apprentices. Eventually she located them, but her joy quickly turned to dismay as she crouched to examine them. They were long solid bars, clearly designed to be driven home with a hammer. There was no way she would be able to move them with her hands alone.

The cage rocked again and pain lanced through her leg, as the satyr reached through with its knife and sliced deep into her calf. She didn't scream. The pain stole her breath and the faint sound that came from her lips was the gasped whimper of a wounded animal. Erinn pulled herself to her feet and managed to limp to the corner of the pit, watching as the cage doors slammed upwards again and again, as the satyr fought against the strength of the springs.

The blood ran freely down her leg, but she ignored it and huddled against the wooden braces that held back the earth surrounding the pit. How long she stood there watching the creature slam into the doors, she couldn't say. Her plan had seemed so simple, almost foolproof. She'd thought that the hardest part would be getting the thing into the pit in the first place. A tear escaped her and, as if the first one had cut a path, the others followed.

The satyr hung from the bars by one gnarled hand, trying to force the cage doors open with the other. The door was giving slowly, only by an inch, but enough to fill her with dread. The creature stared at her with murder in its eyes and forced the door a little further.

"Erinn?" Her father's voice cut through the darkness. "Are you out there, girl?"

"I'm here." Her voice was little more than a whisper, too small to reach the top of the pit. She tried again. "Father!"

The satyr hissed, shielding its eyes from the sudden glare of a lantern at the edge of the pit, and dropped to the bottom of the cage.

"Lord of Midnight, Erinn, what are you doing down there?" His voice, so calm and kindly, broke what little of the dam remained and the river of tears became a flood.

CHAPTER SEVEN

Obair stood close to the edge of the pit and watched as the soldiers secured ropes to the top of the cage.

"You're sure the bolts will hold?" one of them asked Harlen, for what seemed like the fifth time. "I don't want that thing getting loose."

Harlen gave the man a flat, unfriendly look that told him just what he thought of that question. The soldier wilted, turned away and barked orders at his men. A team of four horses moved forwards and the ground around the pit began to crumble as the cage was torn free.

Obair examined the satyr with interest as the cage rose. It was sprawled in a corner of the trap, one leg thrust out before it, looking more like a tired old man than the tormentor from legend and fable. Its eyes passed over the crowd with disinterest, ignoring them as they gawked at it.

Some of the soldiers reached to steady the cage as it was lowered down on its hoist and the satyr struck in a blur of movement, lashing out with its knife. A man fell back with a cry of pain, clutching at his hand.

"Back away, lads," a sergeant called. "It might be in a cage but it's still a vicious little bastard." He turned to the injured man. "Get that seen to. Then you can come back and guard this thing."

Obair moved as close as he dared, studying the thing. It glanced up at him and its eyes seemed to widen in recognition before it looked away.

The crowd parted to let Larson through and he sucked a breath in through his teeth as he got a look at the prisoner.

"Nasty looking thing, isn't it?" Harlen called as he came to meet him.

Larson nodded, his eyes still locked on the beast. "And you say your daughter trapped this thing alone?"

"She did," Harlen's voice was filled with a fierce pride.

"I heard she was injured?"

"A cut to the leg. Nasty, but nothing that won't heal in time."

"Well, now that we have this thing, where do we put it? I don't think we can just leave it," Larson said.

Obair shook his head and strode over to them. "Sorry to interrupt, Sergeant."

"Lieutenant," Larson corrected him.

"Oh my goodness, I'm sorry," Obair said. "Is there much of a difference?"

Larson waved it off, sharing a look with Harlen. "What did you want?"

"Yes, yes, sorry. I don't think moving it is such a good idea. Certainly not inside, anyway," Obair explained.

"Oh?"

Obair nodded. "I'll admit that this is just a suspicion, but I would keep it out of the moonlight as much as possible and make sure the sunlight hits it."

"I suppose we can do that," Larson said, confused. "I need to prepare a report for the captain. I would welcome your input when the time comes."

"Hmm?" Obair tore his gaze away from the satyr. "Oh, yes. Just come and get me when you're ready."

He moved around the cage slowly, ignoring the sounds of the soldiers clearing the streets. Despite all the years he'd spent as guardian of the stones, he'd never had as good a look at one of the creatures as he was getting now.

"What do you want with me, Wyrde weaver," the creature said. Its voice was little more than a whisper, low and filled with malevolence.

He started at that, jumping back slightly, and glancing around at the almost empty street and the guard standing at post.

"What did you call me?" He pitched his voice low.

"Wyrde weaver? Do you think I can't smell the stench of it on you? The reek of corruption and abuse?"

"Corruption?" Obair rolled the word around in his mouth, not liking the taste.

The satyr pulled itself to its feet, its hooves making a dull clang against the bars that pressed into the dirt. "You know nothing of it, do you? You wove it and held it in place, but you don't even know what it was or what you did."

"What do you mean?" Obair asked. He was losing control of the conversation but, at this moment, he didn't care. "The Wyrde? It was a barrier keeping your kind out of our world."

"Your world?" The satyr laughed, the sound dry and scathing. "Even if we let that pass for the moment, the abomination you call the Wyrde was far more than just a barrier, you stupid little manling. Were all the weavers so ignorant?"

Obair shook his head in silence, confusion and doubt battling with the desire to know the truth the creature hinted at.

"You think of the Wyrde as a wall, blocking the entryway into *your* world." It curled its lip as Obair gave a barely perceptible nod. "It did more than just block entry. It closed the passage!"

"I don't understand," Obair admitted.

"Bah! This language. How do you cope with it?" the satyr spat. "It's like a song without music. These dead words are like stones in my mouth!" It met his eyes again. "Try to understand, if your feeble mind can. This world and mine, they are joined." It clenched its fists, clashing them together and then holding them apart. "Anyone with enough of Our Lady's grace and the required knowledge may pass between, from one to the other."

"Yes, yes, this I understand, but…"

"Cease your jabbering, defiler!" The satyr's tone was as harsh as its words, as it slammed against the sides of the cage.

"The way is not a single step, as if through a gateway. It is along a passage. Your sick Wyrde closed it." The hate burned in its eyes, hot and accusing.

"I still don't…"

"It closed *both* sides, meddler, locking us in the passage. In the Outside." The satyr turned away, curling into a ball on the far side of the cage.

"You mean you were locked in the middle? Trapped in the space between your world and ours?" Obair's voice trailed into a whisper, his horror at the notion robbing the strength from his speech.

"For three ages, we were locked in the cold. In the Outside," the satyr said. It carried on speaking, but its words were drowned out by the blast of horns sounding through the village, as soldiers heard the signal and passed it on, sounding their own horns. The Bjornmen were attacking.

* * *

Obair rushed to the walls, more because everyone else was doing it than for any other reason. The sun was just a fiery sliver, edging its way above the horizon, and fires still burned in the Bjornman camp. The invaders were moving forward, though not in the orderly ranks he would have expected. Instead, most of their men stood watching as wooden structures were wheeled into place. He looked down over the palisade and noted Rhenkin had similar devices stationed on the ground before the walls. As he watched, one of the devices hurled a loosely wrapped bundle of arrows into the sky. The cloth fell from around the bundle as it flew towards the Bjornmen and the arrows rained down on them.

He grimaced at the distant screams while men shouted orders and the devices all began firing. The Bjornmen split into two groups, either hanging back out of range or clustering around their devices in a tight formation with their shields raised. Obair looked around and, spotted Rhenkin further along the platform and began to work his way past the men lining the walls.

The man seemed to be surrounded by chaos as he barked orders left and right, the ever-present Larson at his side. Obair glanced out at the distant Bjornmen and froze as he caught sight of the flames licking up from the large bonfires that had been lit beside each of the wooden contraptions.

"What are they doing?"

"Loading their catapults with flaming pitch, if I'm any judge," Rhenkin's voice came from behind him.

Obair spun to face him. "But that could burn the whole village down!"

Rhenkin gave a bitter laugh. "I think that's the general idea, yes." He continued along the walkway, heading for the watchtower built into the corner of the wall as Obair followed him.

"They'd actually burn the village down with us inside? That's barbaric!" Obair gasped, looking out over the walls again.

"That's war, Druid. I think that you've led a very sheltered life locked away in your woods. Mankind can be every bit as vicious and brutal as your fae."

Obair stared at the fires in horror, stepping to the side as men laden with buckets rushed up the steps. Water splashed down the sides of the palisade, pooling in the mud at the bottom, and still the men rushed back to the wells and pumps to fetch more.

The distant catapults lurched and Obair saw at once that Rhenkin had been wrong. There were no burning pots arcing through the skies. Instead, he could see nothing more than clouds of smoke and dust around the catapults. Then the glowing coals and embers began to fall. They passed overhead, far above the palisade, and flew into the village.

Rhenkin swore and waved at Larson, who ran for the steps, shouting at the men to form bucket chains.

"I'm busy here, Druid. What do you want?" Rhenkin demanded.

"The satyr. It's contained but there is much we can learn from it."

"When we start the withdrawal, we'll take it with us. I think it's time you met my duchess."

"When we withdraw?" Obair said, shocked.

"We're not going to be able to hold here, Druid. We simply don't have the men. This village was doomed the moment the Bjornmen advanced. We've been sending small groups out since yesterday."

"But the village...?" Obair protested, looking down at the houses and streets.

"Will burn," Rhenkin finished for him. "The only thing that would stop their advance would be if the king finally committed his armies. Until he does, then North-eastern Anlan will belong to the Bjornmen."

Obair stared at him, but Rhenkin had already turned away and was giving out a steady stream of orders to the runners passing in and out of the watchtower. Obair stepped back onto the walls and looked out over the fields, drawn by a morbid curiosity.

Rhenkin's catapults, positioned at the base of the walls, fired briefly but the operators soon abandoned their efforts. The Bjornmen had pulled back out of range during the night and had not yet advanced far enough again. As he watched, the gates opened, and archers and infantry poured out, forming into mixed ranks before they slowly advanced towards the Bjornmen.

The trebuchets fired again, this time lofting flaming pots. The burning pitch Rhenkin had predicted had arrived. The pots arced across the sky, trailing lines of black smoke as they flew. One fell short, the fragile clay shattering as it crashed into the mud in front of the walls and creating a lake of fire around it.

The other two flew true. One smashed into the wall itself, while its brother flew into the village, turning one of the recently constructed buildings into a pillar of flame. Obair turned away from the sight, gagging as men were transformed into torches and fell screaming from the walls to writhe on the ground, while others frantically emptied buckets of water over them.

Through it all, the Bjornmen stood still, watching.

"Why don't they advance?" Obair demanded of the man stood next to him. The farmer shrugged and fiddled with the bow he held inexpertly in his hands.

"Because they don't want the village," a sergeant said quietly from the other side of him. "They're not looking to take this place. They just want it gone. They can get most of that just by burning it down. Why risk their own men before they need to?"

Obair opened his mouth to respond but then turned his head at a shout from behind him. "Obair!" Larson waved him down from the walls.

The old man pushed his way through the press of men and clambered down the steps.

"I want you in the next group," the lieutenant explained, as Obair drew close.

"Next group?"

"The next group to leave, man! Wake up!" Larson snapped. "The captain wants you to take the cart with that beast and take it to Duchess Freyton."

"He wants what? Why me?"

"We need more support, old man," Larson said. "Look around you. We can't hold against these Bjornmen and, so far, we're the only ones that know anything about the fae. You wanted to warn mankind, Obair. Well, now you have your chance."

Obair nodded. He couldn't really object to that.

The line of carts stood before the rear gates, packed tight with villagers clinging to those few possessions they could carry. They were surrounded by a circle of soldiers looking anxiously at the crowd of villagers pressing in at them. As he walked closer, he heard a commotion surrounding the rear cart. A soldier was bundling a large man he dimly recognised as the miller away from the cart.

"Why can't I just leave now?" the man demanded. "I don't see why that hell-beast gets pride of place while we have to wait."

The response was lost in the noise of the crowd as they surged against the line of soldiers.

"So that thing gets to go while we stay here and burn?" the miller roared, shouting more towards the throng of people behind him than to the soldiers in front. "Who are you protecting here?"

Obair elbowed his way through the crowd until he reached the nervous soldiers, and was quickly grabbed and bundled aboard a cart. The men wasted no time in opening the gates and sending the caravan through. There was an air of panic about the crowd and the guards seemed little better as they resorted to driving the villagers back with clubs.

The gates were shut hurriedly as the caravan went on its way. Their closing creak was muffled by a crash, as a hail of stones smashed against the palisade at the far side of the village.

As the wagon clattered over the sun-baked road, the distant sound of steel on steel carried from the far side of the village. Obair looked back at the smoke, tinged red with sparks and floating embers, that belched up from the palisade where the firepot had struck. He looked at the flames, shaking his head in wonder and disgust. He'd come to try and warn mankind about the fae but, as he watched the Bjornmen surge forward, he wondered who would warn mankind about itself.

* * *

Rhenkin looked on as the Bjornmen drove the line back again. Mixing the archers in with the regular infantry had worked well for a time, but the enemy adapted quickly, rushing his units before they could fire more than once or twice. As he watched, the Bjornman advance forced his line to retreat again or else be overwhelmed, and the sky turned dark with flights of arrows as the infantry units ran back behind the range marker and headed for the gates.

Another hail of rocks struck the palisade and men fell screaming to the ground. He turned to look for Larson before remembering the man was overseeing the evacuation.

"Where did they find the stone?" he grumbled to himself, as he waited.

He didn't have to wait long before the dark-haired man ran up the steps, ducking involuntarily as the wall shook from the impact of more stones.

"Report," Rhenkin said, as soon as the man was close enough to hear.

"The satyr and six carts are away. The villagers are close to panic though, Sir. We'll need to allow a general withdrawal soon or we'll have a riot on our hands."

Rhenkin nodded. "Open the gates and let them go. I didn't really want to do that until those bastards started to advance, but I don't think they're going to until they've breached the walls."

Larson looked out to the battlefield. The Bjornmen hadn't really moved since they'd driven the defenders back, preferring to use their siege engines, but now they were drawing close. "I don't imagine they can have much left in the way of stone, Sir," he shrugged.

As if in response, the trebuchets leapt forward, lofting a barrage of firepots towards the village. Rhenkin threw himself flat on the platform, barely aware that he'd screamed out the order to get down. The pots struck and then a wave of heat passed over him, scorching his skin despite his prone position. The flames soared high as the stench of burning pitch filled the air.

He pulled himself to his feet and staggered back from the heat, one arm flung over his face to ward off the flames. The entire section of palisade was engulfed by fire. Had he been just ten feet farther along the wall, he would have joined the men that had fallen screaming to the earth.

He heard Larson call for water and bucket chains, but he knew it was futile. The logs closest to him were already steaming in the heat. An entire day's work soaking the palisade had been undone in moments. Another section of the wall exploded into flames. The Bjornmen had found the range now.

"Larson, get those back gates open and pass the word for the villagers to go," he ordered, as he staggered towards the steps. "I want all the men off these walls. Squads of archers to form a retreating firing line back towards the inner palisade." One last glance over the walls showed a massive ram being wheeled through the enemy lines.

He grabbed a corporal as he reached the bottom of the steps. "Get some men and dump the earth out of those carts against the front gates. I'll be damned if we're going to make this easy for them. Be sure to get them braced with beams first though."

As Rhenkin made his way back to the heavy gates that would soon seal the inner palisade, he saw his men moving smoothly into position. Almost a third of the front wall was burning now. It wouldn't be long.

The Bjornmen were already surging forwards by the time he'd made it onto the walls of the inner palisade. His men had abandoned the outer wall and moved into their new positions. A glance behind him revealed that the rear gates to the village had been thrown wide open, and a stream of carts and villagers was fleeing along the road.

The soldiers had braced the outermost gates with thick timber beams and then dumped earth from the carts onto the ground in front of them, piling it high and shovelling it against them. Rows of archers standing immediately behind the gates launched volley after volley over the walls. The need for any kind of accuracy was gone as the Bjornmen charged. The archers couldn't help but hit something.

From where Rhenkin was standing, he could see the arrows were having little effect. The Bjornmen were in a tight formation with shields interlocked. Men were falling, but not nearly enough to make a difference.

The gates shook as the ram was brought into play and the impact resounded through the village. Smaller catapults were wheeled into position near the ranks of archers and logs began to fly over the walls. Rhenkin couldn't see the results, but the screams of pain seemed testament enough to the fact that they were hitting their targets.

As he watched, a figure appeared on the outer wall, close to the gates. He was some distance away, but Rhenkin could see that he wasn't in uniform and was too fat to be one of his men. He was running low, trying to make himself as small a target as possible for the crossbow bolts that flew past. He sped through the clouds of smoke carrying something under one arm. As the ram crashed into the gates again, he stumbled, dropping to one knee before throwing the object down over the wall. He tossed something down after it and then the ram was engulfed in bright blue and crimson flames.

Rhenkin grabbed a nervous soldier. "Find out who that is," he ordered, pointing at the wall.

A hail of heavy crossbow bolts rained down inside the gate, dropping the closely packed archers like flies. While the Bjornmen all had shields, Rhenkin's archers were unarmoured and the heavy bolts caught them completely by surprise. He muttered bitter curses as they fell and the survivors scattered.

The catapults lurched forward again, hurling small wooden casks out over the walls. Rhenkin shaded his eyes as he watched the missiles fly, and fresh crimson and blue flames shoot up from the Bjornman lines.

He turned his head at the sound of footsteps to see the soldier he'd dispatched returning with the innkeeper in tow.

"That was you on the wall?" Rhenkin asked, in surprise.

Owen nodded, his face pale and his hands shaking visibly. "My best brandy," he explained. "The bastards might be burning my village down, but I'll be damned if they're going to drink my stock."

Rhenkin grinned and slapped the man on the back. "I thought I caught a whiff of something." He glanced at the rear gates. "You'd better get your family out of here, Owen. It's going to get ugly soon and you want to get a lead on these bastards."

Owen nodded and looked past Rhenkin towards the dark stain of the Bjornman army that extended out to the trees on the horizon. "We'll be gone in half an hour. I've a brother in Kavtrin that I think it might be time to visit."

"Not a bad idea. We'll be pulling back ourselves once we've bled them as much as we can here. The meeting point was supposed to be Carik's Fort, but I won't blame you for going your own way." He held a gloved hand out. "Good luck."

"Luck to you, Captain," Owen said, grasping his hand. "You've done everything that could be done here. Some will blame you anyway, but I want to thank you for it."

Rhenkin nodded once and turned back to the battle.

The gates shook again as a hail of rocks crashed into them, then they slammed inwards against the mound of earth piled behind them as the heavy crossbar tore apart. With a tortured creak, a section of palisade to the right of the gates, weakened by fire and the barrage of rocks, first sagged and then fell away, crashing down into the compound. There was a moment of shocked silence and then cheers rose from beyond the walls, as the Bjornmen began to pour through the breach.

Rhenkin watched in silence. There was no need to bark orders now. For the moment, they were already given. It was time to let his men do their jobs. The archers fired in ranks, loosing arrows and then sprinting through the rows of men behind them to their next position. The constant hail of arrows took its toll and the Bjornman charge faltered as bodies littered the earth until an effective shield wall could be formed.

The outer village beyond the inner palisade had become a killing field. The extra buildings required due to the influx of refugees and the demands of the Rhenkin's own forces, had almost filled the area which had once contained cottages and small fields. The defenders launched furious counter-attacks from the new streets and squares as the Bjornmen pushed their way forward, striking from ambushes when they could but then melting away before the Bjornmen could truly engage.

Rhenkin watched the line of carts as the villagers fled through the rear gates. The village had been neatly bisected by a line of collapsed houses and buildings, with the inner palisade at the centre. Though it might have been possible to clear the debris, it would have taken time and the Bjornmen were pushing directly towards the inner gates. It was obvious they were seeking to neutralise Rhenkin's forces as quickly as possible.

The assault on the inner gates, when it came, was overwhelming. As Rhenkin's troops retreated behind the walls, the Bjornmen pulled back, holding their positions at the outer wall, as the trebuchets were slowly wheeled forward. He could do little more than watch. The range of the siege engines was such that they could fire from way outside of the breached outer walls. First firepots, then rocks and then massive sections of tree trunk were hurled at the inner palisade and the gates.

"Sergeant!" he shouted at a man further along the walkway.

"Sir." The man snapped off a salute. Rhenkin fought back a burst of irrational laughter. A parade ground salute in the middle of a hail of rocks and burning pitch. It all seemed so ridiculous, somehow.

"Find me a corporal, man," Rhenkin barked.

The man rushed down the steps into the village as Rhenkin glowered out over the walls.

"Orders, Sir?" The officer was a fresh-faced man with an immaculate uniform.

"Bloody droos, man, what are you? Twelve?" Rhenkin swore. "Never mind that." He raised a hand as the man sputtered and started to protest. "We're going to lose this wall soon. I want archers on every roof that will hold them, with ropes in position to let them down."

The man nodded smartly and began to turn away.

"I'm not finished yet!" Rhenkin snapped. "No heroics. I want every archer off the roofs and back behind our lines before they are truly threatened."

Another section of tree trunk sailed over village and crashed into the gates. The impact threw them inwards and, already weakened by fire, they gave a tortured groan as they twisted and then fell.

"Don't just stand their gawping, man," Rhenkin shouted. "Move!"

The lieutenant snapped another salute off and hurried to the steps.

"And tell Larson to get back over here!" Rhenkin called after him.

The interior of the village had been almost completely transformed. Piles of logs and debris from collapsed buildings had turned the once open and airy place into a maze of twisting corridors and tiny lanes.

The Bjornmen surged through the streets, meeting no resistance for the first five or ten seconds. A horn sounded and each of the men on the rooftops of the buildings closest to the breach rose to one knee and drew back on his bowstring. The arrows flew at the Bjornmen from all sides and hundreds died in a moment, falling to the ground, their screams mixing with the battle cries in a bizarre chorus.

The mass of raiders recoiled like a burnt snake and they crouched low, reforming their formation of interlocked shields. The advance halted altogether for a moment, while arrows slammed into shields as the archers searched for a weakness.

A unit of pikemen charged around the corner. They threw themselves into the fray, easily finding the cracks in the shield wall with their long weapons and thrusting them deep, decimating the stricken Bjornmen. They withdrew quickly, before the Bjornmen could gather themselves, and more arrows lanced down from the rooftops.

A raider tossed a flaming torch up onto a thatched roof and, as if this was the signal, more followed. Within moments, half a dozen buildings were suddenly alight.

Rhenkin swore as his plans dissolved into chaos. The Bjornmen locked shields and advanced slowly through the streets, touching flame to thatch as they went. The archers did their best but, in one stroke, their time had been cut in half. Barely had they loosed an arrow, when they were forced to flee to the next roof or down into the streets.

"Catapults," called Rhenkin, and a barrage of logs was hurled into the enemy to cover the archers' withdrawal. His plan descended into a bloody brawl as the Bjornmen pushed forward to meet his troops. The narrow streets provided them with no room to manoeuvre and, for the best part of an hour, it was a ugly song of blood and pain, as feet slipped in the mess and swords stabbed down savagely.

The catapults continued to hurl logs at the Bjornmen and, at Rhenkin's order, into the flames as well. Within the space of twenty minutes, the fire had turned into an inferno.

"Larson, it's time. Sound the withdrawal. We've done all we can here. I'll not waste lives needlessly."

The retreat was a hair's breadth from a rout as Rhenkin's force streamed through the village. Rhenkin ran at the rear with hand-picked men carrying heavy mallets. They slammed the mallets into the pinned beams braced against half-collapsed houses as they ran, the dust from the tumbling buildings eclipsing the cloud of smoke behind them as they fled.

The dust rose into the skies, mingling with the darker smoke as the village burned. The palisade and barracks, both constructed of wood, were merely more fuel for the fire and the flames soared high into the skies.

Chapter Eight

She wasn't like the others. It had taken a long time for her to notice it but, once she had, she wondered how it could have taken her so long. They came and went, these brief moments of lucidity, but they were increasing. She now noticed the passage of time, the days that passed. None of the others seemed to. They were lost in the same fog that ebbed and flowed in her mind. The fog that seemed to have flooded theirs.

They rose before the darkness had started to fade, moving by the light of the glowing orbs that hung outside of their huts. It was a pale, watery light, an imitation of moonlight with all the joy and romance sucked from it.

The women were almost sluggish as they moved walking as if still asleep, though none of them ever truly woke from it. They worked to put food together, toasting oatcakes or making porridge by boiling water on the stone plates with strange glowing symbols that each had in their huts.

There was no fire anywhere. She knew she ought to be more curious about this and the fact she wasn't nagged at her like a stone in her shoe.

A cry broke her train of thought. The babies were squalling again. It only took one to wake and they were all at it, joining together in a little choir of hunger and need. She rose with the others to fetch them. They'd all want feeding. They were always hungry.

As she cradled the baby to her breast, his eyes glowed a soft blue in the gloom. She stroked his hair and crooned a tune that seemed to begin at her lips without ever being formed by any thought.

She was one of the few that weren't trying to get pregnant. Those that did were soon moved to a different area, away from the pens. She and two others were there simply to help with feeding the babies. No single woman could hope to keep up with their demand for milk. They simply grew too fast.

There were only women in this pen. The men were kept somewhere else. Their compound consisted of five simple huts arranged in a circle with a well at the centre.

These were surrounded by a low wooden fence which marked the boundary. Beyond that was the unknown. The women were not permitted to go further than the fence and she'd never been curious enough to risk taking a look. Her curiosity came and went with the fog in her mind.

A tear ran down her face as she fed the baby. She always cried and the tears were another odd constant. *What was she so sad about? She had no complaints, did she?* The other women were in bliss. Bliss. The word tumbled around in her mind. It sounded like something. Reminded her of something.

The thought fell away as the baby stirred, protesting as her milk gave out. She frowned. This wasn't right. It was much too soon. He fussed and grumbled, as she turned him and tried the other side, but there was little there either and, before long, he was crying again.

She was dimly aware of the woman beside her speaking. "Give him to me."

The woman reached out her arms and, defeated, she passed the child to over her and fixed her clothing.

The baby settled down to feed, nursing hungrily. She watched for a moment, the sight stirring odd emotions in her. Envy and fear. She puzzled at the feelings, they were unsettling and she frowned again as she rose to her feet and left.

None of the others even looked up as she stepped out of the hut into the half-light. The glowing orbs were kept under the edge of the roof, far away from the rays of the sun. Their weak light didn't extend far into the compound and she moved more from memory than anything else as she made her way to the well.

Her eyes soon adjusted to the darkness and her movements were mechanical, as she hauled the water up and poured it from the bucket into the jugs sat beside the well.

Bliss. The word still echoed in her mind. She found herself whispering it.

"Bliss." The sound wasn't quite right. This wasn't the word she wanted at all. She dropped the empty bucket back down into the water then hoisted it up on the rope again.

"Liss." Her blonde hair tossed as she shook her head, rejecting the noise.

"Riss." She paused, resting the full bucket on the rim of the well as her lips moved. "Riss... Sriss..."

"Essriss." *No, not that.* "Ylsriss." As she whispered the word, her eyes grew wide

97

and the lethargy fell from her as she shed it like an old skin. She looked about her and truly saw her surroundings – the huts, the well - for the first time in months. She caught sight of the satyrs, their lantern-light eyes gleaming as they stared through the fence, and then she screamed.

She was still screaming as the women came out of the huts, carrying the oversized babies with them. Babies that had grown to the size of toddlers in little more than a month. The women looked at her with confusion while the babies turned their heads towards her, their glowing blue eyes filled with a curiosity and an awareness that no baby that age should have, and then she screamed all the harder.

They came for her soon after that, man-shaped creatures with eyes of flame. They spoke to each other in a language that seemed closer to music than words, their hands reaching for her, grasping her. Ylsriss kicked and flailed in panic, as they held her down and studied her intently. Then a hand was laid on her head and everything was still.

She was being moved. Though her mind was filled with a fog, Ylsriss could tell that much. They took her to another place, where gentle hands and human voices cared for her. She lay under thick blankets as they spoon-fed her a thin broth, tending to her body while her mind retreated into a corner to curl up around its wounds.

It was a week before she spoke again. Two before she left the hut and entered a new world. Her mind was still waking, unfolding from the fog of the pens, but a fresh horror was growing within her as memories unfolded. Where was Effan? Where was her baby?

* * *

Her hands ached. Of all the things that might bother her it was the way her hands cramped as she was scrubbing the clothes in the cold water. The wellpumps might produce hot water but it cooled all too soon.

Ylsriss knelt on the rough wooden deck and thrust her hands into the water again. She grabbed the clothes and brought them to the scrubbing board. The water was almost cold now. Tepid would have been too generous a description. The sodden cloth slipped under her hand and she scraped her knuckles against the ridged board.

"Shit!" she swore loudly.

She brought her hand to her lips and sucked at the soapy knuckle as she hurled the rags down. The water sloshed to one side of the tub, causing it to tip, and the remaining clothes and soapy water spilled out over the deck, pouring over the edge onto the soft forest floor.

Her cheeks coloured in embarrassment as she felt the others' eyes settle on her, and she rushed along the deck and down the steps to retrieve the clothes. The eyes drifted away as if she wasn't quite interesting enough to hold their attention. They were passive and docile, and this just served to fuel her anger.

Another pair of hands joined her as she squatted in the soft earth and helped her to gather up the clothes. "I know what it's like," Joran said, as she looked up at his young face in thanks. "It can be hard to adjust to life here. You will get used to it in time, though. Just give yourself a chance."

Ylsriss glared at him, his warm smile a flash of white against a face made dark by the almost endless twilight. "Give up, you mean?" she snapped.

His smile faded as his expression became sympathetic, but this just stoked the fire inside her. She bit hard on the inside of her lip, tasting blood as she fought to contain more harsh words, and felt the guilt rising within her.

"I'm sorry. I didn't mean it like that," she muttered.

"Yes, you did," Joran disagreed, in a kindly tone. "It's the truth, after all. But you need to understand that it will get better. You don't have to live in anger. You can find a joy in serving."

She looked at him for a moment, wondering what he might have been like if he'd grown to manhood in her world, without feeling the touch of the fae on his mind.

A bitter sigh escaped her lips and she looked around the clearing. The huts were rude at best, cobbled together as well as they could be from fallen branches. The fae refused to let them fell trees, only permitting them to use limbs that had fallen in the wind or by some other natural means. They'd provided them with a handful of shaped boards, fashioned with their magic, but the majority of the huts had been made with what the slaves could scavenge.

She'd been shocked when she first arrived. The slaves were kept in conditions worse than any she'd known. They were treated little better than animals but they seemed to accept it stoically and without complaint.

She forced herself to smile as she stood by the tub. "You're right, Joran. I just find it hard sometimes."

He reached out hesitantly and squeezed her shoulder with genuine affection. "You need to give yourself time, Ylsriss. It's only been…what…six months since you came to this camp?"

She didn't answer. A group of children ran around the hut, laughing and squealing. She'd expected the pain to fade, although part of her had hoped it wouldn't, but the sight of them brought the pain of Effan's theft back to her, as fresh and sharp as she had felt it on the day it happened.

How long had she been here? Even after all this time, she found it almost impossible to keep track of the days. Six months sounded possible, but it could have been as much as nine or as little as three.

The sun didn't rise and fall here like it did in her world. That was the reason they called it the Realm of Twilight. The sun and moon were only in the sky for roughly an hour each day. During the rest of the time, the sky was in a perpetual state of twilight or predawn.

"I think so," she shrugged. Thinking of the time that had passed just reminded her of the time she'd lost with Effan. The fae would have taken him to a different camp, apparently. They hadn't even given her the chance to say goodbye to him. She clenched her teeth and fought back the tears. Emotions like that just got you strange looks here.

With Joran's help, she managed to gather up the now filthy clothing and pull the tub back up onto the deck. Ylsriss dumped the clothes out into a pile and turned to take the tub back to the wellpumps. She froze and noticed Joran stiffen too, as a stir passed through the camp. It was not as if any noise had been made, but the atmosphere changed instantly and her eyes were drawn to the far end of the small clearing, to the trail that led into the dense woods.

A fae stood there, its burning eyes slowly sweeping the camp until they settled on her. With an imperious gesture, he beckoned her closer and she obeyed quickly. Despite her anger, the creatures terrified her. It had not yet been her time to be chosen but she knew the day was coming. It had been coming since her milk ran out. Running would be futile. There was nowhere to run to.

As she drew closer, she saw two more figures behind him - a large human man and a young woman. The man held the girl by the wrist and it was clear he had been dragging her along for at least part of their journey. She was short, even shorter than Ylsriss herself, and her long dark hair covered much of her face as she stood, defeated, her head bent towards the ground.

Ylsriss looked questioningly at the fae. It was only when it glowered at her that she remembered herself. "How may I serve you, Blessed One?"

The glower transformed into a self-satisfied smirk. "You will care for this one. Show her the way of things." The large man stepped forwards and Ylsriss realised her first impression was wrong. He had ice blue eyes that shone faintly in the twilight. This was no human. He was one of the fae-born.

She recovered herself quickly and bowed to the fae. "As you wish, Master."

He grunted and turned to leave. The fae-born dropped the woman's wrist and followed. She watched them walk lightly through the forest for a moment before the foliage swallowed them. The woman rubbed her wrist where the fae-born had gripped it. The red finger marks were visible even in the dim light. Ylsriss ducked down slightly to meet her eyes and gently touched her shoulders. "Let's get you inside, shall we?"

The woman nodded mutely. Her eyes were like the rest of her. Shocked. Numb.

Ylsriss took the young woman's hand, half-expecting her to jerk away or flinch, but she seemed unresponsive. She shared a look with Joran over the top of the girl's head. His face mirrored her concern as he shrugged and they led the newcomer into the hut that Ylsriss shared with five others.

The young woman sat on the edge of one of the two bunks that stood against one wall, the extra sleeping pallets tucked underneath. Ylsriss poured water from a wooden bucket into a copper kettle and set it onto the runeplate to boil.

"There's going to be a lot for you to get used to," she said, as she traced a fingertip over the first sequence of glyphs to release some of the stored heat.

She gave the girl what she hoped was a comforting smile and then turned to Joran, who stood watching them from the doorway, nodding to let him know it was okay for him to leave.

"Why don't we start with your name? My name is Ylsriss." The curtain that hung in place of a door fell back as Joran left, leaving them alone.

"Tia," the woman breathed, her voice almost inaudible.

"Tia," Ylsriss repeated. " That's a nice name. Now, how about a cup of tea? It's not real tea, of course, but it's as close as we can get." She waited for the nod and then reached for two of the wooden cups on the small shelf above the window.

"When were you taken?"she asked, with her back still turned.

"Three days ago, I think. The sun isn't right here,"Tia replied, her voice climbing above a whisper.

"I know. It's something they say you get used to, but I haven't yet."

"How long…?"

"Have I been here?" Ylsriss finished for her. "I would think about six months in this camp, but it's hard to say for sure. Where were you from?" she asked, as she spooned out the dried leaves.

"Tigrit on Bresda. You've probably never heard of it."

Ylsriss shook her head.

"It's a little place on the northern coast. More a fishing wharf with a few huts to keep it company than a village."

"I didn't really see anywhere outside of Hesk until we started making preparations for the war," Ylsriss shrugged.

"How were you taken?"the girl asked.

"I followed my baby. They took him." Ylsriss said it quickly, hoping it wouldn't hurt. It didn't work.

Tia looked at her in shock. "They took him? What happened to him?"

"I don't know. He's in another camp somewhere. I know he's being cared for, but that's all I know." She cleared her throat. "What happened to you?"

"They came from the sky,"Tia said. Her eyes were glazed as she remembered.

Ylsriss blinked at that. Every time she thought there was nothing else she could hear about the fae that could shock her, she heard something new. "From the sky?"

"On white horses,"Tia said, softly.

"What happened?"Ylsriss asked, lifting the bubbling kettle from the runeplate and pouring the water into the cups. She deactivated the glyphs quickly. The stored heat was too precious to waste.

"It was late. Later than I should probably have been out and I knew I would get a tongue-lashing when I got in, but you know how it is when you're with a boy."Tia shrugged, her lips curling into a faint smile.

"I remember,"Ylsriss said, with a wry smile herself.

"Harn had taken me for a walk along the clifftop and we'd talked until past sundown."

Ylsriss chuckled at the blush spreading on Tia's pale cheeks. "You did more than just talking too, judging by that face."

The colour faded quickly as Tia continued. "It started like a sound of thunder in the distance. We both looked around because it was a clear night. Then there were pipes and horses, and something was laughing. They tore down out of the sky on white horses, the moonlight shining on their hair. Their eyes…" She glanced up at Ylsriss, her face telling the story of her fear as she relived it.

"We ran. In my life, I don't think I've ever run so hard or so fast. We ran until my breath burned in my throat, but they were just toying with us, charging in from the sky and then veering off. Harn tripped and then grabbed a branch to use as a club but then they took him. There was so much blood, Ylsriss, and it was so fast. One moment he was telling me to get behind him and the next he was on the ground."

Ylsriss realised she was still holding both cups and handed one to Tia, who took it slowly, her mind somewhere else as she continued to speak.

"They took his head. One of them actually took his head and held it high, like it was some kind of trophy, and they all laughed. Even the goat-men laughed. What kind of monsters are they, that they could do something like that?"

Ylsriss sipped at her tea, wondering where to begin.

"That's a good thing to remember, Tia. They are monsters. They'll tell you that you can have a good life here if you give in to it, accept that you're a slave. There are wonders here like you've never imagined. Magic, true magic. It's easy to let the past go and just accept your place here. You have to remember that they are monsters, though. They don't feel things like we do. They don't even look at us as people. We're playthings, toys at best."

Tia blanched and swallowed her tea down, barely noticing that it was too hot and burning her tongue. "Magic?" she asked, trying to take it in.

"Things like this." Ylsriss waved to the runeplate. The glyphs glowed, the gentle orange light showing it was still warm.

Tia gave it a curious look, but then her eyes dropped and her face fell. "What will happen to me?"

"I won't lie to you, Tia. You won't be harmed so long as you work hard but, as a young woman, you must know what's coming?"

Tia looked at her blankly.

"We're breeding stock, Tia," she said flatly. The girl's vacant expression slowly turned to one of horror.

"They don't...?" she gasped, moving one hand to the thong around her neck and grasping at something beneath her simple dress.

"They do," Ylsriss said. The truth was hard and brutal, but she would be better off knowing it from the outset rather than fostering false hopes. "They'll probably give you some time to adjust but, yes, you will be taken and given to one of them. Over and over, until you are pregnant. They normally put women like you straight in the breeding pens. They stay there until they've given birth and their milk gives out. I don't know why you've been put here. This is more of a holding area for women until they're fertile again."

"And you've been here..."

"Six months," Ylsriss whispered. Then the tears came and, this time, there was no stopping them.

Tia looked on helplessly and then tried a tentative hug. Ylsriss hugged her back and gave a bitter laugh. "I'm supposed to be helping you," she protested weakly. "A fine job I'm doing!"

"We must trust in the Lord," Tia said, her soft voice full of calm conviction. "He will bring us through this."

"The Lord?" Ylsriss wiped her eyes with one sleeve. "The Lord of New Days, you mean?"

Tia nodded.

"I wish I had your faith, Tia. It's not something I share. I hope this place doesn't take it from you."

Tia smiled and toyed with the necklace inside her dress. "I'm sure it won't."

"Let's get out of here. I'll walk you around the camp and show you how things work," Ylsriss suggested.

Tia nodded and followed the older woman towards the door. One glance out of the window at the light was enough to prompt Ylsriss to turn back and test the temperature of the runeplate with a licked fingertip.

"Give me a hand with this?" She lifted it from its mounting with a grunt and staggered out of the doorway onto the porch. Once she was through the door, Tia grabbed an end and together they carried the chunk of stone down the three steps to the ground.

"What are we doing?" Tia asked, as they set the stone down.

"It stores heat. We can't use fire here," Ylsriss explained. She dug into the soft earth with her hands and dumped soil over the glyphs, covering them and hiding them from the light.

"The glyphs will absorb the heat that the sun brings to the stone and then we can release it when we want to cook."

"Why did you cover that bit in dirt?" Tia asked, pointing.

"The sunlight stops it working for some reason," Ylsriss explained. "I'm not sure why or how, but we were told to make sure the glyphs never get exposed to it. You could cover them with anything, I suppose. I just find this easiest."

Ylsriss watched the horizon as it grew steadily lighter. At last, the sun crested the trees and she gave a quiet sigh of pleasure, as she felt its warmth fall upon her. As if in response to the light, a flock of birds burst from the forest canopy, their red and green feathers bright against the blue sky.

The camp became a flurry of activity as the others rushed out to leave their runeplates in the sunlight. Tia's gaze fell on the moonorbs that were being swiftly deactivated. She turned to Ylsriss. "What about those? Why aren't they being put out to capture the light?"

"You're a quick one, aren't you?" Ylsriss said, impressed despite herself. "I didn't think to ask that for at least six weeks. We put those out at night to capture the moonlight."

"Moonlight?" Tia asked, her face creasing in a frown. "Wouldn't the sunlight be brighter?"

"It might be but remember what I said? It has to do with the way the magic works. We covered the glyphs in dirt to stop the sunlight from touching them. If we captured sunlight in the orbs and then released it...well...I don't know what would happen. The orbs would probably just wink out straight away. Even if they didn't, the light would affect everything else around them. The runeplates...the wellpumps... everything."

Tia nodded, taking in the scene. "It looks so different here in the sunlight," she marvelled.

"It really does," Ylsriss smiled. "It's my favourite time of day and it always passes too soon."

They wandered around the camp and Ylsriss pointed things out as they passed them: the wellpumps that drew water into the buckets that were lined up and waiting beside the odd-looking contraption; the small but well-tended vegetable plot that extended from behind the small ring of huts; and, in the distance, the barely visible fence line.

"The fae hate most of the things that we take for granted. They allow us to farm these vegetables out of necessity, but they won't touch them themselves. I suspect they also know what we keep in this pen but choose to ignore it."

Tia followed her through the long wild grass. She caught flashes of russet through the trees and peered over the fence, trying to get a proper look.

"What are they? Some kind of cow?" she asked.

"Deer, actually," Ylsriss replied, with a shrug. "As far as I know, there are no cows here and the only pigs I've heard of are wild boar. The fae keep us as their servants... well, slaves, if I am honest about it. They make use of the people that aren't breeding for them in other ways. The men hunt for them. The fae will only eat meat taken on the hunt."

"If they have to be taken on the hunt, why do you keep these?" Tia asked.

"Let's just say it's not a good thing to come back from a hunt empty-handed," Ylsriss said.

"So you lie?" Tia gasped. "Isn't that dangerous?"

"It's not something we do all the time. We hunt the deer for them. We just keep these as backups, just in case. Joran thought this up a couple of years ago, apparently. It's never been questioned."

Tia leaned on the fence and looked out at the deer flitting through the trees. "Joran. He's the boy you were with earlier?"

"He's one of the ones who's been here the longest. I expect they'll come for him soon."

Tia gave Ylsriss a sideways look at that. "Come for him?"

"For the same reason they come for us, Tia. Men are used just the same as women. We're slaves...or servants, if that sits better with you...but primarily we're breeding stock."

"But why?" Tia brushed the hair out of her face. "I mean, if they're taking men then there must be female fae?"

"Oh, there are," Ylsriss explained. She leaned on the fence and looked at the young woman. "This is guesswork, you understand? None of us know very much for certain, but I think that maybe the fae don't reproduce very quickly. The man who brought you in. You remember him?"

"I'm not likely to forget," Tia muttered, rubbing at one wrist.

"No, well, he's what they call a fae-born. Half-human, half-fae."

"He seemed a little...well...simple," Tia said. "Why would they want to breed a new race of half-breed idiots?"

"I don't know," Ylsriss admitted, "but you saw how strong he was. Maybe they want them for soldiers. Maybe they have something else planned. It's not really important." She reached out and took hold of Tia's hands. "What's important is that you understand what's going to happen. Everyone copes differently. Some, like Joran, have just accepted that this is what their lives are going to be like. He and some of the others almost seem happy. Me, well, I keep a little place locked away inside myself. A place where I can keep the hope burning, no matter how futile it may be. I know I'm lying to myself. It's not like I could escape and run away. This is a whole other world. But I have to do something to stay sane. Does that make any sense?"

Tia nodded. "Yes, I think it does." She looked back towards the camp, an odd expression on her face, and then turned in a slow circle.

"What is it?" Ylsriss asked.

"There are no guards or anything," Tia said, in surprise.

"No," Ylsriss agreed. "I'm surprised you noticed. Most are too affected to."

"Affected? What do you mean?"

"Have a good look at the people in the camp, Tia. They wouldn't think of escaping, even if it were an option," Ylsriss said.

Tia looked at her in shock. "Why?"

"I'm not sure how it works. I've taken to calling it the Touch. I haven't spoken about this to anyone else. Most of the others are too far gone to even notice. I'm sure some of it comes from being a prisoner. The rest of it is something else, though. It's to do with what the fae are. It seems to come on quite quickly with some people. They become pliant, docile. They're almost like cattle. Whenever a fae comes near them, they get this look."

"They are pretty terrifying, Ylsriss. I don't think I've ever been so scared of anything," Tia confided.

"No, that's not it. It's not fear, it's…"

"It's what?"

"It's closer to adoration." She sighed and stepped away from the fence. "You can't predict it. Some just become content with their lots here. Others… well, it barely affects them at all. Then there are those who practically worship the fae. They dream of being chosen to breed with them." She spoke with venom. "I despise them. I know it's not their fault, that they can't help it, but I do. It's disgusting."

She moved towards the path, "Come on. The sun will be gone soon and I still have a lot to show you. We ought to be getting back."

* * *

Ylsriss was woken by the smell of tea and toasting nutcakes. She sat slowly, rolling her shoulders and neck to work out the kinks, then turned to see Tia stood by the runeplate in the soft glow of a moonorb.

"You've picked that up quickly," she said quietly, so as not to wake the others.

Tia smiled. "It's amazing."

Ylsriss looked at her closely for a second, then clambered out of the tangle of blankets on the thin sleeping pallet. She arched her back and grimaced at the knotted muscles.

"Are you sore? I should have taken the floor. I'm sorry." Tia's dark eyes were filled with concern.

"Don't be silly. Besides, we all take turns. There aren't enough beds for all of us. You can sleep on the floor tonight." Ylsriss stepped in behind her, looking over her shoulder at the glyphs.

"Ease it back a touch," she instructed. "You'll burn through the heat too fast like that."

"Sorry. Maybe you should show me again?" Tia moved to the side to let Ylsriss at the glyphs.

"The stone itself will hold a lot of the heat you need once you've got it warm." Ylsriss traced one of the inscriptions, bringing down the intensity of the glow with deft fingers.

"If you weren't careful, you could use an entire day's heat in one moment. It'd probably burn right through the floor." She stepped back, letting Tia get back to the food. "That ought to do it."

Tia nodded and turned the nutcakes over again. She touched the glyphs as Ylsriss had taught her, deactivating the hot stone of the runeplate.

"Here." She handed Ylsriss some nutcakes on a wooden board with a cup of hot tea.

Ylsriss thanked her and sat on the edge of the girl's bunk. Chewing on a nutcake, she reached out her foot and nudged the others gently with it to wake them. The five women ate in silence, as was their morning ritual, each with a distant look in her eyes and her thoughts in another place, another time. They were changing though. Ylsriss looked from face to face as casually as she could. With some of them, it was more pronounced than others, but the signs were there in all of them. Soon they would be just like Joran. Some would be worse.

She felt stifled all of a sudden. The cramped conditions were too much when they were awake. Standing abruptly, she brushed the crumbs from her legs and reached for the pale clothing they all wore. She nodded towards a chest in the corner. "You should find something in there that will be roughly your size, Tia. You'll be forbidden from wearing anything else from now on. Get changed quickly and then meet me at the wellpumps. We have a busy day today."

Ylsriss didn't have to wait long. The girl already seemed to have changed since yesterday. She was eager to fit in, to learn how things worked. She'd seen this happen before. Two of the girls who'd been brought in just after her had both accepted their new lives readily. Despite the time they'd spent in the pens and the babies that had been taken from them, they were happy. Tia seemed set on the same path. The thought depressed her and she had to force a smile as Tia came to meet her.

"Here." She handed the girl a roughly woven wicker basket and a bulging waterskin. "You'll need this today. Stick with me and try to keep up."

Tia took the basket and studied the straps. The basket was well-made, but worn and heavily stained with dark red, almost purplish, smears.

"Berries for their wine," Ylsriss explained, as she hoisted her own basket onto her back. "We juice them in the shed over there and then set them to ferment." She led Tia out of the camp, following the other women and children who were making their way along the well-worn path through the forest.

Ylsriss looked back now and then to make sure Tia was keeping up, but the girl was right behind her. Her eyes were wide with wonder, as she took in the sights and sounds of the world around her. She gasped in delight as a flight of carrow moths fluttered out of the bushes, their black and white wings flashing in the dim light as they flew up above the trees.

"Come on, Tia!" she growled. The girl's joy was irritating her. This was not a holiday. It was not a pleasant stroll through the woods. It was slavery.

The trail led up into the hills and Ylsriss was soon sweating from the heat and exertion. It was never truly cold in this place. There seemed to be no seasons to speak of, but the weather was muggy. The undergrowth grew thicker the further they travelled and it seemed to generate a humidity all of its own.

Finally, they broke free of the trees and emerged on a hillside that was densely carpeted with low bushes, which the women made their way into without hesitation. Tia watched them, her forehead creasing into a frown.

"The fae are a bit inconsistent, really," said Ylsriss. "We pick these terel berries so we can make wine from them. They insist that their meat must be taken in the hunt, but they have no problems with us planting more of these bushes." She motioned to Tia to follow her as she worked her way into the fields.

"Watch closely. There's a knack to it, but it's not all that hard to pick up." Ylsriss lifted a leafy stem carefully. "Watch out for the thorns," she muttered, twisting it to show Tia the vicious-looking spikes concealed beneath each leaf. "The berries come away with a twist." She plucked one from the stem and reached over her shoulder to drop it into her basket. "Now you try."

Tia reached for another low-hanging stem and lifted it, trying to match Ylsriss's smooth motion. She jumped and uttered a small cry of pain as she dropped it. Several children looked at her and giggled, as she sucked her finger.

"I told you to watch out for the thorns," Ylsriss said, irritation creeping into her voice. "They are poisonous. Not enough to kill you," she added quickly, as Tia's eyes grew wide and she pulled her finger from her lips. "It'll just give you a mild fever if you get stuck enough times and then you're no good to us." She gestured towards the bush. "Try again."

This time, Tia managed to pull the berry off without incident and pop it into her own basket.

"Good," Ylsriss grunted. "Now, stay close to me and try to do it a bit faster. You'll speed up in time, but we're supposed to fill these baskets at least twice today." Tia nodded and smiled again. Ylsriss pressed her lips together, trying to hide her frustration, and turned to the closest bush.

There was a rhythm to the work. Grab the vine with one hand, stroke back the leaves with the other, twist off the berry and then drop it over one shoulder into the basket. Grab, stroke, twist, drop. Ylsriss settled into a pattern, and her hands were soon flickering here and there over the bush as her basket grew heavier.

"Be sure to drink," she called back over her shoulder to Tia, as she stopped to pull the waterskin up to her lips. "You won't notice yourself getting dry until it's already too late."

Tia nodded gratefully and drank deeply from her own skin. Her fingers were already stained a deep purple from the juice of the berries and covered in small cuts from the thorns.

"It'll come," Ylsriss said. "Just try to keep at a steady pace. We don't expect you to meet quota today."

"Quota?" Tia began but the sound of a horn in the distance cut her off . She glanced at Ylsriss, who looked up in alarm as it sounded again and then again.

The other women and children on the hill stood and set their baskets carefully down on the ground. "Leave your basket here, Tia," Ylsriss said. "We have to go."

"What's going on?" the dark-haired woman replied, catching Ylsriss's worried tone and eyes.

"I'll explain as we go." She motioned to Tia's basket impatiently and then led her swiftly back to the trail.

"We have a quota. An amount of berries we have to provide each week. Sometimes they want us to collect other fruits for them. Once, it was a particular kind of leaf. If a camp hasn't met the quota, they summon us like this."

"Wait a minute! You mean there are other camps?"

"You didn't think we were the only humans the fae have taken, did you?" Ylsriss spoke more harshly than she'd intended to and the girl flinched back from her.

"I'm sorry. I didn't mean it to come out like that. Yes, there are at least eight or nine, judging by the numbers at these gatherings. Remember I told you my son is in another camp?"

"So what happens if we don't produce enough?" Tia asked. The women were moving along at much faster pace now and she was struggling to keep up.

"One of us is given to the fae. If it's a woman, she is given to a satyr. If it's a man, he is given to a female fae and then, when she's done with him, to the satyrs for the chase," Ylsriss said, her tone matter-of-fact.

"Satyrs?"

"You called them goat-men, I think."

"What would they want with a woman?"

"What do you think, Tia?" Her look was direct, and Tia's face reddened and then paled, as she moved from embarrassment to horror.

"The chase?" she asked, in a soft voice.

Ylsriss ducked under a broken branch that hung from a tree. "I don't know all the details, but they are given a full day to run and then the satyrs hunt them. They never survive it. Few women survive their time with the satyrs either."

The trail split and they passed further down the hill, away from the camp. The trees became less wild as they travelled. They didn't look as if they had been planted deliberately or pruned, but almost seemed like they had been sculpted, as if the entire forest were a part of some gigantic artwork. The sweeping arch of a bough here seemed to complement, and even mirror, the twisting line of a trunk there. It was a subtle change and one that was easily overlooked at first, but Ylsriss couldn't fail to notice it now. It marked the shift from the wild woods into the home of the fae.

The trees seemed to be spread further apart, although there was no evidence of them having been cultivated or tended. The canopy altered too. Instead of the branches growing where they could, fighting for the light, they worked in harmony, the broader limbs of some trees supporting the lighter, weaker branches of others.

The soft voices of the women, and the chattering and giggles of the children ceased as the lights became visible. They were far paler than the light shed by the moonorbs of the camp and, as they crested the small hill and looked down into the fae city, their glow added a ghostly feel to it.

Ylsriss heard Tia gasp as the scope of the city became visible and remembered her own reaction at first seeing it.

"Is that it? Their home?" she asked in a whisper.

"That's it," Ylsriss replied, her voice filled with dread. "Tir Rhu'thin, the home of the fae."

The city filled a massive area of the forest. It was unlike any other place Ylsriss had ever seen. Whilst many of the buildings were constructed of stone, some had been fashioned from living trees. They rested in the embrace of the branches, raised high above the earth.

There was no uniformity in the construction. Some trees cradled fully constructed stone and wooden buildings, while others held simple platforms strewn with pillows and billowing silk curtains. Other buildings seemed to be formed within groups of four or five trees. Somehow, the trees intertwined to create enclosed spaces.

Ylsriss glanced over at Tia and reached out gently to take her arm. The woman was reacting just as she once had, her feet barely moving as she looked about her in wonder.

The group huddled together as they approached the yellow-stone wall and passed through the ivy-covered archway that led into the city. Not for the first time, Ylsriss noted the crumbling stones. Despite the newly-built appearance of some of the tree homes, the place had the feel of a ruin that had been brought back to life.

The city was riddled with small winding paths paved with the yellow-stone slabs, which stretched out through the trees. Ylsriss and the others followed a wide central route that led into the centre of the city.

Suddenly, the fae were everywhere as if someone had sounded a bell. They perched on tree limbs, stood in doorways and waited by the side of the winding path, watching in silence as the women and children passed.

Ylsriss no longer needed to hush Tia or hurry her along. The young woman pressed close to her for protection. The fae did not move but their faces were filled with animosity and derision.

The group followed the broken paving stones into a central square. At its centre was a garden of sorts, although it was little more than a wide circle of grass with a huge willow tree in the middle. Fae clustered around the tree, their musical voices falling silent as the women approached. The crowd parted and the creature at its centre strode forth.

Tia gave a barely audible mewl of terror as the figure walked slowly towards them. A man's head and torso extended out of the lower body of a massive stag. The creature had a thick beard and hair that hung down to its shoulders, and a pair of huge antlers sprouted from its head.

It extended one arm and invited them closer with a sweeping gesture. Tia moved in with the crowd and then sank to her knees in the grass, following the lead of the others. They waited in silence. She noticed that the children were silent and still. They didn't need to be hushed. She edged closed to Ylsriss and whispered, "What is that thing?"

"That's Aelthen. Their leader or king, or something. Be still!" Ylsriss hissed.

Others began to file in, first groups of women and children, and then smaller groups of men, until the garden could hardly contain them and the square groaned with the numbers.

"You, who have been summoned, will bear witness." The creature's voice was deep and powerful, reaching the furthest edges of the crowd with ease.

"You all know your tasks and the consequences of not performing them well." He turned and beckoned into the crowd of fae. A tall female emerged from it and dragged a man out towards the creature. He looked spent. Not just tired, but drained, as if he hadn't eaten in weeks, although he showed no signs of gauntness or weight loss. It was as if the very essence of him had been leached away, leaving little more than the husk.

Aelthen's burning amber eyes swept across the crowd as if searching. Finally, they settled on Joran and a faint smile touched the creature's lips. "You will take him. Prepare him. Tomorrow, he will be quarry for the chase."

Joran stood and nodded respectfully, before stepping forward to the female, who dropped the man at his feet. A sneer of contempt tainted her beautiful but alien face.

With that, Aelthen turned away. Ylsriss pulled Tia to her feet and herded her back with the others. They filed through the streets, passing through the ivy gates and heading back into the forest in silence.

CHAPTER NINE

Ylsriss walked on in silence. Tia had already tried to speak to her several times but she'd ignored her. Her attention was on the man who staggered along beside Joran, leaning heavily on his arm. Despite Joran's smaller stature, he managed to support him easily. It took some time for it to sink in, but Ylsriss was slowly becoming aware of a resemblance. The man was older, certainly, but he had the same facial structure as Joran, the same set to his eyes and cheeks. She thought of the way Aelthen had smiled at him and she wondered. By the time they had made their way back into the camp, she was certain they were related.

She sent Tia off with some of the other women to retrieve the berries they'd harvested that morning and then hurried to Joran's small hut. She tapped on the door frame and waited until the thin curtain was pulled back. Joran looked calm as he peered out at her.

"Ylsriss," he said, "I'm a little busy right now."

"You know him, don't you?" Her question was deliberately blunt.

"Know him? I don't think so. How could I?"

She ignored his protest and pushed past him into the hut. It was smaller than her own and designed to house only two or three people. The man lay on the bunk closest to the window, his eyes closed and his face pointed towards the dim light filtering through the white cloth that Joran had hung where glass panes would be in another life.

She studied his face and turned to Joran, who looked at her with an expression of mild confusion. She knew his emotions were probably dulled. On the face of someone so affected by the fae it was equivalent to looking at her as if she'd gone mad.

"How can you not see it, Joran? This man looks just like you!"

"You're being ridiculous, Ylsriss. Besides, what does it matter?"

"Where were you taken?" she asked, as a thought occurred to her. *Just how far did the Touch go? What if it were challenged, pushed?*

"It was a long time ago," he replied, looking slightly uncomfortable. Ylsriss felt a surge of triumph. Any display of emotion was a mark of success.

"How can you not remember? It was your home." Her tone was blunt, as she deliberately goaded him.

"I was young. You don't think about things like that when you're young."

"Like what? Where you live? Of course you do," she scoffed. "How old were you when you were taken?"

"I must have been about eight or nine, I suppose," Joran muttered, his face creased in concentration.

"Are you sure? Tell me your mother's name," she demanded.

"My mother's name? What?"

"It's simple enough, Joran. Tell me her name."

"What are you doing, Ylsriss? What's all this about?"

"This shouldn't be this hard, Joran. This isn't normal. Tell me her name." Her voice was harsh, ordering him.

His usual pliant look fell away, as his confusion slowly gave way to frustration and then panic. "I... I can't."

He trembled as the emotions came flooding back into him, and his face was etched with pain and fear. She took him into her arms then, as his tears began to fall and he uttered a cry of anguish. "How can I not remember her name? I can't even picture her."

"It's this place, Joran. It's them. They're doing something to you. To all of us," she said, brushing his hair from his face as he clung to her.

He cried for a time and then pushed her away gently. He coughed and rubbed his face. "I'm sorry, I didn't..."

"Don't be silly," she said. "Do you still think it's strange you can't picture her?"

"What? Of course I do. She's my mother, for crying out loud!"

"Good!" Ylsriss snapped. "Now, look at him!" She stabbed a finger towards the man on the bunk, who was snoring softly.

"Lord of the New Days, Malik!" Joran gasped. "How could you know?"

"It's like looking at a man next to a mirror, Joran. It's as plain as day."

"So why didn't I know? How could I forget my own brother?"

Ylsriss sat him down on the edge of the other bunk. "I meant what I said, Joran.

They're doing something to us."

"How do you mean?"

"Well, it's subtle, but people just don't behave as they should," Ylsriss explained, trying to put something she had only really made guesses at into words. "Like Tia. She was only taken about a week ago, I'd guess. Look at her though, she's happy and smiling, and taking joy from the magic and sights here."

"Isn't that a good thing? Life here is hard enough," Joran said, with a frown.

"Yes, but it's not how she should be acting. She should be screaming, terrified, looking to see if there is a way to escape." Ylsriss paced as she spoke. "We're all so passive. Why is that?"

"It's not like we have anywhere to go, Ylsriss. We don't have any way we could resist them or fight back. We're slaves!"

"You're right, we are," she agreed, "but I think we're almost slaves of our own making. Do you know it took Tia more than an hour to notice that there aren't any guards here?" She caught the shocked look on his face. "You hadn't even realised, had you?"

He shook his head. "It's not that I didn't know. It just… this sounds ridiculous, but it just didn't seem important, for some reason."

"It's the Touch," insisted Ylsriss. "It's more than just something that makes us compliant. It's slow, subtle, but in the end we almost worship them."

Joran nodded, his face thoughtful. "The Touch?"

"It's as good a name as any for it." Her speech became faster, excitement building in her. "You fought this thing off . Perhaps the others could too."

"And then what?"

She stopped at that. "I have no idea. Something. Anything!"

"We'd need to find out what causes it first," Joran mused, his face more animated than she could ever remember. "Is it the food? No, we grow most of it ourselves. The water, maybe? Like a medicine a hedge woman gives you to make you sleep?"

"It's not the water," a soft voice came from the corner. Malik sounded exhausted but his eyes were wide open and his words were clear.

"You're awake!" Joran knelt at his side.

"Obviously," Malik replied, dryly. "It's not the water though. Speaking of which, I'm as dry as bone here."

Ylsriss filled a cup from the bucket by the runeplate. "Here," she said.

He sipped the lukewarm water slowly at first, then drained the cup in three large gulps before handing it back for more. The water seemed to help and, after another cupful, he was able to push himself upright.

"It's not the water. It's not the food. It's something about the fae themselves," he explained, taking a nutcake from Ylsriss and picking at it.

"How though?" Ylsriss asked, intrigued.

"I don't know. It gets worse the closer you are to them, the more time you spend with them. I could feel myself becoming lost, losing all sense of who I was." His face clouded and he shook his head in disgust.

"I can see it all now, as if I'm looking at myself from the outside, seeing how I acted, what I became." He looked up at them, anger in his eyes. "They make us into something no better than dogs. No, worse than that, we're like toys to them, something to entertain them in their idle moments. I was filled with adoration for Byrlian, the female I was given to. I worshipped her."

"You loved her?" Joran asked.

"No...yes..." Malik shook his head. "It's more than that. I literally worshipped her, like she was some kind of goddess. I would have cut off my own arm for her if she'd asked, or even if it would have made her favour me with a smile. The things she made me do, though. You can't know how cruel they can be. The games she played with me..."

"So it was deliberate, then," Ylsriss mused.

Joran looked at her, "What was?"

"It's not a coincidence that you were picked to prepare him, Joran. Aelthen knew exactly who you both were. They're still playing their game with you now."

Malik nodded with a sigh. "You're probably right. Joran would never have noticed if you hadn't brought him out of it, whatever it is, but I would have known. They delight in this type of thing."

"I still don't remember it all," Joran muttered. "It's like half of my memories have gone. I know you're my brother, but I can't remember our family or where we're from. I don't even know when we were taken or how."

"You'd soon forget it all again, anyway," Malik said, quietly.

Joran paced the three steps to the doorway and back. "We can't just let them do this, though. We have to do something. You could run early. You could go now!"

Malik's lips twisted into a small, tired smile. "I can't, Joran. They'd just come for you."

"I don't care about me. It's not about me," Joran cried, waving his arms.

"And what about Ylsriss or the others in this camp? What about the children here? Do you think they'd stop with just you? No. If I am not there as expected, they will come for all of you. I won't let that happen."

"You can't go early," Ylsriss said. "But that doesn't mean you have to be unprepared."

"What do you mean?" Malik propped himself against the wall, his eyes now bright and interested.

"Well, they'll expect you to be tired, with no food or water. Easy prey." A nasty smile crept across Ylsriss's face. "What if you were none of those things?"

"I don't get you."

"Well, you have to be at the Whitestone. They're expecting you." She spoke slowly, still forming the plan in her mind as she was explaining it. "We don't though. We could meet you with provisions. We could all run!"

"No." Malik was adamant. "They'd find us and kill us all."

"What do you think is going to happen to us all in the end, anyway?" Joran demanded. "What do you think is going to happen to Ylsriss?"

"You don't know that. Life is hard here, but at least it's life," Malik protested. "What you're suggesting is a life of running. It would probably end with Joran and I just being killed, but you, Ylsriss, you must know how it would end for you. Alone in the woods, chased down by a horde of satyrs. You'd be passed around among them until it killed you."

They fell silent at that. Ylsriss sought Joran's eyes. They were bright and clear, filled with determination. It was more than that, though. They were filled with life, with a fire that hadn't been there before.

A thought came to her. "Fine. If you won't let us run with you, at least let us help you when you do run," she said.

"How are you going to do that?" Malik asked, with a scowl.

"They expect you to arrive rested, but with no supplies. That's how you're supposed to run, isn't it?"

Malik nodded and motioned for her to continue.

"What if we left early and put some supplies out for you? Nothing too heavy. Just some water and food. It could make all the difference."

"She's right!" Joran said, grabbing Malik's arm. "They'll think that by the time the satyrs start to run, you'll already be tired. They'll expect you to be thirsty and weak."

"It's a big risk. What if they catch you with the supplies?" Malik hedged.

"We're doing it, Malik. You can stop me from running with you, but you can't stop me from doing this." Joran jabbed his finger at the air in front of Malik's face as he spoke. "Get some rest. I'll be back in a few hours."

"You're going now?" Malik gaped.

"Soon. The sun will be up in an hour or so. It makes sense to go then, when the fae are all inside."

"Joran, I..." He reached for the younger man.

"Save it for when I get back."

* * *

Ylsriss rose as silently as she could and made her way out of the hut onto the deck. The others were still asleep and Tia's snores were loud enough to mask her passage. The sky was shifting from the true black of night to the silvery twilight that would last all morning until the sun rose for its hour near noon. They would be coming for Malik before too much longer.

She passed through the camp and tapped lightly on the wall of Joran's hut. The deep, steady breathing coming from within it carried on rhythmically. Ylsriss shook her head and smiled. *Were all men this hard to wake?* Klöss had been just the same.

"Klöss." She whispered his name. She hadn't allowed herself to think of him or their baby in so long. She clenched her fist and dug her nails into her palm in an effort to stem the rising tears. She *would* find a way to get Effan back, to get back to her own world. It was a hope she'd hidden from herself, one too distant to indulge in, but now...now that Joran had changed...perhaps it was possible. She stopped herself. "One thing at a time, Ylsriss," she whispered.

She knocked again, louder, and the splutter from inside told her she'd been successful. Joran pulled the curtain aside and peered out . His relief at seeing Ylsriss spoke volumes about his fear that it would be someone else waiting. "Ylsriss, it's still early. What do you want?"

"It's not that early. They'll come for him soon." She looked back over her shoulder, half expecting to see movement in the trees. "We should make sure he is well fed before they do."

"He probably needs sleep to more," Joran said, stepping out onto the deck.

"No, Joran. She's right." Malik's voice carried from inside the hut.

Joran shot her a black look and then held the curtain aside for her to enter.

She cooked quickly and they ate mostly in silence as the sounds of the camp waking drifted in through the door and window. Conversations started and ended almost before they began, stifled by the situation. The sound of distant voices prompted Ylsriss to pull the curtain aside and she turned back to the pair with a grim expression that said all that was needed.

"You remember the directions?" Joran whispered, with a sudden urgency.

"I remember." Malik rose and stepped through the curtain with a quiet dignity. Two fae faced the hut while a small group of satyrs stood behind them, laughing and speaking in their musical tongue.

"Come," the fae said simply, while reaching a hand out to Malik.

Curtains twitched in the other huts as the men and women watched, their eyes filled with nothing more than a dull curiosity.

Malik turned once as he was being led away. The expression on his face was calm but he managed a smile. Ylsriss knew, as they followed at a distance, that it was the only goodbye they would get.

The Whitestone was close to Tir Rhu'thin on a hill at the end of a well-trodden forest path. The stone itself was a massive grey boulder, shot through with veins of white. Ylsriss was reminded of the cheeses she used to steal from the market in Hesk, and had to fight down a wave of nervous laughter as they stopped at the very end of the path.

The forest seemed to have shied back from the hill that held the stone at its summit. The image stuck with Ylsriss and she found herself looking down at the trees and trying to decide if they actually were growing at an angle leaning away from the stone. It was an odd thought but it helped to distract her from the horror of the moment.

The hilltop was packed with satyrs, their eyes filled with anticipation. Aelthen waited at the stone, surrounded by a small ring of fae. The growing crowd parted as Malik was escorted through and presented to Aelthen. They were too far away for Ylsriss to hear any of the words but, even at this distance, the massive creature's voice carried.

"What happens now?" Tia's voice was low.

Ylsriss glanced at her. She hadn't realised she was so close. "We wait," she replied.

"Wait for what?"

"The sun." Ylsriss spoke without looking at her, her eyes searching the crowd for Joran. They'd become separated on the walk to the hill. "When the sun rises, Malik will start to run. He has the whole day. When the moon rises, he'll loose the satyrs on him." She nodded to the antlered figure next to the stone.

"Aelthen?" Tia guessed. "He's magnificent, isn't he?"

Ylsriss gave her a sharp look. It was there, in her expression. The admiration in the girl's eyes was plain for anyone to see. It wasn't quite adoration yet, but she knew it soon would be. She bit back a retort that would have been wasted anyway and sighed.

The fae and satyrs waited in silence. Slaves filed in to join the crowd. Ylsriss guessed that almost every human in the camps was in attendance. Was Effan somewhere in the crowd? Or was he still in his camp with whoever cared for him? Any murmur of conversation was stilled by cold looks from the fae and even Tia's whispered questions eventually stopped. The sky grew lighter by degree as they waited and, finally, the first rays of sunlight fell upon the hilltop.

The satyrs hissed and flinched as the sunlight hit them, and a faint green mist began to rise from their bodies. The fae were more stoic, Ylsriss noted. They initially grimaced but then ignored the deeper green vapour trailing from them. Aelthen stood as before, silent and impassive, simply waiting.

Only when the sun had crested the trees and the whole of it could be seen in the sky did he move. A cheer rose from the massed satyrs as he turned his head to speak to Malik. The crowd parted to allow the condemned man to walk through, and he made his way to the edge and then began to run down the hill and into the forest.

They watched for a time, long after he had passed into the trees and out of sight. The humans began to drift away soon after he faded from view. Despite their summons to bear witness, there was still work to be done.

Ylsriss spotted Joran and walked over to him, reaching for his hand. Eventually, they were the only two humans left. The satyrs stood, as if frozen, the mist boiling from them in a great green cloud. They would remain there until the moon rose. "Come on, Joran," Ylsriss said. "We should go."

The walk back to the camp seemed very quiet and very long.

* * *

The day passed slowly. The mindless drudgery of the work was bad enough, but Ylsriss itched to be able to speak to Joran. Her basket was filling slowly with berries, but she wasn't really putting any effort into picking them. The longest anyone had lasted on the chase was until the moon had begun to set the same night. At least, that was what they had told her.

The satyrs were fast and they wouldn't tire in the same way that a man would. Usually, they would find their quarry quickly. The dehydrated and terrified slaves must be easy to chase down. She wondered whether the supplies that Joran had hidden for Malik would make any difference.

When it was time to head back, she set her own pace and passed the others with ease. It was impossible to run whilst wearing the basket without spilling the precious berries, but she moved as quickly as she could. Tia was silent for once, walking with the group, wearing the same vacant look as the worst of them. Ylsriss was driven on as much by the desire to get away from the sight of her as she was to speak with Joran.

When she arrived in the camp, she immediately saw that she needn't have bothered rushing. It was silent. The men must still be out on the hunt. She dumped her berries into the vat in the storehouse and made her way back to her hut. The runeplate lay on the ground outside where she'd left it to absorb the sunlight, but she ignored it, stormed into the hut and threw herself onto the hard bunk. Sleep was an escape, the only place she had left she could run to.

Morning marked the surreal return of the camp's daily routine. Tia had retrieved the runeplate and breakfast was the usual silent ritual. Ylsriss ate as quickly as she could, then gathered up the soiled clothing and the washbasin, taking them out to the deck.

Washing the clothes was a chore she privately despised, but it would give her some time to herself and, hopefully, the opportunity to see Joran.

She ferried the bucket to and from the wellpumps, filling it with steaming water which she then transferred into the tub. The glyphs on the pipe running out of the well-mouth shone brightly in the twilight as she slid back the sleeve to activate them. They must have recently been renewed, although she hadn't seen a fae enter the camp.

Ylsriss kept an eye on Joran's hut as she scrubbed the clothes against the ridged board. She was up earlier than most of the other slaves, but she knew it wouldn't be long before they started work. As if on cue, the first of the men emerged from their huts, their eyes downcast and their voices subdued when they spoke at all.

Joran came out of his hut and she gave up all pretence of working, watching him openly. He moved just as the others had, slowly and without meeting anyone's eyes. Her heart sank. Surely he hadn't drifted back under the influence of the fae already? The thought of being truly alone here, the only person not smothered by the Touch, was too dreadful to bear. He glanced over at her. It was little more than a flicker of the eyes, but it was enough to give her hope.

She groaned inwardly as Tia approached and handed her a basket. "Come on. You're really slow today."

There was no avoiding it. She drained the water away and quickly hung the washing on the lines behind the huts before following the women and children out to the trails.

It was the last hours of twilight before true dark when they finally heard it. Ylsriss had returned to the camp and was working the press in the fruiting shed, crushing the berries down and setting the juice to ferment. The horn cut through the stillness, its haunting note made all the more poignant by what she knew it signified. Malik was dead. They had found him after all.

* * *

Ylsriss looked around the dark hut in confusion. She listened to the soft sounds of the others sleeping for a moment, trying to understand what had woken her. A soft tapping came from the wall next to the door opening, barely loud enough to hear.

She picked her way through the tangle of the two women sleeping on the pallets on the floor and stepped out into the darkness. A dark figure loomed next to the door. She jumped back in shock, before a soft green glow illuminated Joran's face.

"You scared me!" she whispered.

"I'm sorry. I couldn't think of a way to wake you and not the others."

"How did you know it was me?"

"You're the shortest one in there." His smile was an eldritch green in the glow of whatever it was he held in his hand.

Ylsriss grunted her acknowledgement. "It's not polite to point it out, though."

"I've been thinking about Malik. I think we need to talk."

She glanced back into the hut, then nodded. "Not here, though. Let's not run the risk of waking anyone else up."

He reached for her hand. The darkness was absolute. No moonorbs still glowed and the clouds blocked any starlight that there might have been. They moved carefully, by the tiny bit of light Joran was shedding. He led her through the camp and behind the juicing shed.

"Behind the sheds, Joran? If we were home, people would talk," Ylsriss said, with an impish grin, before realising he couldn't see it. "What is it you've got there, anyway?"

He ran a finger over the glyphs and the moonorb began to glow more brightly, giving off enough light to illuminate them but not enough to extend beyond the shed.

"The glyphs themselves gave off enough light for me to see my way through the camp," he shrugged.

"Clever," she said. "I tried to talk to you earlier. I've been trying to find a way to talk ever since we got back from Tir Rhu'thin."

"I know." The darkness hid his features but it couldn't cover the misery in his voice. "It's stupid, but I feel like everyone is watching me now. That they'll notice I'm different."

"You're right. It is stupid." Ylsriss was only half-joking. "Most of them wouldn't notice if you burst into flames."

Joran grunted at that. "You heard the horn?" It was a foolish question. Everyone had heard it.

"Yes." There wasn't much else she could say.

"It was a good three hours after sunset. He lasted more than a full day." There was a note of fierce pride in his voice.

"It was the only revenge he could have against them," Ylsriss said, in a hoarse whisper. "He spoiled their game."

Joran cleared his throat and shook his head. "I'm not sure he did. They might have just seen it as a greater challenge. That's not my point, anyway. My point is he lasted three hours past sunset. Longer than anyone else ever has. He achieved that even though he had no real supplies, and when they knew where his trail began and how fresh it was."

"What are you saying, Joran?" Ylsriss already knew the answer.

"We could run." His eyes were bright in the night. "Think about it. I mean, it's only really the Touch that keeps us here. There are no guards. They might not even notice we've gone for days. Not until the quota was missed."

"Run?" She kept her voice neutral. "Where would we go? What would we survive on?"

"I don't know where we'd go. Maybe in search of a way out of here. A way home." He shrugged. "Just away from here. That would be enough to start with. I can't go back to being the way the others are. I know I won't notice once it starts, but I can't bear the idea. I know if we stay here, eventually I will, though. As for what we'd survive on, what do we survive on now? I could take a bow. We could hunt and forage."

"And what about Effan? What about my son?"

"We don't even know where he is, Ylsriss. But maybe, in time, we could go in search of him too," Joran said.

Ylsriss tried to ignore the excitement rising in her. He probably didn't mean it about Effan. He was just humouring her. He was young though and, much as she didn't like to admit it to herself, she was not above using him if she had to. Not if it meant getting Effan back.

"When would you want to go?"

"You'll do it then?" He practically squeaked with excitement.

"I didn't say that, Joran. I just asked when."

He paused for a moment. "I think if we're going to do it, it should be as soon as possible. I know it would make sense to wait until the Wild Hunt when more of them are in our world, but I don't dare."

"What are you afraid of?"

"I don't think you ever fell under the Touch, Ylsriss, not really. You don't know what it feels like." His voice was harsh, raw. "It's like being numb inside your own mind. Nothing matters except for the fae. You live only to serve them, to please them. I can't let it fall on me again. It's not just that, though. We have no idea how this works. I mean, what if they can tell somehow?"

"Tell what? About you, you mean?" The thought hadn't even occurred to her.

"It's no more outlandish than stoves powered by glyphs and sunlight, is it?" He laughed suddenly. The sound was too loud in the night and his teeth clacked together as he clamped his mouth shut.

"I hadn't thought of it like that," she admitted, softly. "You're wrong though. I felt the Touch as strongly as anyone when I was in the pens." She fell silent, studying his eyes in the dim glow of the moonorb. "Tomorrow?" she whispered.

"That soon?"

"Why not?"

He couldn't think of a reason.

"We'll need to gather some things," he said.

* * *

Ylsriss stabbed herself on a thorn again and swore under her breath as she sucked at her finger. She sucked and spat, then sucked again. The poison was very minor but it would be enough to make her clumsy and more likely to scratch herself again. She'd heard tales of women dying in the berry fields, scratching themselves over and over until they finally collapsed. It wasn't something they spoke of any more. The Touch seemed to have affected the rest of the women more powerfully recently. Maybe it was just the events of the last day or so that made it seem worse to her, but they seemed even quieter, even more docile. "Like stupid sheep", she muttered, spitefully.

She spat again and began picking once more, moving slowly, deliberately. *Why hadn't she volunteered to work the vegetable patch instead?*

Tia stood to her left, humming contentedly as her fingers flickered over the bushes. Ylsriss shot her a sour look. The young woman disgusted her now, although she knew that it was irrational. It didn't seem likely anyone could resist the Touch once it was upon them, but some were just more susceptible than others.

Tia was different though. She seemed to have opened herself to it, to have welcomed it to her. She'd been entranced almost from day one. From the moment she first saw the runeplate and the other magical items around the camp, she'd given up any thoughts of home or the fact that she'd been taken by force. It wasn't just the Touch, although that had very clearly taken hold. She actually wanted to be here.

There were women in the camp who'd actually looked forward to being taken by the fae, who had welcomed the chance to try and carry a child for them. Tia would be one of these women, Ylsriss knew it. She would go to the fae with open arms and be willing, possibly even eager, to be bedded.

She glanced up at the sky. The day was dragging. Sunset had been hours ago, but the afternoon twilight seemed to be lasting forever. Her basket was less than half-full, but that wouldn't matter, not if she and Joran were to escape that night. The thought brought both excitement and fear in equal parts and she forced herself to take a deep breath and calm down as she looked around nervously, before picking another berry.

Joran was right. Despite knowing that no one was watching her, that the weight of the Touch stifled any real curiosity in those affected by it, it was hard to quell the paranoia. She glanced at Tia again and then turned back to the berries in front of her.

It was the silence that first alerted her to the fact that something was wrong. The Realm of Twilight was usually alive with the sounds of birdsong. Ylsriss straightened and looked about her, trying to pinpoint the source of her unease.

The terel berry field was really just a collection of small clearings that were connected by gaps in the trees. She caught a sudden blur of movement and then a woman screamed. It wasn't a scream of fright or surprise. It was a scream of pure terror and indescribable pain.

Ylsriss could see something thrashing around in the bushes. The screams ended almost as quickly as they began, but they were followed by a visceral growling, and the terrible sounds of cracking bones and ripping flesh, as whatever it was devoured the remains of the woman it had killed.

The other women ran through the berry patch, screaming, heedless of the scratches they were receiving from the thorns. The Touch might make them pliable, but it didn't override something as primal as the survival instinct. Ylsriss didn't move. Her eyes were still fixed on the thrashing bushes.

The creature emerged from them and then pounced, reaching out almost lazily to hook one of the fleeing women with its claws. It seemed to be a thing of purest darkness. Even the claws that extended from its paws were ebon. Its eyes burned a flaming green, but what caught Ylsriss's attention the most was the dark streak that extended out behind it as it leapt. It was as if the beast left a trail of mist behind it as it moved. A mist which seemed to be slowly catching up with it again and coalescing with its form.

The thing emerged from the bushes again, blood dripping from its powerful jaws. It was some kind of cat-like creature, although its head had a definite canine quality to it. Ylsriss didn't stop to study it. This time, she fled. It wasn't really hunting them, she realised. It didn't stop for long enough to eat its prey. It was just killing. She sped along the rows of bushes rather than through them, as the other women had. They were low, little more than waist-high, but they offered some chance of concealment.

The bushes ahead of her shook wildly as the cat-thing landed, crashing into the leaves and branches. It moved casually, almost slowly, its eyes burning with a cruel intelligence as it turned to regard its new prey. The long streak of darkness extended from its pelt, back over the bushes.

This time Ylsriss screamed. She couldn't help it. The thing sat back on its haunches, flinching away at the noise, then almost seemed to smile at her terror. It tensed, ready to spring. Even as she turned to run, she knew it would catch her. She threw herself forward through the bush in front of her, falling to her knees as she tumbled through the stubby branches. She tried to clamber to her feet, but then felt the wind of the beast's passage as it leapt completely over the top of her. There was a wet thud as it landed. She closed her eyes tightly and waited for the end.

It didn't arrive. After a moment, she opened her eyes again. The cat lay on its side, a long arrow shaft protruding from the top of its foreleg, just behind the shoulder joint.

Ylsriss stood and looked around. It had to have been Joran. None of the other men could have hoped to make that shot. She searched the bushes looking for him, but then her gaze fell upon the fae as he strode towards her.

He was one of the tallest of the fae she had ever seen, over a head and a half taller than her. A bow that was even taller than he himself was slung over his shoulder. He knelt down beside the cat, ignoring her completely. His hand stroked the beast gently and, as he did, she realised it was still breathing, painful and laboured breaths. With one swift motion, he grabbed the arrow and forced it deeper. The cat jerked once and then was still. The fae closed his eyes tightly for a moment and his lips moved silently.

"Take this."

Ylsriss blinked. "What?"

"The bow. Take the bow." He thrust it at her, then hauled the cat up onto his shoulders and stood with a grunt. Now that it was dead, the creature looked even bigger than it had before and it hung down to his knees. "Take me to your camp," he ordered, looking at her expectantly.

"Yes, Blessed One." Ylsriss suddenly remembered herself and dropped her eyes, adopting the subservient manner of the other women in the camp.

They did not speak on the trek. It would have been out of character for a slave to speak to a fae and he was clearly not interested in talking to her. She watched him carefully out of the corner of her eye and he looked at her curiously on more than one occasion.

They passed the first of the huts and went to the centre of the clearing, near the wellpumps. He dropped the cat to the ground, where it landed with a loud thump, and then held his hand out for the bow.

He waited in silence as the women of the camp assembled. They flocked to him like moths to a flame.

"A magnificent beast, Blessed One," breathed Tia, admiration clear in her tone.

He glanced at her and smiled. "A shade-cat. One of the largest I've seen. Certainly the largest I've seen since the ret…" He cut off, stopping abruptly and frowned at Tia as the women on either side of her whispered for her to be silent.

"You will skin this creature for me," he said to the group. "I will return in three days for the pelt. Be extremely careful with it. I do not want any of it to be wasted."

He glanced around the village. "Are your glyphs all renewed?"

The women looked at each other, whispering quietly. "There is a single moonorb, Blessed One," said one.

"Bring it to me."

He fingered his bow as he waited. The weapon was fashioned from some form of horn, leather and a white wood. His eyes fell on Ylsriss, as if he had felt her watching him and she dropped her eyes to the ground, bowing her head and fighting to hide the sudden panic.

The woman returned with the moonorb and he took it in one hand as he traced his other over the glyphs. He closed his eyes and a look of concentration came over his face as a thin green mist, barely visible in the dim light, trailed from his fingers and sank into the glyphs, which began to glow brightly in response. It only took a moment and he handed the device back to the slave woman.

"Three days," he said, with a nod down at the cat's body, and then he left without another word.

Ylsriss let her breath out explosively. The creature had been curious about her. Could he sense something? Did he know something?

"Did you see the way he looked at me?" Tia gushed, taking her upper arm.

"What?"

"He smiled at me, Ylsriss. Didn't you see him?"

Ylsriss forced herself to smile. "I didn't, Tia. You think he's taken a liking to you?"

Her eyes grew wide. "Oh, do you think he might have? Oh Lord, please say he did." She clasped her necklace through her tunic.

Ylsriss turned away then, barely able to disguise her disgust. She made her way to the hut. The others could go and collect the baskets. In a few hours, it wouldn't matter anyway.

* * *

She looked at the runeplate carefully. It was formed from a single slab of black stone with the glyphs etched into a section close to one end. "Do you think it will work?" She looked up at Joran who was keeping watch at the door.

"I don't know, but it's worth a try. We'd be much better off if we didn't need to try and make a fire. Hurry up, though. The sun's almost up."

Ylsriss examined the plate again. It wasn't very thick, only a thumb's width, so it ought to work. She lifted it out of the setting and lowered it to the floor, placing it on top of the rock she'd set there. She put one foot on the end with the glyphs and then stamped down hard on the opposite end with the other. The runeplate shook under her, but refused to crack. She looked over at Joran, helplessly.

"Let me try it. Come and watch the doorway." He switched places with her and stamped down hard. There was a loud crack as the thin basalt sheet snapped.

She jumped and whipped her head round to look at him for a moment, before peering through the gap in the curtain.

The jagged diagonal fracture in the runeplate was perilously close to the glyphs. Joran stepped back carefully and crouched to examine the runeplate.

"Does it…?" She trailed off.

"I don't know yet. Hold on." He moved his fingers over the weakest of the glyphs. The light bloomed for a second then sputtered, wavering and flickering before it went dark again.

"Try again. Try a stronger glyph."

He scowled at her and touched a different series of inscriptions. This time, the light bloomed strongly and stayed on, and Ylsriss could feel the heat as it radiated through the small section of the plate.

He smiled at her in triumph and quickly deactivated the plate. She grinned back at him. "Stick it into the pack. The sun is almost up anyway. We should go."

"Last chance to back out," he said, his tone serious.

"I think we just passed that point when we broke the plate." She took the pack from him, then watched as he took up the other one and his bow. A small quiver filled with horn-tipped arrows hung at his hip.

"Let's go," he said.

They stepped out of the hut and moved along the side of it at a steady pace, although they didn't break into a run. It was unlikely that anyone would pay them any real attention, but a man and a woman going off together when they should both be working was peculiar enough. They didn't need to make it worse by running.

Ylsriss fought against the temptation to either look around or start to sprint. The short walk into the forest seemed to take an age and she breathed a loud sigh of relief when they eventually passed into the shade of the trees. She met Joran's eyes and they shared a tense smile. "Let's get out of here," she said, and sped off without waiting for him to answer.

They ran hard for ten minutes. Neither of them was in especially poor condition, but life at the slave camp didn't lend itself to fitness and they were soon forced to fall back into a walk, their chests heaving.

The fae would be inside, away from the magic-draining touch of the sun while it was in the sky. This gave them an hour, at least, when there was almost no chance of them being caught.

They walked as fast as their breathing would allow, then settled back into a jog, a pace they could both maintain for hours. As the sun began to sink and the sky returned to twilight, they slowed and she looked back over one shoulder. She could see nothing of the camp, just trees and ferns. For now, at least, they were free.

* * *

She moved into the bedchamber hesitantly, his insistent hand on the small of her back, urging her along.

"This needn't be unpleasant for you, Tia." His voice altered. He sounded like Harn, all of a sudden.

She turned in shock. There he was. The sweet young man from her village.

"Harn!" she gasped. "What are you doing here?"

The vision flickered and vanished as the fae revealed his true form again, wearing an amused smile. "I can make this easier for you, should I choose to."

The Touch lay thick upon her emotions, manipulating them, calming her fears and inflaming her lust. "You don't need to do that, Blessed One," she breathed in a husky voice.

He grabbed her roughly by the throat and kissed her, and she moaned into his mouth, a gasp of both pleasure and shock. The fae threw her backwards onto the bed, his hand ripping away the necklace from her throat as she flew.

He crouched and lifted the leather thong, turning the carved wooden figurine around in the light of the moonorbs. "What is this?"

"It's nothing, Blessed One," Tia said quickly, clutching the remnants of her dress to herself. His attention had been diverted and she felt less sure of herself all of a sudden. *What had she been thinking? Offering herself up to this creature! He wasn't even human.*

His head snapped around as she spoke. "It's clearly not nothing, Tia. What is this trinket?"

"It's a keepsake, Master," she explained. "A carving of Our Lord, that's all."

"Your Lord?" The expression on his perfect face twisted into one of cruel amusement. "The Lord of New Days?"

She nodded and then frowned as he burst into helpless laughter.

"Have you pathetic creatures not realised the truth of this yet?"

Tia shook her head in confusion. "I'm not sure what you mean, Blessed One."

She worked her way to the edge of the bed and perched there, holding her dress to her chest as a shield.

"This Lord of the New Days that you so revere, the one that will lead you to a better future. There is no such thing."

"You're wrong!" she snapped. The anger coursed through her, somehow slipping free from the pen it had been forced into along with the rest of her emotions, her true self.

"Wrong?" He laughed again. "Oh, you poor little rabbit. You don't know easily we have manipulated you all. Did you really think some all-powerful god had come to save your race from itself? Didn't you ever question just how fast this religion had spread?"

She shook her head, confused.

"Tell me, Tia, this 'Lord' of yours. Is he supposed to look something like this?" He flickered again and then he was a tall figure in black. Soft, velvet robes hung from his arm as he extended a hand to her, as if to lead her onto a path." Tears sprang to her eyes as she began to understand what he meant.

He returned to his natural form again, a cruel smirk upon his face. "Do you know we managed to instil this ridiculous faith across most of the lands in your world? We wiped away your traditions, persuaded you to remove the horseshoes and iron from your portals and windows, the iron pennies from under the pillows of your children."

She shook her head mutely. It was simply too much to bear.

"There is no Lord of the New Days, Tia. There never has been. There is only us. These gullible men that you call priests follow the thinnest of lies, learning the tenants of a faith we created with the briefest of whispers into the right ears. So desperate are your kind to believe in something that even now you send your children to us to be our slaves."

"I don't believe you," she cried, rising to her feet and looking at him defiantly.

"Your belief is irrelevant. You are a tool. Your kind always has been. You don't even know the best of it. It was one of your own kind that first let one of our number through the Wyrde. This religion was simply the next step. You let us free of our prison yourselves and then accepted the one we created for you with open arms." He reached for her again but she skipped to the side, slipping past his outstretched hand.

His amber eyes grew cold and the smile slipped from his face. "I could have made this easier for you, Tia." He was little more than a blur as he darted across the room to stand in front of her. "But, you know, now that we're here, I don't see why I should. You're here to breed, human." He spat the word at her.

She moved her arm without thinking, the slap aimed for the side of his face. He caught it easily, without even breaking eye contact.

"The livestock needs training, apparently," he muttered. "Well then, if you won't obey willingly, then I suppose I'll just have to break you." He threw her onto the bed again, and ripped her dress and his own clothing away in a moment, whilst he held her down with his other hand. As he moved between her thrashing thighs, she let out a whimper. He pulled her arms up above her head, somehow holding them in place with one hand. And then he was taking her, and the whimper became a scream.

CHAPTER TEN

Devin looked back at the line of wagons and the villagers walking alongside them, as they climbed the hill. Widdengate had long since faded from view, but the dark smoke that stained the sky told a tale he wasn't sure he wanted to listen to. The satyr was silent in its cage on the third wagon behind theirs. Obair sat beside it, his eyes a mystery.

On a whim, Devin hopped off the edge of the wagon and headed back towards the old man. Hannah glanced at him without interest, then dropped her gaze to her lap. She hadn't spoken in days and, as hard as it was for him to admit it to himself, he couldn't bear to be around her. It was easier just to pretend it wasn't happening.

Obair shook himself from his reverie, as Devin climbed up onto the cart and sat beside him. Unlike the others, this wagon was not crammed full of villagers. Few were willing to be near the satyr and those who had originally been on the cart with Obair had either opted to walk or managed to squeeze themselves onto one of other wagons.

Devin nodded in greeting and looked back at the satyr curiously. It sat on the floor of the cage, scratching idly at the bed of the wagon with one clawed finger. It met his eyes briefly before looking back at the floor.

He glared at it. This thing represented everything that had gone wrong in his life, from his mother being torn away from him, right the way through to Khorin being killed. One had been taken alive, the other with a blade, but both had been stolen from him. He stared at the creature, willing it to look at him, to do something. It ignored him, comfortable in its indifference.

Khorin. The thought stilled him, took his anger and replaced it with a guilt as sharp as his rage had been hot. He hadn't even really had time to process what had happened. The man had been the only father he'd ever known, and the void he'd left behind was as cold and bitter as the harshest of winter frosts.

"Do you want to talk about it?"

Devin jumped. "What?"

"You looked sad," Obair replied, with a shrug. "No. Worse than that. You looked tormented. It might help to talk about it. I could use the practice anyway. I've not spent much time talking to anything that can talk back in recent years."

Devin gave him a quizzical look and the old man chuckled. "I used to talk to my animals. The goat, in particular, for some reason. Anyway, it might help, you know?"

"I suppose," Devin replied, in a non-committal way. "I'm not really sure how to start."

"It's Khorin?" Obair guessed, waiting for Devin's nod. "Well, why don't you start by telling me about him. I never really had the chance to speak to him properly. What was he like?"

Devin fiddled with the corner of his cloak, twisting it through his fingers as he thought. "He saw to the heart of things," he said, finally. "There was no fooling him, not ever. If I was trying to shirk chores by blaming it on this tool or another, he'd always know without even looking at it. If I'd had an argument with Kainen or Erinn, or anyone else in the village, he could cut through it with two quick questions."

"He sounds like he was a wise man."

"Oh, he was. It could be bloody annoying at times," Devin laughed. "He had a way of speaking that always let you know when you were being foolish or acting like a child. He never said anything, never rubbed your nose in it, but you just knew. For all that, I loved him. He's my father. He was my father." He fell silent, watching as the road slipped by them like a muddy river.

He enjoyed the silence for a time, wrapping it around him like a comforting blanket, as he thought. "Do you think we'll ever be able to go home?" He glanced back at the distant smoke.

Obair followed his gaze. "I don't know, Devin. I don't think there would be much left to go back to." Devin's expression grew grim as Obair continued. "It's an interesting concept for me, though, because I can't say I ever had a place I could call a home. I lived in the glade, but it was never a home. Homes are safe and comforting, somewhere you want to return to."

Devin mulled that over for a while as the wagon rattled over the dusty road. "You think I'm being selfish then? Childish?" he said, finally.

Obair chuckled. "No. That's not how I meant it. I never had a home. Not that I can remember, anyway. My earliest memories are of working with my master at the stones, learning to feel the Wyrde."

"What was he like?" Devin asked, curiosity getting the better of his manners.

"Severe," Obair said, in a quiet voice. "He was a perfectionist. He used to drill me on the ritual for hours, until I had it absolutely perfect. I wouldn't get to eat until I'd done it three times without a mistake."

"It doesn't sound like much of a childhood," Devin said.

"No, I suppose it doesn't. Not in the conventional sense, anyway. But then I didn't really get a choice."

"Did you never leave then? You spent your entire life in that cottage?"

"Most of it," Obair replied. "We travelled twice, as far as I can remember, although I was so young the first time that I don't really recall much of the journey."

Devin shifted on the seat and tucked a leg under him. "You must remember something, surely?"

"Not really. I remember more of the second trip. We saw the sea, although I suppose it could have been a large lake. I remember being shocked at there being so much water in one place. My master was meeting with some others at a cabin in the woods. It was a bit like my own cottage, except for the lake. I was pushed outside so they could talk and even eavesdropping grows boring after a while, so I spent my time at the lake. I'd waste hours just looking at it, watching the sunlight play on the surface."

"Eavesdropping?" Devin grinned.

Obair shrugged with a shamefaced smile and let out a chuckle.

"Do you suppose the others were droos too?"

"I wish you wouldn't use that word, Devin. It brings a host of silly tales along with it wherever it goes."

"Droos...druids? What does it matter? They're just words."

Obair gave him an odd look and then sighed in defeat. "I suppose they must have been."

"Then they might still be around somewhere? Maybe they could help us?"

"Devin, calm down," the old druid began. "You need to understand this was all a very long time ago. I was barely half the age you are now. Those people will all be long gone by now."

"But if they were anything like your master...?" Devin persisted.

Obair cocked an eyebrow at him. "Yes?"

"Well, wouldn't they have had someone like you? An apprentice?"

"An apprentice?" Obair said, softly. "Do you know, I never thought of myself like that before? But you're right. That's exactly what I was."

"Well, wouldn't they have?"

"I suppose they might have done. Oh, look, if I'm honest with you, Devin, I know they did. Well, one did, at least. I haven't heard anything from her in many years though. For all I know, she's dead and gone."

"You can't just leave it at that," Devin burst out. "I mean, if there's even a chance that we could discover something, we have a duty to, don't we?"

Obair's head shot round at that, his eyes dark and angry. "Don't presume to lecture me. I know my duty, boy."

Devin recoiled as he realised what he'd said. The old man, usually so passive, looked furious as he glared back at him. "I'm sorry, Sir," Devin stuttered. "I didn't mean it like that."

Obair took a deep breath, then puffed out his cheeks as he exhaled. "It's alright, Devin. I overreacted, is all. It's just something my master used to lecture me about for hours. I got very tired of hearing it over the years."

"Tell me about her? The apprentice, I mean." Devin asked, speaking quickly before the silence could fall and smother the conversation.

"There isn't much to tell." Obair smiled. "Her name was Lillith. After my master died, she was someone I used to ask advice from. That's how it started, anyway. We were in touch a couple of times a year, sending messages back and forth by bird."

"So what happened?"

"Advice turned into conversation. It was a lonely life, performing the ritual, and our messages soon became just chatter. It was frivolous, I suppose, and we both knew it. She drew a halt to it."

"Why? I mean, this was the only contact either of you had with anyone, wasn't it? Why would anyone choose to end that?"

"Because it was dangerous, Devin." Obair sighed and stared blankly at the horse's back. "The druids were hunted almost to extinction, our records and histories burned. Those of us that were left couldn't risk being found. It's more than just that, though. To perform the ritual, you need to be in a certain state of mind. One way of describing it is that you need to concentrate, but that still doesn't really explain it. It's more a state of emptiness. Lillith decided that exchanging messages with me was making it too hard for her to focus and she was also terrified that someone would follow the birds."

"What did you think?"

"It doesn't really matter what I thought, does it? I didn't have any choice at the time. Her messages grew further and further apart, and then eventually they just stopped. I wrote to her a couple of times, but the birds just came back with the message unopened. I haven't heard from her in fifteen years now. She was a good bit older than me, so I expect she's gone now too."

Devin picked at his sleeve, avoiding the old man's eyes. The pain came without warning and he gasped, as his hands flew to his head.

"Headache again?" Obair guessed, with a wince.

"Feels like somebody's driving a spike through my eyes," Devin managed through clenched teeth.

"Chew this," Obair said, as he pressed something into Devin's hand. "It'll taste dreadful, but it will help after a bit."

Devin chewed for a moment and spat at the bitter taste. "What is this? It feels like a piece of wood."

"It is," laughed Obair. "It's a bit of willow bark. I used to get headaches too. The Wyrde takes it out of you."

They fell silent as Devin nursed the pain away with equal parts willow bark and water. The first elements of Rhenkin's forces had caught up with them by mid-afternoon, their horses barely slowing as they passed them. The wagon made slow progress, thanks to the weight of the cage and, by the first signs of evening, the infantry had caught up too.

Devin roused himself as another horse approached and Rhenkin drew level with their cart. The man's uniform was covered in ash and a bloodstained bandage was bound tightly around his upper arm, mute testament to his own part in the fighting.

"Is this as far as you've got?" he said.

Obair waved vaguely at the horse and the cage. "We're not exactly loaded for speed here, Rhenkin."

He received a grunt in response that could have been a grudging acceptance but which probably wouldn't admit it in public. "Well, they don't seem to be pursuing us anyway. I half expected a harrying force, but the last word was they were making camp."

"Well, that's good, isn't it?" Obair said.

Rhenkin looked back over his shoulder at the distant plume of smoke. "They are the most damnable people. I half-think they'd have let us all leave without even drawing a sword if we'd just burnt the place down ourselves. Who conquers a nation like this?" He glanced at Obair, then shrugged as he realised what he'd said, but didn't have the energy left to care.

"The others are all headed to Carik's Fort, but I'd like you two to accompany me to Duchess Freyton," Rhenkin said, after a moment. "She's going to want a full report on what's going on." He fixed his gaze on Obair. "I think it would be best if she hears about the fae from someone with more answers than I have."

Obair nodded, though the expression on his face was far from happy.

"Why me?" Devin asked.

"It was your idea to fight back. Besides, from what I've heard, there's a connection with you too."

Devin slowly turned his head to fix Obair with a cold look. The old man had the grace to look embarrassed.

"I won't go without my mother," Devin said, looking back at the captain. "She can't be on her own right now."

"This is hardly a family outing, lad," Rhenkin protested.

"She was the first one to see a satyr. The first to fight one too and, in truth, she was the first to think about fighting back, not me." Devin's voice was firm, leaving little room for argument.

"Fine," Rhenkin gave in. "She won't be far behind you, anyway. Stop and wait for a bit until she catches up."

Darkness fell as they waited. Hannah seemed confused as Devin waved at the wagon driver to stop and then coaxed her out of the cart. He led her up onto the middle of the bench seat, so she sat between himself and Obair. They carried on through the night, stopping only to switch horses. The moon peered fitfully through the clouds, painting the road ahead of them in shades of grey, but most of the time they were driving only by the light of a single lantern.

"Why don't you try and see if you can sleep for a bit?" Obair said, in the soft tones people seem to use in the darkness. Hannah had dozed off almost as soon as night fell and was slumped against Obair's arm, wheezing a soft snore.

Devin nodded. "Wake me when you've had enough and I'll take over." He climbed into the back of the wagon and pressed himself into the corner, close to the seat. The satyr was silent, its eyes shining faintly as it lay, curled up, on the floor of the cage. Devin's mind churned as he thought of the events of the past week, but true exhaustion is a tenacious force and, despite it all, he slept.

He was woken by Obair shaking him gently. "I'm sorry, Devin, but I don't think I can drive any longer. I'm likely to put us into the trees."

Devin sat up and rubbed his eyes. His neck was stiff from the angle he'd slept at and it felt like several people had spent the last few hours walking across his back.

"It's alright." He yawned. "Get some rest. I'll take over." Obair had pulled the cart in at the side of the road and Devin noticed there were few, if any, people still walking in the glow of the lantern. A glance behind them showed a sparse trail of lanterns from other wagons still trundling along in the darkness.

"What time is it?" he asked, as Obair settled into the space he had left.

"A few hours past midnight, if I'm any judge," Obair replied.

Devin was about to climb into the front of the cart, when the moon came out from behind the clouds and shone brightly onto the wagon. There was a flash of blue light and a faint clang from the cage, and he whipped his head around. The satyr crouched, bathed in the moonlight, with blue fire flaring from its hooves as it scrabbled around for something on the base of the cage. Tiny green sparks flickered under the surface of its skin on its shoulders and back where the light touched it.

"Obair!" he said, in alarm, as the satyr glanced up at him, its eyes glowing brightly.

Obair stood and pulled his cloak off his shoulders. In a smooth motion, he flipped it up over the top of cage, blocking the light. The creature hissed and screamed at him in its own language, its face a mask of fury. Through it all, Hannah slept on.

"Well, that seemed to work," Devin muttered, recoiling from the creature's rage.

"It was just a guess, really," Obair replied, "but it does seem to have worked."

"What has it got there?" Devin pointed at the satyr's clenched fist, ignoring the stream of incomprehensible abuse flowing from its mouth. Blue sparks still flew from the creature's hooves but also, now that they looked, from its fist, where it gripped something tightly.

"I don't know. Something iron, if the sparks are anything to go by." Obair shrugged. "Whatever it is, I can't see it being much use to the beast. Let it have it. This cage doesn't even have a lock now. I watched Harlen hammer the pins in. It's not going to get out."

Devin climbed over the seat into the front, keeping his eyes on what was visible of the creature under the cloak. One cloven hoof sparked faintly where the moonlight touched it. He glanced at Obair, who gave him a reassuring smile and settled down to sleep. Devin gathered up the reins and clucked the horses on.

Behind him, the satyr muttered softly as its fingertip traced the tiny design it had managed to scratch into the iron bar on the base of the cage. Its eyes dimmed slightly and it shuddered as a faint wisp of green light passed from its fingertips into the etched symbols. The row of markings began to glow gently in the darkness and the satyr's face broke into a grim smile of satisfaction, as it covered them with its hand and settled in to wait.

* * *

Selena stood on the small balcony that overlooked the grounds and watched them approach. Rhenkin was accompanied by a small number of troops and followed by what appeared to be a circus wagon.

"You never fail to surprise," she murmured to herself, as she turned to the doors. Selena swept through the halls, excitement mounting at the thought of seeing him again. She noted, with satisfaction, that the garish wall hangings had been removed. It might take a while, but she was determined to inject some class into this stuffy mansion, even if it killed her.

She paused halfway down the staircase, taking a moment to compose herself. *It wouldn't do to appear overeager now, would it?* She fought down a girlish smile and made her way sedately to the foot of the stairs as the voices carried through from the entrance hall.

"Rhenkin," she said, with a warm smile, as Evans, the footman, escorted him in. "You're back a lot sooner than I expected. Clearly I'm either not paying you enough or not giving you enough to do."

"Your grace." He gave a stiff bow. "The news I bring is not good, I'm afraid."

Her smile wilted like a flower in a summer drought. She looked past him and his soldiers to the old man and young peasant standing at the door. The young man was supporting a frail woman and all three looked as if they might bolt at any moment.

"Go on," she ordered.

"The Bjornmen have even greater numbers than we were led to expect. I would estimate they put an army of more than sixty thousand into the field. Despite our efforts, we were forced to abandon Widdengate and fall back to Carik's Fort."

She nodded silently and chewed her bottom lip in thought. "Losses?" she asked, finally.

"Moderate, your grace," he replied. "We fought a retreating line from the outset. I would imagine somewhere in the region of two to three thousand, but I'll have a better figure for you once I've been able to speak to my officers again."

"And the peasants?" she prompted.

"Successfully withdrawn, your grace. Most of them have travelled to Carik's Fort, although some have dispersed to other villages."

"Very well, Major." She nodded. "Now, why don't you explain to me why you've brought me a circus wagon?"

"Captain, your grace," he corrected with a cough.

"You held against a vastly superior force, managed to successfully evacuate the residents of half a dozen villages and lost only two thousand men in the process?" She shook her head. "No, these do not sound like the actions of a captain. Besides," she added, with a wicked smile, "Major Rhenkin sounds so much more impressive, wouldn't you say?"

Rhenkin coughed again. "I'm flattered, your grace."

"Don't be, Rhenkin." Her voice had a hard edge to it. "You'll have earned it twice over by the time we're through this." She glanced past him at old man again. "Let's move this into the parlour, shall we? I want a full report." She looked at Evans, "Have Rhenkin's guests settled into suitable rooms and then ask them to join Rhenkin and I in an hour."

"Very good, your grace," the silver-haired footman replied, as he bowed.

She led the way to the parlour and poured Rhenkin a brandy before motioning to him to sit down on the divan. He wore a perplexed expression at the treatment.

"I'm going to make this easy for you, Rhenkin," she said softly, casting a glance at the door. "I'm with child."

He froze with the glass halfway to his lips, his usually stern features made soft by shock.

"For various reasons, the child has to be Freyton's. I thought twice about telling you at all, I'll admit. No, don't speak." She pressed a finger to his lips as he drew in a sharp breath.

"This isn't ideal, I know that. It is, however, very necessary and it is the way things will be done. You can be as involved as much you wish or not,. The child will need advisers, after all. For now, just let it slide and let us deal with the matters at hand."

He downed the brandy in one quick swallow and stood to move to the windows, looking out in silence for a time. When he turned back, his face was coldly professional. She felt a sharp stab of loss and searched his eyes for something more, but he may as well have been wearing a mask for all that they revealed.

She sat opposite him on the settee. "Take me through it all then, Rhenkin, before your companions join us."

The old man and the others were escorted in by Evans before Rhenkin had managed to get halfway through his report. Fewer than five minutes after he had delivered it, however, they were all standing in the stable yard, as Selena stared at the creature. The satyr met her gaze as it lounged on the floor of the cage, leaning on one hand.

"What did you call it?" she asked.

"A satyr, your grace," Obair said.

"And you say they're dangerous? Do you think there would be any way to reach an accommodation with them against the Bjornmen?"

The woman, Selena had never caught her name, drew in a surprised breath with a sharp hiss.

"They are extremely dangerous, your grace." Obair didn't hide the shock in his voice.

"And?"

"And I think that might be the single most horrifying suggestion I've ever heard, your grace."

She raised an eyebrow at him but he plunged on. "The fae are the single most deadly threat mankind will ever face. War? Disease? Famine? These are nothing when compared to the fae. They would grind us to dust beneath one foot, merely to provide themselves with passing amusement."

"So that's a no, then?"

"No, your grace, I do not believe they would consider an accommodation." Obair shuddered visibly.

"Oh relax, man, I wasn't seriously considering it anyway." She turned to Rhenkin. "So you ride off to deal with one enemy and come back bringing me two."

"So it would seem, your grace."

"How do we deal with them then, Druid?" she said to Obair. "What is your plan?"

"Plan, your grace?"

"Well, yes. Rhenkin tells me you came out of the woods with a warning about these things. What do we know about them? What do you suggest?"

Obair sputtered, looking for all the world like a landed fish, as his mouth first gaped and then closed again.

"If I may, your grace?" Rhenkin put in.

"Oh, Rhenkin, these titles are starting to give me a headache. You know my name. Use it."

"I suspect Hanris might suffer some manner of fit, were I to do that, your grace."

"Well, that sounds like it could be rather entertaining. Shall we send for him?"

"I was about to suggest that perhaps we might adopt a stronger position in seeking aid from the king," Rhenkin said, ignoring her.

"I can't see what stronger steps could be taken, Rhenkin," she replied, all business once again. "I've had message after message dispatched. Short of actually going to petition him in person..." She stopped mid-sentence. "Surely you're not suggesting that?"

"It would at least ensure a dialogue, your grace."

"It would take weeks to get to Celstwin, Rhenkin! By the time I have travelled there and sought an audience with him, there will be nothing left to come back to."

"Frankly, your grace, if you don't go, there will be nothing left anyway."

She glared at him but he held her gaze with cool assurance. "Damn it, Rhenkin, I can't just up and go like that!"

He started to speak but she stopped him with a raised finger before looking back at Obair. "You've told me about the need for iron weapons, but what of their motivations? What do these creatures actually want?"

He studied the satyr for a moment. "I'm not sure it's as simple as that, your grace," he replied.

"I know what it wants," Hannah said, in a soft voice that skulked low by her feet. "What they all want."

They looked at her expectantly, but she ignored them and muttered to herself before abruptly walking back towards the palace as they stared after her.

"Oh, come now, everything wants something," Selena said, looking back at Obair. "Even a dog has wants and needs. Can you communicate with it?"

"Easily, your grace," Obair said. "It's understood every word we've said."

Her eyes widened, then narrowed in thought as she looked the satyr over again. "I will be leaving for the capital in two days. You have until then to get me some answers from the creature. Find out what it wants. You can get anything you require from my staff." She turned on her heel and motioned for Rhenkin to follow her back inside.

Obair watched her go. "Two days." He turned to Devin and spread his hands helplessly. Devin shrugged and stepped towards the cage, crouching down so he was level with the satyr.

"Careful," Obair warned, but the young man was easily outside of the reach of the creature, even through the bars.

"They say you can understand my language," Devin began. "Is there anything you need?" The satyr glanced up at him curiously for a moment and then let its gaze drop.

"Different food? Do you have enough water?" He glanced at the metal bowl of dried meat, which the satyr had left untouched. He had yet to see the creature eat anything at all, but it didn't seem to be suffering any ill effects. He gave Obair a questioning look, but the old man motioned for him to continue, an odd expression on his face.

"Are we so very different?" Devin persisted, feeling more than a little foolish as the grooms and stable hands stopped their work to watch him.

"You will get nothing from me, human." The voice was barely more than a whisper, but it held such venom and contempt that Devin took a step back from the cage.

"I just want to know what is it that you want," he said.

"Ask the defiler," it spat, glaring at Obair. "He can tell you of the vengeance that is owed to your kind."

Devin cast a confused glance at Obair, but the old man simply shrugged. He looked down at the iron bars of the cage floor, remembering the blue sparks. "Doesn't it hurt?"

The satyr followed his gaze. "Like a thousand tiny thorns twisting in my flesh," it hissed, "but my pain is nothing to what will be done with you. Once I am free, my brothers and I will pen you as you would a pig and keep you for our pleasure. For every hurt you have visited upon me, I will grace you with a thousand torments. I will rend your flesh, manling, and starve you until you beg to eat the strips I slice from your body."

"Come away, Devin," Obair said, his voice steady as he pulled him away. "We'll try again in the morning." He grimaced in sympathy, as the young man's face contorted with pain and he pinched at the bridge of his nose. "Again?"

Devin nodded as Obair waved a stable hand over to them. Through the fog of pain, he heard the druid giving instructions about the satyr. "…not been eating or drinking anything anyway, so far as I can tell. Throw a tarpaulin over it and stake it tight. Don't let it get into the moonlight. It's supposed to be a full moo…" He trailed off and turned to Devin with his eyes full of wonder.

"Full moon," he finished, in an awed voice. "Devin, when did your headaches start?"

"What?" Devin replied, as he walked away from the cage and massaged his temples.

"When did they start?"

"Does it matter? A few days before Erinn found you at the tower, I suppose."

"That was a new moon," Obair muttered. "But this doesn't make any sense! It's not possible!"

"Fine," Devin gasped, in a pained voice. "Then let it not be possible more quietly."

"Sorry," Obair said, reaching out to steady him. "Let's get you back inside."

The kitchens were a massive four-roomed affair, joined together by wide archways. Obair pushed him through the crowd of cooks and assistants, and guided him into an empty corner at the end of a long table. The old man clambered around the table and sat, before asking a brown-haired girl with huge eyes to bring tea and honey.

"How are you feeling now? Has it eased any?"

"Some," Devin said, sitting up more and blinking at the light from the window.

The mugs of tea arrived and Obair pushed one across the table to him. "Drink this," he said. "The sugar in the honey ought to help." He looked at the boy appraisingly for a minute. "Are you up to listening to me talk at you for a while? There are some things I need to explain."

Devin sipped cautiously at the tea and nodded.

"I don't remember being chosen by my master. I told you my earliest memories are of learning the ritual with him. That was the way it was done. A master would seek out someone young enough to learn from him or her. We're not anything special. We get sick, we grow old and we die. The Wyrde was too important for us to allow it to fail though, so each of us was supposed to find someone to carry on the work."

"So why didn't you ever take an apprentice?" Devin asked.

"Because there would be nobody left to perform the ritual while I was looking," Obair replied. "Don't interrupt."

"Sorry," Devin said quickly.

Obair flashed him a small smile. "Anyway, they would search out a child young and sensitive enough to learn to maintain the Wyrde. The first step was to learn how to feel the cycles of the moon."

"Feel the moon?" Devin failed to keep the scathing tone from his voice.

"Feel the moon through the power of the Wyrde," Obair repeated, with a serious look. "My point is that this took many years to perfect and the first signs of progress started with headaches."

"Headaches?" Devin repeated, dumbly.

"Headaches, like yours, which came and went with the phases of the moon."

Devin pushed himself back from the table, his pain forgotten as he looked at the old man. "So what? You're saying I'm some kind of druid?"

"No, that's not what I'm saying at all. I don't know what you are. It doesn't make sense. I felt the Wyrde fail, felt it wither and die. There is nothing there for you to feel. That's why this doesn't make sense. I can't even feel it myself now."

"Then how could I feel it?"

"I don't know. It might be that you're not feeling it at all. It's too much of a coincidence to dismiss though. There are a few things I want you to try once your head is better. If you're willing, that is."

Devin nodded. His head was throbbing so badly, he'd try anything at this point.

* * *

"Focus on the moon, Devin," Obair whispered, as the candle flickered. "Look at every shape and shadow. See how the light surrounds it as well as shining from it. Look at the moonlight, how it's unchanging, constant, unwavering. Feel it, know the shape of it until you can see it without using your eyes."

The two of them sat cross-legged in Obair's room, beside the windowed doors that led out to his balcony. The candle between them was the only light source in the room, and it guttered and danced in the evening breeze.

"Use the pain in your head," Obair instructed, "as it throbs in time with your heartbeat. Make it your own. Reach out with it."

"I feel stupid, Obair," Devin muttered.

"This is serious, Devin," Obair growled.

"I don't know what I'm feeling for."

"Concentrate." Obair reached over and brushed Devin's eyes closed. "Combine the pain you're feeling with the image of the moon. Once you have that, you're halfway there."

Devin sighed. He could certainly focus on the pain, that was no problem. It throbbed, pounding in his temples and behind his eyes. As he ignored Obair, the man's endless droning fading into the background, he fancied he could hear it too, a faint, rushing screech, like tortured metal in the wind. He opened his eyes a crack and looked up at the moon again, embracing the pain, reaching out with it. There was something there, something indefinable, unlike anything he'd ever felt before. He pushed the feelings towards it - the pain, the throbbing, the sound filling his ears and then...

He gasped and sat back, staring at Obair in shock.

"What?" the old man demanded, his face lighting up with excitement. "What did you feel?"

"I don't know. Something cold. Lords and Ladies, I can't explain it." Devin felt a chill run through him. "I could feel it as though it were almost passing through me. A cold wind almost, bitterly cold, and all over me. At the same time though, it felt like I was just brushing the edges of it, as if I'd barely touched it."

Obair wore a grim smile. "And the phase? The need for it to move on?"

"Yes, that too. It felt like the tide was about to turn. More than that, though. I felt it reaching out. It was like part of it was trailing off, stretching out. Does that make any sense?" Obair nodded but looked confused, rather than pleased.

Devin felt his face relax as he looked at the old man. "I thought you said this couldn't happen? Didn't you say you can't do this without the Wyrde?"

"I did and you're right. I don't know how you are able to do this. You shouldn't even have these headaches. It took me three months of focusing on the moon to get the headaches and another six before I could really feel it. I was always taught that it's the Wyrde that lets us feel the moon. If that's true, what you're doing is impossible. I didn't ever feel anything like a wind, so maybe it's something else you're feeling. Maybe this is nothing more than a coincidence. We need answers."

Devin was silent for a long time before he spoke again. "Maybe the satyr?"

"I'm not sure it would tell us or that it would even know. The satyrs are a race apart from the true fae and not terribly bright."

Devin grunted, rising to his feet and flexing his stiff legs. "That leaves Lillith then, I suppose. If she's still alive."

"I doubt it," Obair murmured. "We were little more than children when we met. Seasons seem to last forever at that age. By the time you've noticed that they're flying past like the autumn leaves, most of them have already gone." He stared into space.

"Do you think you could find her?" Devin asked. "It was a long time ago."

"I think so. I might need to look at some of the duchess's maps, but I think I can work out where she was."

"How long will you be gone?"

"A goodly while I expect and I really think you ought to come along. If, by some miracle, Lillith is still alive, she might be able to answer some questions. She will certainly want to speak to you."

"I'll talk to my mother," Devin replied. "I don't know where we were going to go from here. Carik's Fort, I suppose. That's where everyone else went. To be honest, I haven't really caught up with everything that's happened."

Obair pulled himself to his feet. "It can't have been easy for you, these last few weeks. Try to get some sleep. We can talk to Hannah and the others in the morning."

CHAPTER ELEVEN

The palace stilled, like a great machine with cogs whirring slowly and grinding to a halt. Horses were settled, fires banked in the kitchens and lamps snuffed. The servants eased out of the halls and slipped into their own realm below stairs. Two guards were all that remained on duty, standing post at the main gates with only the guttering torches for company.

The moon rose over the horizon, a silvery eye peering down at the world with few taking note of its gaze. The satyr sat alone in the stable yard. A large tarpaulin had been draped over the cage and staked tightly at each corner to prevent the creature from pulling it down.

The creature couldn't see the moon, but the silvery light on the ground below the edge of the tarpaulin was sign enough. Its eyes glowed faintly in the darkness and a smile curved its lips. It had waited in silence for the last three hours, listening to the sounds from the mansion as the activity taking place within it slowed. As the moon rose higher and the palace grew quieter, it crouched to examine the gently glowing glyphs it had scratched into the bar at the base of the cage.

It traced the symbols with a gnarled fingertip, bringing them to life. It was a crude work and one which a fae would have sneered at, but satyrs were not known for being gifted at crafting. It touched the final sigil and moved back across the cage, pressing itself against the hated iron. The metal burned where it touched him but he had none of the Lady's grace that might result in sparks and flames.

The satyr watched eagerly as the runes began to release the heat. The cage had been bathed in sunlight for days, both on the trip to this place and once they had arrived. The hated defiler had insisted that he should be exposed to the light as much as possible. The man had thought himself so clever, allowing the sunlight to rob him of any of the Lady's gift he might have absorbed, but now his foolishness would be shown.

The cage had been absorbing heat for days, transferring it into the glyphs. The cage had grown so cold, it had frost on it. It was a wonder the manlings hadn't noticed it, but then they were merely prey.

The heat waited, lurking inside the glyphs, with only one command needed to release it. Runeplates were constructed and designed to release the heat under careful control. These glyphs had none of that and the heat poured out of them and into two vertical bars at the side of the cage. It came like a lightning strike, flooding into the iron and heating it almost instantly. A dull ruddy glow bloomed within the metal, growing brighter until the iron was almost white and began to sag under its own weight. With just two swift kicks from the satyr's hooves, the bars flew outwards and the creature managed to force itself through the gap, ignoring the pain of the metal, and the stench of seared flesh and fur. It was free.

It moved quickly, heading into the deeper shadows at the edge of the yard. The heat from the runes was dwindling already, the dull green glow fading to the black of iron as the grace was expended. The satyr licked its lips and sniffed, turning its head this way and that, as it sampled the night air. Snorts came from the stables as the horses caught its scent. It eased itself out into the moonlight in the corner of the yard, closing its eyes as the Lady graced him and the green sparks danced on its skin.

* * *

Hannah lay on her bed, sleepless. Her mind was like a wounded animal, curled up and licking at a hurt it couldn't cope with. She'd grown numb since they fled the village, barely noticing the passage of the days. Her only thoughts were of Khorin's death. The image of him and the sound of his voice thrashed around inside her head like an eel in a trap.

She lay in the bed and stared at the dark ceiling above her. Sleep would not come. Clearly, it had things to do elsewhere. Hannah pushed the blankets aside and padded to the window.

Her rooms were opulent, more luxurious than anything she'd ever seen, with deep rich carpets and paintings on the walls. She even had a separate room just for dressing in. She pulled the thick curtains aside and looked out at the moon.

"I'd never have thought you would be something to fear." Her voice sounded strange to herself, taut and strained. She looked down at the grounds of the palace. The ponds gleamed with the reflected moonlight in the gardens. Her eyes drifted over towards the stables, and she frowned as a green light flared and shone through the tarpaulin on the satyr's cage.

Her room was a fair way from the stables, but she still caught sight of the shadow as it darted out from under the tarpaulin. She blinked, shaking her head as if to clear away the cobwebs. Had she really seen that? Her feet seemed to move on their own, taking her to the door whilst her mind was still processing what she'd seen.

All but one of the lamps in each of the hallways had been snuffed and those that still burned had been turned down low. The thin nightgown she wore provided little protection against the cold. The stone walls beneath the tapestries and paintings seemed to have sucked all the heat from the air, and she found she was hugging herself as she scurried through the palace.

It was a blessing that her rooms were not far from the servant's staircase, or she'd probably have been lost in moments. The steps took her to the ground floor and she padded through the halls. A noise brought her up short and she pressed herself flat against a doorway, without really knowing why, as a pair of servants crossed at the end of the corridor. Shaking her head, she moved on. She found her way to one of the side doors quickly, more by luck than anything else, and stepped out into the night. The skies were clear and the moon lit the grounds almost as well as the sun might have done.

She ran, sticking to the grass where she could to avoid her feet slapping on the stones. The stable yard was still and the faint noise of horses shifting restlessly mingled with the distant sound of the leaves rustling in the light breeze. For some reason, the sounds made it seem quieter than if it had been truly silent.

The cage bars were broken, their ends bent and twisted, and the iron stretched thin as if it had been melted and then hammered out. The stupidity of having come to the cage alone struck her with an almost physical sensation. *What was she doing? She hadn't raised the alarm or anything. She'd just rushed from the palace to confront the satyr alone.*

She backed away from the cage towards the edge of the yard. A door, the latch not fastened properly, caught in the breeze and slammed back against the wooden wall. She spun with a scream and pressed herself to the wall before edging around towards the open door as her eyes flew about the stable yard, darting in and out of the pools of shadow as she searched the darkness.

The door led into a farrier's, the walls thick with tongs and tools. The moonlight parted the gloom enough for her to make out the large anvil set near the forge and a smaller one on a stump close to the door. She reached for one of the hammers. Harlen had killed a satyr with a single blow from his hammer and, if ever she needed a weapon, it was now. She managed to lift the hammer with both hands, grunting at the weight before setting it back. She might be able to lift it, but she'd never be able to swing it. There had to be smaller tools in here, but the darkness made it impossible to find anything.

A faint sound drifted in from the yard. It was as soft as the crunch of dry leaves, but any noise sounds loud in the night. She whirled around and fixed her gaze on the entrance. A dull glint came from a stack of old horseshoes by the door and, in desperation, she grabbed one up, the cold metal comforting in her hand.

The wind caught at her hair as she crept back out into the yard, blowing it across her face, and she clawed it away with her free hand. The satyr saw her almost as soon as she noticed it. It was pressed into the corner of the yard, bathed in the moonlight. Its eyes, which had been dull and dark for days, now shone as bright as any lantern's flame.

Hannah froze in the doorway as it took a single step away from the wall. It seemed unsure, hesitant. It was a good hundred feet from her, but then she'd seen how fast the creatures could move when they wanted to. The distance would be no protection from it. She glanced to either side of her. The presence of the doorway was no help to her either and the building would soon become a trap. Hannah stepped to her right, keeping her back against the wall, and sidled towards the way out of the yard.

It sprang towards her, somehow managing to shift from a standing position into a sprint without passing through anything in between. Hannah let out a breathless scream as she ran, although she knew it was useless. She felt the satyr closing on her and fancied she could feel its breath on her neck. A whimper, made more from fear than noise, passed from her lips and she sucked the breath in, ready to scream for help, as the hand buried itself in her trailing hair.

A sharp yank brought her up short and the satyr hauled her backwards, throwing her to the ground. She landed hard and the breath blasted out from her lungs, as the horseshoe in her hand was driven into her stomach.

Rough hands flipped her onto her back. Her arm was pinned awkwardly beneath her as she looked up into the hateful thing's face. Its features were twisted in fury as recognition flickered across its face.

"You! The silent one," it rasped. "You dare to trap me like some kind of prey?" It grabbed her throat, its movement fluid and as fast as drawing a breath. "Your snare has failed, foolish She, and now I claim you, as is my right." Its meaning was clear as it leered at her looking her up and down in the thin nightgown.

It pulled her up, its hand still firmly around her throat, and her feet scrambled beneath her as she struggled to stand before it choked her. All at once, the fear that had filled her was replaced with a blind rage. This thing, or some other like it, had killed Khorin. One of these beasts had driven her half-mad with nightmares and grief, and now this one saw her as some prize for the taking. She clawed at the hand at her throat with her fingers, her eyes flashing as the satyr laughed at her efforts.

It sniffed at her, its laughter dying as its eyes widened in first surprise, and then in fear. In that instant, she knew the time had come. It was act now or lose any advantage she might have. She whipped her hand around from behind her, clenching it into a fist around the horseshoe and smashed it into the side of the satyr's face. Blue fire flared, just as it had all those months ago in her kitchen, and the creature flew back from her, crashing to the ground with a visceral scream.

She was on it in a second, not wasting time on shock or fear. Those things were beyond her now. Hate had consumed her, reforging her into a creature of purest rage, and she flew at it, her knees slamming into its ribs as she drove the horseshoe down into it again and again.

Her screams filled the air as fire burned them both and the satyr raked at her with its thick nails.

It kicked out at her and she hurtled through the air, crashing to the ground fifteen feet from it. She pulled herself to her feet as the world span around her in crazy circles. She could just make out the blurry image of the satyr getting to its feet. Her vision cleared to reveal that its face was a bloody, charred ruin. It glared at her out of its one remaining eye, hatred reaching out from it and enveloping her. Her rage flared anew, running through her like a river of molten steel, as her mouth filled with the taste of her own blood.

She charged, screaming, at the satyr, as it stood in a twisted stance, hunched against its own pain. Her blows came fast, and she struck it with fist and horseshoe in equal measure. Fire flared anew and she followed its body down to the ground as it collapsed under the onslaught. The flesh gave way below her, as bones broke and then shattered. This beast would pay. They would all pay. With a final howl, she raised the bloody horseshoe high above her and drove it down into the remains of the satyr's head, hardly feeling the gore that hit her as it spattered upwards. Then there was silence. The blue flames guttered and died, and she pushed herself away from the body.

Her hands shook as she became aware of the blood, flesh and fragments of bone that covered her body. Her knees sagged and then buckled, unable to bear her own weight as she sank to the dirt. The horseshoe tumbled from her numb fingers and the wail that tore from her throat was far more primal than anything that the satyr had uttered. Darkness found her. A blackness that wrapped itself around her and bore her away to a safer place, a comforting embrace far away from the horrors of the light.

* * *

Devin followed the soldier that had been sent to fetch him. Curiosity had quickly driven away the gritty eyes he'd had when he was woken and rushed from his bed, but still he stumped through the corridors in a foul mood. The soldier had been less than forthcoming. Given that he seemed to be little older than Devin, he probably didn't know the reason for the summons himself. It would be unfair to blame him, really. Devin did it anyway.

They passed through the corridors, following some convoluted route that seemed to have taken them both up and down stairs in equal measure, while Devin shot the man black looks and wondered if he'd managed to get them both lost. Finally, he was delivered to Rhenkin's office.

The young soldier knocked and then entered. "The Widdengate boy, Sir," he announced. Devin found himself strangely irritated by that. He was no more a boy than this private. He walked in to find Obair and Rhenkin sat back in their chairs in a way that showed they'd just been in deep conversation. Rhenkin was calm and impassive, as always, but Obair looked distinctly nervous.

"What is it?" Devin demanded, after a long moment of silence. There was a tension in the room that would have been hard to miss.

"The satyr escaped last night," Rhenkin began. "How, we don't know. It managed to break some of the bars in the cage by the looks of things."

"It's dead, Devin." Obair interrupted, shooting the major a look that spoke of vast disapproval. "That's not important, though," he said quickly, holding up a hand to stop Devin before he could speak. "They found Hannah with it. She's alive," he added, as Devin sucked in a sharp breath. "Just in a bit of a state."

"Can I see her?"

"Of course," Rhenkin said. "The druid here thought it might be best to warn you first, that's all. She managed to kill the thing with a horseshoe. Stove its skull in. The most amazing thing, really."

"The point is, lad," Obair said, through clenched teeth, "that she's not going to be in any condition to travel for some time." He looked from Devin to Rhenkin, his eyes passing a message.

There was more to it. Devin was certain of that. Things that they weren't saying, things they thought him too young to cope with, perhaps.

"Don't," he said.

"Don't? Don't what?" Obair replied, his old face creased into a confusion of wrinkles.

"Don't protect me. Don't talk to me like I'm a child. Like I need the truth laying out for me, all nice and neat, with the sharp edges filed off."

Obair opened his mouth to speak, but couldn't find any words.

Rhenkin snorted at the old man and looked at Devin appraisingly. "You're right. You're not a child, no matter what your age is. You deserve the truth, plain and simple." He took a deep breath and let it out in a long sigh.

"Stable hands found her at first light and alerted the guards. She's got some nasty cuts and, I suspect, one or two broken ribs. That's not the worst of it, though. She's not making sense. It's like her mind is as damaged as her ribs. Obair told me some of the things she's been through. It sounds like she's already been dragged through hell backwards. I've seen it happen a few times. Young men in battle, wondering when all the glory is supposed to start, up to their eyebrows in blood and filth, tripping over limbs in the mud and covered in their own piss. Sometimes they just snap."

He looked up from his hands and their eyes met as he tapped his temple. "The thing is, son, it's not like a wound you can patch up knowing it will heal with time. She might be fine in a week but she might not, and you need to realise that now, before you go in to see her."

"Take me to her." Devin's voice was firm and steady.

Rhenkin raised an eyebrow. "Now? You're sure?"

Devin nodded. "I can't put this off. It'll only be worse if I have time to think about it first."

Rhenkin looked at him for a long time before he spoke again. "You're probably right." He stood and held the door open, then glanced back at Obair. "Coming?"

Hannah was tucked into clean sheets in her bed. The curtains were closed against the morning's light and a maid sat in a chair in the corner, reading a book as her charge slept. She stood as they entered and, at a word from Rhenkin, slipped out into the hallway.

Devin moved closer and look down at the battered figure in the bed, being careful not to wake her. Her eyes were closed and she lay so still that he worried for just a moment until he caught the faint rasp of her breath. One side of her face was already dark with bruises, and the flesh that wasn't swathed in thick bandages was swollen and misshapen.

Looking down at her was a surreal experience. He felt dispassionate, wooden. The entire scene felt like it was happening to someone else, as if he were merely an observer, a member of the audience at a travelling mummers' play. He wondered at it, prodding at his feelings like a tongue worrying at a sore tooth. *Why wasn't he more upset?* He wasn't sad. If anything, the only feeling he could muster was a faint anger. It glowed dull and sullen like banked coals, needing only fresh air to flare back into life.

Her hand was limp and cold as he took it in his own. It lay in his hand like dead flesh. "Do you think she can hear me?" he asked.

"I don't know, son," Rhenkin said softly. "I expect she can, even if she doesn't answer."

Devin looked at her face. She looked so old all of a sudden. No. Not just old. Tired too. The bruises and scratches made it worse, but she seemed to have aged a decade since the fae had come. He glanced back at the others, suddenly self-conscious. "It's me, Ma, Devin. I need you to know you're going to be okay. I'm fine too, so don't worry about me. You just concentrate on getting well."

He broke off. It all felt too unnatural and forced. "What will happen to her?"

he asked Rhenkin. "It's not like we have a home to take her to."

"Don't worry about that, lad. You're both here as my guests. She can stay until she's on her feet. We'll work it out from there."

Devin nodded at him gratefully.

"You realise that this changes a few things?" Rhenkin said to Obair.

"Well, I can hardly question the beast now, can I?" Obair replied, with a shrug. "I suppose we'd best talk to your duchess."

"She's your duchess too, old man."

"I suppose she is, at that. I'd never thought of it that way."

Devin gave Hannah one last look and patted her hand, before following the others out of the room and through the corridors. Obair was a strange man, he mused, so confident in his purpose on one level, but as ignorant as a child in other ways.

Rhenkin spoke quietly to a guardsman stationed outside a dark oak door before knocking. The duchess was sitting at a desk in the book-lined study talking to a short man in brass-rimmed spectacles when they entered.

"Rhenkin," she purred. "So nice of you to seek me out."

"Your grace," the major said, with a stiff bow. He looked around curiously. "A new base of operations?"

"Base of operations. I like that," she said. "You military types always have the best titles for things. Yes, I decided I needed to move out of the parlour. Absolutely everybody could find me there."

Rhenkin favoured her with a wry smile and she waved them all into chairs. Devin jumped visibly when she addressed him.

"I am so terribly sorry to hear about your mother, Devin. I want you to know that you can both stay here in the palace until she is well enough to move on."

"Thank you, My Grace...I mean...Your Lady..." She let out a warm, throaty laugh as he sputtered to a halt. Her eyes were warm and filled with compassion, and Devin felt a sense of relief. It was good to have had assurances from Rhenkin, but it wasn't really his house.

"Now then," she said, looking back to Obair and Rhenkin, "these recent events have obviously changed matters. Were you able to obtain any useful information from the creature?"

"None of any consequence, your grace," Obair replied. He seemed perfectly at home speaking to the woman. Despite living in isolation for all those years, being in the presence of a member of the aristocracy didn't seem to faze him at all.

"So we're back to square one then, Rhenkin." She picked up a letter opener and tapped it absently on the leather writing set on top of the desk. "The Bjornmen outnumber us and we still know next to nothing about these fae creatures."

"Not entirely, your grace," Obair said smoothly, before Rhenkin could speak. "There have been some developments with Devin here which were entirely unexpected."

"Oh?" She raised an eyebrow at him as she continued toying with the knife.

"It's a bit complicated, but Devin appears to have some talent that requires investigating."

"Don't spoon-feed me, Obair." She smiled sweetly. "I'm a big girl. I can take it all in one go."

Devin's mind wandered, as Obair explained about the Wyrde and the role he had played in maintaining it. It was amazing how quickly the fantastical could become mundane, how fast the dead could be forgotten. His head still throbbed. The pain had become a dull ache that he had almost learned to ignore. It made a counterpoint to the welter of emotions he felt about Hannah and Khorin.

With a guilty start, he realised that he'd not even thought about Kainen, Erinn and their families, or any his other friends in the village. He'd wrapped himself in a blanket of hurt and misery, and was shocked he hadn't been able to see through it.

"And you believe there might still be information there that we can use?" The duchess's voice cut through his thoughts and he jerked his eyes back to her.

"There may be nothing, your grace," Obair shrugged. "My hope is that either she, or her student, still lives and can help with this. The fact that Devin can feel the moon through the Wyrde is something that I cannot ignore."

"And you, boy?" She turned her attention to him. "How do you feel about this? After all you've been through, are you willing to leave your mother and go in search of something which might not even exist?"

"She's not my mother." The words left his lips before he'd really thought about them. "Hannah has been a mother to me for longer than I can really remember, but she's not my real mother. The fae took my mother from me. My mind has been broken and twisted for so long that I'd almost forgotten it all. Now they've killed Khorin, the only father I've ever had, and broken Hannah so her mind is as shattered as my own was. If I can find a way to hurt them, I will."

She looked at him with sympathy but, rather than comfort him, her pity just fuelled his anger. He felt it rising in him and the look he returned pushed at the outer edges of politeness and bordered on belligerent. She raised an eyebrow at his expression before turning to address Obair.

"When do you leave?"

"As soon as possible really, your grace." He glanced at Rhenkin. "I don't suppose we would be able to impose upon you for some supplies?"

"You may have whatever you need," Selena said, before Rhenkin could open his mouth. "Rhenkin, I will be travelling to Celstwin with Hanris to try to talk some sense into King Pieter. I want you to gather our forces and engage the Bjornmen. Bleed them slowly." She ignored his intake of breath and carried on before he could speak. "I know we can't match their numbers and I don't expect you to hold lands. Fall back as they advance but, Major, I expect you to make them pay in blood for every mile they take." Her voice was calm but her eyes were savage.

"As you wish, your grace." Rhenkin rose and stood to attention.

CHAPTER TWELVE

Ylsriss sipped the water from the skin and grimaced at the leathery taste. A bird, startled by something in the trees, burst from its cover and crashed up through the leaves into the purple twilight sky. She froze, the waterskin still pressed to her lips, as her eyes searched the bushes and leaves around her.

The woods had grown still and it was only as the quiet noises of the birds returned that she felt herself relax. Joran hissed out a sigh of relief behind her and she turned to see him lowering the bow. She hadn't even heard him move to retrieve it from the packs.

"Do you still think we should be resting during the daylight hour?" she asked, for what she knew must be the hundredth time.

"It's the only time we can be certain of being safe, Ylsriss. You know that." He stepped closer and held her gently by the shoulders. "Look at me. I mean, really look. You look as bad as I must do. We can't sleep properly at night, not when we have to take turns on watch and we jump at every sound."

"But we could be so much further away…" She trailed off. They'd already been over this. There was little point in listing the pros and cons of the rest stops again.

She could tell he knew what she was thinking, as he hunkered down beside the remains of the runeplate to make sure the glyphs were covered. The sun was already shining through the trees, although it had yet to crest them.

"They're fading," he said.

"It will last a bit longer. I'm surprised it's lasted this long, really." Ylsriss shrugged. "When it's gone, it's gone. We can make a fire easily enough."

Joran lowered himself to the earth with a groan. "Lords of Blood, Sea and Sky, I'm tired."

Ylsriss dug through the pack to find their few remaining oatcakes. "We're going to have to stop and hunt something soon, Joran. We're running out of food."

"I know," he sighed. "I don't want to stop here, though. It just doesn't feel safe yet."

She nodded, though he wasn't looking. It didn't feel safe yet. That much was as true for her as it was for him. They'd seen no sign of pursuit or any sign of a threat but the menace hung in the air. It had done for days, but it was nothing she could put her finger on. It felt similar to the sensation of being watched, but not quite the same.

"I've lost track of the days again," she said softly, as she handed an oatcake over.

"It's been three weeks now, by my reckoning."

"Another week then?"

"Hmm?"

"If we go another week, then we ought to be safe, don't you think?"

He paused, the oatcake held to his lips. "I suppose so. If they haven't caught us by then, they either can't find us or they don't care."

She swallowed down the last of the cake, forcing it down though she didn't really want it. She knew she would need the strength it gave her. It was odd sleeping in the sunlight. There was so little of it in this strange land that it felt wrong to waste it. The pack was lumpy under her head as she lay back. No matter how much she shifted it, it didn't seem to make a difference.

Glancing across at Joran, she saw his eyes were closed, and his chest was rising and falling rhythmically. The man was already asleep. Ylsriss muttered choice words under her breath and shifted again in an attempt to get comfortable.

It didn't take long for her to give up. Patience had never been something she could lay claim to having. Climbing to her feet, she headed to the edge of the small clearing. As an afterthought, she went back and picked up the waterskin. Maybe she could find a stream or something.

She kept a careful note of where the clearing lay but, other than that, she wandered without any real purpose. The sun shone onto the trees, making the leaves radiant with bright reds and golds. Here and there, the silvery bark of a tree gleamed in the golden light.

The distant sound of water drew her around the side of the hill and she caught her first clear view in days, as the ground dropped steeply away in front of her. The canopy burned in the sunlight, the red and orange leaves forming a blanket of flames. A flash pulled at her from the corner of her eye but when she turned to look in that direction it was gone. She stared, eyes scanning the distant trees, but it did not come again.

The stream was clear and the water icy. She knelt awkwardly at the edge, as she held the skin under the surface and tried to fill it. The water was cold enough to burn her and her hand swiftly went numb in the flow. It was probably the only cold thing she'd come across since she had passed into the Realm of Twilight.

Her eyes caught the flash again as she stood and this time they locked onto it. The distant images blurred and shifted before slowly forming a clear picture. It was a small section of wall. The yellow stones were stained with moss and half-covered in vines, but it was a wall nonetheless. She had no idea what had been flashing, but she was so shocked by the sight of the structure that she didn't care. The waterskin banged against her side, the water within it sloshing about, as she jogged back to the clearing and shook Joran roughly awake.

He jumped as he came to and his eyes were filled with panic as he stared up at her. She immediately felt guilty and hushed him with one finger, shaking her head and smiling gently. "No, it's not that. There's nothing to worry about."

"Why did you...what's going on then?" he asked, through sleep-fuddled lips.

"I found water..." she began.

"That's great, but did you need to wake me to tell me?"

"Shut up for a minute." She laughed. "I found water and, as I was filling the skin, I saw buildings."

"What do you mean, buildings?"

"You know...four walls... roofs?" She didn't bother to temper the sarcasm.

"Funny," he said, in a flat voice.

"Alright. I'm not sure it was buildings, actually. It was just a wall," she admitted.

"But we have to be at least a hundred miles from Tir Rhu'thin," he protested.

"Exactly!" Her excitement was contagious and his smile grew to match her own. Abruptly, however, her expression was one of panic. "Do you think it could be more fae?"

"I don't think so." Joran frowned. "They always made it clear that Tir Rhu'thin was their home. If they had other cities or towns, wouldn't they have mentioned them?"

"Who knows?" Ylsriss shrugged again. "I think it's worth taking a look though. We might find something we can use or, at the very least, some shelter."

"How far away would you say it was?"

"I don't know, really. It's hard to judge. Maybe two days?"

"Show me." He clambered to his feet, and gathered up his pack and bow while she retrieved the chunk of runeplate, splashing water over the glyphs to make sure the dirt was stuck fast before she shoved it into her pack.

"What about resting?" she asked.

"This is more important. I just have a feeling about it." He looked away, embarrassed.

"I know what you mean. I thought I was just being silly but…" She spread her hands helplessly.

They paused as they reached the stream and she pointed out the distant wall. He looked at it for a second, then strode through the icy water without so much as a flinch. Ylsriss shook her head and headed further downstream, where a fallen log had formed a natural bridge. Men were idiots. She'd always had to nag Klöss to bathe, but show him something that promised adventure and he'd wade through the surf without batting an eyelid. It seemed Joran was cut from the same cloth.

The wall vanished from view as they travelled, obscured by the trees. Joran increased his pace and she found herself struggling to keep up.

"Damn it, Joran," she yelled, in frustration. "It's not going to vanish on us. Slow down! Either that or take this damned skin, so I can walk properly."

He looked back at her and she fought down the wave of guilt as she saw his crestfallen expression. He was like an overgrown child in so many ways, but she hadn't the time to coddle him.

"I'm sorry, I didn't mean to yell at you. Just take the skin. The strap is too long for me, anyway. I'll take your pack until we've used some of the water up."

The twilight was darkening by the time they stopped for the night and she lay in the dim light thinking about the distant wall. Joran's deep, steady breaths were the soft accompaniment to her imagination's travels as she wondered about the wall and what it might enclose. In her time in the world of the fae - at least, once she'd broken free of the Touch - she'd only ever heard any mention of Tir Rhu'thin. Now that she thought about it though, it did sound odd. An entire world with only one city? She gave a mental shrug. It was no wonder she'd accepted it; this was how the Touch worked. It was as if part of your mind went to sleep. Things like this just didn't seem important, even when they should have been screaming out at you.

She shook her head in the half-light. How could they have been so stupid, so befuddled, that they didn't question it? She felt a moment's fear at the prospect of another city of fae, but it was soon overridden by her desire to know the truth. If the wall surrounded a city of fae, surely they would have been discovered and captured by now?

Joran murmured and she glanced at him, jealous of his ability to sleep. She examined his features in the gloom. He looked like a grown man or very close to it. In many ways, he acted like one, and in some ways he seemed even older, but there were other parts of his personality that marked him as little more than a child. His ability to sleep whenever he needed was something that any oarsman from the Barren Isles would have envied. For him, though, it was just natural. She also knew that, at some level, he still thought of the fae as benevolent. Despite what he said, it hadn't yet occurred to him that they were in any real danger.

* * *

He knelt and examined the tracks; just a scuffed patch of moss and a broken twig, things most others would have missed. He was patient for his kind, but then he was far older than most of the Revel. More importantly, he didn't fear the leaching rays of the sun as they did.

The leaves on the twig were just starting to wilt. It hadn't been broken for long. The damage could have been done by any number of creatures, but the scuff in the moss was a clear sign. Humans really were the clumsiest of creatures.

He rose from his crouched position and looked about for Sabeth. The fae'reeth was almost unique amongst her kind, more focused than many of the tiny creatures were capable of being. He caught sight of her purple form as the setting sun reflected off her wings and waved her over.

"This way." He pointed. "They are little more than a sunrise ahead of us."

"They are an interesting quarry." Her eyes gleamed as she stared off in the direction of the trail. "Do you imagine any of your brethren still continue the hunt?"

"I doubt it." Thantos glanced back in the direction of Tir Rhu'thin. "Most are too careful hoarding the Lady's gift." His lip curled as he spoke, the derision thick on his black tongue.

"I confess, my brother, that I will never understand this obsession with the Lady."

Thantos permitted a rare smile to twist his lips. "Your kind rarely does, Sabeth."

She shrugged, the movement causing her to bob in the air as it interfered with the motion of her wings. "How far do we travel to then, Thantos? You realise we are close to the boundary? Aelthen will be incensed, should we be discovered."

The old satyr tugged at his beard. The dark wiry hair was shot through with silver streaks. "We will go on. We can turn back easily enough if need be, but I'll not let the quarry escape when we're this close."

"You're as bad as those on the chase," Sabeth chided.

"As are you, dear sister," Thantos replied, with a dry chuckle. He waved a gnarled hand forward, inviting her to lead the way, and ran behind as the purple creature no larger than his hand flew through the trees.

He ran lightly, a gait that was little more than a trot but which allowed him to scan the ground ahead of him as they travelled. Sabeth would be looking for trail signs anyway, but only a fool left a task totally to the fae'reeth. More than any of the fae, they were a fickle people.

The sun dropped below the trees as they travelled and he felt their pace quicken in response as the drain of the sun fell away. It was subtle, but he'd been running in the daylight long enough to appreciate it. His chest felt lighter, his body relaxed as he ran and every muscle was that little bit more responsive. He might mock the others for their reliance upon it, but he would never argue the Lady's Gift wasn't potent. The difference lay in appreciating the benefits of the Lady's Gift and reliance upon the Grace it imparted.

Sabeth flared her wings and spun in place ahead of him, pointing into the bushes to his left. Her warning came a fraction of a second before his own ears caught the rustle and his nose was filled with the feline scent of the cat. He threw himself to the side and ripped his curved knives free of their sheaths as the beast crashed into the earth where he'd just stood.

He rolled and came smoothly to his feet with his knives extended before him. The shade-cat was young and inexperienced, he could tell. It hadn't long been free of its tree by the looks of things. He tried a feint to see what it would do and was surprised as it backed away, giving itself space to react, rather than falling for the motion.

The pounce was a thing of beauty. Its powerful muscles rippled as it launched itself into the air and flew at him. The thick trail of darkness extended out behind the cat and into the trees, a testament to its youth and lack of control.

Thantos rolled to the side again, lashing out with his knives and cutting deeply into the cat's side. It let loose a yowl of pain and landed awkwardly, the trail of mist pouring in and encompassing it. The satyr could see two green eyes glowing malevolently amidst the darkness.

He didn't pause. Waiting would just give the beast enough time to heal itself. He threw himself at the cat, his knives moving in a blur before him, as he slashed and thrust deep. A flash of purple heralded Sabeth's entry into the fight as she plunged into the mist.

The mist faded almost at once as the cat twisted and recoiled from the tiny cuts Sabeth's knife inflicted. It lashed out at the flitting fae'reeth with its black claws, but it might as well have been trying to catch the wind.

As Thantos shifted back a step and waited for an opening, the creature soon became covered in a web of tiny slashes that oozed blood. The wounds that the fae'reeth inflicted with their blades were seldom designed to be immediately fatal. Instead, they preferred to drain their victims slowly, as a source of amusement for the swarm.

Sabeth, however, was alone and the cuts she made were the actions of instinct let loose. Despite this, they proved a useful distraction. Thantos waited as the cat grew more and more frustrated, its large paws slashing futilely at the air behind Sabeth as she darted around it, under it and through its legs.

The cat reared up in a rage, batting at the fae'reeth with its forepaws, and then Thantos struck. He lunged in and rammed both of his knives into the base of the cat's throat. Blood ran in torrents as the cat lurched backwards, forcing itself off the blades. The shadowy mist flew in again from where it had trailed out through the trees, surrounding the cat, but Thantos did not back away. Instead, he struck again, slashing and thrusting with the horn knives, as Sabeth thrust her thorn-sized blade into one of the creature's glowing eyes.

Silence fell as the cat collapsed. Its body was a bloody ruin, a mass of cuts and hideous wounds. It was a gruesome sight, evidence of a fight of necessity become a slaughter, a killing devoid of grace or beauty.

Thantos wiped his knives on the thick moss and glanced at Sabeth. "My thanks, sister. Your warning was timely."

"It seemed appropriate." She shrugged, licking the blade of her small knife.

The satyr looked at the body of the shade-cat again. Their mother would have been delighted to receive the pelt, but it had been sliced to ribbons. He shrugged away the loss, met Sabeth's eyes with a nod and moved away from the corpse as they continued to follow the trail.

As they left, the earth near the body of the shade-cat heaved, as the roots from the nearby trees began to burrow through the blood-soaked earth, drinking greedily and worming their way towards the corpse, until they could thrust themselves deep inside of it to reclaim the nutrients.

* * *

Ylsriss swatted away the branches that seemed determined to bury themselves in her hair, and tried to see through the undergrowth to where Joran was up ahead.

"Joran, damn it, wait for me!" she called out. He probably wouldn't hear her and she doubted that he'd stop if he did. He had been like a man on a mission since they'd seen the wall.

She rushed on, stumbling over tree roots which had been half-buried by fallen leaves. *What if she'd lost him? What if she was alone?* The idea came to her unbidden, but she stopped dead for a moment as it struck her. A haste born of fear spurred her onwards and she cried out his name again, an edge of panic touching her voice.

The slope was fairly gentle, but she hadn't been expecting it, so when the root caught her foot, she fairly flew before hitting the ground and starting to roll. The runeplate slammed into the base of her skull as her pack was thrown forward on her back, and she cursed as she came to a halt at the bottom of the small hill.

She pulled herself up onto her knees as she spat the leaves out from her mouth and probed gingerly at the back of her head, checking her fingertips for blood.

"Joran!" she yelled, anger in her voice this time. She spotted movement in the trees ahead of her and forced herself to her feet. The pain was a dull ache now, more remembered pain than anything else, but it was enough to maintain her sour mood and fuel her irritation.

He stood beside a towering pine. The tree had grown far taller and broader than it ever would have done in her own world. She called out again as she approached, but he ignored her until she reached for his arm.

"What is it?" she demanded, his silence telling her more than words might have done.

"Look." He pointed down through the few remaining trees. The stones were cracked, and grass and ferns pushed their way through the gaps between them, but they had clearly been part of a road at some point.

"It's just a road," she said, with a frown. "I know we haven't seen one here before, but ..."

"Not the road. Look!" He pointed again and she followed the road with her eyes. She'd taken it as a break in the stones, but now she saw it clearly – it was a ravine. It slashed through the forest, extending out of view in both directions, and cutting directly across their path. She sucked in a breath and took his hand as they walked down towards it.

It took longer than she'd thought it would to reach the edge, though she stood a good way back from it. He held onto her as she looked down, as if fearing she'd fall. Ylsriss was grateful despite her amusement. If anyone was likely to not take a danger seriously, it was him. She was never likely to be at risk of falling. The sides fell away, revealing rocks and tree roots, before extending down into the darkness.

"How deep do you think it is?" he asked, in a hushed voice.

"Too deep for me," she said, with a shudder. "It's too wide for us to cross too." The far side was at least fifty feet away.

"So now what?"

She looked at him curiously. He'd taken the lead since they'd fled the camps, guiding her through the woods long after they'd left the lands he knew.

"Left or right, I suppose." She waved her hands vaguely. "It has to end at some point, or at least get shallow or thin enough for us to cross it."

He peered through the trees in both directions before looking back at her, his eyebrow cocked in a silent query.

"Left, then," she decided. "I imagine either direction is as good as the other."

He nodded and set off, heading slightly away from the edge of the cliff. She didn't blame him. The sight of the empty air beside her was enough to make her skin crawl. She'd always hated heights.

"Can you still feel it?" she asked, raising her voice so he could hear her.

He glanced back. "Feel what?"

"The Touch."

He waited for her to catch up. "Not really," he replied, falling into step beside her. "I can remember the feeling of it, of almost worshipping them, but it's almost as if it happened to someone else now."

"At least we know it can be broken," she said, ducking under a thorned branch. "Can you remember much from before?"

His confused look prompted her to continue. "You never really spoke about your life before you were taken. It was hard to get any kind of detail from you. I thought it might have been the Touch. I suppose I'm asking if you remember anything more now?"

"I do," His words were slow as he tried to grasp the memories. "It's very strange. Everything has a dreamlike quality to it."

"How so?"

"Jumbled." He laughed suddenly, the smile looking out of place on his face for some reason. "That's not the best explanation, is it?"

She grinned and shook her head.

"The memories have no sense or order to them, like how a dream jumps about from place to place. I can remember being cold. I was on a fishing boat. I was wrapped in furs, but I was still cold. I remember the smell of the sea and the taste of salt on my lips. I can even remember the feel and the smell of the fish as we tipped them out of the nets. But I have no idea what fish tastes like. Isn't that crazy?"

"Give it time," she said, reaching for his hand. "You've been here a long time, most of it under the Touch. It will probably take a while for your mind to recover."

"You make it sound like I'm crazy." His voice was steady, but his eyes had grown hard, accusing.

"You're not crazy, Joran. I think I'm going to lose it soon though, if we don't get something to eat other than stale oatcakes!"

Their laughter was forced and false to begin with, but it felt good and genuine laughs followed from both of them. They fell silent for a while as they walked, looking through the trees from time to time to be sure they still followed the edge of the chasm.

"Joran?" she asked, quietly. "Do you remember your mother?"

He looked at her with sympathy. Her tone had been light but he'd clearly seen through it. "I'm sorry," he replied. "I don't. Not really. I remember the idea of her and sometimes I think I remember the smell of her. Sort of a combination of baking bread and flowers." He shrugged and looked over at her. "It's been such a long time though. I'm sure it will be different for you and Effan."

"Don't," she said, glaring at him.

"Don't? Don't what?"

"Don't humour me, Joran. Don't patronise me." She spoke softly but the irritation was plain in her tone. An angry dog waiting to be set free.

"I wasn't," he protested, holding his hands up in front of him. "I…"

"You what?" she snapped. "You told me you're sure it won't be the same for me. How is that not patronising, when you can't know anything of the sort."

His voice stumbled into silence and he looked down at his feet as they walked, thinking carefully before he spoke again. "I'm not trying to humour you, Ylsriss. I suppose I'm just hiding from the truth. I'm lying to myself as much as I am to you. The chances of us getting home are tiny. You must know that as well as I do. The chances of finding Effan aren't much better. And even if we did, would you even recognise him? It's been…what…the best part of eight months or so since you saw him? It could be even longer."

She drew her breath in sharply and opened her mouth to retort before forcing it closed again. He was right. After so long, Effan would bear little resemblance to the baby she'd had stolen from her. With a whole world to search, would she really be able to find him? "The lies we tell ourselves," she whispered to herself.

"What?" Joran looked at her, catching the edges of the whisper.

"I was talking to myself." She gave a humourless laugh. "I said these are the lies we tell ourselves. The things we need to believe to stay sane, to keep going."

His smile was tinged with sadness. "So we're both crazy then, in our own ways."

"I suppose everyone is." Her gaze slipped past his face, drawn by a flicker of light from the ravine.

"What?" She ignored him and pushed past him towards the clifftop. He followed in silence, confusion stilling his tongue.

Ylsriss clung to the tree. It was a good five feet or more from the edge of the cliff, but the drop was terrifying and she gripped the rough bark, digging her fingernails in.

The flash came again, yellow-white, and reflected up from the rocks on the far side of the ravine. She forced herself to let go of the tree and dropped to her hands and knees, crawling towards the edge.

"Ylsriss, what are you doing?" Joran asked, amusement in his voice. She ignored him and lay on her belly, squirming closer to the edge until she could peer over it. The ravine wasn't really worthy of the name any longer. Ylsriss could see the bottom of it clearly, no more than a hundred feet or so below her. The sides that sloped down towards the centre were no longer the sheer face they had once been. It would be a tumbling fall that would probably kill any but the luckiest of men, but it was far better than the endless drop into darkness that she had seen earlier.

There was another flash and she looked to the left. A huge metal bar, pitted with rust, reached from one side of the ravine to the other, some fifty feet away from her. Far below it, a jumble of stone blocks and columns lay broken and collapsed against each other. Rusted rods of iron jutted out of them, as though they'd formed a net and the stone had been wrapped around them.

A small section of pipe protruded from the wall of the ravine amidst the tumbled blocks and, as she looked, sparks erupted from its mouth in a burst of yellow and white.

"What in the world...?" Joran's voice made her jump. She hadn't heard him approach.

"What is that thing?" she asked.

"I have no idea. I know one thing, though," he replied.

"What?" She already knew what he was going to say and the thought filled her with dread.

"It goes in the right direction. We can use it to get across."

"You have got to be joking me!" She pulled herself away from the edge and up onto her knees as she stared at him in dismay. "It's not nearly as deep as it was. It's probably coming to an end. If we carry on, we could cross it much more easily."

"We don't know that, Ylsriss," he replied. "It could just as easily drop down again. We could waste days walking in the wrong direction, looking for a way across that isn't even there."

"How would we even get down there?" she asked. She felt sick to her stomach at the thought of crawling across the beam.

"It's not that far down to it and the edge isn't a sheer face, like it was. If we got some vines, we could probably just slide down to it."

"Probably?" Her voice was shrill with fear and he gave her an amused look.

"There's another very good reason for going down there, Ylsriss."

"I haven't heard the first good reason yet, but go on." She folded her arms and hugged herself tightly, as if the air had suddenly become cold.

"That's rust on that thing, and rust means iron or steel," he explained.

"So?"

"The fae can't abide the stuff. There was an old man in a camp I was in, years before you arrived here. He had found a sliver of iron in the woods. It looked like a bit of nail to me, but I never thought to question what it was doing there at the time. I remember he was acting so strangely. He was so excited about it. He kept wanting people to hold it at first, then he was talking about making a spear with it."

"What happened?" Ylsriss asked.

"He'd only had it about an hour before they arrived. Three fae, they just appeared at the edge of the camp with horn bows. They didn't speak, or warn him or anything. One minute he was rushing about, trying to get people to touch it, the next he had three arrows in his face."

"What?"

"They killed him, Ylsriss, just for having a tiny scrap of the stuff. They made one of us scoop it into a little pouch for them and then they took it away without a word. They wouldn't touch it or even go near it. They treated it like it was a live snake or something."

"What do you think it was about it?"

"I have no idea. But if it can make them so scared that they need to hunt a man down just for having it, then I think we should get some if we can."

She drew in a long breath, then looked helplessly at him before shaking her head. "I can't do it, Joran. I can't climb across that thing. Not for iron, not for anything. Not if there might be another way." She stopped him as he was about to speak. "Just give me one more day, okay? One more day to see if we can find a different way across? We'll carry on the way we've been going and, if we don't find anything, then we'll do it your way."

He looked at her in silence. She was pale in the fading twilight. The sun couldn't be more than half an hour away, but her skin looked bloodless as she bit at her lip and pleaded with her eyes.

"Fine." He gave in. "We'll give it a day. I want to go slowly though. I'll use the time to try and hunt something."

She gave him a wan smile of thanks and he led her off through the trees, keeping the ravine in sight as a point of reference. The woods came slowly alive as the sun rose. Despite the fact that it was only in the sky for an hour, birds became more vocal and the distant rustles made by animals in the undergrowth became more obvious.

Joran walked with his bow in hand, arrow nocked and held ready, though the string was relaxed. He'd instructed her to follow him, telling her it was so they didn't disturb any game before he had a chance to shoot, but she was making so much noise she doubted it would make a difference.

He managed to move almost silently, keeping to moss or exposed tree roots. She'd listened attentively as he'd explained the best way to avoid making noise but it didn't seem to work for her. She had an undiscovered talent apparently, or maybe she was just destined to be a city girl.

Joran froze ahead of her and sent an arrow flying into the trees. There was a muted crash, then he flashed a grin at her and ran ahead to collect whatever it was he'd shot. For a moment, she was shocked by just how boyish he seemed, worse than ever. By the time she caught up with him, he was holding a fat bird in one hand. He waved the body at her like a grisly trophy, before stuffing it into a sack he'd pulled from his pack.

They moved more swiftly after that. Joran had pulled the pack open slightly to allow the sunlight to hit the runeplate and warm it. It would be good to get some meat again. The oatcakes that they'd brought with them had long gone and the rest of their supplies were almost exhausted. Although they'd managed to forage some berries as they travelled, it was not enough.

The sun fell swiftly and they slowed as the light faded. It was always hard to adjust to the twilight again and she made more noise than she had before. She was concentrating on trying to keep quiet, looking down at the ground ahead of her, when she sensed Joran stop.

"What is it?" she asked finally, unable to bear it.

"Come and see this," he called back, a frown of confusion on his face.

She hurried to his side and then stopped. The ground fell away ahead of them, dropping down in a steep cliff. Beyond the cliff was nothing but skies and wisps of cloud, as if the land simply ended there. She looked to the left and right of her, tracing the cliff with her eyes as it extended out of view in both directions.

"Shit." She spat and sat on the thick grass that grew between the trees and the edge of the cliff. He stared off to the right, stepping closer to the edge, then his eyes bulged and his mouth fell open.

"What?" she asked, although part of her didn't really care.

He pointed wordlessly and waved a finger ahead of him at the cliff as he looked at her. "Seriously, Ylsriss, look at this."

She sighed and pulled herself back to her feet. The cliff that sank away below them was a combination of white stone and small patches of exposed earth. For the most part, it extended down away from them in a steep slope before dropping off into darkness. Far to the right of them though, the bottom of the cliff was clearly visible. Where the ground should have been at the base of the cliff, there was nothing, a twilight expanse filled with wispy clouds. Another sky extending out from underneath the ground on which they stood.

As she tried to make sense of what she was seeing, a break in the clouds below her revealed the pinprick lights of stars. She rocked back and staggered away from the edge as her eyes grew as wide as Joran's had been.

"Those are stars!" she gasped. "How can there be another sky underneath us?" Her only answer was the stunned face of her companion.

The trek back was silent. They'd talked about it until confusion drove the words from them and there was nothing left to say. A sky beneath them, visible underneath the bottom of the cliff they stood at the top of. The concept made her head hurt but set her vertigo screaming. She shuddered away from the notion of the land she stood upon resting on nothing but empty space far beneath her. Was this entire world just floating in the twilit sky?

Joran was equally silent, not even bothering to hunt. Despite all of the alien oddities of this world of the fae, nothing had prepared them for this. He led the way through the trees, retracing their steps until they returned to the ravine and the strange metal beam that would be their way across it.

Now that she was closer, she could see it was as straight as any fashioned stone. Odd nodules jutted from it in places like the heads of massive screws. She couldn't say how long she stood examining it, but as Joran arrived back beside her with a tangle of thick vines, she realised it must have been some time.

He set about wrapping the ends of the vines around the thick trunk of a tree that stood close to the ravine edge, before letting a length of it down towards the rusted metal. The vines were not made from single strands, like ropes or lines. Instead, they were tangles of wide green and brown plants that lay as wide as her outstretched arms, extending down over the edge of the ravine like a poorly-fashioned rope ladder.

"Are you ready?" he asked.

"Me?" she demanded. "Why do I have to go first?"

"Alright, I'll go first."

"Well, I don't want to be left here alone!"

He chuckled. "Fine. They should be strong enough to hold both of us. We can go together."

"Should be?" she asked, a dangerous lilt in her voice.

He laughed again. "Look at the slope, Ylsriss. Most of your weight will be on the ground itself, not the vines. They're only there so we can control how fast we go down and to help us to balance."

"Right." She didn't sound convinced.

"Trust me."

"I do trust you," she replied. "It's the scraps of plant that you've pulled out of the woods that I don't trust."

He ignored her and sat on the edge of the ravine, his hands grasping the vines on either side of him. "I think it makes sense to go down like this, sort of sitting down. That way, you can use your feet to slow yourself too and you put less weight on the vines."

"That would be the vines you're sure will hold us?" Sarcasm dripped from her words as she looked at him.

"Those are the ones, yes." He grinned at her and then pushed himself over the edge, kicking up dirt and small stones as he slid down on his rump.

"Joran!" she screamed. He slowed then stopped himself with his feet, grabbing onto the vines with his hands.

"It's fine," he called up. "Now you."

"Oh yes, my turn now. Joy!" she muttered to herself as she swung her legs over the edge. He looked up at her expectantly and she took in a deep breath before she pushed herself over the edge. The breath was gone in a moment, used all at once in one long scream, as she slid down towards him.

CHAPTER THIRTEEN

Selena strolled through the rooms of the villa, ignoring the maids as they frantically darted about trying to make the place ready for human habitation. Although they'd sent word ahead, the house was far from ready for them.

She gave a snort of amusement as the distant barking of the mistress of the house sent the maids scurrying again. The woman had the soul of a rottweiler and was not anyone Selena would ever want to cross if she could help it.

A wave of nausea struck her, coming from nowhere, and she rested a hand on a cloth- covered piano to steady herself. She closed her eyes tight and bent to rest her head on her hand. Biting her lip seemed to help her, for some reason, although nothing else had. She winced at the remembered taste of the herbal teas and the ginger-laced foods she'd eaten in an effort to quell the urge to throw up.

Swallowing was helping today as well. Last week, it had been more likely to send her scrambling for a chamber pot. She took a deep breath as she fought it off and circled the room, lifting a cloth to examine a harp before stepping out into the hallway.

"Ah, your grace." Hanris smiled with that facial grimace that all staff seem to use with their employers. "Do you find the villa to your liking?"

"I presume the villa is under a dust sheet then, Hanris? Everything else seems to be."

"Yes, your grace, it does rather seem that the staff are somewhat behind schedule."

"No, Hanris. Behind schedule implies that some work was due to have taken place. What we have here is a complete failure to even begin it before our arrival." Two maids hurried past bearing mops and buckets. "Should we present ourselves at the palace? I don't think there will be much opportunity to relax here for a while."

"Are you sure that's wise, your grace?" Hanris pursed his lips and looked at her midriff meaningfully. "In your condition, I mean?"

"My condition?" Selena laughed. "Hanris, women have been tilling fields in my condition for thousands of years, sometimes with another child strapped to their chests while they do it. I'm sure I can cope with a brief carriage ride and the poor hospitality of the palace."

Hanris was unfazed. "I'll have the carriage brought round for you, your grace."

"Do." Selena paused, tapping her lips with one finger. "I think some attendants and an escort would be a good idea, as well. We must send the right message, after all. See if you can round up some suitably strapping young men in uniform to trot along beside me, would you?"

"An honour guard. Yes, your grace." He gave a tight bow and strode down the marble-tiled corridor. Selena watched him for a moment, before making her way to the central staircase and up to her suite. The villa was relatively new, in the sense that Freyton had acquired it along with the rest of the duchy. Each of the major political players retained a presence in the capital. She presumed that, at some point, the Browntree family had owned its own villa here too.

At least the staff had managed to bring in the trunks and get them unpacked, she noted, as she made her way into the suite. She glanced out the window at the sun shining above the marble-clad buildings, judging the time by the light.

Changing alone was a relief. For once there were no foolish women seeking to help her to do something she'd managed by herself since she was knee-high. She selected simple, yet elegant, clothing from the wardrobes and began to dress. The full-length mirror on its stand threw her reflection back at her. Older than she remembered. Stronger, certainly, but was she wiser? Time would soon tell, she supposed.

She placed a hand on her stomach, looking at the woman in the mirror. It was starting to show more obviously. She'd have to have a dressmaker brought in while they were here. For now, however, it would probably help her cause to exaggerate things a little.

The gown was just a touch too tight, a fact exacerbated by the bow that tied at the back and lay atop the bustle. She shook her head, laughing at the spectacle of herself in the mirror. Who had even come up with the idea of a bustle?

Her hair, at least, wouldn't need much fussing with. She reached for the bell pull with one hand while she fumbled with the pins with the other.

"Is the coach ready?" she asked the servant as she entered the room.

"Yes, your grace."

"Lead the way then." Selena flashed the woman a bright smile. "I'm sure His Majesty is breathless with anticipation."

"Does he know you've arrived, Ma'am? Were we supposed to have sent word?" The maid's expression was panic-stricken.

"Never mind," Selena said, with a heartfelt sigh. Why was she doomed to be surrounded by people with no sense of humour?

Hanris awaited her beside the carriage, opening the door for her himself and shooing away the efforts of the footman. She graced him with a warm smile before climbing in and perching on the edge of the seat.

The carriage clattered through the city. It was not yet midday and the streets were still covered in a sheen from the rains of the night before. Selena forced the bustle into the backrest and managed to find an almost comfortable position as she leaned against the cushioned wall of the carriage.

"Is this your first time in Celstwin, Hanris?" she asked, more to break the silence than from any desire to speak with the man.

He jumped slightly, roused from a half-doze, and coughed before replying. "The first time in many years, your grace. I travelled here as a young lad. It is quite as fine, as I remember it."

She glanced out at the pristine buildings. "You do know that's by design, don't you?"

"Your grace?"

"The city was designed and constructed so that the poor could be kept off the streets and out of sight," she explained. "The broader avenues that carriages pass along are deliberately grand in order to drive up the prices of property. You won't find any but the most successful tradesmen on the main streets of Celstwin."

He stared at her. "Surely that's the same in any city, your grace."

"Not really, Hanris. Other cities have rich and poor areas that have sprung up over time. Celstwin was built with them already in place. In order to buy desirable property in Celstwin, you either need a title or a writ of patronage. The slums hold more than four-fifths of the city's population, but you'll never see them unless you go into the poor quarters."

He nodded in understanding. "And if you go into them looking like you don't belong, you'll be lucky to leave with your purse."

Selena smiled grimly. "Or your life."

"Surely it's rather foolhardy to create social divisions like that, though? I mean, to intentionally put the citizens at odds with each other?"

"Oh, Hanris, you are so delightfully naive at times." She reached over and patted his hand. "The people who live in the poor quarters have never been unified. You could fill a book with the names of the various guilds, thieving gangs and crime syndicates. That's not the point, though. The poor generally leave the elite of Celstwin alone, because the king wishes it. In return, he ignores them."

"And while he's ignoring them, they are ruling themselves," Hanris finished for her.

"Exactly!" She beamed like a proud parent, despite the fact he was easily twice her age. "And where there is division and conflict, there are pressure points. Kings have been manipulating the various factions in Celstwin for generations. Anlan is little different. A push here, a prod there. Turn a blind eye to one faction to balance out the other. Ruling is a balancing act, Hanris, one our present monarch does not seem to be adept at. Either that or he is far more adept at it than I imagined."

She fell silent, looking out at the pampered people as they strolled idly through the well-manicured avenues, past decorative columns and topiaries. Their arrival at the palace came almost as a welcome relief. Celstwin was very much like a spoilt child and Selena found her hands itching to teach it a lesson.

Palace footmen rushed forward to open the door for her and set a small plush stool beside the carriage for her to step down onto. She waited whilst Hanris clambered out and stood beside the coach before she climbed out herself.

The grounds of the palace were grand. It would be odd if they weren't, of course, but these were grand in a brash and ostentatious fashion. What one king had built, another had let fall into disrepair. As a result, the grounds and, indeed, the palace itself were a garish mishmash of half a dozen architectural styles.

She cast an appraising eye over the palace as she brushed down her gown. It had been many years since she'd seen it and she found herself reclaiming half-forgotten snatches of memory as they proceeded into the building itself.

Her own escort, she noticed, had been smoothly diverted. As she walked towards the palace entrance, with only Hanris to accompany her, she suddenly felt very small and alone.

As a duchess, she was required to present herself at the palace whenever she arrived in the capital. It was a convention that few followed, but today it suited her needs. Putting on an air of confidence and entitlement that she did not feel, she strode into the building, ignoring the guards that stood to attention with their long polearms.

A stuffy-looking steward in a spotless crimson livery intercepted them in the entrance hall.

"Can I help you?" he said, in a manner which indicated very clearly that not only did he not wish to help them, but also that he resented the implication that he ought to, or that they should even have dared to enter the grounds.

Selena gave the man a withering glance and nodded to Hanris.

"And you are?" Hanris replied, looking the man up and down.

The man bristled, smoothing his red moustache with one finger. He ignored Hanris and addressed Selena. "I am His Majesty's house steward. Kindly ask your man to moderate his tone."

"And I am Duchess Freyton of Druel, The Wash, and the Eastern Reaches. How dare you address me in that manner!" Her eyes were ice as she spoke in a dreadfully quiet voice.

The man held her gaze for a full second before he began to wilt. "I'm sorry, madam. I had no idea."

"Your grace," Hanris said, in a stage whisper.

"I'm sorry?"

"The correct form of address." His words were drenched in condescension and pomposity. "Your mode of address ought to be 'your grace', not simply 'madam'. This is not some simple washerwoman you are speaking to."

A red flush appeared at the man's collar and spread until it began an assault on his cheeks. "My apologies, your grace," he began again. "Is there something I might assist you with?"

"I'm not sure," Selena replied, as she fought to keep a smile from her face. It was hard not to enjoy the sight of the arrogant little man deflating. "Is there?"

He cleared his throat and clasped the thick black ledger to his side. "I am tasked with overseeing His Majesty's appointments, your grace. As such, I am required to announce those that have arrived for scheduled meetings with the king."

"Oh," she said, drawing out the word as if suddenly understanding. "You're the doorman!"

Hanris made a noise that could conceivably, in some other time and place, have been a cough and the steward's face became, if possible, redder, as he pulled open the ledger and rested it on one arm.

"You do not appear to have an appointment, your grace," he said, biting off the words. "I'm afraid His Majesty's calendar is simply too full for social visits."

"I believe you will find that all members of the higher nobility are required to present themselves to the king upon arrival in the city, as is required by convention and privilege," Hanris replied smoothly.

"Well, yes, but nobody follows those silly traditions in this day and age." The man waved away the suggestion.

"Are you suggesting that Her Grace does not have the right to present herself?" Hanris asked, with no small measure of incredulity.

"I take it you're going to insist upon this?" The steward sighed. "Very well. I'll find you somewhere you can take refreshments. I'm afraid it might be a lengthy wait though." He looked at Selena. "My apologies, your grace."

Selena nodded, acknowledging the words, and then fell into line behind him as he led them deeper into the palace.

The parlour was comfortable but held the smell of a room that was rarely used. It was probably one of a hundred forgotten lounges and sitting rooms littered throughout the place. She made her way around the room, idly inspecting the paintings on the walls. The oil had grown so dark in some that it was hard to make out the images.

"I'm not entirely sure that was wise, your grace," Hanris said. He perched on the edge of the divan. He may have conceded to her demand that he sit, but he clearly had no intention of relaxing.

"Hmm?" Selena turned away from the portrait. "Oh, the doorman? He doesn't have any power to speak of, Hanris."

"Be that as it may, your grace, he will not be inclined to assist us with obtaining an audience."

Selena snorted. "I'll not crawl and scrape to every petty-minded bureaucrat scurrying about the palace. We'll have our audience one way or another and I'll not beg to exercise my own rights."

Hanris's sigh was quiet but just loud enough to reach her ear.

After a few hours, a servant brought them refreshments but they were then studiously ignored. Selena grew bored and then irritated before falling prey to self-doubt. Had the silly little steward actually managed to block her? He wouldn't dare, surely?

Finally, as she was about to give up hope, they were escorted to a marble bench outside the king's audience chamber. Her initial excitement faded quickly, however, as it became clear that they had simply been moved to another place to wait. She glared at the door as the hours passed, attracting more than one curious look from the servants as they hurried past.

"Come, Hanris," she said, standing abruptly. "We'll not be party to this."

"Your grace?"

"The king is clearly not going to see us this day, and I'll not sit here whilst the servants peer around the corner and snigger at us."

"As you say, your grace."

The ride back to the villa was silent.

They were not seen the next day or the day after that, and Selena perfected the art of quietly seething. She exuded an aura of politely contained rage that sent the servants hopping when they came too close. Appointments for the king came and went, looking at her with barely concealed derision, as their attendants identified her as an 'eastern noble' in the same manner as one might classify a dog as a mongrel.

It was late in the afternoon on the third day when she heard someone call out to her.

"Selena? Is that you?"

She turned to see a refined-looking man peering at her from under his bushy white eyebrows. "Uncle Thomas!" she exclaimed, rushing to her feet.

"We've both been too old for you to call me uncle for years, my dear," the old man said, with a laugh. "Besides, I was never really your uncle anyway."

"Uncle sounds better than cousin," Selena said, with a toss of the head.

"And both sound better than Earl Salisbourne," he said, with a grimace. "What are you doing here? I heard you were married off to some eastern fellow. Slayton or something?"

"Freyton," Selena corrected him, ignoring the way he'd curled his lip when he said 'eastern fellow'. "I was. He died recently, I'm afraid."

His face fell and the twinkle in his eyes was replaced with guilt and sympathy. "Oh, my dear, I am sorry."

"Don't be," she replied. "It was not a happy marriage. We all know it was one of convenience and necessity, anyway. I'm only sorry his son won't get to meet him." She put a hand on her midriff, looking down so he couldn't fail to catch her meaning.

"A child?" The smile flew back to his lips immediately. "Why, that's wonderful news!" He pulled her into a hug and, just as quickly, pushed her back, placing his hands on her shoulders. "Look at us! A pair of gossips chatting away for the entertainment of the staff. What are you doing here?"

"I was rather hoping for an audience with the king," Selena said, rolling her eyes.

"Few and far between, these days, I'm afraid," he replied, with a sidelong look at the doors. "Would it be terribly rude of me to ask why?"

"The Bjornmen," Selena grated. "They're taking whole counties at a time and he doesn't seem to be inclined to do anything about it. I've sent missive after missive and, frankly, my own forces are not up to the task. If we're to have any chance of repelling them, I need the king's armies."

Thomas nodded soberly. "Listen, I'm having a little meal tomorrow evening with a few people you might like to meet. Rentrew is going to be there. I suspect you have a lot to talk about."

"Baron Rentrew?" she said, in shock. "What on earth is he doing here?"

"Much the same as you, by the sound of things," Thomas replied. "Must dash, my dear. I'll send a coach for you tomorrow evening." He gave her another twinkling smile as he left.

* * *

Pieter was a pale man with dark, lank hair that was no friend to a bath. They were only nodding acquaintances at best. It hung down past his cheekbones, framing his sallow face, as he looked down at her with bored indifference in his dark shadowed eyes.

His was not the face of a king. Not a king that would ever inspire his subjects, anyway. It was a cruel face, the face of a child grown to adulthood who had never quite stopped pulling the wings off flies. He lounged in the throne, his head propped up on one hand as he leaned his elbow on the armrest.

"Freyton," the king said slowly, as if testing the word to see whether or not it was to his liking. "Freyton is one of my newer dukes. He holds my lands in the Eastern Reaches, I believe. I wasn't aware he'd taken a wife." He looked over to the large table set against one wall and received a nod from one of the red-robed men there. They were huddled together, speaking quietly as another man scribbled into a thick ledger.

The scribbler was wearing a black robe with red trim. He stood and moved to his usual place, beside and slightly behind the throne, as Selena spoke.

"Yes, My Liege." She was not quite sure what to make of the man. It had been a shock to be admitted after all this time spent waiting. Hanris had been forced to wake her, as she'd dozed and she hadn't quite found her feet yet.

"So why has this man sent his wife in his place? I have little respect for a man who hides behind his woman when making requests."

"Nor should you, my lord," the dark-robed man murmured, just loud enough for the words to carry.

"Requests, Your Majesty?" Selena found herself parroting the man and turning the words into a question. It was a habit she'd always found intensely annoying when used by her own staff and she inwardly chided herself for it.

"Nobody sits outside waiting for an audience for three days without wanting something, girl," Pieter said. His voice was little warmer than his eyes, and they were as cold as winter's kiss. "Where is he?"

"My husband died recently, Your Majesty," Selena said simply.

He sat in silence for a moment, digesting the news. "And why was word not sent? One of my own dukes dies and you see no reason to inform me?"

"Word was sent, Your Majesty, both by bird and messenger." She met his eyes. Not defiantly, that would be stupid against such a man, but yet refusing to be cowed.

He ignored her, changing tack as if she hadn't spoken. "Why are you here? Not to tell me Freyton is dead. You Browntrees are all the same, money-grabbing schemers. What do you want now?"

Selena ground her teeth. She was being toyed with, baited. There could be no way the man was this ill-informed. "My duchy, your lands, have been invaded by a large force of Bjornmen, Your Majesty. Their numbers are such that we cannot repel them. They are taking lands. Driving off your subjects and settling the lands for themselves."

"*Your* duchy?" he asked, cocking an eyebrow at her as the robed toady tutted beside him, shaking his head in disapproval. "What makes it your duchy? By your own admission, Freyton is dead."

"He left the title to me, to act in his stead until his unborn child is ready to take the helm." She swallowed, fighting to keep the act as unobtrusive as she could. A sign of weakness before the man would be tantamount to suicide.

"He left you the title?" Pieter's voice rose with his anger and he stood up in his seat. "Am I not king? I decide who my lords and dukes are, not some semi-literate scratchings."

The grey-haired man bent to whisper into Pieter's ear, his words too low and swift for Selena to hear, although she did catch the word 'regency'.

She drew breath to speak, but the king waved a hand at her in disgust as he retook his seat. "Enough, woman. I'm done with your prattlings. Go to your villa and remain there until I send for you. We will consider your request to allow your regency."

"But, Your Majesty…" she began, in desperation.

"You're dismissed." He cut her off, his eyes narrow in thought, as he watched her make a hasty curtsy and step backwards before turning and making her way out.

She ignored the guards at the door as they turned their eyes away from her, embarrassed on her behalf. She clenched her fists at her sides to stop them from shaking and made her way out into the small antechamber.

Hanris stood as she entered, a question on his lips, but she stopped him with a curt shake of the head and marched out into the hallway.

"Your meeting was not a success then, your grace?" Hanris asked, once they were in the privacy of the carriage.

"You could say that," she replied, in sick voice. "There is a game at play here, Hanris, we are late arrivals it would seem. Our task is to find what moves have already been played."

"Indeed, your grace, and if I might interject, it would be beneficial to know who the other players are as well."

She raised her eyebrows at that. "Indeed. Our esteemed monarch has commanded us to remain at the villa until summoned. It would seem he isn't quite finished with us yet."

"That's something at least, your grace," Hanris said.

"It's his seeming lack of knowledge about the Bjornmen that concerns me most, Hanris," she admitted, shaking her head. "I cannot truly believe that he has not received word. What motive could he possibly have for feigning ignorance?"

"What indeed?" Hanris muttered. "I take it the fae were not mentioned?"

"Hardly!" she scoffed. "The man seems not to believe the Bjornmen have invaded, I was not about to bring up monsters escaped from fable and legend."

"A wise move, your grace," Hanris replied but she didn't hear. She was already staring out of the window, her mind churning.

* * *

"Are you certain this is appropriate, your grace?" Hanris asked, as the coach passed through the gates into the Salisbourne estate.

"Appropriate, Hanris?" she replied, with an amused smile.

"My accompanying you, your grace," Hanris explained, as they approached the mansion.

"I've already explained, it will be fine." She took a closer look at the man and realised he was genuinely worried. "It's really quite common, Hanris. You're a professional and, as such, it's expected that you will attend and meet with your counterparts in Salisbourne's household. If Freyton hadn't been such a frightful bore, you'd have done this half a dozen times each year." She paused and looked at him. "Surely you've done this before? Not in Freyton's employ, obviously, but prior to working for him?"

Hanris cleared his throat and looked away. "Not as such, your grace. I've...well, I've never been what you might call a people person."

Selena nodded. "Well, I think it's time that changed. Can't have you spending your whole life tallying figures now, can we?"

"Apparently not, your grace." His response was almost lost in the crunching of gravel as the carriage slowed to a halt and Salisbourne's men opened the door for them. Selena took the hand of a young footman and stepped out carefully, so as not to stand on the hem of her elegant evening gown.

The dressmaker's fee had made Hanris blanch, but she had to admit it was worth it. The deep forest green colour set off her flaming red hair and the cut almost, but not quite, concealed the fact she was pregnant. It had taken her some time to explain what she wanted to achieve there. Designing a dress to look as if it had just failed to conceal a pregnant waistline, whilst still ensuring that she looked fabulous, was no easy task. It was also cut almost scandalously low, obviously so. This again, was by design. An overly blatant attempt to draw the eyes away from the waist.

Selena felt the blood rise in her cheeks as she stepped out of the carriage and felt the eyes of the footman upon her. She murmured her thanks, something Freyton would never have done. The man had possessed the social graces of a sewer rat, often present, but seldom welcome.

Salisbourne himself came out to greet them on the front steps, beaming as he took in her dress. "You look positively ravishing, my dear," he said, as he bent to kiss her cheek.

"Why, thank you, Thomas," she purred. "Impending motherhood allegedly gives a woman a certain glow. I've yet to notice it myself. It's possibly because most mornings lately I spend more time clapping a hand over my mouth and searching for a chamber pot than looking into mirrors!"

The earl gave her a startled look and then burst into laughter. It was a deep, genuine laugh that came from the belly. "Selena, you always were the most fun to sit near at dinner. It doesn't look like anything has changed." He looked past her to Hanris. "And is this your man here?"

"My chamberlain," she explained. "Hanris, this is my cousin, Thomas."

"You honour me, my lord," Hanris said, with a short bow.

The earl smiled a polite acknowledgement. "I believe my staff have their own modest dinner planned which, of course, you are welcome to attend. My man, Adams, is always looking for someone to sample the wine cellars with. Be careful though, I have it on good authority he can talk your ear off."

He took Selena's arm and escorted her through to the dining room. Salisbourne's home was warm, both from the décor and from the large fireplace that almost filled one entire end of the dining hall.

The rich carpets and dark oak panelling provided a sense of homely comforts. Neither were especially in fashion these days, but they drew Selena's mind back to happier times, to a childhood she barely remembered, a time before things had gone so terribly awry for the Browntrees.

"It's a quiet affair this time, my dear," Thomas explained, as he waved her into the room. "Agnes is away at the country house and so I could dispense with half of the insipid toadies she seems to delight in surrounding herself with. I think you'll probably recognise a few faces, though."

The room was awash with conversation and at least forty people sat at the long table. He waved away the steward and pulled the chair out for her himself, before moving to his own place opposite her.

She smiled at the older lady on her left and glanced at the empty seat on her right, before beckoning the wine steward over. She gave him discreet instructions for her wine to be extremely well watered, then turned as a portly man in his middle years took the seat on her right.

"You must be little Selena, then," he said, with a broad smile on his red face. "Tommy told us all about you last night." The room was warm, but not so warm as to justify the faint sheen of sweat on his brow. "Jantson," he said, by way of introduction. "Earl of someplace you've most likely never heard of, but we don't bother with those things at Tommy's dos. Stuff and nonsense, anyway." His laugh was infectious and was already relaxing her.

"Oh," he said, peering past her at her other neighbour. "A word from the wise. Don't bother trying to talk to her. She's as deaf as a post. Isn't that right, Agatha?" He raised his voice to almost a shout, leaning into the table and waving at the elderly lady.

"What's that?" she replied, with a bemused look.

"Deaf!" Jantson yelled again, as Selena looked on with an uncomfortable smile.

"Me?" Agatha asked, loudly. "Oh, yes. Deaf as a post. I only come for the wine!" She burst into laughter and raised her glass again, motioning to the servant to refill it.

"She'll be snoring into her plate before the third course," Jantson snorted.

The first course was served at that moment, saving Selena from the effort of trying to respond to the odd man. A cold beetroot soup, exotically spiced.

"It's cold!" protested Jantson, grabbing for a napkin.

"It's supposed to be," Selena laughed, unable to help herself. "It's called 'pasha', I think. I believe it's from Feldane."

"I know it's supposed to be warm down there, but surely they still need to cook?" Jantson muttered, pushing the bowl aside. "We'll all be peeing pink in the morning, if we eat this." He snorted at his own joke, missing Selena's slightly repulsed expression.

"So tell me, Selena, what's it actually like over in the Eastern Reaches. You hear such stories about endless winters and raiders coming from the sea all bundled up in bearskins."

"I don't know that it's as barbaric as the tales say. It does take a little getting used to. Not quite the pinnacle of civilisation, you might say," she replied, sipping at her wine. The servant had paid attention, she noticed. Though it was as dark a red as Jantson's, she could barely taste the wine itself.

"That's right, Tommy mentioned you'd spent some time here in your youth."

"My youth?" A dangerous smile curved her lips.

"Not to say you aren't young," he sputtered, as his face turned red.

"Of course not," she murmured. "That would be outrageously rude." She glanced up at him and then burst into laughter at his stricken expression.

Dinner was pleasant, with Jantson proving to be an entertaining companion, and it was almost with regret that she pushed away the remains of the last course, a deliciously light lemon torte.

"Shall we adjourn, gentlemen?" Thomas called out across the table. Selena groaned to herself. She'd forgotten this ridiculous tradition. The men would now sequester themselves drinking brandy and smoking stourweed in their pipes. Meanwhile, she would be trapped with a collection of old dears and trophy wives with nothing to talk about save the latest fashions.

She rose with the others as Thomas left the table, and stepped backwards away from the crowd and into a corner as she pondered what to do. She lost sight of Jantson and sipped her wine as she tried to avoid being drawn into conversation. A few guests had remained at the table, nibbling on a selection of cheeses and nuts. She wondered if she should join them.

A tap on the shoulder and Thomas was there again. "I thought we'd get the gossips busy and then slope off for a private chat. There are a couple of people I want you to meet."

Selena tried to conceal her relief, but his wry smile as he escorted her to the door told her plainly that she'd failed.

Jantson was in the hallway with two other men she didn't recognise. One seemed vaguely familiar, but she couldn't place him.

"You've met Jantson, of course," Thomas said, as the fat man smiled. "This is Raysh and I expect you've probably heard of Rentrew?"

She smiled politely in greeting before it clicked. "Baron Rentrew?"

"So very nice to meet you, your grace," Rentrew said, with a small bow.

"The pleasure is mine, I assure you, my lord," she replied, with genuine pleasure.

"Oh, don't start all that nonsense, Rentrew," Salisbourne sighed. "We're all titled here. If we start Gracing and Lording, we'll never get to the end of a sentence." He turned to Selena. "I've a nice private study where we can all have a proper conversation. I have a feeling we have a few mutual interests that should be discussed."

Salisbourne's private study was filled with the smell of old books, whiskey and stourweed smoke. He arranged some chairs around a small table and poured drinks for them. Selena shook her head behind her raised hand as she refused the offer.

"Selena here, as I'm sure you know, Rentrew, has been trying to get in to see our beloved king for the past three days."

He looked at Selena, nodding towards Rentrew as he spoke. "Rentrew has been trying to get in for over a month now. He began by sending missives, then emissaries and finally upped sticks and came himself." He looked back to both Rentrew and Raysh. "She managed to get in to see him this morning."

"How could you possibly...?" Selena burst out, before managing to stop herself. Salisbourne gave a dry chuckle when he saw her expression. "Because it's my business to know, my dear."

"I'm going to be frank, Selena," Rentrew said, leaning forward to set his glass back on the table. "I know all about the Bjornmen. I've had to deal with some attacks myself, though nothing on the scale you've been facing. I've lost five or six villages and more troops than I really care to put a number to. What concerns me far more, however, is the lack of any response from Pieter."

Selena glanced around the table. Everyone's attention was fixed on her. What exactly had she wandered into here?

"The response has not been what I would have expected," she replied. It never hurts to be cautious.

"What was his reaction today?" Salisbourne asked, resting his glass on his leg as he leaned forward.

"He dismissed it," Selena replied. "As I recall, he branded it a Browntree scheme to grab crown funds."

"Bloody fool," Raysh snorted into his glass.

"That's it? He just dismissed it entirely?" Rentrew said, his eyes betraying just how shocked he was. This was a man who should never play cards, Selena decided.

"As I've said, he implied it was a scheme. To be honest, he spent more time questioning my right to the regency."

"Foolishness," Raysh muttered. "Something must be done, Salisbourne. The man has spent months ignoring the business of the kingdom. If Feldane presses north now, who knows where it will end?"

"Calm down, Raysh." Thomas held his hands out as if slowing a startled horse. "We've all been hearing rumours about the Bjornmen, Selena. We've been hearing other things too. Fantastical things that I can't bring myself to believe."

"What is this?" she asked, looking from face to face. "What have I been pulled into here?"

"Call us a small collection of concerned lords," Salisbourne said, with a grim smile.

"You can't have moved that far already," she breathed, sensing the meaning behind the words.

"In thought, perhaps," Raysh spoke up. "Not yet in deed. Tell us the truth, Selena. What is really going on in the Eastern Reaches?"

"Before I do, tell me who I'm speaking to here? Is it really just you three?"

Raysh and Salisbourne exchanged wry smiles. "I told you she was never one to tangle with," Salisbourne chuckled.

"No, you've seen right through us all, Selena. We each represent certain interests. No, *represent* is too strong of a word. We have the ear of certain interest groups. Rentrew is in close contact with a group of eastern lords and landowners. Jantson has the ear of a group in the west. Raysh is part of a stronger, more influential consortium of merchants and lords reaching down into Feldane. As for me, well, I have my fingers in many pies, but my main interests have always been here in the capital."

She took a breath and collected herself. A push here, a prod there, she told herself. "Fine, gentlemen. Let's see if I can't bring you all up to speed with things. Before we begin though, I think perhaps we ought to discuss just what it is that you can offer in return. My duchy is, after all, on the front lines, as it were." Their eyes widened. Apparently, none of them would be any good as a card partner. They were already invested in the potential knowledge though, she could see that. This was just another round of games and she had always excelled at games.

CHAPTER FOURTEEN

Ylsriss clung to Joran, her fingernails digging into his flesh like claws. The drop yawned beneath her. She could almost feel it calling to her, whispering to her to just let go and allow it to embrace her.

She forced herself to open her eyes and look down. The rational part of her mind tried to tell her that it wasn't that far to the bottom. The impact would hurt, it might even kill her, but the ravine wasn't the bottomless chasm her fear was trying to convince her it was.

"Ylsriss," Joran rasped again. "You've got to let go of me. We'll both fall." He reached up, leaning awkwardly to the right to compensate for the loss of support, and began to prise her fingers away from his throat.

"Just hold on to the vines for a moment." He pulled himself onto the huge metal beam and twisted to face her. "Just take deep breaths for a minute. We're in no hurry, okay?"

She did as he said. Lords of Blood, Sea and Sky, she hated herself like this. The loss of control was enough to make her scream. She wasn't this weak. She wouldn't allow herself to be this weak, not again. Ylsriss drew a deep breath. She could use this, take the anger and let it consume the fear. She opened her eyes again and glared at the metal span, ignoring the way that Joran flinched away from her.

"Let's get this over with, shall we?" she said, from between clenched teeth.

She examined the span, forcing herself to ignore the drop. It was ancient and pitted deeply with rust, but so large that it was unlikely it couldn't support them. The beam was easily two feet wide and three feet thick. Another section extended below them at a right angle, dropping into the ravine before burying itself into the side of the chasm. The weight of the beam alone would have pulled it apart, had it been anything less than sound.

"This must have been here for centuries. Look at the rust!" She prodded at the metal, testing its resistance.

"It will be fine, Ylsriss," he said, reaching for her.

"I can't walk across that, Joran." She snatched her hand back as he started to pull her onto the beam again.

"We're not going to walk. Look, we can sit on it and pull ourselves forward." He lowered himself down until he sat astride the metal, tilting slightly to the left to make up for the angle. She cursed and followed his lead.

It was slow-going, but they managed to move themselves across the beam reasonably well. The main problem, she noticed, was that the rust caught on the thin fabric of their leggings, scratching and rubbing at the flesh beneath.

"Talk to me, Joran," she panted, as she shifted forwards again. "I need the distraction. What do you think this thing is?"

"I don't know. It's clearly been made by somebody, but I can't imagine why. Or who. That's the real question, isn't it? Who?"

"How do you mean?" she grunted, as she shifted forward again. He didn't answer, but turned slightly to look past her. She followed his gaze, but there was nothing to see except the trees at the top of the slope they'd come down.

"I thought I heard something," he muttered, in response to her look. He shrugged and began shifting forward once more.

The feeling began as she started to move again. It was vague and nebulous at first, but soon coalesced into the knowledge that they were being watched. Before she'd moved another few feet forward, she was certain and she froze for a second before twisting around to look again.

It stood at the top of the slope, staring down at them with fascination in its black eyes. It was different to the others she'd seen. The horns were longer, about a foot in length, and extended out of its hair and curved towards the back of its head. Its short beard was shot through with grey and a slow smile spread across its face as it saw her looking.

"Joran!" she hissed, and pointed up at the satyr.

"Shit," he gasped.

The creature seemed content to watch them for the moment and made no move towards them. As she looked, she realised it was not alone. A tiny purple figure was floating in the air next to it. It was only as the leaves of the trees shifted, sending down a shaft of sunlight, that she caught sight of its wings.

Realisation hit her. "Joran, it's daylight!"

He grunted in response and continued to move forward. "Let's get off this thing. If they decide to come for us, I'd rather be on solid ground," he said.

She saw the sense in this and shifted forwards again. They were more than halfway across the ravine now. The shock of seeing the satyr and whatever it was with it had eclipsed her fear of falling.

Joran had stopped ahead of her and she glanced over her shoulder at the creature before she spoke. "What are you doing?"

"Just give me a second," he grunted, his shoulders straining as he worked at something in front of him.

"Joran, keep going!" she cried, as she saw the winged figure soar up into the air and then swoop towards them, ignoring the cry that came from the satyr.

Joran glanced over one shoulder, then jerked backwards as whatever he was pulling on gave way. He started to make his way along the beam again. Ylsriss hurried behind him, wobbling as she traded balance for speed. She swivelled slightly to take a fleeting look at the thing flying slowly through the air towards them. It had the form of a tiny woman, perfect in every detail, albeit winged and with skin tinted pale violet.

Suddenly, Joran turned and shoved her sideways off the beam. She just had time for a startled scream before she crashed into the jumble of tree roots and packed earth that made up the side of the gorge.

Ylsriss thrust her hands into the tangle of roots, grasping blindly as her feet scrambled and kicked, trying to find purchase. She caught hold of one and, as she came to a halt, she realised that the slope was far less steep on this side of the ravine. She would have stopped soon anyway.

She glared up at Joran but the angry words died on her lips. He stood on the beam, his knees bent for balance, using a long sliver of rusted metal as a makeshift dagger. Blood ran freely from half a dozen wounds on his face and body, as the purple creature darted around him, the snarl of hate seeming out of place on her beautiful face.

"Sabeth!" the satyr screamed, from the far side of the ravine. He seemed to be unwilling to cross it. Joran slashed at the tiny woman with his blade, missing again, before jerking backwards in pain. A line of blood appeared on his cheek, just a finger's width from his eye.

It's playing with him, Ylsriss realised, like a cat would toy with a mouse for hours before finally killing it. As Joran staggered back from another lightning quick slash, she looked frantically about for something she could use to help him. There was nothing. She could throw mud at it, or even a stone, but the thing was so fast that she could barely see it most of the time. The chances of hitting it would be tiny.

The satyr was still screaming out the single word over and over, a note of panic in its voice. It was the creature's name, she realised. Wrapping one hand around a loose root, she grabbed up a clod of dried earth with the other. "Sabeth!" she screamed, as she hurled the mud in its direction. She missed. Not by a few inches, but by a foot or more. The creature slowed for just a second, as it glanced in her direction, and Joran swung hard with the rusted shard of metal. The blow tore the tiny figure out of the air, like a stone striking a butterfly, and she landed in front of Ylsriss in a broken heap. The creature lay still, twisted and ruined, but beautiful even in death.

The satyr screamed like a wounded animal and then fell silent. He looked left and right before fixing them with a venomous glare, then ran back into the trees.

They made their way up the bank and collapsed onto the soft grass. Ylsriss pulled herself up and looked at Joran. His wounds, whilst painful, looked superficial. They were shallow cuts and none were bleeding excessively.

"You *pushed* me!" she said, as she pulled a horn knife from the pack and used it to cut strips of material from a spare shirt to make bandages.

"I'm sorry, Ylsriss. I couldn't think of any other way," Joran managed.

"You could have warned me first!" He looked up at her, silent for a moment, and then began to laugh.

"I can't see how this is funny, Joran," she protested, but he just laughed all the more. Finally, she kicked at him.

"Damn it, Ylsriss," he howled, as he jerked away from her. "That hurt!"

"Try being pushed off that thing!" She stabbed angrily with one finger in the direction of the beam.

"Alright, I'm sorry. I had to do something to get past you."

"Hmmm." She had nothing to say to that, but she'd be damned if she was going to let him know that.

"Come on, we should get going," he said, wincing as he stood.

"Are you sure?" Ylsriss asked. "I mean, you're in a bit of a state."

"It's not going to get any better here." He shrugged.

"But doesn't it hurt?"

"Like tiny ribbons of fire, but that's not going to stop just because we do." He shouldered his pack and made his way into the trees. Ylsriss paused, shooting one last look at the forest that had swallowed the satyr, then followed.

She caught up with him easily. "Joran, do you realise that it was still daylight when they attacked?"

"I hadn't thought about it, but yes, I suppose it was," he replied.

She ducked to avoid a branch. "Doesn't that strike you as weird? I thought the fae avoided the sun? And the satyr...did you see its eyes?"

"I was a little busy at the time, Ylsriss."

"Oh, sorry. Well, they were dark, almost black."

He nodded, unsurprised. "Yes, it means that he doesn't have any power. I've only seen it once before, in satyrs returning from the chase. They get so intent on the hunt that they ignore the fact the sun is leaching the power from them."

"What about the other thing? It looked like a fairy from a children's tale." She gave him a funny look as he snorted with laughter.

"Where do you think the tales came from, Ylsriss? It was one of the fae'reeth. They're quite rare, I think. It's only the second one I've ever seen."

She nodded. "Every time I think I've started to come to terms with being here, I realise how little I know." She said it as a joke, expecting a laugh in reply. It was only when the laugh didn't come that she realised how true it was.

They passed through the woods at the fastest pace that Joran could manage. His wounds didn't slow him much, but Ylsriss was reluctant to hurry him along. She spent as much time looking over her shoulder for the vanished satyr as she did watching where she was going.

The wall reappeared late in the afternoon as they rounded a low hill. They drew to a halt, peering out around the tree trunks like mice peeking into the grain store. Now that they were closer, Ylsriss realised that what she'd seen wasn't a city wall at all. It was the wall of a building itself. A city, some of it in ruins, stretched out before them and the breath caught in her throat as she took in the sight. No wall surrounded the city, or ever had, from what she could see. It made sense though, she realised. What was there here for a wall to defend against?

The city extended further than they could see, with grand buildings and soaring towers in the distance. The peaked roofs of the strange, yellow-walled houses were covered with red tiles and sprouted stubby chimney pots. Trees appeared to be growing out of some of the dwellings and large sections of the city had tumbled down, the stones scattering on the ground.

"What do you think?" Ylsriss asked.

His sigh said it all. "I don't know. It looks abandoned but can we really be sure of that from here? What if we're just walking into another Tir Rhu'thin?"

"Surely we'd have seen some sign of life by now?" Ylsriss glanced at his face. He was chewing his lip, something he always seemed to do when he couldn't make up his mind. "Look, if there was anyone living there, we'd see smoke from the chimneys." She stopped, the last word falling dead from her mouth.

"Chimneys. Why are there chimneys?" she whispered to herself.

"What?" Joran asked, looking at her as if she'd gone mad. "Why does that matter?"

"Think about it, Joran," she said, her eyes sparkling with excitement. "When have you ever seen the fae use fire. *We* don't even use fire! Why would there be chimneys?"

"There wouldn't be," he said slowly, drawing out the words as he puzzled through to the end of it, "unless it wasn't a fae city at all."

"Exactly!" She beamed at him.

"It's still a risk," he insisted.

"Everything can be a risk, Joran. Sometimes even breathing can be a risk." She held his shoulders and forced him to look at her. "Look, that satyr is still out there somewhere. If this place really was a human city, maybe we can find something to help us. If nothing else, we'll be able to rest up for a day or two."

"Fine, have it your way." He growled at her.

"I usually do." She smiled into his scowl and led the way.

As they drew closer to the city, the sheer age of the place became more obvious. Ylsriss soon realised that it had not known ruin through war or anything similar, but had simply crumbled due to the passage of time. Plants, similar to ivy but with bright purple leaves and sapphire blue flowers, snaked over the walls, thrusting their tendrils into the gaping holes that had once held windows.

The forest seemed hard at work reclaiming the city. Trees now stood in the middle of roads, having shouldered the thick stones aside as they searched for the fleeting sun.

Ylsriss exchanged an awed look with Joran as they stepped onto a street which was half-covered in moss. Grass poked through the cracks between the stones. "Which way?" she asked, in a low voice, although she couldn't have explained why she felt the need to speak so softly.

"Let's stick to the main roads for now," Joran suggested. She nodded. That made sense. The city was far larger than it had looked from the trees and the last thing they needed was to get lost.

They wandered deeper into the heart of the place, gawking like children at the moss-covered fountains and leaf-strewn squares. She was still leading the way, despite having asked him which way they should go.

They both froze at the sound of hooves clattering on stone. She pulled him behind her as she slipped into a doorway, only to emerge laughing, as a herd of deer stared at them inquisitively with liquid eyes. Ylsriss gazed at them in wonder. They seemed utterly unafraid - they had never learned to be fearful of man.

The arrow flew past her ear and buried itself into the throat of the closest beast. She screamed as the creature fell to the cobbles. It bucked and writhed as the rest fled. Ylsriss gave Joran a shocked look, as he lowered the bow and rushed forward to retrieve the arrow. "What?" he asked, as he noticed her expression. "We need the meat, Ylsriss."

He was right. She didn't even know why she'd reacted like that. She might be a city girl, but she was under no illusions as to where the food from the markets came from.

"I'll go and find us somewhere to camp," she said. The grisly work of butchering a deer was not something she wanted to watch. He grunted in response, without looking up from the task.

She wandered along the streets. The doorways of the partially collapsed buildings hung open, the doors themselves having long since gone to rot. As she moved farther along, however, she could see the state of the buildings steadily improving, as if the outer edges of the city had born the brunt of the decline.

Popping her head through one of the closest doorways, she saw a home from another age. It had been empty for so long that any smell of decay had long since gone. All that remained was a faint mustiness. She made her way into the building, glancing nervously at the roof once or twice, although it seemed sturdy.

A kitchen and two small bedrooms complete with the crumbling remains of the furniture. Mounted high on one wall, a moonorb hung, dark and forgotten. Exploring the house was like being in a family's grave. This had once been a home, not just a building. People had lived, loved and laughed here. She looked around, half expecting to see shadowy figures lurking in the doorway. Hugging herself against the sudden chill, she made her way back out onto the street.

They sheltered in the remains of a shop of some kind that night. The contents had mouldered away but the counter was still in place. Joran had raised an eyebrow and even argued a little when she had insisted on staying there rather than in one of the houses, but she was not about to spend the night surrounded by other people's memories. Wood, at least, was plentiful as the shop still had more than one door in place. They roasted hunks of venison on sticks over the fire, and she felt warm and full for the first time in weeks.

Joran fell asleep almost before he had swallowed his last mouthful and Ylsriss stared into the fire, listening to the distant sounds of the crickets. How odd that, in this other world, there would be crickets. The sound took her to another place, another time. Memories of nights with Klöss, in their cabin above the shipyards, played through her head. She followed the thought onwards, though she knew where it would lead, to loss and to pain. Joran slept on, snoring a soft accompaniment to the sound of her tears, as she allowed the barriers to fall. She let herself think of Klöss and Effan. She could almost smell her baby and feel the softness of his cheek, the way his fingers would open and close over her skin as he fed from her. The pain was an ache inside her. Part of her soul was missing. It had been taken from her and that theft had left a wound that would never heal.

Morning brought fresh wonders. The city was a place of awe, a bizarre combination of the everyday and the exotic. Wells stood in squares, the remnants of decayed buckets still sat beside them under arches of giant moonorbs that hung from curved stone supports.

In one house, they found a large runeplate that covered a section of the kitchen counter. The glyphs were dead and unresponsive but, at first glance, they were identical to the ones on the segment they carried. Ylsriss compared them with interest, while

Joran waited impatiently at the door.

"Look, Joran," she called. "It's not quite the same. This section here was never on our runeplates in the camp." She pointed to where the glyphs extended over the edge of the plate, trailing down to create a sequence of sigils on the side of the device.

"I wonder why they are so rare here? It's like these people relied more on wood for heat and cooking."

"Yeah, interesting," he said, his eyes still on the street. She sighed and followed him out.

On several occasions, they discovered charred stones at the end of a street. A blackened area extended out from a small crater, as if the ground had been scorched by some unimaginably hot fire that had burned down into the very stones.

Other times, they discovered large circular stone plates set flat against the stones of the streets. The plates were surrounded by glyphs as dead as those on the runeplate. They were obviously important and their placement close to a wall implied they had been used regularly, but Ylsriss couldn't puzzle out what they were. Joran spent a full five minutes trying to make one of the stones move. He could see the direction that they were supposed to shift in from the scars in the stones but, try as he might, he couldn't budge it. Ylsriss tried hard not to let her smile show when he gave up in disgust.

They moved each night, never sleeping in the same place twice. As they explored the city, Joran frequently checked behind them to make sure they weren't leaving tracks. He needn't have bothered, so far as she could tell. The cobbled streets carried no sign of their passage that wasn't erased with the next gust of wind.

They'd split up on the third day. They could cover the ground faster and, if Ylsriss was honest with herself, Joran's constant nagging to move on from the things that intrigued her was beginning to wear.

She'd found she enjoyed the solitude. It was hard to explain, but the silence of the city had a peaceful quality to it, as if the city itself was sleeping, waiting only for someone to wake it. Something else was niggling away at her though, and she stopped to look behind her on more than other occasion, certain she was being followed or watched.

It was towards the end of the first week that Joran came to find her. Ylsriss looked up from the runeplate she was studying in the kitchen of the large house as she heard her name echoing. She sighed in frustration and looked closely at the runes on the side of the plate and then at the block in her hand. It was made of a strange black stone, almost glass-like, and she'd never seen anything like it before. Glyphs were etched into three sides of it and she'd just discovered that the series on one side bore a striking similarity to the glyphs on the side of the runeplate.

"Ylsriss!" the call came again, closer this time. She muttered darkly and made her way out, taking the glass block with her. He turned into the street just as she stepped out of the house, a lucky coincidence that would stop him yelling any more, at least.

"Ylsriss," he gasped, as he drew close. His face was flushed and he'd obviously been running. She felt fear touch her for a moment, as she wondered if the satyr had found its way around the ravine, but then she realised his eyes were glinting with excitement.

"What is it?" she asked. His enthusiasm was contagious and a smile lit her face.

"You have to come and see this!" He grabbed her hand and led her down the street at a run.

"What?" She laughed, tugging at his arm, but he wouldn't let go.

"You'll see soon enough. I wouldn't do it justice if I tried to describe it, anyway."

They raced through the silent streets, kicking up wind-tossed leaves as they made their way towards the centre of the city. The buildings grew steadily grander and more opulent, reaching up to three or four floors in height. He'd obviously explored far more of the place than she had, but then he didn't stop to examine things. He looked at something once and then moved on.

The square was huge, easily the grandest she'd seen, and showed almost no signs of age. A few doors hung off their hinges and there were empty windows in some of the frames where glass should have been, but the area was in a far better state than the outskirts of the city. The buildings around the edge of the square looked as if they had been fine shops and she could pick out at least one inn. Joran ignored all of them and pulled her towards the largest building.

It was a massive edifice, fully five floors high, and constructed of brilliant white stone, set with columns and ornate carvings. One end of it appeared to have collapsed completely and rubble spilled out into the square.

He led her up the steps and in through a gaping hole which, from the look of the scraps of rotten wood that still remained, had once contained large double doors.

The entrance hall was grand. Even with the leaves that had blown in littering the floor, and the centuries' worth of dust and grime clinging to the walls, Ylsriss could see how opulent this place had once been. Joran fell silent and walked backwards so he could see her expression.

The dim light of the twilight sky soon faded as they proceeded inside, and Joran shocked her by producing a moonorb, activating it by tracing the glyphs with a deft hand.

"Where did you get..." she began.

He stopped her. "In here. It's the least of it, trust me."

They made their way through a maze of passages and corridors, passing through rooms filled with semi-rotten furniture and rugs turned to a rotten ruin. Finally, he led her up a set of stairs and stopped in front of a thick wooden door. He gave her a broad smile and pushed it open.

The room was lit with burning moonorbs which had been hung up at regular intervals. What caught Ylsriss's attention, however, were the books. The walls were lined with shelf upon shelf of books.

She rushed over and pulled out a heavy tome at random before Joran could stop her. The pages crumbled like ash between her fingers as she opened it, until she held little more than the binding.

"They almost always do that. Leave them. This is what I wanted to show you." He ushered her over to a workbench in the middle of the room. A small block of stone, carved with intricate glyphs, lay in the centre of it. The work was clearly unfinished and chips from the stone were scattered on the bench. Next to it, there were racks containing high-quality chisels and other tools. Further to one side, there was a lectern with a huge book lying open upon it.

She moved closer as he held the moonorb over the pages. "It's not paper," he said, grinning. "It looks like it, but it's something different. Look!" He reached out and turned the page. The material held together. It was as strong as if it had been made yesterday.

She lowered her eyes to the writing. The page was filled with huge sections of text, as well as diagrams. She looked up at him in awe and then back to the book. The pages were thick and had an almost metallic feel to them. A tiny series of glyphs was etched into the uppermost corner of each page.

"I can read this!" she gasped. "Not every word, but I can understand some of it. It's like a really old kind of Islik, a bit like they speak on the Far Isles."

He pointed behind her to a stone rack set against the wall. "There are more there too."

His smile lit his face and his eyes were filled with a joy at having surprised her, but she barely noticed it. Her attention was already being drawn back to the archaic script.

From that moment on, she spent almost every waking hour in the library. The book was like a gateway to another world. It hinted at a power she was only just beginning to perceive and she devoured the information on the pages with a hunger that surprised her.

Joran lost interest in it quickly. He visited with tales of the things he'd discovered, and forced her to eat and drink. After a day or two, he nagged her into taking breaks to join him for walks around the city, but she barely registered the things he took her to see. A bridge over an empty riverbed. An ornate garden, the plants running wild around the circle of tall stones that stood at its centre. An entire section of the city with buildings that were fire-scarred and blackened with soot. All too soon, her eyes would drift back in the direction of the library, and his voice would trail off in mid-sentence before he took her back to the library and the books.

It was another three days before she left the library. She'd studied late into each night, reading by the fading light of a moonorb. She'd drained four already and there were only two more remaining. The text was maddening. Some sections were so close to Islik, it was like talking to Tristan. Others had barely a recognisable word, using odd letters she'd never seen before, or additional syllables added onto the beginnings or ends of the words.

"Where do you want to go?" Joran asked, a cautious smile on his face. He didn't seem at all surprised by her desire to wander the city that early in the morning.

"There's something I want to try," she replied, as she picked up a small bag and headed towards the entrance.

He hurried to keep up with her as she marched through the square and into what had clearly once been a residential backstreet. She stopped at the end of a row of houses. The sky was still a pale twilight. Sunrise was still four hours or more away. She moved towards the wall, her steps small and slow. Joran frowned as he watched her. Then he saw it.

"You opened one?" he blurted, pointing at the circular stone that had somehow been shifted to one side. "How did you even move it? When did you do this?"

"Last night. It was a full moon and I didn't want to miss it," she said, her tone plain and matter-of-fact.

He gave her a hurt look and muttered something to himself, but she ignored it. She was already moving towards the shallow hole that had been revealed when she had moved the stone plate. It contained a silvery circle of metal which was completely covered in glyphs, most of which were a mystery to her. The glyphs that were etched into the stones surrounding the hole, however, these she understood.

She set down her bag and pulled the curious stone block that she'd found near the runeplate out of it. "Here goes," she breathed, as she traced the series of glyphs.

Joran yelped and leapt back as they flared to life, the characters burning bright green or amber as she traced them. She looked back over her shoulder to make sure he was clear, before touching the final glyph. The circular cover stone slid back over the silvery capture plate, making a sullen grinding sound as it slipped back into position.

She grinned at Joran's wide eyes. "Watch this but please keep quiet. There's a lot for me to remember and plenty of things that could go wrong here." A mute nod was the only response she got.

She examined the glyphs again before setting the glassy block down in the small depression at the edge of the series of characters. Her fingers moved slowly, carefully, and she became aware she was chanting under her breath as she worked, naming each sigil in turn as she activated the sequence.

Joran cried out again, as the channel that had been cut into the stone blazed with light for a moment before dulling as the conduit awoke for the first time in untold ages. The glassy block began to pulsate, as the glyphs on it drank the power in greedily. In a matter of moments, it was done and the illuminated symbols grew darker before finally fading completely.

Ylsriss picked up the block and turned it over in her hands, before looking at Joran in triumph. "Well?" she asked.

"Well, what?" He sounded frantic, like he might bolt at any moment.

"Aren't you going to congratulate me? It worked!"

"I don't even know what you did. Except nearly blind me."

"Don't be such a big baby," she snorted. "It wasn't that bright. What I did was infuse this." She waved the block at him.

"In-what?"

"Infuse," she repeated, drawing out the unfamiliar word. "Look, come back to the library with me and I'll show you."

She led the way back, almost at a run, as the day grew brighter.

"Okay, how much do you know about the glyphs?"

"Not much," he shrugged. "The same as anyone, really. The fae have a way to make them work. They take some of the power they get from the moonlight and somehow put it into the glyphs. It works for a while and then they have to put more power in."

"That's one way of putting it, I suppose." She pointed up at a dark moonorb. "Fetch that one down for me, will you?" He took it off the wall without comment and passed it to her.

"The people who lived here knew an awful lot about glyphs. The things that I've read suggest that they knew far more than even the fae. Most importantly, they learned to power their glyphs directly."

She knelt, setting both the moonorb and the glassy block down on the floor before her. With the fingers of one hand, she traced a series of glyphs cut into the block and a soft light flared from them. Lifting the moonorb and turning it over in her hands, she muttered to herself, searching for the right place. "Ah, here it is."

She pressed a small section of the base of the moonorb onto the glowing block. Lights pulsed both within the block and on the base of the moonorb, as different glyphs lit up and, within a matter of moments, the orb was glowing brightly.

"Lords of Blood, Sea and Sky, Ylsriss, that's incredible!" he gasped.

"It's more than that, Joran." Her smile shone as she spoke. "Don't you see? I could create a moonorb, if I had the time. The people who lived here powered their own glyphs. They didn't need the fae at all!"

Chapter Fifteen

They stayed in one of the finer mansions close to the library again that night. Since Ylsriss had begun studying there, it had made sense to stay within easy reach of it. She suspected that the only reason they moved house every night was because Joran was bored.

"Do you ever wonder what happened to the people here?" he asked, looking up from his plate.

"How do you mean?" she said, when she'd finished her mouthful of venison.

"Well, think about it. The city is largely intact, isn't it? Some things are broken or have fallen down, but others are fine. This house. That plate." He pointed as he spoke.

She sat up at that, her jaw frozen mid-chew as he continued. "It's not a city that looks like it was taken by force. I mean, I don't really know what that would look like, but if there had been fighting, I'd expect more damage. Even the section that's all fire-scarred looks like it was burned more by accident than as the result of an attack. If there was no war, then where are all the people?"

"I don't know," she admitted, swallowing hard and reaching for the water. "Maybe they left for some reason? For that matter, we don't know for certain that we're even alone here. We've not explored all of it."

"I have," he said, chuckling as her eyes widened. "Well, I have to do something while you're wrapped up in those books all day long." Another laugh, this one short and uncomfortable, escaped him. "As for being alone, I'm not entirely sure that we are."

"What do you mean? The satyr?" She set her food down, no longer hungry.

"No," he replied. "At least, I don't think so. I've had an intense feeling of being watched a few times now."

"Oh, we all get that from time to time." Her laugh sounded as false to her as she was sure it did to him.

"Maybe you're right. I'll admit I had the same thought to start with. It happened too often for me to just brush it off though, so I started being careful. Setting traps.

Nothing harmful," he added quickly, seeing her expression. "I just wanted to prove to myself that I wasn't going mad. I wanted to know, one way or the other, if there was anything out there. So I scattered some leaves behind me in a few places, put down some dust. Things like that."

"And?"

"And nothing. The wind usually fouled them anyway." He held up a finger as she sniggered. "Until today."

"What happened?"

"I'd scattered some bits of wood across the road behind me, but I was pretty sure that whoever was following me was avoiding those easily. So this time, I made it obvious. I spread leaves across the road, totally covered it, leaving just a narrow path through the middle. Then I left some really clumsy piles of dirt. Anyone would have seen it, hunter or not. It was obvious that it was put there as a trap of some kind. Anyway, they avoided that easily enough but what they didn't see was that the dirt I'd covered in leaves was wet. I got a clear footprint."

Ylsriss was silent for a moment, thinking. "A foot though, right? Not a hoof?"

"Yes, definitely a foot. A bare foot, though."

"So, what do we do? Do you think it's a human?" Ylsriss asked, drawing idly in the ring of liquid her earthenware cup had left on the wooden table.

"How would I tell?" Joran shrugged. "I think your first question is a better one, anyway. What do we do? I think it's time we moved on from here, Ylsriss."

Ylsriss sat back in her chair. The suggestion shocked her and, from the look on Joran's face, the panic rising within her was visible on her own. "Not yet, Joran." She spoke quietly, as if confessing something dreadful.

"Why not?" he asked. "There's nothing here, Ylsriss. We were only supposed to be staying here a day or two to rest up. We've been here too long. We have meat now. We have food to take with us. What if that satyr comes back? What happened to finding Effan?"

"I haven't given up," she said, glaring at him. "It's just…"

"Just what?"

"I don't know. I feel like I'm right on the edge of something. Of discovering something huge." She shook her head, unable to find the words.

"Like what? I mean, it's amazing that you found out how to power the runeplates and moonorbs, but is it really that important?" he asked.

"It's not that. The book hints at it, at there being some purpose for this city." She pushed her chair back and made her way over to the runeplate to make tea from the leaves he'd gathered. It wasn't quite the same as nettle, but it was close enough.

"This city had a design. There are channels of power running under the streets. They ran all over the city, taking the energy from the capture plates to neighbourhoods. But then there are others. There are stronger power channels that make those first ones look tiny, and they all head in the same direction, to the same place." Her eyes were bright with excitement.

"Where do they lead?" he asked.

"You don't have to pretend to be interested for my sake, Joran," she said.

"I'm not," he said, with a sigh. "I still think it's a mistake to stay. I think we should move on. But if you're set on this, then let's find whatever it is as soon as we can and then we can go."

He looked tired, older somehow, she noticed. "Are you sure?"

"No." The years seemed to fall away from him as he laughed and he looked like the young man from the camps again. "No, I'm not sure at all, but if that's what you want, that's what we'll end up doing anyway. Why fight it?"

"Am I that bad?" She wasn't sure whether to be amused or upset.

"You're... tenacious," he said.

"You said that very carefully, Joran." She folded her arms and fixed him with a look.

* * *

Joran wandered the streets in silence. The morning was bright, or as bright as the twilight ever got, with only the smallest clouds in the sky. Birds whistled to each other as he walked and he smiled at the faint noise.

He drifted without direction or purpose, letting his feet take him wherever they would. Ylsriss would have been into a dozen buildings by now, poking around and sticking her nose into things. He preferred to let the city offer its marvels up to him itself. It had become a game he played with himself, wandering aimlessly until the city provided him with a reason to follow a particular path.

His feet took him through now familiar streets, past some of his failed attempts to prove the existence of his watcher. He crossed a twig-covered patch of ground and stepped to the right to avoid the piles of leaves he'd left. He made it halfway down the path, then stopped.

He glanced at the leaves and then up at the roofline. The feeling of being watched had hit him like a wave in strong surf, breaking over him and threatening to drag him under. He could feel the eyes boring into him. It was more than that, though. The passage through the leaves had been on the left when he'd made it. He was being toyed with. He shrugged his bow off his shoulder and nocked a bone-tipped arrow, chiding himself under his breath for not fashioning some tipped with iron, as he'd intended to. Seconds stretched to minutes as he stood, eyes sweeping the street.

He sighed as he let the bowstring relax. His arm had begun to cramp and it was shaking from the tension. The feeling of being watched had eased, anyway. Three careful steps took him out of the leaves, searching the rooftops for any sign of movement, and then he ran. He fled without thought, sprinting through the streets like a panicked child or a small animal. He took corners at random, speeding through streets he'd never even stepped into before until, finally, he collapsed gasping against a doorway.

"Either it's playing with me or I'm going mad," he muttered to himself, as he drank deeply from the small waterskin he carried. He stood and forced himself onwards, eyes and ears alert for any noise or movement.

He crossed the bridge he'd come to with Ylsriss just the other week and stopped beside the gardens. Although they were overgrown, it was still just possible to make out their design. They must have been an impressive sight at one point. The flower beds were still visible, though most of the plants had either spilled out and grown into the pathways, or been smothered by weeds. He made his way down the short flight of stone steps and into the gardens, forcing himself to relax as he walked.

The pillars were massive. Made from roughly hewn stone set on end, they had been arranged in a rough circle. They were a grey stone, contrasting with the pale yellow rock from which the rest of the city was constructed. His fingers traced the surface of the first one as he circled it, wondering at the sheer size of it. It must have taken more than a hundred men to even move it. How they had been transported here was anybody's guess.

There were nine stones in total, each angled slightly so that its broadest side faced the centre. Twelve steps took him into the middle of the circle. He didn't see the stone until he was almost upon it. The grass had grown tall and obscured it. Joran stopped as his foot touched it and he knelt immediately. It was actually a stone plate, wider than his outstretched arms, and every inch of it was covered in tiny, precise glyphs carved deep into the surface. Four stone posts thrust down into the grass at points surrounding the plate, overlapping so they pinned it to the ground.

"The manling's folly." The voice carried a note of sadness, but Joran was so shocked to hear someone else speak, he didn't notice. He spun towards its owner awkwardly from his crouched position and his leg slipped out from under him, tipping him onto his backside.

The fae regarded him evenly for a heartbeat and then began to laugh, a musical sound that held nothing of malice, but which was filled with simple amusement and delight.

Joran scrambled backwards and got to his feet, fumbling with his bow. The fae didn't move, but watched him with mischief dancing in her amber eyes. "Do you see a deer or some other game, little hunter?"

"What do you want with me? I won't go back," Joran managed. The words of the fae tongue felt awkward in his mouth and he spoke haltingly, conscious of how clumsy his phrasing was. The creature wasn't acting as he'd known them. He felt panicked and off balance.

"With you?" the fae asked, mulling the question over, as she leaned against one of the tall stones. "Nothing. Unless you are suggesting something?" Her look was direct and she laughed again as the blush spread over his cheeks. "Put away your weapon, manling. I mean you no harm and your arrow offers me no real hurt anyway." She smiled at him, radiating calm as she spoke.

"Stop it!" he grated, as he felt the edges of her influence working on him.

"I apologise. I had forgotten the tales of how sensitive your kind is. It's been a very long time since any of you dwelt in our realm," she said.

He felt her presence withdraw, the feather-light touch being pulled away. "What do you mean, since my kind dwelt here?"

"It was an age past, by your reckoning. Enough that even I would regard it as long ago." Her voice held something he almost couldn't identify. It sounded so odd coming from the voice of a fae that he couldn't place it until she finished speaking.

It was gentle regret.

He looked at her, expecting more, until she caught his expression and sighed. "Your kind seem much unchanged, manling. Still asking for every little thing to be explained when there is no need. You are the first manling I have encountered in our realm. I believed all your kind had fled."

"I don't understand," Joran admitted.

"This is not unexpected." She gave him a small smile.

Joran shook his head and fought down a laugh. She was nothing like any of the other fae he'd ever met. There was no condescension, no sense of his being worthless when compared to her. She was curious, he could tell that much, but it was only curiosity – just a desire to know. He found himself relaxing and knew there was no hint of the Touch about it.

"What's your name?" he asked, without thinking about it.

"I am named Aervern. Do you yet have your name?" she replied, eyeing him up and down as if unsure of his age.

"My name is Joran," he replied, defensive in spite of himself.

She sat on the grass and patted the ground beside her, motioning for him to join her. He looked around for a moment, although he had no idea what he was looking for, and then sat.

"Will you tell me how you came to be here, young Joran?" Aervern asked. She was cross-legged in the grass, and her tunic was pulled tight against her body. Joran swallowed hard and made a conscious effort to look at her face.

"I escaped the camps near Tir Rhu'thin with a friend, a woman. We've been on the run since then. We spotted this place a few weeks ago and we've been here ever since." His speech slowed as he drew to the end of his sentence, and he became aware of what he was saying. His face went pale, and he gasped and he jerked back away from her, his eyes filled with horror.

"I am sorry, Joran." She appeared as horrified as he did. "Please, you must know that it was not my intent. For us, this is just another part of speech. We use this the same way you would use a smile or raise your eyebrows. Or even touching another." She reached out and stroked his arm as she spoke, and he moved away from her.

"I will work hard to restrain my instincts around you, sweet manling." She shot him a devilish look, and eyed him up and down with an exaggerated leer.

She looked so ridiculous that he couldn't help but laugh. She soon grew serious and his laughter died on his lips.

"I will speak truly to you, Joran. I know nothing of any camps at Tir Rhu'thin. The place is a ruin. It was abandoned more years ago than I can put a number to." Aervern looked more human than fae at that moment and Joran sat in silence as he wondered what to ask first.

"Aervern, where do you come from?" he asked, finally.

"Tira Scyon," she replied. "Far to the kielth."

"The kielth? I don't know that word, I'm sorry."

"That way," she waved vaguely.

"It's a long way then?" he pushed gently.

"A very long way, yes." She seemed distracted by something and kept looking over his body and his arms.

"Aervern?" He drew her attention back to his face.

"Yes?"

"What are you doing here? If it's so far away, I mean?"

She looked affronted and drew away from him. "I travel. I sate my curiosity. I do not feel that I need to explain myself to you, manling."

He felt his face redden. Though he didn't understand what he'd done, he'd clearly caused great offence. "I'm sorry, I didn't mean to insult you."

"It is no matter, I will forgive you perhaps if…" she stopped, a speculative look on her face.

"If?"

"Are you yet full grown, Joran? You seem short to me. Though all manlings must seem short to us when compared with a fae man."

Joran coughed. He was blundering through the conversation, as lost as a blind man in the woods. "I suppose I am."

"Well then, I will begin to forgive you…" she paused, her lips curving into a wicked smile. "I will begin to forgive you in exchange for a kiss."

"A kiss?" He felt the heat of the blush in his cheeks as it rose to the roots of his hair.

She laughed at his reaction, a delighted chuckle but one without mocking. "Is it really such a terrible thing to ask?" She looked down at herself. "Am I unpleasing to your eye? Or perhaps you are sworn to the She you travel with. I seem to remember your kind has strange ways like that."

"Yes...I mean no..." he blurted, as she laughed again. "No, you're not unpleasing. I mean...Oh, Lords of Blood, Sea and Sky!" He moaned before drawing a deep breath, "I think you're very beautiful, Aervern."

She grinned at that, her teeth shining white in the predawn light as she moved towards him on her hands and knees, her hips swaying dangerously. "I believe you owe me a kiss, manling."

He froze as she approached, suddenly realising how a deer must feel as it spots the hunter. Her arms snaked around his neck and she pulled him close. Her lips were soft but insistent, and she tasted of grass, honey and something he couldn't place. She leaned into the kiss and devoured it, hungry for the pleasure and sensation. When she pulled away, he found his heart pounding.

She smiled at him in satisfaction as she knelt back on her heels. "You show some slight promise there, manling." She lifted her face up to the light as she squinted up at the sky, then stood in an easy motion, brushing the grass from her leggings.

"I would speak with you some more, Joran. Would you meet with me here again?"

He didn't need to think about it. "I will, happily, Aervern."

"Tomorrow then. I will wait for you. There are questions I would have answered. I think you may need to practice some more also." She gave a wicked chuckle as his face coloured again, and then she disappeared between the stones.

He sat for a time, savouring the fading taste of her on his lips and the memory of her hot breath on his skin. The rising sun came swiftly and he roused himself, crouching to collect his bow from beside the tall stone. The glyphs were clear in the face of the stone and he wandered to the centre of the circle, looking down at the circular stone plate and the myriad of tiny carvings in its face. It was untouched by moss or lichen and showed no sign of weathering. Ylsriss would be fascinated by it.

"Shit!" he swore out loud, startling the birds into silence with his outburst. It was daylight; half the day was gone and he'd not done a thing. They would need water to be drawn from one of the three clean wells he'd found and they would need food. Hunting for meat was relatively easy but a man gets sick on a diet of just meat, he knew. He'd taken to foraging in the outer edges of the woods for what nuts and berries he could find. He gathered up his quiver and pack, and set off at a run.

* * *

She was waiting for him, just as she'd promised she would be. His breath caught as he saw her, leaning back against the tall stone. Her short tunic seemed even shorter than it had been yesterday and her long legs were bare. The wind tossed her pale golden hair as she raised her face to the sky, her lips parted slightly as if she yearned for a kiss.

Her head turned towards him and that same wicked smile curved her lips as she caught sight of him. It seemed as though her form shimmered and then she was reclining on a rich rug strewn with pillows. Her tunic had been replaced by a garment made from the thinnest gossamer that worked more to enhance her raw sexuality than to conceal anything.

Joran gasped and shook his head, refusing to accept what he was seeing. She pouted prettily and the image vanished, revealing her as she had been before, leaning against the stone.

"Didn't you like it?" she asked, in a throaty voice.

"It's not real." Joran said, hoping the tremor in his voice didn't carry to her.

"What does that matter? I made it for you." She laughed at his expression and sat down, patting the ground as she had before. "Did you like what you saw, Joran?"

"I think any man would like it," he replied, trying to sound casual.

The compliment was oblique, but she accepted it anyway, smiling at him as she stretched her legs out. "Do you know how many times I have kissed a manling?"

He blinked. *Where had that come from?* "No, how many?"

"Only once." She put on a sad face. "I have mated with fae by the score, but it is a cold thing. A thing of purpose only. I have long ceased to find any pleasure in it."

He nodded, not sure where this was going.

"But you, my Joran, with you there is a passion that has been lacking for long years."

She let herself down to the grass and lay on her side. "Will you gift me with another kiss, sweet manling?" Her lids were low over her eyes and her voice almost purred. He could feel her using the Touch. It was subtle but it was there. There was a difference, though. This was simply enhancing her seduction, rather than compelling him and he found he didn't care at all. He followed her down to the grass, her arms

217

reaching for him as her lips sought his and then he was lost to the taste of her lips and the feel of her skin. She tore at his clothing, savage as the most rabid of wolves and as she pulled him to her, wrapping her legs around him. Her nails raked at his back and he was hers.

* * *

It was days later by the time he fought his way out of the fog of lust that clouded his mind. They had met each day, talking briefly before she pulled him down to her. Each day he had left her in a rush, to hunt and gather some food for Ylsriss and himself. He never thought of food with Aervern, not until afterwards.

She lay on the grass beside him in a half-doze and stroked his arm lightly. He looked up at the sky. Sunrise couldn't be more than half an hour away. "Don't you need to avoid the sun?" he asked.

"It is not that important," she replied, with a shrug.

"But doesn't it hurt?"

"No, there is no real pain to speak of," she replied. She sat up and picked grass from his hair, an unreadable expression on her face. "In times past, it was not uncommon for a fae to do it intentionally. If you wish, I can show you."

"Show me what?"

"It is easier to simply do than to explain. Be patient, manling, the wait will not be long."

He nodded and began to pull his clothes back on. Despite having been naked for the last few hours, he now felt terribly exposed. She watched him, making no comment, but she made no attempt to reach for her own clothes.

"Come. Sit." She knelt facing him.

The flirtatiousness had evaporated as easily as the glamour she'd worn the first time he'd come to meet her. He wondered briefly if he had ever seen the real person at all.

"Will you tell me of your time in Tir Rhu'thin, Joran?"

He frowned. It was a blunt way to start a conversation and it put him on guard, suspicious of her in a way he hadn't been in days. "What about it?"

"I will speak plainly with you, Joran. I wish to know about your time in these camps and about the fae you met there. We both have information we seek. I will trade with you fairly if you agree."

His nod was slow to come. This all seemed too easy, for some reason.

"You do not trust me." It was a statement of fact; her voice was neither accusing or offended.

"I have not had good dealings with your kind in the past, Aervern." He worked to keep his voice level and meet her eyes, but their colour alone was enough to unnerve him, despite the time they'd spent together.

"That is honest and good." She nodded her approval. "Know this then. If I but chose, I could take this knowledge from you and leave you a hollowed out husk, drifting with the wind. I choose instead to ask."

Joran swallowed hard and briefly wondered if there was an easy way to get back to the kissing instead. "A question for a question, then?"

"This seems fair." She nodded her acceptance.

"Where shall I begin?" he asked.

"The beginning seems a likely place." She didn't laugh but her smile was close enough.

"I don't remember a lot of it clearly. I was under the Touch for a long time."

Her head cocked to one side. "The Touch?"

He frowned and gave her an odd look. "It's what we call it when we fall under the influence of the fae. I lost my own will, my own wants and desires. I even forgot my own brother. All that was important to me was pleasing the fae."

She nodded in understanding. "I can see how that could be possible. I had just not heard the term before. An apt description, I suppose."

"I was taken when I was about ten years old. I have scattered memories of being kept in the pens for a long time and then being moved to the camps at Tir Rhu'thin. They didn't keep us in the same camp for long. We were moved every six months or so. The last camp, where I was with Ylsriss, was the one I'd been in for the longest stretch of time. I think I was there for about a year before she arrived."

He paused for a second. "The fae didn't talk to us much, not beyond explaining their expectations. Their satyrs set up the chase not long after I arrived, so that those that were disobedient could have the glory of being killed in a hunt." His lip curled in derision as he spoke and he fell silent, waiting for the backlash.

"Taken?" She leaned forward, her eyes so intense that he barely noticed she was still naked.

"I think I was one of the first. I can barely remember it, it's just a hazy memory of being chased and scared..." He trailed off, looking out into the city and staring at nothing.

"It is my turn. Ask and I will do my best to answer," she announced, shifting slightly to make herself comfortable.

"Where are you from?" he asked, after a moment's thought. "You don't seem to be like those fae at Tir Rhu'thin."

"This is a good question. Like a flower's petals closed tight against the night, it is one with many others enclosed within." She smiled in approval.

"As I told you once before, I am from Tira Scyon, far from here. You are right, I have nothing to do with those at Tir Rhu'thin. The return of those at your camps has not gone unnoticed, although we have yet to have contact with them directly. The fall of the Wyrde is a wondrous thing, but one which we must approach with caution. Like young shade-cats, they test their strength, these others that have returned to the Realm of Twilight. It must be seen if they will take a suitable place in the court once they reach out to us, or if they will seek to dominate it. They have a value. There is much they might still know. Things that we have forgotten."

Joran shook his head. "I don't understand most of what you've just said," he admitted.

She laughed. "As I said, questions within questions." She stood and arched her back. Joran made no attempt to hide the fact he was admiring her body. He might be on another world but he was still a man.

The sun was rising, the smallest crescent just visible over the rooftops. "Here is an answer to an earlier question, one you might enjoy." She reached for him and pulled him to her. "Stay close. It will not last for long."

He let her press herself against him, wrapping her arms around him, and they waited as the sun rose. As the first touch of sunlight played over her skin, she hissed and tensed, but then seemed to relax. A thin green mist rose where the sun touched her, coiling and swirling like smoke. Joran watched in silence, fascinated.

"Try breathing it in," she whispered.

He met her eyes, unsure as to whether or not she was serious until she nodded. He breathed in, slowly at first. The smoke tasted of her, of her lips and her skin. He breathed more deeply and then rocked as it hit him. His awareness grew until the city was uncomfortably bright, his hearing enhanced to the point that he heard the ruffle of feathers on the birds that flew overhead. More than this though, his sense of smell magnified, revealing nuances of scent that he had never known existed. He looked at the slight fae in his arms in wonder, sensing her power and the speed with which it was being leached by the sun.

"Take more. There are things you should see." The strain in her voice was clear to him now and he knew that her earlier statement about this being painless had been less than truthful.

He breathed in again, sucking the mist deep into him. There was an echo of power in the city. As he became aware of it, he wondered how he had never noticed it before. It was almost like a dull throbbing, just beyond the point of hearing. He could feel its tendrils running throughout the streets, and then the larger channels leading in from all sides of the city and converging on the stone circle. Joran turned, tracing the lines of power under the ground until they met, deep below the gardens he stood in, lying sullen and dormant.

The power left him all at once, leaving him gasping and sagging in her arms as his knees buckled. She knelt and lay him down onto the grass, shifting to the side so she could lie beside him.

"That was…" Words failed him, but she knew what he meant. She lay watching his face with an indulgent smile.

"What was it?" he managed, after a while.

"That was the Gift the Lady grants to us. The Grace passed from me to you. I'm told it is lesser in manlings. You are unused to the Grace it gives and it pales swiftly, but it gives you a glimpse of my world."

He pulled himself up and turned. "What about the things in the city and this under here?" he said, waving at the streets surrounding the gardens, and the ground beneath them.

"The manling's folly," she said, with a sad smile. "It is a long and sad story. Perhaps one that is best saved for another time."

"No. Please?" He forced himself to sit up.

"Please? What is it you would give in exchange for this tale then, sweet Joran?" Her eyes sparkled with suppressed mirth.

"Anything," he replied simply.

Her smile fell away and she met his eyes. "You should be more careful with your offers, Joran. Not every fae is as forgiving as I."

"Kisses then?" he suggested.

"Are you so sure of your skill all of a sudden?" She laughed. "Very well. I will tell you the tale but take note that you have put no limit on your kisses. You are not a good bargainer." She smirked and then began.

"Our history goes back much farther than most realise. Fae and man once dwelt here together. They were our servants. Slaves, if you will. I will make no apology for this, for it was long before my time. It was simply the way of things." She stood and began to pace as she spoke, her feet stepping lightly, barely leaving any impressions in the grass.

"They served us in all things. They hunted for us, made wine for us, entertained us and serviced us. It is troublesome for we fae to beget children. True children, that is. More often than not, a union between fae produces satyrs or fae'reeth."

She noticed his expression. "You did not know this, did you? Are the fae at Tir Rhu'thin not taking humans to mate with? Did you never question why? Your face speaks louder than your voice, Joran. Yes, the satyrs and the fae'reeth are fae themselves, after a fashion. I have many brothers and sisters among both."

He glanced at the stones, not wanting to rush her, but the memory of that lake of power was fresh in his mind. She caught his glance and grimaced. "Do not hurry me, manling. A tale is something that should be savoured slowly. Like mating, if it is done too quickly then much of the pleasure is lost. There is a lot to be said for drawing out the experience."

She paused for a long moment before continuing. "The manlings were gifted in one area above all others. A union between manling and fae would produce a cross-breed, what came to be known as the fae-born. These were simple creatures with short lives and little intelligence. Less than the satyrs, in many ways. They would, however, always produce a pure fae from a union with a fae." She met his eyes to stress her next words. "Every time."

"Our numbers were never great," she said. "Before we encountered the manlings and took your people to serve us, we were a fading people. Your folk had another gift, however. You were uncommonly gifted with the art of glyphs.

Joran watched her intently, entranced by her story.

"We had long been able to imbue simple things with the Grace of our Lady," she said. "Moonorbs for light, runeplates for heating and cooking, for example, so we could remove the need for us to deal with hateful flame. Creating glyphs for such things is a simple matter and maintaining the power they need to function is no real chore for any fae. You creatures though, you cannot simply accept what is. You have this need, this compulsion, to dig to the root of things, to tear them open and find what it is that makes a thing so. It was this way with glyphs." Her tone had a reproachful edge that made Joran avoid her eyes.

"I can recall tales of wonder, stories I was was told as an infant, about things that the manlings created that defied our understanding of glyphs and the limits of their power. Perhaps all would have been well if those limits had been accepted." She looked at him sadly. "But your people would not accept them. They continued to dig until they unlocked the power of Our Lady herself. At first, it was hailed as a wondrous thing. The manlings could power their own glyphs, without the need for fae to imbue them. This was the beginning of a new age, some said. And so it was."

She looked down at the grass, avoiding his eyes as she spoke. "It began with the discovery of the Otherworld, the place Our Lady can take us to if we but know the way. It was an empty, dull place, but it led you to push further, until we reached the Land of Our Lady itself."

Aervern spoke the words with such a hushed reverence that Joran was hesitant to speak, but she seemed to notice anyway. "Ask your question," she said bluntly.

"I don't understand. What was this place?"

"The Otherworld? It is a place between the two worlds, an awful place. Some call it the Outside. As for the Land of Our Lady, it is the world the manlings fled to. For, you see, there were those that rejected the changes that the manlings had brought. The ability to create and power glyphs without the need for our help made your kind question your place. There were those who thought that the manlings no longer accepted the rightful order of things." She glanced at him but he motioned for her to carry on.

"The war was short and barbaric. There are things I have been told which are terrible to recall. The manlings fought back as best they could against my kind, but you must know that we are not evenly matched. They were forced to leave their cities and towns, fleeing as the silver banners of the fae moved ever closer. It was here that the manling's greatest feat was accomplished, and their greatest folly. The few that still lived tore open the sky and fled this land, claiming the Land of Our Lady as their own. This was the land you were taken from, the land your kind locked us away from with your Wyrde."

She fell silent and gazed into the distance, a worried look on her face. Then, without a word, she gathered her clothes and dressed quickly. Ignoring his calls, she disappeared into the distance.

Chapter Sixteen

"Well?" Joran asked again.

"I don't know!" Ylsriss snapped back at him, as she knelt over the stone. "Sorry. Look, just give me some more time to look at this, okay?"

"Okay. I'm sorry too. Do you think it's what you were looking for, though? You said this city had a purpose," he persisted.

"I'm not sure. There is an activation sequence here. I can see the start of it. It's as obvious as the ones on the moonorbs." She pointed out a series of glyphs near the centre of the stone. "But then there are all these other glyphs leading out from it. I have no idea what they do at all."

"Is there no mention of any of them in your books?"

"It's only one rack of books, Joran." She stood to face him. "You seem to forget that there is an entire library in there that we can't read. I'm piecing together the tiny scraps that I can understand, but there are huge sections that I don't. You're expecting miracles from me."

He stepped back from her as she spoke and lifted his hands. "Look, I didn't mean it like that. I'm just excited to see what this is, okay?"

"Why this?" she asked, as she knelt again, tracing the glyphs with a finger as she tried to read them.

"What?"

"Why this thing?" She looked at him again. "I mean it's impressive, I'll grant you, but you've shown no interest in any of the other glyphs in the city. Why now?"

He looked away for a long moment. "I...umm...well, I just want to get moving, you know?"

He was lying about something, that much she could see clearly. What it was, she couldn't tell, and why was an entirely different question. "Fair enough." She shrugged and knelt down to examine the stone disc again.

Eventually, she rose to her feet in defeat. "I have no idea," she admitted. "I can see the start of the activation sequence, but honestly, it could be anything."

"So let's find out," he suggested.

"What? You mean just activate it and hope for the best?" Her eyes were wide with the shock that she couldn't fit into her voice.

"What's the worst that can happen?" He shrugged as he spoke.

"A painful death? A signal calling down an army of fae?" She waved her arms wildly at the stones. "It could do anything, Joran. Anything!"

"You know you're not going to walk away from something this big, Ylsriss," he said, with a knowing smile. "Let's just try it and see."

She muttered to herself as she glared at him. He was right, though. There was no way she could leave without finding out. The glyphs were calling to her, speaking much louder than her common sense. She crouched before she could second-guess herself and examined the first activation sequence. The symbols were laid out in an arrangement that was far larger and more complex than anything she'd seen before. Despite this, she could see where it began. "I can't believe I'm doing this," she whispered, as she reached out for the stone.

The sigils flared a dull red under her hands and the standing stones around her seemed to shimmer for the briefest moment. Then the light of the glyphs sputtered and died.

"What happened?" Joran demanded. "It just stopped."

"I don't think it has enough power," Ylsriss said, guessing. "If this is the thing we were looking for, it has power channels running to it from all over the city."

"So what do we need to do?" Joran asked.

She looked down at the glyph-inscribed stone, then back to his eager face. "This is probably a bad idea, you know?" she said, although she wasn't sure if she was speaking to Joran or to herself.

* * *

It was two full days before she let him talk her into trying again. She'd barely seen him. He was usually gone for most of the day anyway, but he had always come in to see her before these last couple of days. There had been days lately when he hadn't visited once. She was curious about it, in a vague, distracted way, but also glad for the uninterrupted study time.

They left the library before the sun had even gone down. She'd marked out a route through the streets that would pass as many of the capture plates as possible. Now, as she examined the book and reread the passages, even though she knew them by heart, she wished she could learn more.

She wandered over to the other shelves and ran her hand along the wood. They were mostly bare now. She'd worked her way through the books, lifting them as carefully as she could, but only one in ten had held together long enough for her to open it. She had collected the pages that had survived together, but she could only understand a tiny fraction of what was written on them.

She glanced over at Joran who was practising drawing glyphs in the dust. "Are you sure you know the sequence now?" she asked, for what felt like the tenth time.

"I'm sure, Ylsriss. Do you want me to show you again?" Joran sighed and walked to the door. He was the very picture of impatience as he waited, his hand on the door frame and a sack tossed over one shoulder.

"Fine, if you're sure," she said. "It's just that if they aren't all open, we probably won't have enough power."

"I know, I know," he said, boredom clear in his voice. "And if I do it wrong, they might explode or lock open. You've explained all this, Ylsriss."

"Okay," she laughed, as she let him lead her through the hallways. "I'm turning into an old nag, aren't I?"

"You're not a nag," he said, with a grin.

She caught the implication and scowled. "Just old?"

"I didn't say that," he replied, failing miserably in his attempt to look innocent.

"You just didn't use the word, that's all." She wagged a finger at him. "You'll pay for that one."

They worked on the first three capture plates together. Ylsriss watched carefully as he traced the glyphs that would start the mechanism and send the heavy stone cover plate grinding loudly over the cobbles as it shifted to one side.

After that, they split up, working as quickly as they dared. Joran had discovered more than thirty capture plates throughout the city, but there were probably many more. They split them evenly between them, but still it took time.

The moon was already rising as Ylsriss finished the sequence on the last capture plate and the silvery metal flared even as the heavy stone shifted into its resting place. The plate dimmed, but continued to glow faintly to show it was active as it absorbed the moonlight.

"What now?" Joran asked, watching her.

"Well, if we've done it properly, then they should close on their own as soon as the moon goes down." She frowned down at the plate. "I think we'd better check them anyway. This first time, at least. I'm not sure if I trust it to work. Letting sunlight hit them when they're full of power like this doesn't strike me as a good idea."

"Why do I know I'm not going to like the explanation to that one?" he groaned.

"Hmmm?"

"When you said 'this first time.'"

Ylsriss chuckled. "It's not that much of a chore, Joran. I think we need to do this at least twice before we try the glyphs at the stones again, though."

They returned to the mansion hours later, with eyes gritty from lack of sleep. The capture plates had all glowed brightly as they'd covered them under the heavy stones that hid them from the sun. It irked her that she couldn't find a way to make them close on their own, so they didn't need to be there to trace the sigils. The glyphs were all there. It ought to have worked. There was just something missing in the sequence she'd traced out. She chewed at the problem as they made their way back to the mansion and their camp.

By the time she woke, the sun had already risen and was close to being gone. Joran was nowhere to be seen but that was nothing unusual. She climbed out from the tangle of blankets she used as a bed, blankets stolen from the camp at Tir Rhu'thin when they'd escaped. The mansion was comfortable but it was still essentially a ruin. She sipped water from her waterskin to wake herself and pulled a handful of nuts from the dwindling supply at the bottom of a sack. For the first time, she shied away from the prospect of spending another day alone in the library.

The steps were strewn with fresh leaves which she supposed had been blown in by the night winds. There were few trees in this part of the city. Statues were commonplace, as were the myriad of fountains, but the only garden she'd ever seen had been the one Joran had led her to.

Her footsteps echoed through the empty streets as she made her way along. She wasn't quite moving aimlessly. She was drifting in the direction of the garden. Joran was probably hunting, either in the areas closest to the forest or amongst the trees themselves. The deer that had once roamed the streets had long since learned not to venture too far into the city.

She stopped and glanced behind her more than once, as she felt eyes upon her. Most of the time, she could ignore the sensation. It never truly went away, although she felt it less often when she was working in the library. She shook her head and pushed herself onwards.

She caught sight of him long before he noticed her. He was beside one of the tall stones in the centre of the garden. Ylsriss started to call out but stopped herself. There was something odd about the way he was standing there. He wasn't resting or looking at the stones. He was waiting for something.

His guilty start when he noticed her only served to make her more suspicious. He looked around as she approached, his eyes searching the gardens around the stones for something.

"Lost something?" she asked, as she climbed the grassy bank.

"No. I… what do you mean?" He stumbled through the sentence, tripping over his guilt.

"You just seemed to be looking for something or someone. I don't know." She shrugged. Why did she suddenly feel like she was in the wrong, as if she was trespassing or unwelcome? Joran stiffened and she followed his gaze. The fae stood at the apex of the arched bridge, watching them calmly with her amber eyes as the wind tossed her pale hair.

Ylsriss plucked at his clothing. "Joran!" she said, in a hoarse whisper. "Joran, we've got to run."

He didn't move. His face was frozen in an expression of dismay. Ylsriss grabbed his arm and pulled hard. "Come on!" She glanced over one shoulder and saw the fae was walking into the garden towards them.

"We don't need to run," Joran said, each word its own confession.

His meaning was lost on her and she looked at him as if he'd gone mad. "What? Let's go!"

"Joran," called the fae. "You have company already. Perhaps I should go?" She spoke the language haltingly, with an odd accent that placed emphasis on the wrong syllables, but it was clearly Islik.

Joran looked stunned. "You speak Islik?"

"Your languages are not to hard for my kind to puzzle out, sweet manling. Our own is a rich melody, but yours are a simple blow of the flute." She laughed, as if she had made a clever joke.

Ylsriss looked from the fae to Joran, shaking her head as her face twisted in disbelief. "You know her?" It was barely more than a whisper, but the accusation echoed louder than it would have if she'd screamed it into his face.

He gripped her upper arms, turning her to face him fully. "I meant to tell you, Ylsriss. I couldn't think of a way how." The betrayal she felt was clear on her face as she looked at the approaching fae.

"Really, she's no threat to us," he said.

"Let me guess. She's not like the others? She's different?" The sarcasm was thick in her voice as the initial shock began to fade. "You're Touched again, Joran!" She stepped back as the fae drew closer.

"You need not fear me," the fae said.

"Thanks," Ylsriss scoffed, taking another step away from the creature. "Lords above, Joran! What were you thinking! We only just got away from the satyr and now this?"

"What is this?" Aervern rounded on Joran, laying a possessive hand on his arm. "Why did you not mention this?"

He shied away from her furious expression "It was weeks ago. I didn't think it was important anymore."

"Foolish manling! Have you learned nothing from your time here?" the fae spat. She spun away from him, her eyes searching the horizon.

"Aervern, seriously," Joran began, "it was weeks ago. We lost him at the ravine on the other side of the city. It won't be able to track us now."

Her laugh was a mocking sound, devoid of mirth. "You fool. You believe a manling could hide his passage from a satyr? They live for the hunt. You risk everything!" The willowy creature turned to Ylsriss. "You need not fear me, but fear those that hunt you. Gather what things you have and prepare to leave." She stabbed a finger at Joran. "This one cannot be trusted with such things."

Joran looked stricken as he met the eyes of first Ylsriss and then Aervern, his mouth gaping as he sought words that would not come. The fae gave him a withering look, then turned and ran through the garden towards the empty streets.

* * *

Ylsriss walked through the streets in an icy silence, ignoring Joran as he followed her. "Prepare to leave," the fae had said. It wouldn't take long to gather their things. They didn't have much. The jagged shard of runeplate, some food. Some moonorbs would be useful. The books! She stopped in her tracks as she realised she'd been preparing to leave them behind.

"Come on!" she snapped at Joran, who'd stopped beside her, looking at her warily. She threw her arms in the air with a sigh of disgust and began to run.

The library was only minutes away, but she tore through the streets as if all the satyrs from Tir Rhu'thin were already at her heels. Joran kept pace behind her.

"Make yourself useful," she shot at him, as they marched into the library. "Fetch down those moonorbs. We'll take whatever we can carry."

She walked to the far end of the room without bothering to check to see if he was doing as she'd asked. The books were not small. Each one measured about two feet along the spine and was as thick as her spread fingers. Even before she'd lifted one, she realised that the idea was foolish. She'd managed to stagger from the rack to the lectern with them before, but there was no way she could run with one. Which one would she take anyway? The knowledge she'd only just begun to get to grips with was spread throughout them all.

She picked one up anyway, but quickly dropped it again. It was useless. It was simply too heavy.

"Shit!" she spat, in frustration. Joran looked on in awkward silence.

With no other options, they gathered what little they had together and waited. The sun had risen and set again by the time Ylsriss could bring herself to speak to him.

"Explain," she said, as they sat on the steps outside the building.

"It was a couple of weeks ago," he began. Ylsriss hissed a breath in through her teeth, but he plunged on. "She came to me at the stones in the garden and we… talked."

"Talked?" Ylsriss would have been hard-pressed to raise her eyebrow any higher.

"Yes. She was interested in hearing about our time in Tir Rhu'thin." Joran spoke quickly, hoping the blush would fade. "She's not from there, Ylsriss. There's a whole other sect of the fae that we know nothing about!"

She sat in silence as he recounted their time together and told her the things the fae had shared with him. He was less than half of the way through his story when Aervern came to find them.

She stalked across the square and glared at Joran. "Your satyr has returned from Tir Rhu'thin with his brethren," she growled, holding up a hand for silence as both Ylsriss and Joran started to speak. "The ravine is known to us, although probably not to those so recently returned here. There are numerous places to cross, if you know where to look. They have not yet located your tracks, but I expect them to be within the city before the moon rises."

Ylsriss blanched. "What do we do?" she asked Joran.

"There is little you can do," Aervern said, answering for him. "If you run, they will inevitably find you. There are too many for you to fight. If it had been just the one, I might have been able to aid you, but even I cannot succeed against so many."

"So we just die?" Ylsriss demanded.

"He will die," Aervern pointed. "You, I expect they will have other uses for first. But yes, you will die eventually."

Joran gasped as the thought struck him. "The stones!"

"What?" Ylsriss said, in confusion.

"We can use the stones!" He grabbed her by the shoulders, shaking her lightly in his excitement.

"We don't even know what they do," she protested.

"Aervern does." He gestured at the fae, who stood watching them, unconcerned. "She called them the manling's folly. It's a path home, Ylsriss."

"Even if that's true, and even if it still works, we don't know how to use it," she replied.

"But you said you'd found the activation glyphs, didn't you?"

"I did, but there are whole sections that I don't understand," she admitted.

"How is it you have knowledge of these glyphs, She?" Aervern demanded.

"My name, is Ylsriss, *fae*," she spat back.

"Ylsriss then," Aervern replied, in her thick accent. "How is it you know of glyphs?" The mollifying tone seemed out of place coming from this creature from legend.

"We were taught how to use runeplates and moonorbs at Tir Rhu'thin," Ylsriss explained. "Nothing advanced or complicated. But then we found the library here, with books about the art."

"A listing of glyphs then?"

"Yes, but it's much more than that. The writing talks about the theories, the construction of glyphs. I've barely scratched the surface, but I've already learned so much." Ylsriss smiled briefly, before remembering who she was speaking to.

"This *writing*." Aervern struggled with the unfamiliar word. "It can do this? Impart knowledge with no need for an elder to recount it?"

Ylsriss nodded.

Aervern sucked in air through her teeth. "This is an alien thing to me. There is so much we have forgotten about you. Knowledge that has been lost." She glared at Joran. "Now there is no time to regain it." Joran's attempts to look apologetic went unnoticed, as Aervern looked back to Ylsriss. "If you can make use of the manling's folly, you should do so. My own designs are largely thwarted now." She shot Joran another black look. He seemed to be working hard to crawl into the stones. "I can slow the satyrs, but I dare not be seen. If they approach in any real numbers, I will not risk myself."

"We'll need to be fast, Ylsriss," Joran warned. "You know as well as I do how fast those things can be. We'll need to get as many capture plates open as we can before we try the stones."

Ylsriss nodded in silence as her eyes glistened, a terrible realisation coming over her. She buried it down deep. It would be of little help to them now.

* * *

They ran through the empty streets as fast as they dared. The city was quiet at the best of times and any noise seemed to echo on forever. The satyrs might be there already and they knew they couldn't risk doing anything that would draw the creatures to them any faster.

Aervern ran beside them, moving in long easy strides, her bare feet making almost no noise whether they struck stones or dried leaves. She led them to an innocuous-looking house, ducked inside and emerged with a bow, as tall as she was and fashioned of polished black horn, and a quiver of arrows.

"If it comes to it, my little hunter, aim for the eyes. The satyrs cannot really be harmed by your weapons. You might cause them pain, but no more. A shaft into the eye will have more of an impact." She smiled as she spoke, her own eyes glowing softly in the fading light. Ylsriss shivered in spite of herself.

They kept close to the sides of the street, darting in and out of the growing shadows. They opened the first capture plate and Aervern gasped, almost in awe, as it slid back over the stones.

The fae left them after they had opened the third plate, stopping to look back at them once as she loped along the street. She made a strange gesture, touching her hand to her forehead, her lips and her stomach, before running into the growing gloom.

Joran's face was unreadable as he watched her vanish. "Come on, let's go," Ylsriss said. She led him off towards the next capture plate without looking back.

She traced each set of glyphs as fast as she was able to before speeding off to the next plate, sometimes leaving before the grinding of the stone cover plate had even really started. They worked separately where they could, but only split up when they wouldn't need to move out of earshot of each other. Ylsriss was hesitant to lose sight of him as it was.

Time seemed to be slipping away from them. It was already growing darker and several times she fancied she'd heard distant noises in the city. Joran knelt to trace the glyphs, his face turning ruddy in the dim red light of the sigils as he moved his fingers through the sequence. Ylsriss stood behind him, chafing at his slow pace. She'd already finished the plate she had been working on. She glanced back along the street. It was already growing harder to see as the twilight began to turn to true night. Something seemed to move in the lengthening shadows and she squinted, trying to decide if it was just her imagination. A staccato clack of hoofs on stone came first, then the pinpricks of amber became visible as the satyr charged towards them.

Her scream echoed off the walls, probably carrying across half the city, and she clamped her lips shut tight to trap in the sound. Joran spun, one hand still on the glyphs as he finished the sequence.

"Shit, shit, shit!" he muttered. He snatched up the bow and strung an arrow with shaking hands. He pulled back and released. The arrow flew wide and deflected off the wall of a building before falling to the ground and skittering along the stones.

"Shoot it!" screamed Ylsriss, scrabbling at his belt for the knife. The satyr was now less than a hundred feet from them.

Joran's second arrow bounced off the creature, causing it no visible damage. It slowed, seeming to enjoy their panic, and stalked towards them, long knives held low in its fists.

"I should thank you. You've led us a merry hunt," it said, with a delighted grin.

Ylsriss backed away, holding the knife before her in one hand, and pulling Joran backwards by his shirt with the other. The arrow came from nowhere, hissing through the gloom and burying itself in the satyr's eye. The creature let out a scream then, piteous and dreadful, as it clutched at the shaft. The sound put Ylsriss in mind of the tortured cries she used to hear from the abattoir close to her cellar in Hesk. The satyr staggered, then fell to the cobbles and was still.

Joran stared at it in amazement and then spun, tracing the roofline until he spotted her. Aervern was pressed into the shadow of the chimney pot, barely visible. She raised her bow once in salute and then ran lithely along the roof, leapt easily to an adjacent building and was gone.

"Come on!" Ylsriss urged him, as she shifted into a sprint. They ran towards the garden, passing unopened capture plates as they sacrificed the increase in power in order to put more distance between them and the unseen satyrs. They stopped three times to frantically trace glyphs, but had to abandon their final attempt and flee at the sound of hooves on stone.

Screams rose intermittently, the echoes carrying to them through empty streets, as Aervern fired her bow from the rooftops. If anything, the noises seemed to be spurring the satyrs on, and Ylsriss felt panic rising in her as they entered the gardens.

The light had faded almost completely and a tiny sliver of moon was making feeble attempts to illuminate the skies. The gardens extended for some distance and the faint sounds of animals that came from beyond the stones did not help her nerves.

Joran paused to glance towards the bridge. "Come on," she said, and reached for his hand. He seemed to have left all his self-assurance on the streets of the city, and he let her lead him along as though he was one of the children from her cellar in Hesk, all those years ago. *No*, she corrected herself, *he was nothing like those children*. They had been hard. Beaten down by a life that either makes you strong enough to bare your teeth back at it, or broken and damaged enough not to care what happens to you.

Joran was neither. He was a child newly emerged from the cocoon that the

Touch had forced him into. So much of his life had been lived through a fog, it was a miracle he could function at all. She gave his hand a quick squeeze and turned the corner, passing the last overgrown hedge that obscured the stones.

They charged up the grassy bank and made their way to the stone disc that lay at the circle's centre. The moonlight shone faintly onto the stone, a pale watery light, but just enough to work by.

Joran stood behind her, watching in silence as she squatted and then moved, crablike, around the stone, reading the glyphs and muttering to herself as she whispered the names of the symbols.

It looked different in the moonlight, but not just because it was harder for her to see it. The symbols seemed unfamiliar, as if something had changed.

"I don't understand this," she whispered to Joran.

"What?" His response was shrill.

"No, not like that. I can read it, but it's like there's more here than there was before."

"You're imagining it," he told her. "Hurry!"

She shook her head and traced the first of the runes. It flared into life, bright and strong, bathing her face in a golden light as she moved onwards.

The disc had glyphs that worked inwards in a spiral, but also some grouped into circular patterns that she couldn't understand. This was so much more complicated than anything she had ever looked at before. Runeplates and moonorbs had a simple activation sequence, releasing some of the energy they had stored within them, be it light or heat. The glyphs were almost the same on both of them.

The stone disc had glyphs she'd never seen before, interspersed with sigils she recognised but in arrangements she'd never considered before.

"Hurry up!" Joran hissed at her.

"It's not like lighting a fire, Joran!" she snapped back. "Give me a minute."

He didn't respond but she felt him stiffen. The satyr approached slowly, in no hurry and obviously savouring the moment. The moonlight picked out the grey in the fur on its legs and its beard, reflecting off the horns that seemed longer than those of the other satyrs she'd seen.

"A blood debt is owed," it said in a calm voice. Its eyes, however, radiated a fury that far outshone their dull amber glow.

"Blood debt?" Joran said, nudging Ylsriss with his foot as he spoke. She didn't need to be told twice and bent over the disc again, searching for the next of the glyphs that had seemed so simple to read in the daylight.

"Keeping your kind was always a mistake," Thantos said. "More than once have I told Aelthen this. You are fit for the hunt and no more." Its knives were long and curved, the bone blades pale in the light. Joran plucked the knife from Ylsriss's belt. It looked tiny and shook in his hand as he faced the satyr.

"You spilled the blood of a fae'reeth. One who abided with me in the Outside for untold years before the return. To meet her end at the hands of a creature as low as you is something that cannot be borne. I will not accept that Sabeth will not go to the Realm of Our Lady, whilst the manling that stole her life still walks. No, I will not permit it!"

It moved in, not in a rushed charge like Joran would have expected, but slowly, almost formally, offering a tight bow before falling into an odd stance.

When the attack came, he didn't even have time to move before the creature was upon him. The bone blades slashed twice, cutting into his side and slicing his forearm open before the satyr moved off to one side. Joran staggered, reaching for the closest stone to steady himself. He was going to die; it was simply a matter of how long the satyr would toy with his prey before he let it fall.

He clasped a hand against the deeper cut in his side, bending into an awkward crouch against the pain as he faced the satyr again. The creature staggered forwards as the arrow smashed into the back of its head. Two more followed, so close together that they seemed to strike it almost at the same time. The missiles did not penetrate the satyr's skin, but splintered as the force of the impacts shattered the shafts.

The creature spun round, snarling in fury as it sought the source of the attack, and another arrow hurtled out of the darkness, exploding against its chest. Light poured from the glyphs as Ylsriss traced sigils furiously, squinting against the light that erupted skyward.

A figure emerged from the darkness, blades held ready as she nodded towards the two within the circle. "These manlings are bound to my purpose, satyr."

Thantos gasped in shock and fury, then narrowed his eyes as he looked at her. "I do not recognise your face. How can this be?"

"It is not important," Aervern replied, her voice filled with icy rage. "I am fae, you are but satyr. You will obey."

"You are not of the returned!" Thantos gasped in recognition. "I owe you no allegiance. You and yours had not the honour to follow in the hunt. You are lesser in the eyes of Aelthen than even these manlings." He raised his blades again and took a step towards her, dropping into a low stance.

"You dare!" Aervern gasped. Her shock did nothing to slow her as she dropped into a stance herself, her knife weaving intricate patterns in the air before her.

The satyr bared his teeth in fury and launched himself into the fight, slashing at her with his blades. He moved almost faster than Joran could follow, yet Aervern stepped casually aside, her eyes blazing bright with amber as she moved out of the line of attack. Thantos shifted his own line in response and the blades made a soft hiss as they slid against each other.

The fight was fast and Joran realised in moments that he could have been killed before he could even react, had the satyr wanted it. The two fae creatures moved back and forth before the stones, slashing at each other in an elegant but deadly dance. The blades did not clash against each other, that would have wasted an opportunity to redirect the force of the attack. Instead, each blow was met with the barest touch, as it was guided past the defender.

The satyr growled and cursed in the lyrical fae tongue as he fought. Aervern fought in silence, an icy calm radiating from her as she stepped and shifted in the flow of the fight.

She leant backwards as the twin knifes of the satyr thrust at her throat, arching almost until her pale hair brushed the grass. A twist of her torso and she shifted out from under his overextension, her eyes growing dimmer as she drew on her Grace to move faster than the satyr could ever hope to. The knife's thrust, imbued with the same power, parted the flesh like the water of a millpond and buried itself to the hilt in his side, just under the armpit. Blood fountained from Thantos's mouth as he sank to the grass, the light already fading from his eyes. Aervern pulled her knife from the body and met Joran's eyes for just one moment before she disappeared into the night.

Joran slumped against one of the stones as the fae vanished. The rough stone behind him shuddered as Ylsriss traced glyph after glyph, activating the complex sequences, and then the entire circle burst into light.

"You did it!" he cried, his pain forgotten as he pulled Ylsriss to her feet.

Her cheeks were wet with tears as she smiled sadly at him. "I can't," she said, in a voice thick with anguish, as she shook her head.

"What? What do you mean?"

"I can't go, Joran. I can't leave Effan here."

He looked at her incredulously. "This could be our only chance to get home, Ylsriss. The whole city must be crawling with satyrs. We'd never make it out of here alive."

"I know," she whispered. "I know, but I still can't leave him. You go. Just walk out onto the disc. Leave me."

"But you don't even know where he is, Ylsriss!"

"It doesn't matter, Joran. I can't leave my baby behind. If I go, I know I'll never see him again. I can't do that." She had never been more certain of anything in her life.

He stared at her for a moment. His mind was suddenly cold and clear. He knew exactly what he had to do.

He fixed his gaze on something behind her. She couldn't help but turn her head to follow his gaze, and he smashed his fist into the side of her face with all the force he could manage. Ylsriss dropped to the grass, her eyes glassy and unseeing as the impact drove the tears from her cheeks.

Joran snatched her up, clenching his teeth against the pain as he walked onto the disc with her in his arms. The lights of the glyphs blazed around him, and then all was brilliant light and a bitter cold that drove the breath from his lungs. He felt the stones of the world pass through him and then they fell into darkness.

Chapter Seventeen

Selena climbed down from the carriage, accepting the footman's hand as he guided her down to the gravel path. Her gown was stupendous, pale crystal blue with touches of white that made her look as if she were encased in ice. Combined with her hair, she was the perfect storm of frost and fire.

She had arrived alone. Hanris would have been more than welcome, but she couldn't be seen to be leaning on a man, even a servant.

The villa was decorated for the occasion, with banners of red, gold and flaming orange giving it an autumnal flavour. She thought briefly of the farmers that had been forced from their newly leased farmlands by the Bjornmen. What would they think of the attempt by the Celstwin nobility to celebrate the harvest and the turning of the seasons?

"Selena, you look simply stunning!" Jantson gushed, as she swept in.

"You're really very sweet, Jantson," She looked down at herself with a pained frown. "You're an awful liar, though. I'm starting to show. I look like an iceberg in this dress."

"Nonsense," he scoffed. "You look better than my wife did on our wedding night."

"Didn't you tell me, just the other night, that your wife was chronically overweight when you married and that you put your back out trying to carry her over the threshold?"

Jantson coughed. "I may have mentioned something to that effect."

She laughed, taking his arm as they made their way into the villa and through the halls towards the ballroom.

The group had met on several occasions since that first dinner, each time at a grand affair, a dinner or a ball. She was beginning to suspect that Raysh was just using the need for them to get together as an excuse to throw more lavish and grandiose events.

"Another ball," she muttered, in mock complaint, to Jantson.

"Oh, they're not that bad," Jantson said, as he looked for the others. "It gives me an excuse to dance with a beautiful woman, after all."

"Well, could you at least wait until we've found the others before you abandon me?" Selena joked.

He chuckled. "Shall we?"

She nodded and allowed him to lead her out onto the floor. The musicians were playing a muted piece in a minor key. It made for a slower dance, allowing for quiet conversation, making it perfect for their needs.

"Rentrew has dispatched his forces, I hear," Jantson said. He spoke softly, behind a broad smile.

Selena laughed as if he'd told a particularly good joke. "Yes, some time ago now. They ought to be reaching Rhenkin any day, I believe. Have you heard anything about the king's army?"

"No movement still," Jantson said, his expression grim. "He'd have to send out a general muster order if he were going to respond in any significant fashion."

Selena let him guide her through a complex promenade, forcing a faint smile onto her face as she ranted. "What is he thinking? Our troops are never going to be enough to stop the Bjornmen. The best we can hope for is to slow them down and the losses will be terrible."

"Perhaps that's the point," Jantson quipped with a snort. He stopped as her face went white. "Are you quite well, my dear?"

"Let's find Salisbourne." She strode off the dance floor, ignoring the surprised looks people were shooting her.

"This is less than subtle, Selena," Jantson muttered, as he followed her. "There are bound to be at least one or two of the king's spies here, in addition to the usual sycophants."

"Some things can't be helped, Jantson."

Salisbourne was in the study with Raysh and Rentrew.

"It occurs, Salisbourne," Selena said, as she was shown in by one of Raysh's staff, "that there is little point in throwing these elaborate functions if we all end up sequestered in a smoky study."

The older man shrugged and drew on his pipe. "Sometimes I wonder if we aren't wasting our time with this subterfuge anyway, Selena. There is little in Celstwin that our esteemed monarch doesn't know about and less still that he can't uncover."

"That doesn't mean we should simply be blatant about these things," Jantson said, as he edged around Selena to find an empty chair.

"Relax," Raysh muttered into his drink. "The king doesn't seem interested in anything much at the moment. Except his pet projects, that is."

"Gentlemen, if I can drag this back on track for a moment?" Selena turned to Rentrew. "Jantson tells me your troops have been dispatched and are well on their way."

He nodded. This was not news to anyone present. "The question is, then, why is the king not acting himself? The Bjornmen have taken a sizeable chunk of land and, whilst it is part of my duchy and encroaches on your own lands," she nodded to Rentrew, "it is, perhaps more importantly, part of his kingdom."

"Did you have a point, Selena, or were you just going to meander through until you tripped over one by accident?" Raysh asked, as he drained his glass.

"I do, as it happens," she replied, giving him an arch look. "Even with Rentrew's forces added to my own, there is little we can do to stop the Bjornmen taking more lands. We can slow them, certainly, but the costs in terms of both men and finances will be enormous. So what is it that Pieter stands to gain from this? The pact demands he act, yet he ignores this invasion."

"Selena, please?" Raysh groaned.

"I'm getting there. Don't be so impatient," she chided. "What's making him so boorish?" she asked Salisbourne.

"The treasury found an irregularity in his tithe," Salisbourne said, from behind a smirk.

"It's not an irregularity." Raysh snapped. "It's a levy based on laws that weren't even in place at the time of the trade. They're making up rules as they go along, just to gouge any merchants who might be making a small profit."

"Just how small is small?" Selena asked, her curiosity peaked.

"Enough to run your duchy for a good few years," Salisbourne snorted. "Raysh here managed to steal the march on a number of people and corner almost the entire Suraman wine export market some years ago. If you listen carefully, you can still hear the echoes of the howls of protest."

"The bean counters couldn't touch it since the trades were all made in Surama, so they decided to levy a retrospective import tithe on wine. It's blatant!" Raysh stopped, realising he'd stormed to his feet and sank back into his chair, still muttering.

"Anyway, my dear, I believe you were making a point?" Rentrew smiled.

"It was more of a question than a point, but thank you." She turned back to Salisbourne. "I think it's so obvious, it's been staring us in the face. What does Pieter gain from us being forced to act in his stead, throwing our own wealth and forces in the path of this invasion? We're not equipped to stop them and all that results, unless he acts, is our impoverishment."

"That's true, but if he continues to ignore it, he risks outright rebellion. He flies in the face of a thousand years of tradition. This defiance of the tenets of the pact will never be allowed to stand," Jantson said.

"And if there is outright rebellion?" Selena asked.

"Well, then I expect he would have to bring in his own armies to crush it. You know that. That's why we've never considered acting in open opposition," Salisbourne replied, his tone mirroring the confusion on his face.

"Suppose, for a moment, that we were forced into outright rebellion. Even if we had the majority of the lords on our side, Pieter would respond in force. He'd most likely crush us under his boot." Selena ticked it off on one finger. "Then, with his armies already mustered, he could engage the Bjornmen and drive them out. That would leave him with newly recaptured lands, noble houses that had either been weakened or destroyed outright, and a populace that sees him as their saviour. What, gentlemen, do you think he might do in such a situation?"

"Anything he pleased, I imagine," Raysh said. "It's any politician's utopia. He could do anything."

"I don't think it's as broad an opportunity as all that. He's king already. The scope of ambition narrows the more power you attain. He really only has one place left to go."

"You don't mean...?" Rentrew gasped.

"Emperor." Selena nodded. "What's to stop him? Abaram's Pact will be dead in the eyes of the peasantry. Most of the nobles will have shown themselves to be unable to protect them. They will even have risen up against the king, the very man who then overcame the rebellion and drove the Bjornmen invaders from his shores. Why not rebuild the empire and concentrate the power?"

"Why not simply declare himself emperor and not risk the lands?" Raysh asked.

"Because the lords would oppose him. He couldn't be seen to just seize power like that. Aside from anything else, it would fly in the face of Abaram's Pact," Salisbourne said softly.

"It's still a hell of a risk," Raysh argued. "What if he can't retake the lands?"

Selena went to the drinks cabinet and lifted a crystal decanter, sniffing at the wine whilst holding the heavy stopper. "It wouldn't matter. He'd still be emperor. With all the armies of Anlan at his disposal, I expect he'd be able to retake the lands at his leisure. Unless he underestimates the Bjornmen hugely, of course. Even if it took years though, he'd still have massive support."

"So what do we do? We seem damned either way," Rentrew interjected. "If we openly oppose him, we play right into his hands. If we ignore him, the Bjornmen continue to take our lands."

"I would suggest a measured response," Selena said, setting the wine down untouched. "Outright rebellion is risky at best and doesn't really meet our purpose. No, the core of this is the pact."

"The pact?" Raysh scoffed. "It's a political measure. Does anyone here even know what it says? It's simply an agreement that we pay the tithe in return for his protection."

"I rather suspect it might be more than just that," Selena replied, pursing her lips in thought. "The pact is more than some obscure document. It's become a convention without most people knowing what it really says. We're bound to the concept of it, as is Pieter. His whole kingdom functions on the basis of it. Perhaps with a little research, it can be turned to our advantage."

"You want to go and poke your nose into dusty old books?" Raysh was scathing. "The king has ignored the fact that your lands are being invaded, and levied taxes that defy sense and reason. He dismisses the missives of his nobles asking for aid and even rejects your requests when you petition him to his face. He does all this and *that's* your response?" He swept his legs off the desk and stood, brandishing his glass at her.

"I thought you were serious about this," Raysh grated. "How much more land do they need to take from you before you're willing to act?"

He pushed past Salisbourne and gave them all another dark look before he left.

"Well, that was spirited," Jantson said, with a forced chuckle.

"He's drunk," Salisbourne said, with a shrug that was almost an apology.

"How much was his tithe?" Rentrew asked, looking at the open door.

"Upwards of ten thousand marks. He didn't tell me the exact figure," Salisbourne admitted.

"Ten thousand," breathed Selena. It was more than half her annual tax revenue.

"Yes, well, you can see why he might be upset," Jantson murmured.

"I think it's time we got back to the ball, gentlemen." Selena said, becoming businesslike again to move past the shock of Raysh's tithe. "We're going to become conspicuous like this. Salisbourne, why don't you come for dinner in a day or two. It's not necessary for us all to meet at once and if, as Jantson says, Pieter has spies here, we need to be more careful. I'll see what I can discover about the pact and if there is a way we might be able to use it. I would suggest it might be an idea to see to your own forces, gentlemen. We might need them all if things go wrong here."

She opened the door and swept out into the hallway, before looking back over one shoulder with a crooked smile. "Coming, boys?"

* * *

"Where is it?" Selena muttered to herself, as she flipped the page over. "Mention after mention of it, but where is the document itself?"

She strode to the doors of the study, wrenching them open and moving through the halls to the staircase.

"Get me a carriage," she snapped at the first servant she saw. "Oh, and fetch Hanris. He's going to accompany me."

She stood at the entrance to the villa and tapped her foot until the carriage was brought around, then tapped it some more until the sound of running footsteps heralded Hanris's arrival.

"your grace," he greeted her, in between puffs and wheezes. "Had I known of your excursion, I would have planned accordingly."

"You didn't know because I didn't know, Hanris," she said. "I can't think what keeps you so busy here, anyway," she said, as she made her way out into the grey afternoon and down to the carriage.

She clambered into the carriage and waited while Hanris climbed in. It really was so much simpler for a man, she noted. Gowns might look fine, but they really were impractical in many situations.

"So, Hanris," she said brightly. "Tell me what you know of Abaram's Pact. I thought we might go to the royal archives and see if we can find a copy."

"Abaram's Pact?" he burst out.

She looked at him calmly. "You know, Hanris, if I didn't know better, I'd say you were genuinely irked. What is the problem here?"

"your grace, might I speak freely?"

She nodded.

"Your grace, whilst your holdings are not quite as extensive as they were before the Bjornmen incursion, there is still a significant amount of land and holdings. All of which produce revenues and costs which must be properly logged and accounted for. I am hampered by distance as it is." Hanris sighed.

"Do you mean to tell me, Hanris, that you are still doing the accounts for the entire duchy? From Celstwin?" She normally adopted a rather playful, teasing manner with Hanris. He was so much fun to torment. This news, however, had thrown her completely.

"Such are the requirements of my position, your grace."

"Lords and Ladies, Hanris," she exclaimed. "I didn't bring you all this way so I'd have an accurate tally of the corn taxes! I brought you because you happen to have a rather keen mind buried underneath all those dusty reports and figures."

"But, your grace..." he began.

"Hanris," she snapped, raising a finger between them. "I realise, now, that you must be drowning in tiresome reports. Understand, however, that I no longer retain you on my staff for that. Frankly, any child who knows to count past his fingers could do much of this work for you. Find some suitable people and bring them on board. Delegate, Hanris, delegate!"

He deflated then, although she was sure she saw the ghost of a smile haunting his lips.

"Now, tell me what you know of the pact," she said.

"To be honest, your grace, not a great deal," Hanris admitted, taking his glasses off his nose and polishing them with a pristine white handkerchief. "I know it is an ancient document dating back to just beyond the fall of the empire. I believe it was an agreement between the regional barons and Earl Abaram, designed ostensibly to obtain his support against the Feldane invasion. In practice, it formed the basis upon which the Kingdom of Anlan was formed."

"Top marks." Selena clapped her hands together. "Now, tell me this. Why is it I cannot find a single reference in any of the histories as to the contents of this agreement?"

"I have..." He paused. "I honestly have no idea, Youryour grace. I must confess, however, that I was never really a scholar of history. No mentions at all? That seems very strange."

"Oh, there were mentions." She waved her hand dismissively. "Broad strokes discussing the impact on the form of the state and the monarchy. That was all, though. There were no specifics, no meat to it."

"And it's 'meat' you require, your grace?"

She laughed then, a tinkling delighted laugh that filled the carriage. "Hanris, you are a delight sometimes."

"Indeed, your grace," he said, without a trace of a smile. "If I might be so bold, your grace, I notice you are spending a great deal of time with the Lords Salisbourne and Jantson, and their associates. Attending balls and the like."

"Yes?"

"I have always found it odd that the man leads in a dance. The woman cannot help but go where the man leads, even if it results in the dance going poorly."

She smiled. The man was genuinely worried about her. It was actually quite touching. "Dear Hanris, your concerns are sweet but really not necessary. A man might lead in the dance, but any woman who truly knows what she is about can direct a man without him ever knowing."

He fell silent at that and she watched the streets pass as they moved through the city. The trouble with manipulating people, she thought, is that you can never be entirely sure you are not on the wrong end of the marionette's strings.

The royal archives were not actually in the grand library, as she'd expected. Instead, it was a small, drab building in a side street. Selena looked out of the window with a puzzled frown as she waited for the driver to open her door.

"Are you sure we're in the right place?" she asked, as the man opened the door and extended a hand to help her down onto the stepping stool set by his feet.

"The royal archives, your grace," he said, with a short, tight bow.

She raised an eyebrow and shrugged before heading for the doors. "Coming, Hanris?"

The interior was poorly lit, the narrow windows in dire need of a good clean. Lamps were strung on the walls to compensate, and the smell of the oil mingled with the musty smell of old paper and parchment.

A balding man in brown robes, behind a desk, half stood as they entered. "Can I be of some assistance?"

"Perhaps," Selena said, with a warm smile. It never hurts to start off on a friendly footing. "I have been doing some research into Abaram's Pact and I wondered if you had an extant copy?"

"We may have a duplicate stored away." He stopped and frowned. "You do realise, of course, that this is not a library. These documents are extremely fragile and not available to the common public."

She sighed, and it had been going so well for a moment. "Hanris," she muttered.

Hanris stepped forward and cleared his throat. "Might I have your name, Sir?"

The archivist stepped out from behind his desk and drew himself up. "My name is Brent, Second Assistant Archivist."

Hanris flashed a cold smile before turning to Selena. "Your grace, Brent, Second Assistant Archivist." He turned back to the man and gestured towards Selena. "Allow me to introduce Her Grace, Selena Freyton, Duchess of Druel, The Wash and the Eastern Reaches."

He stepped a little closer, speaking in a low voice as he leaned in towards the man. "As you must realise, she is far from the 'common public'."

"It is a pleasure to meet you, your grace," Brent said, swallowing hard. "I'm afraid, however, that the archives are simply not open to visitors."

Hanris gave the man a look which clearly called into question not only his competence, but also his parentage and his grip on reality. He drew in a breath but stopped as Selena placed a hand on his arm.

"Second Assistant Archivist?" she queried, in a mild tone.

"That's correct, your grace," Brent replied. "As I said, I'm sorry but..."

She cut him off. "Do you think I might meet the First Assistant Archivist?"

"Well, I...err...," he managed. "I'll see if he has a moment to spare."

"Do," Selena said, allowing a hint of steel to fall into her voice.

They waited in silence, listening to the distant voices grow steadily in both volume and urgency. Hanris raised an eyebrow at Selena at the sound of hurried footsteps and she gave him a brief smile.

The man who entered with Brent was short and thin, with close-cropped, silver hair. He smiled warmly and gave a small bow. "My apologies, your grace," he said. "I am Ditton, the head archivist here. I am so sorry. Brent has clearly misunderstood the situation."

"I quite understand, Master Ditton." She favoured him with a dazzling smile. "Working with a small staff can be so challenging, can't it?"

He gave Brent a sour look. "One problem of a reduced budget, your grace. Rest assured, Brent will have ample opportunity to reflect on certain realities. I understand you have an interest in Abaram's Pact?"

She nodded her agreement.

"The original document is far too fragile to be moved, I'm afraid. Simply opening the case could cause irreparable damage to it."

"Surely there are copies?"

Ditton raised his eyebrows and flashed a look at Brent that spoke of a temper barely contained. "Of course, your grace. We have several. If you'll follow me?"

He waved them through the double doors leading into the archives, pausing long enough to whisper something hard and short to Brent as he passed.

* * *

Jantson burst into the room, not waiting for the servant to announce him. "They've taken Raysh," he blurted.

Selena sat back in her chair, placing a hand on the large book to mark her place. "They've what?"

"Raysh has vanished. His servants don't know where he's gone. They say he was there in the evening but the next morning, when one of them brought in his breakfast, he'd gone."

"Perhaps he simply went for a walk?" Selena suggested.

"Oh, don't be foolish, Selena. He's been gone two days now," Jantson said, his manners rushing out of the way to let his worry through.

"What makes you think he's been taken, though? Taken by who?"

"Oh, who do you think, Selena? Honestly, this isn't some game we've been playing here!"

Her eyes turned hard at that. "I am quite aware of the stakes, thank you, Lord Jantson. My people are being butchered as their homes burn. Can you say the same?"

He suffered her gaze for a silent minute before sagging down into a chair. "I'm sorry, Selena. This has caught me on the back foot and I've not steadied myself yet. If Pieter has taken Raysh, he could come for any of us. I keep looking behind and expecting a hand to fall onto my shoulder."

"Calm down, Jantson." She reached for the bell and rang it loudly.

"Bring some brandy for the earl," she instructed the young man in livery who appeared in response.

She waited in silence until the man returned with a snifter already filled with the dark amber drink, together with a crystal decanter containing more. He passed the glass to Jantson and, after a nod from Selena, set the decanter down on the table.

"Now, tell me," she began, after he'd managed a shaky swallow, "what makes you think Pieter has him?"

"He hasn't just left, Selena. He's quite literally vanished," Jantson explained. "His servants are panicking. They have no idea where he is. Salisbourne even tells me his business associates are looking for him because he's missed meetings. He runs almost everything himself. He can't simply walk away for a day or two. His entire business would collapse."

"Well then, I suppose we'll just have to locate him, won't we?" Selena smiled.

"How? Pieter won't be holding him openly. He could be anywhere in Celstwin." Jantson emptied his glass and poured another, the neck of the decanter clinking loudly against the glass.

Selena thought for a moment. "You've hit on it yourself. He can't be held openly. A lord can't simply be dragged out of his home, not even by the king. Pieter has changed the tune, thus we must change the dance."

"What?" He shook his head with a frown. "What are you talking about?"

"I'll deal with it." She smiled again. "Trust me. In the meantime, though, I need you to pass word to your associates and to Salisbourne that I'm going to issue a call for a Council of Lords."

Jantson coughed and threw his palm in front of his face to keep from spraying brandy across the room. "A what?" he blurted. "There hasn't been a Council of Lords in more than two centuries!"

"Well then, I suspect it's high time we had one, isn't it?"

Jantson pulled himself to his feet, downing the brandy in one long wincing swallow. "I'll get on to it now. You really think you can do something for Raysh?"

"Leave it with me." Selena walked him to the doorway. "Don't forget to tell Rentrew for me too." He gave her a worried nod and left.

Selena settled back into her chair and pulled the book closer, reaching for her cup with the other hand. She sipped at the tea, then pulled a face. It was cold. How long had it been sat there?

"Thompson?" She raised her voice rather than reaching for the silly bell.

"It *is* Thompson, isn't it?" she asked, as the servant came into the study.

"Sanderson, your grace," he replied, with the faintest hint of a smile.

"Oh, I was fairly close." She smiled her apology. "Do be a dear and have some fresh tea brought up, would you? This has gone cold on me again."

"Very good, your grace." He gave a bow which went unnoticed as she sank back into the book.

"Oh, Thompson?" she called, as the door swung closed.

"Your grace?"

He really was very good. Not the faintest hint of temper. It almost took the fun out of it, really. What was the point in baiting the staff, if they wouldn't rise to it?

"Have you lived in Celstwin long?" she asked.

"All of my life, your grace," he replied.

"And your family? Are they all in Celstwin, as well?"

"My brother and youngest sister, your grace. My parents passed on some years ago."

She nodded, pausing in thought. "And would you say you know the city well, Thompson?"

"As well as anyone, your grace," Sanderson said. It was starting; he wasn't totally immune. There was just the faintest hint of a clenched jaw.

"I wonder if you could arrange something a little unorthodox for me, Thompson?"

"Of course, your grace?" His acceptance was automatic, with just the slightest lift of tone to make the statement a question.

"I'd like you to find me someone of less than savoury character. I need to speak to a cutpurse or someone of that ilk."

"Your grace?"

"Find me a thief, Thompson." She smiled. "Do you think that could be arranged?"

"I... err..." His perfect control cracked at the request, allowing emotion to leak out for the first time.

"Well?"

"I expect that could be done, your grace," he managed.

"Excellent. Please arrange it as soon as possible. I'll receive them here."

"Very good, your grace. I'll have tea brought in momentarily, your grace." He bowed again.

"Thank you, Thompson, that will be all." She smiled again and then looked down at the book.

"Sanderson, your grace," he corrected her.

"I'm sorry?" Selena glanced up, with a confused frown.

"Sanderson, your grace," he repeated.

"Who?"

Sanderson drew a visibly deep breath. "Never mind, your grace." He sighed and left the room.

Selena clapped her hands and stifled a laugh, but her smile faded too soon. Anlan might be at war, her people themselves threatened, but taking on her own king? That would require nerves she wasn't sure she possessed.

Chapter Eighteen

Gavin fought down the wave of nausea and wished the damned door would just open. The press of menand the stink of sweat and tar, were enough to make anyone's stomach lurch, but it was the swaying of the ship that was making him green.

"Still got your lunch on the inside of you, Retcher?" a voice jeered from behind him.

Gavin glanced back over his shoulder. He couldn't put a name to the man that grinned back at him. The pig-eyed idiot was so impressed with his little dig, it looked to be all he could do to keep the smile from splitting his cheeks.

He ignored it, though. Pig-eyes was right. Managing to keep food down aboard ship was a rarity for him and he didn't dare open his mouth to respond for that very reason.

The wall of leather-clad flesh in front of him pushed back, forcing him tighter into the crowd. There was a muffled thump, followed by a waft of fresh air, as the ramp thudded down onto the long dock. "Finally!" a voice breathed from behind him. Gavin grinned, his seasickness forgotten, as they began to move forward.

It hadn't taken him long to work his way onto a ship headed for the Farmed Lands. The haulers that travelled back and forth through the Vorstelv no longer just carried trained oarsmen and settlers. These days, so long as you could swing a sword and follow directions, you were accepted.

Gavin sighed as he took deep breaths of the cool air. "Lords of Blood, Sea and Sky, what am I doing here?" he said to himself. It was a hell of a gamble, coming all this way to find Klöss, but then what other choices had he had?

He fought down a wave of guilt that was just as strong as any of the seasickness he'd suffered. The creature had followed him. He'd been a fool to lead it to Ylsriss. Because of him, Ylsriss had lost her baby. Because of him, Klöss had lost Ylsriss. His debt was not something he could pass off. Anyone would see where the blame lay, if they knew the facts. If they believed them, that is.

Rhaven had not believed him about the creatures in the park, not even for a moment. He'd scoffed at first, then grown angry, demanding to know what Gavin had done with Ylsriss and the baby. Gavin didn't blame him. He almost didn't believe it himself. His face warmed with remembered shame as he thought of the way the man had thrown him out of his house. The shouts had drawn almost as many stares as the picture - a crippled old man hurling a boy less than half his age out onto the streets. Gavin could still feel the wet cobbles under his hands. He'd scrambled to his feet and fled, Rhaven's curses echoing down the street after him. His time at sea, retching over the side of the ship, wasn't nearly penance enough for what he had done.

He stamped down the ramp onto the docks, following the other men. The city seemed a strange sight to Gavin. He was used to the narrow alleyways and tall buildings of Hesk. Wood was almost a rarity there so, if something could be constructed of stone or slate, it was. This place was a confused mix of wooden and stone structures, most of which appeared to be in the process of being replaced, repaired or, in some cases, rebuilt. He looked around as he made his way along the dock. The tightly-packed crowd of men filing out of the ship gave him little choice as to where he was going. Participating in extended military service had never been a goal of his, though. He was going to need to find a way to get out of this line, and soon.

The harbour was crammed to capacity, thanks to the newly arrived fleet. The ships' jet black sails provided a stark contrast to the blood red sails of the reavers that had already been at dock. The line shuffled down the docks towards a small group of people who were sending them off in different directions. Assigning billets, Gavin realised. This was no good. The moment he was assigned a billet he would be on their records. It would be that much harder to disappear. He hadn't come all this way to play at being a soldier.

Crates were stacked up beside the line of men; cargo waiting to be shipped back to the Barren Isles, by the looks of it. If he could somehow slip out of line and in amongst them, he could be gone in moments.

The line crept forwards. Sweaty men shuffling inside sweaty leathers; it was not pleasant. It was also the worst circumstance for him to try to duck out of line, with the men barely moving. He needed to do something. He staggered and fell hard into the man in front of him, pushing himself off, then stepping back and to the side as the man turned.

The man stumbled, then caught himself and spun to face the line behind him. "Watch yourself!" he snapped at Pig-eyes, as Gavin shifted to the side.

Pig-eyes looked back at the man with a flat stare. "Yeah, I'll do that."

The line moved onwards. As they drew level with the crates, Gavin allowed himself to slow, moving into the space at the edge of the piled cargo as he drew level with Pig-eyes. A well-planted foot and a good shove sent the idiot staggering forward until he crashed into the back of the man in front.

Gavin drifted into the space between the crates as the voices rose. "I. Told. You. To. Watch. Yourself!" A series of fleshy thumps punctuated the sentence. Gavin wore an evil smirk as he eased himself around the boxes and stepped into an alleyway. It couldn't have happened to a nicer man.

He ditched the boots first, pulling his own soft-soled pair from the sack that held the rest of his greys. The leathers he wore would do a better job for blending in with the crowd, but the boots were just too clunky for him to move in easily. He tossed them into the gutter and made his way along the alley before pausing, swearing and then retrieving them. It was never a good idea to just toss part of a disguise away, no matter how much you hated it.

It took just half an hour for Gavin to decide that he didn't like Rimeheld. The place was too ordered, too structured. This wasn't a city that had grown naturally over time. It had been made and designed this way. Someone had thought about where the streets should go and how the alleys should intersect. Its design probably had something to do with overall defence plans but, to Gavin's mind, it was profoundly unnatural.

It was also, so far as he could see, almost completely devoid of places to skulk and hide. He had no need to hide, of course. Nobody knew he was here. A city formed of broad avenues, though, with each alleyway as straight as a die and well-lit, thanks to regularly positioned torch brackets? Well, that was just wrong.

After less than an hour, he'd got a feel for the city. It was actually more of a fort, but every place has a soul, a flavour, and he quickly had the measure of it. It took him longer to find the right kind of inn, however. Finding someone to get information from subtly requires a particular type of place. Somewhere quiet enough for a hushed conversation, but loud enough not to make it look suspicious.

The dockside inns, he dismissed immediately. Not only was there the slim chance he'd run into someone from the ship, places like that were also renowned for fights. It's very hard to get information from someone whilst dodging glasses and flying fists.

He passed three more taverns that were busy with soldiers of one form or another. The places were loud and rowdy, with patrons playing table games and laughing. He'd have had to shout to be heard.

Eventually, he settled on a small tavern in a quiet backstreet. The paint was already peeling from the sign hanging from the wall. The Golden Goose looked to be just the place.

A barman looked up from where he was making a half-hearted effort to polish the bar and nodded at him as he came through the door. Pig-eyes had been useful in more ways than one and Gavin smiled to himself as he opened the man's purse. He looked around at the dingy interior and turned to a small man huddled over a tankard. "How's the mead?"

"I'm right here," the barman said.

"He's drinking it. You're selling it," Gavin replied, unabashed.

"S'not got any rats floating in the keg, if that's what you're asking," the small man muttered, giving him a gap-toothed grin.

"Good enough, then," Gavin nodded. "Mead," he said brightly to the barman, who shook his head.

"You with the fleet then?" he asked. "That'll be four farthings."

"Four!" Gavin sputtered. It was extortionate by Hesk's standards.

The small man chuckled over his tankard. "He's from the fleet, alright. We ain't really got mead here yet. S'either ale or pay for what gets brought over on the haulers."

"Ale it is, then," Gavin muttered, and handed the single copper farthing to the barman. He sipped at his drink and winced at the sour taste.

The small man chuckled again. "You'll get a taste for it." He drank deeply from his own tankard and sighed in appreciation.

"Buy you another?" Gavin asked.

"S'very kind of you...?" He paused, waiting for Gavin's name.

"Gavin," he supplied, holding a finger up to the barman.

"Scarit," the short man replied. He took the tankard quickly before Gavin could change his mind. "How is it you're not with your men, then?"

"My men?" Gavin asked.

"You're fresh to Rimeheld. It's written all over you." Scarit shrugged. "The only ships that have arrived lately have been the Black Fleet. That makes you the sealord's man."

The man was sharper than he looked. So much for subtlety. Gavin drank some ale. His companion was right. It didn't take long to get used to the taste. Either that or his tongue had gone numb.

"I'm looking for someone," he admitted. "The fleet was just a way to get here."

"You must need to see 'em awful bad," Scarit snorted. "It's a long way to come just to collect a debt."

"It's not a debt," the barman said.

"How d'you know, Rolant?" Scarit demanded.

"No man's going to cross the Vorstelv just for a debt," Rolant explained, picking up the rag and scrubbing at the bar again.

"Well, s'got to be sommat like that," Scarit said.

"It's not a debt," Gavin said. Their bickering was getting on his nerves. "There's a man here I need to see, that's all. I need to tell him something."

"Think I'd have just sent a message," Rolant muttered to Scarit. The short man snorted and set his drink down quickly, before clapping his hand to his face to catch the ale that was dripping from his nose.

"Dammit, Rolant!" Scarit cursed, between laughs from behind his hand. "You can't wait until I swallow 'fore you come out with sommat like that?" The barman, for his part, did his best to keep the grin from his lips as he shrugged.

"You might know where I can find him," Gavin said. It was a risky move but he had little choice but to try now; he'd gone this far. "An oarsmaster called Klöss?"

"He's no oarsmaster. Don't know who told you that!" Scarit scoffed. "He's shipmaster and second to bloody Frostbeard himself!"

"Shipmaster? Frostbeard!" Gavin moaned and took a long drink. "How am I going to get to see him?"

"You're not," Rolant stated flatly.

"Send a messenger," Scarit advised, waving his ale at Gavin. "S'what I'd do."

"Won't help," Rolant said. "He's not here. Or at least he won't be for long."

"What?" Gavin gasped, his persona slipping a little as shock set in. The possibility of Klöss not being at Rimeheld had never occurred to him.

"He'll be headed inland. Last I heard, he was, anyway."

"You'd be better off with your company, lad," Scarit observed. "Some of them are bound to be sent to join him, anyway."

"You think?"

He waved his other arm and Gavin noticed, for the first time, the fabric of the sleeve was pinned over what must be a stump. "I didn't lose this hand threshing wheat, lad. I didn't fall off the last fishing boat either. S'obvious to anyone with eyes that you're lying about sommat. I don't want t'know. You need to find Klöss, you say. Your best bet would be with the company you left. I'll tell you this for free though, lad, you'd best not tangle with him. His is one reputation that was earned."

Gavin nodded and sipped at his ale as he thought. It didn't improve over time, he decided, as he failed to keep the grimace off his face.

"Thanks for the advice," he said to Scarit.

The man shrugged over his near-empty tankard. "Din't cost me nothin'."

"You want this? I don't think I'm thirsty." Gavin nodded at his ale.

"You don't know what you're missing, son," Scarit said, as he snatched up the drink.

Gavin snorted and nodded a farewell to Rolant, as he made his way to the door and out into the sunlight. He moved further into the alleyway before he started swearing. They'd not told him much he didn't know already but, of all the damned bad luck, he'd managed to sneak out of the very unit he needed to be part of.

* * *

Klöss fought down the obvious response and listened in silence.

"It's totally out of proportion. He couldn't have made it more obvious if he'd just swanned in with a proclamation!" Frostbeard ranted, pacing back and forth behind the desk.

"Have you considered that it might just be exactly what it appears to be? Simply that he has sent reinforcements drawn from the islands?" Klöss suggested.

Frostbeard sank into the chair behind his desk. "They aren't just reinforcements, Klöss," he sighed. "He could have sent reinforcements without those colours. Sending the Black Fleet only means one thing. That he's taking a direct hand."

Klöss sipped at his keft, savouring the bitter taste. "Let him. It's all politics, Uncle. What difference does it actually make?"

Aiden ran a tired hand over his eyes. "I don't know," he admitted, with a sigh. "You're right. As a people, we'll still have these new lands, the new opportunities."

"So it's vanity then?" Klöss asked, aiming the shot over the rim of his cup.

"Vanity!" Aiden sat upright as if he'd been slapped. "You dare?"

Klöss laughed at the reaction, watching as Aiden's face grew darker by the second. "Hear me out," he managed, before taking another sip of the keft. "Think about it. The sealord sends the Black Fleet and you see this as him seizing control of the lands we've taken. But what is the Black Fleet? In theory, it's the thane's own force. In reality, though, it's a relic of a bygone era and hasn't been used, or really even existed, in two hundred years. What he's really done is take some of our own haulers, fill them with whatever men he could scrape together and then put black sails on the ships."

Frostbeard grunted and waved his hand in a motion that Klöss took to mean he should continue.

"For that matter, who is the sealord? He's the servant of the thane, but then aren't we all? These lands we've taken, the fleet we built, that was all done under the auspices of the thane. The sealord is just trailing in your wake, picking up the scraps."

Aiden looked at him from under his bushy grey eyebrows. "When did you get so clever about politics?"

"Probably around the first time I sailed out as shipmaster," Klöss sighed. "You see my point, though? It's all about how you look at it. You're here and the sealord isn't. You're in charge, not him. For crying out loud, Aiden, you have your name hung over the door!"

"Door? I'm not following you."

"What's the city called, Uncle?"

"Now, you know that wasn't my idea!" Aiden started, holding up a warning finger.

"No, I know it wasn't. And *that's* the point!" Klöss took his last sip and set the cup down, a tiny measure of black sludge remaining in the cup. He ran a finger over his teeth to wipe away the grounds that had made it into his mouth.

"Fine, you've made your poi…" He cut off as a knock came at the door. "Your point," he finished, before turning to the door. "Come!"

A head poked round it hesitantly. "Beg your pardon, Seamaster, but there's a man here says he needs to see Shipmaster Klöss. Something about billeting and a message?"

Klöss groaned. "Tell him to go and find Tristan. I'm busy." He waved a hand in disgusted dismissal, but the door was already closing. "Honestly, half the time I don't know if I'm leading men or if I'm a damned nursemaid!"

Frostbeard laughed. "It doesn't get any better, you know." He leaned forward, serious now, and all remnants of the complaining old man fell away. "What's your feel for it out there?"

"You've read the scout reports." Klöss pointed at the pile of papers on another desk.

"Bah! You know my opinion of them!" Frostbeard said.

"Never trust an opinion on troops from a man who's been trained how to run away," Klöss recited.

Frostbeard scratched at his cheek through his coarse beard. "No, not troops. They can count troops easily enough. I say it as a joke, but I'm serious. The average scout has little feel for a battlefield or a battle." He turned in the chair so he could look at the map pinned to the wall. "What do you feel about it at the moment?"

"I expected more," Klöss admitted. He sat up, leaning his arms on the desk. "Look, we didn't know what this land was like. In truth, even though we scouted as much as we could, we didn't know what to expect at all. We've pushed inland for... what, about twelve leagues? We've driven off their people and we've burned their villages. So where are their armies? Where is the response? I keep waiting for the door to crash open with word that they're on the march." He walked around the desk to point at the map.

"After the battle at that last village, I expected more from them. They were good, very clever. Their commander made good use of the land and improvised to compensate for what he didn't have. Using logs in the catapults was genius. His forces, though, were nothing compared to ours in terms of numbers."

"You think they hold back?" Aiden asked.

"They have to be. The plan was to engage them, defeat them and then pull back to the lands we'd taken. To discourage them from trying to retake lands. That 's not going to happen unless we meet, and defeat, a significant force."

"That was more or less what the sealord was saying in his last letter," Frostbeard snorted. "Fine. I want you to push inland in force. You'll have the men from the sealord's fleet but I wouldn't put any faith in their ability. Take ten companies with you, and go and find me their armies. Bring me back a victory we can drink about."

Klöss nodded, concealing a smile at his uncle's refusal to name the Black Fleet.

"Oh, and Klöss?" Frostbeard called him back as he headed for the door. "Try to keep the supply lines as short as you can. We don't have the men to leave whole armies guarding your supply dumps."

Klöss grunted. To be fair, that was all the response it deserved.

* * *

Gavin pulled his cloak closer against the rain. It was more than a misting drizzle, but less than a light shower. If it had been any heavier, he'd have just been wet and been able to ignore it. As it was, it managed to seek out those parts of him that were still dry, sending the occasional fat drip running down inside his leathers in search of them.

He trudged. It was a particular type of walk that he'd been forced to develop over the last three weeks. The men in front of him never moved fast enough for his liking, but there was no point trying to pass through the line. Gavin muttered and tried to kick his boots into a more comfortable position as he walked.

Klöss would be somewhere up ahead of them. His troops had left Rimeheld days before Gavin and the others with him had even been organised.

The arrows came from nowhere, whistling from the trees in a little chorus of hate.

"Shields!" someone shouted, though they needn't have bothered. Any man with any sense was now huddled down behind his shield, trying to make himself as small a target as possible. Then the line was moving towards the trees and Gavin bit his lip to keep from screaming.

The men of the Black Fleet or, as he thought of them, the Dead Men, were mixed in with experienced oarsmen. What the oarsman acting as their leader had done to deserve this duty, Gavin had no idea.

He was surrounded by a pocket of Dead Men, a tight phalanx of oarsmen on each side of them. The differences were obvious and immediate. The oarsmen moved their shields as a unit, working together to provide themselves with the best cover possible as they headed for the trees. The Dead Men moved sluggishly, receiving the occasional kick from the oarsmen that were acting as their squad leaders to keep them moving.

He saw first one man, then two more, go down as arrows found the gaps between the shields and he looked to either side of him. The man on the left was too far away, so he reached out to the right, grabbed the edge of the man's shield and yanked.

The Dead Man gave him a look of pure terror, and then moved closer as he saw what Gavin was doing. Overlapping the shields provided them with slightly more cover, although two alone made little difference. He looked to the left again to where his neighbour scuttled along, hiding more behind other men than taking cover from his own shield.

"You!" Gavin called. "Come over here."

The man gave him a startled look and then shook his head violently. "Fuck that!" he hissed back.

"Get your flea-ridden hide over here or I'll gut you myself!" Gavin spat back. He flicked his cloak aside to reveal the long, curved dagger at his belt and pulled it an inch from the sheath. The man, now more frightened of him than of the arrows, moved within reach.

Gavin stepped back slightly, so the second man's shield overlapped the first. With his own shield held high, they had an improvised wall. The arrows thudded into it with a regularity that was both terrifying and oddly reassuring. He relaxed slightly and looked about for the rest of the squad. They had melted away like mist in the morning sunlight and their leader was nowhere to be seen.

Gavin swore to himself and thought for a second. The wall enabled them to move faster and he saw some of the other Dead Men grouping into threes and fours to copy what he'd done. It would have worked better if they'd worked as a single unit, but they hadn't the training for that.

A cry went up from ahead of them and the oarsmen broke into a sprint, charging into the trees. Gavin watched them go for a second, before lowering his own shield for just long enough to gauge the distance to the trees. "Come on!" he shouted, and raced for the closest trunk. Let the oarsmen have the fight; he had his own agenda and, at the moment, that included having a good two feet of tree trunk between him and the next arrow.

He threw himself into the undergrowth close to the trees as arrows continued to hiss past. His leather armour was bulky and it felt alien to him. Despite wearing it during the weeks of training they'd been given before the sea voyage and for the week or more that they'd been pressing into enemy territory, it still felt wrong. He forced himself to ignore it and squirmed on his belly towards a tree.

Men surged past him, running blindly into the trees with their weapons drawn. *Let them*, Gavin thought. He was no coward and would fight when he needed to, but to run blindly towards flying arrows crossed the line between bravery and stupidity, as far as he was concerned.

The arrows first slowed and then stopped, as the distant sounds of fighting carried through the trees. He moved towards the sound, although he was in no hurry. Keeping his sword sheathed at his side, he pulled out his long dagger. They might have forced him to drill with the sword, but really it was just an oversized knife. Once you got the first inch of any blade into someone, they ended up just as dead anyway.

He could move far faster with the smaller weapon than he would ever have been able to carrying the sword. Even sheathed, it was getting in the way. After a moment's indecision, he drew and then dumped the heavy weapon. He kept his shield for now. It was large, heavy and made moving with stealth almost impossible, but it was rather good against arrows.

He came across the first body moments later. It lay in the ferns, face up, as if the man were just taking a nap. The feathered shaft jutting from his chest told another story, however, and the fact that his armour hadn't stopped the arrow was not lost on Gavin.

"Waste of bloody time," he muttered, picking at the heavy leathers he wore. He found himself wishing, not for the first time, that he had other clothes with him so he could be rid of the hateful stuff.

The sound of the fighting grew louder and he ghosted from tree to tree as he approached. He stopped as he caught sight of them and pressed himself close to a broad tree trunk to take stock.

The men in green cloaks were easily distinguishable from the leather-clad Bjornmen. They were clearly better trained as well, he noted, as the one closest to him held off two Bjornmen with ease. They were probably Dead Men, he realised, as he saw them waste several opportunities to strike.

He knelt to ditch his shield and move in closer but, as he did so, the green-cloaked man's sword dipped, almost delicately, into one of the stomach of one of the Bjornmen. The man fell like a stuck pig, screaming as he rolled in the leaves. Gavin swore to himself and moved quickly before the fight could turn the two men round to face him.

The leaves were dry but the noise of the fight covered his approach as the Bjornman puffed and wheezed. Green Cloak, for his part, didn't even appear to be winded. He turned at the last second, sensing something, and twisted as he spotted Gavin. By then, however, it was too late and Gavin thrust his long knife deep, sinking it into the man's kidneys. He was moving again before the man hit the ground, drifting forward, seeking the cover of the trees, while the surviving Bjornman sank to his knees in the leaves, shaking and sobbing.

Gavin knew how to kill. You didn't live long amongst the Wretched unless you did. His training hadn't come from instructors in ridiculous schools, though. It had come in the shadows of back alleys at the hands of boys trying to kill him for a warmer shirt, for the bread he carried or even just because he was there, in that place.

He moved on through the trees, killing where he had to. Some of the time, he could just step past the skirmishes. Getting killed in a senseless fight after he'd travelled all this way would be beyond stupid.

Any sense of order amongst the Dead Men seemed to have gone out the window as soon as they had entered the trees. They were scattered, fighting a thousand small fights alone or in twos and threes. If it weren't for their obviously greater numbers, Gavin knew they would probably have been slaughtered to a man by now. As it was, the death toll was horrific and every empty space seemed to be littered with bodies.

The sound of a twig cracking was the only warning he had, and he ducked purely on instinct as the sword hacked at the air where his head had been. Gavin followed his movement through and turned it into a tight roll, before coming to his feet and turning.

His attacker was already pressing in, his longsword held low and his large wooden shield ready. He was dressed for speed and wore none of the ridiculous metal armour that Gavin had been warned to expect.

Gavin pulled his knife and stood ready, weaving it through the air. The movements were purely for show; it was a trick he'd picked up from long years on the streets. .

Show the enemy your weapon. Let the light catch it, shine off the edge, so they focus on it and see the sharpness of the blade, the cruelty of its point. A man imagining the feel of a knife slicing into his vitals is not a man concentrating on the fight.

The swordsman struck, with a feint and then a thrust, and Gavin spun to the right, pushing the sword blade to the side with his knife and moving in close to the shield. His intent was to spin again and then be behind the man, so he was utterly unprepared for the blow when the shield slammed into his face.

The impact sent him reeling and he fought to keep hold of his knife as the world spun around him for a second. The man gave him no time to recover though and moved in, his sword held high to strike.

Gavin backed away, giving ground to keep the steel outside of his skull. The swordsman grinned at him, the contempt he felt for the weapon in Gavin's hand clear in his eyes. A knife has one advantage over a sword though, and Gavin gave a snide grin back as he flipped the weapon over in his hand and hurled it into the man's throat.

The skirmisher clutched at the knife and made a tortured, gurgling noise as he fell. Gavin stepped forward to retrieve his blade, then froze as another man emerged from behind the fallen body and charged, his sword ready to thrust. Gavin dived for the knife, knowing he'd never reach it in time, and tensed for the blow he knew must come.

Instead, he heard a grinding, slicing crunch, followed by a crash as the man fell to the dirt. Gavin lifted his head to see a large Bjornman oarsman wiping a double-headed axe on the dead man's cloak.

"A good trick with the knife," he observed, "That, he was not expecting, I think." He held a hand out to help Gavin up.

"Thanks," Gavin said, as he pulled himself up. "Good timing."

"I was watching," the big man confessed with a shrug.

"Watching?" Gavin didn't attempt to keep his feelings from his face.

"I had never seen a man attack a swordsman with just a knife before." He shrugged. "Stupid but interesting. Perhaps next time use your sword?"

"Swords are slow," Gavin muttered and stooped to retrieve the knife.

"We are falling behind. Come." The big man slung his shield over his back and strode off through the trees, hefting the axe in one hand.

"Wait! I never got your name," Gavin called after him.

"Tristan." The voice carried back to Gavin as he ran to catch up.

The Bjornmen seemed to have managed to push the skirmishers back through the woods, thinning their numbers, by the looks of things, but never quite managing to fully close with them. Gavin followed Tristan through the trees and they made their way out of the woods. As they stepped out into the field, Gavin looked around in confusion. He had been expecting to emerge into a battle. The signs of fighting were all around them, from the torn and muddied grass to the bodies lying on the ground like discarded toys, but the scene was nothing compared to what it should have been.

Tristan examined the grass. "Horses," he grunted. "Clever."

"I don't follow," Gavin admitted.

Tristan glanced over to him. "These men. They attack us from the trees, yes?"

Gavin nodded.

"They goad us, allow us to push them back through these woods, picking us off with arrows as they go, staying out of any real fight." He turned, waving at the torn ground. "Then here, they escape on the horses they left." He pointed off to the south.

Gavin nodded again, struggling slightly with the man's thick Far Islander accent. It was a clever plan. The Dead Men, in particular, would have been easy pickings for the archers as they moved back through the woods.

Men were forming back into their units and Gavin watched them for a moment, making no move to join them himself. He looked to the south, where the grassy hillside dipped down into a shallow valley. He could just make out the horses in the distance, as the skirmishers made their retreat.

"What would you have done?" The question caught him off guard and he was silent for a time, while Tristan looked at him appraisingly.

"I would never have put the Dead Men all together," he said, finally. "They should have been dispersed throughout the other units."

"Dead Men?" Tristan asked, with a snort.

"This lot." Gavin waved his arm in their direction. "The men from the Black Fleet."

"Why Dead Men?"

"The training is a joke," Gavin explained. "These men are more used to threatening people with their weapons than actually fighting with them. As fighters, they're dead already; they just haven't found a sword to stick themselves with yet."

Tristan stared at him long enough to make him wonder just who this man was, and whether or not he'd just shoved his foot all the way down his own throat.

"Come," he said, finally. "There is someone I want you to talk to."

"What about my squad?" Gavin ventured.

Tristan gave the Dead Men a scathing glance. "You do not belong with them. Come."

They travelled west, pushing faster than most of the other men. The fact that nobody stopped them or even raised an eyebrow as they went past was not lost on Gavin and his concerns grew by the minute.

They had passed the foremost elements of the column by evening and made a rough camp in a stand of beech. Tristan was quiet and offered little in the way of conversation beyond asking Gavin his name and what training he'd had. They rose early and pushed on. During late afternoon, the shallow valley through which they were travelling opened up into a vast grassy plain and Gavin suddenly saw a sea of white tents and men in leather armour. The Bjornman army was like nothing he could have imagined and the camp stretched as far as he could see.

Tristan moved through the troops unchallenged, although several men offered nods of greeting and respect. He led them into the very heart of the camp, to a cluster of tents surrounded by guards, and entered one of them without pause.

The tent was cramped. Two men were consulting maps and papers that had been spread out across a camp table. Another stood apart from them, reading over a crumpled note with a sour look on his face. His expression brightened slightly as Tristan entered.

"I thought you'd still be pulling arrows out of your skin," he said, the scars on his face twisting as he smiled.

Tristan didn't bother to respond, although his glare spoke eloquently to the scar-faced man, managing somehow to curse, insult, and suggest an unhealthy inclination towards farm animals, all at the same time.

"I have someone you should talk to, Klöss," Tristan said.

"You're Klöss?" Gavin blurted out, drawing questioning looks from both of them.

"What of it?" Klöss asked.

"I came all the way from Hesk to find you. I need to talk to you in private."

Klöss let out a sigh as he rolled his eyes. "Listen, lad, I'm a bit busy for tales at the moment. Most of the things you've heard are crap, anyway."

"What?" Gavin looked confused. "No, it's about Ylsriss."

His despairing expression faded at that. "Ylsriss? What do you know about her?"

Gavin noted the other men's eyes were on him. This was not the way he wanted to do this. "You and I have met before. Years ago, in Hesk. You chased a cutpurse into an alley and got coshed. You woke up in a cellar filled with street children."

Klöss's eyes widened and he nodded. "Carry on."

"I was one of those children. Something's happened to Ylsriss. I came all this way to explain it to you."

"I already know she's vanished," Klöss growled, clenching the note in his fist.

"That's probably from Rhaven, isn't it?" Gavin nodded at the note. "I tried to talk to him first, but he threw me out. I've travelled all the way from Hesk to tell you the truth about what happened."

"Alright boy, you've got my attention. What is it?"

"Not like this." Gavin motioned at the others in an exaggerated manner. "I need to tell you in private."

Klöss sighed. "Fine. You've got two minutes."

CHAPTER NINETEEN

Rhenkin stood in the rain, absently patting his horse's flank as he watched the men file in. His mind churned through the figures in his head - men, supplies, units. Were they going to have enough? The numbers would be close, but it was too good an opportunity to pass up.

"Larson!" he shouted, without turning.

The footsteps were more squelches in the wet ground than anything else. "It's Kennick, Sir." The man sounded apologetic.

Rhenkin swore silently to himself. Larson was a resource he was going to find hard to replace. "Sorry, Kennick," he muttered. "Force of habit."

Kennick nodded in silence. It was probably as hard for the new lieutenant as it was for him, Rhenkin realised. Trying to fill someone else's shoes was never a pleasant experience.

"How well do you remember your academy strategy, Kennick?"

"Well enough, I suppose, Sir," the man replied, scratching at his moustache as the rain ran down his face.

"Accepted ratio for victory over a force with unknown composition?" Rhenkin snapped out the question.

"Your force must outnumber theirs by a minimum of a third, Sir," Kennick replied. "That is, unless there are significant strategic enhancers, such as true surprise, terrain or defensive structures."

Rhenkin looked at him. "Did you do well in strategy, Kennick?"

"Top of my class, Sir," Kennick replied.

"How much stock do you put in what you learned?" Rhenkin asked.

"Honestly, Sir? Not a great deal. Some of the tactics are useful, but I don't really believe you can break a battle, or a war, down to numbers and ratios."

"Is that so?" Rhenkin kept his voice level.

"There are too many factors that the books don't take into account, Sir. You can break a battle down to numbers in terms of troop levels, training and so on, but you also need to consider things like morale shifts or necessity."

"Necessity?"

"It's all very well saying it's strategically unwise to attack unless you outnumber your foe by at least a third, Sir, but you can't give ground forever," Kennick said, with a slight wince.

"Very good, Son." Rhenkin favoured him with a tight smile. "Necessity drives every campaign. Necessity is why we must attack now, rather than giving those bastards any more land." He looked at the sea of tents and men. "Are Rentrew's men set up?"

Kennick nodded. "Some are still on their way, Sir, but most of the officers have arrived and have been brought into the command structure."

"What have they sent us? I see mostly mounted troops."

"It is largely mounted heavy lancers, Sir. A fair number of mounted archers as well, though the infantry is not an insignificant force."

"And the skirmishers?"

"Still making their way back to us, Sir. They sent a man ahead to report."

Rhenkin pulled off his helmet and scratched at his hair. How the hell did the rain work its way in underneath it? "I want you to send out some scouts. All on horseback and with orders not to get even close to being within arrow range. I want to know where the Bjornmen are going and how they're being deployed. Get reports to me every day, without fail."

"That will require messenger relays, Sir," Kennick warned.

"So the men will need to sit and wait in the rain for a while," Rhenkin sneered. "We're doing that now!"

"I'll see to it, Sir."

"In the meantime, I want your analysis of the terrain around here. We're going to do this on our terms and I'll be damned if I'll let them choose the battlefield." Rhenkin waited for the man to nod before speaking again. "For now, I'm going to get out of this pissing rain and get some sleep. Send a man in with something hot and wake me if anything happens."

"Who shall I report to in your absence, Sir?"

Rhenkin gave the man an evil smile. "You're my second now, Son. While I'm sleeping, they report to you." He walked away, chuckling to himself as he headed for his tent. Kennick seemed to be a good man and he had no doubt he could do the job well. He was no Larson, though.

That attack had come from nowhere. They'd not seen or heard a thing from the fae in weeks. A man could almost have been forgiven for thinking the whole thing had been a fever dream. But then they'd come, charging down out of the moonlit sky on horses as pale as a dead man's face. Larson had been at the forefront of the battle, screaming orders for iron weapons. He'd probably never even seen the one that took him. Rhenkin shook his head as he ducked into the tent and sat on a camp chair to prise his boots off. The mud was thick and oozed between his fingers as he worked.

"Bloody waste," he muttered to himself. Years of training and excellence had ended on the bone blade of one of those lantern-eyed monsters.

He pulled some camp shoes on and went to the table, pushing the reports aside so he could see the map properly.

"We ought to be killing these bloody hell-beasts, not fighting each other," he muttered. "Damn it though, if you want a fight, by hell, you'll have one."

Location, that would be the key. His force was now split evenly between mounted troops and infantry, and there are few troops more useless than a mounted unit with no room to move.

Rhenkin traced his fingertips over the map. The local area was sketched in rough shades of charcoal. The woods, valleys and hillsides were useless for his needs. Even the plain was barely large enough for the manoeuvres they'd need to make for this to work.

"This has been a shit-storm from the start," he muttered, before stomping over to the torture device known as a camp bed.

He was asleep long before the young soldier arrived with the food and didn't wake as he set it down on the table. Sleep had been slow to find him, missing him entirely these past two nights. Now that it had him, it would not let go.

* * *

The Bjornman army covered the land like a dark blanket as it moved towards them, out of the trees. Keiron could just see the smaller contingent that he knew contained their supply wagons making its way around the edge of the woods to the north. They'd been moving steadily for three days now.

"Gutsy bastards," he muttered to himself.

"What's that?" asked the dark-haired man beside him.

"They came directly through the woods." Keiron pointed. "I know it's a small wood, but look, their supply wagons had to go all the way around. They took a hell of a risk. What if we'd raided them?"

They'd worked together four times now, staying for a day and a night before one of them headed back to give their report to the next pair in the line. The scouts surrounded the Bjornmen and watched their every move. It was three days hard ride to their own lines, so a messenger relay line had been strung out over twenty miles, with men stationed a day apart, rotating the line and sharing the scouting duties.

Fallon had been sour with him from the outset. He spoke little, offering up nothing about his past or his experience. The only thing Keiron really knew was that he didn't care for him or his superior attitude.

"You think too much, Keiron," Fallon said. He hawked and spat into the grass. "You be just as keen as you like. Lick that corporal's boots until you can see your fawning little face in them. It won't help you. You're a messenger boy dressed up in a scout's uniform, plain and simple."

Keiron felt the blood rise in his face. "Screw you, Fallon. I'm as much a scout as you. Captain said so himself."

"Well, scurry off and deliver your message then, *scout*," Fallon spat, his words dripping with contempt.

Keiron glared at him and swung himself up onto his horse, only turning back as Fallon sniggered at him.

"What now?" Keiron snapped. He was done with this self-important idiot.

"You might want this." Fallon waved his travel sack at him, with a sneer.

Keiron shook his head, despairing at himself as much as at the annoying man. He nudged his horse forward and snatched the sack out of Fallon's hand.

It was probably only because he was so sick of the man and wouldn't meet his eyes that he was looking beyond him. He frowned as he tried to make sense of what he was seeing. Something wasn't right. Then the grassy plain simply stood up and levelled crossbows at them.

It must have taken them three full days to crawl through the long grass. The blankets they'd draped over themselves were covered in thick tufts that blended with the grass on the plain. They wore only light clothing under them, so as not to hamper their movements.

Keiron noted all of this in a second, but his attention was focused on the large crossbows the pair carried. "Fallon, move!" he finally managed to shout. It was too late. The loud twanging report of the weapons seemed quieter than the sickening crunch the bolt made as it tore into Fallon's chest, and even quieter than the sound of the second bolt as it passed his face.

Wheeling his horse, Keiron dug his heels in and urged the beast for more speed, bending low over its back. He had no idea of the effective range of the Bjornman crossbow or how long it took to reload. The hollow sensation between his shoulder blades drove him to turn the horse wildly as he charged through the long grass.

The horse was coated in lather and blowing hard by the time Keiron reined her in. His hands had stopped shaking about five minutes before, but his legs felt like they'd barely support him. He climbed down out of the saddle, but clung onto the pommel as his knees threatened to buckle.

There were no signs of the Bjornman scouts, although their army still loomed in the distance. Of course, there'd been no sign of them right up until the second they'd attacked either. Fear forced him to move, whispering into his ear, and he led the horse through the grasses. After an hour of walking, he stopped and allowed her to drink from a small, stream-fed pond before mounting her again.

He rode steadily, careful not to strain the horse too much, running her hard for only short periods before permitting her to drop down to a canter and then to a walk.

By evening, he was exhausted. The riding was taxing enough, but the fear was visceral and it ate away at him. He hadn't really stopped for any rests, other than to walk the horse. He'd tried to, on several occasions, but soon found he was glancing back or staring nervously at the grasses as they blew in the wind, so he'd pushed on.

Navigating by the stars was simple enough when all he had to do was to go in a straight line, but the darkness was total. Keiron wasn't a city boy, by any means, but there is a huge difference between the darkness inside a town or village and the darkness found in the middle of nowhere.

The stars seemed very bright and the moon, although not yet quite full, hung fat and heavy in the sky, lighting his path. When the wind blew the clouds across the sky, however, they cloaked the glowing orb and the night enveloped him. The darkness swallowed him, taking him down to that place every child has visited and which every man carries with him in a small, secret part of his soul; the place where the night holds a touch of terror.

He slept twice, waking with a lurch each time and nearly falling from the saddle. On both occasions, he also discovered that the horse had strayed off course and he had to search frantically to find the constellation he should have been heading towards. He felt a sense of true relief when the darkness finally began to lift, revealing the grey light of dawn.

The hill was miles to the south. He must have drifted off track during the night and never really corrected course. It was visible, however, and that was enough. He let the horse graze while he ate a handful of something dried and tasteless from the sack, then set off again. The warning couldn't wait. The Bjornmen were coming.

* * *

Klöss moved forward towards the front lines, muttering an almost rhythmic stream of curses. It was a low song of frustration, one that he sang to himself as he watched the hated horsemen peel off and retreat again. Their riders were lightly armoured and were, as far as he could see, wielding only bows. They would be easy prey if his men could ever get close enough. Every attempt they had made, however, had been met with a hail of arrows and the riders had eventually simply broken off without truly engaging.

His army was spread out behind him, company after company of men awaiting his orders. He ignored them, however, focusing on the horses and the endless sounds of arrows striking shields as his men crouched against the onslaught again.

The bows of the riders were small and didn't really have the power to penetrate the thick leather armour of his men, even if they did make it past the broad shields. Despite that, there was a scream of pain with every hail of arrows, as either an archer was lucky or a Bjornman wasn't.

"These horses, they are effective." Tristan spoke conversationally, as if they were just taking a stroll.

"They're a pain in the arse, is what they are." Klöss looked at the low-lying hills and the army in the valley between them. The horse archers had been harrying them for days as they'd advanced, riding in and raking them with their bows, only to peel off and retreat as soon as an advance was ordered. The one time he had allowed a force to truly pursue them, riders in heavy steel armour had come thundering into position and charged into his troops, their lances devastating the exposed Bjornmen, while the fallen were churned under the steel-shod hooves of their mounts.

"I'll be damned if I'm going to play his game," he muttered.

Tristan gave Klöss a wry smile. "His game?"

Klöss waved at the view before them. "Look at the hills there. He's basically set himself up with a fortress. He expects us to come plodding along and walk right between them as his archers slam arrows down onto us and the rest of his troops charge."

"A good plan, as far as plans go," Tristan acknowledged, with a grunt.

"And one I don't plan on following," Klöss muttered, waving an arm to catch the attention of the man following him. "Gerrig, find out if they have assembled the catapults yet. Oh, and pass the order to bring the arbalests to the front line."

The young man nodded and left at a run.

"A good lad, you have there," Tristan noted, watching him vanish through the lines. "Needs a sense of humour, though."

Klöss gave him a long look. "A sense of humour? Tristan, you do understand we're about to have a battle here?"

"Then it is required even more." He laughed as Klöss treated to him to an icy stare.

The army undulated as the men shifted and those carrying the heavy arbalests moved towards the front.

Klöss gave the order and waited. The army had halted now, a high wall of shields protecting those in range of the arrows that flew towards them. The horse archers continued to worry at the army like flies at a horse's eyes.

The weaponsmaster stood beside the long rows of catapults that were situated in an otherwise clear space in the middle of the army. The weapons were too valuable to risk by leaving them exposed to an enemy attack, but nobody wanted to be that close to them. They threatened a violent death, involving flying shards of jagged wood and ropes lashing fast enough to cut through flesh, to anyone within reach, if anything should go wrong.

The older man scowled down at his crews as they made adjustments, then finally raised the white baton.

"Let's go and spring their trap, shall we?" Klöss said to himself.

The order was given and the men moved forward, organising themselves into three companies as they trotted towards the enemy lines. After only a few minutes, volleys of arrows began to fly towards them, but it was nothing close to the storm that they had been expecting. Very few of the arrows managed to cover the full distance, and the Bjornmen simply closed ranks and raised their shields as they drew closer.

The hillside before them erupted as the men stood, throwing off their concealing blankets and setting arrows to strings. The Bjornmen reacted instantly, clustering together and overlapping their shields to form three protective domes.

"Now!" shouted Klöss, raising his sword to give the signal to the weaponsmaster.

He watched as the storm of arrows engulfed his companies. They huddled low, all forward movement forgotten as the arrows slammed into the wooden shields or shattered as they hit the steel central bosses.

The sound of the catapults was thunderous as their operators launched them almost in unison. Stone was hard to come by on the plains and even harder to transport with any speed, but Klöss had learned the lessons his battles had taught him and the woods they had passed through had provided amply.

A hail of rocks, hunks of wood and broken weapons tore into the poorly armoured archers. His arbalests would never had managed the range; the enemy archers were using the height of the hills to add to their reach and they were probably at their limit, as it was.

Those that hadn't already fled at the sight of the incoming storm were torn to pieces as the deadly barrage struck. The huddled Bjornmen dropped their shield wall and formed back into lines again. They all knew there could be only one response from the enemy.

Klöss waited in silence. It was always a risk to assume your opponent thought the same way as you did, but he couldn't imagine anyone passing up the opportunity. The men trotted forward, their heavy shields raised in front of them and long spears in their hands. Arbalest men followed, pressing close to the spearmen so they could use the cover from their shields.

The horse-borne heavy lancers came in a wave, passing out of the enemy lines and forming up as they began their charge. A blur of thundering hooves and shining steel, they bore down upon the seemingly hapless companies of Bjornmen, who were now far from the rest of their lines.

The spearmen shifted their heavy shields slightly to the side as the horses flew towards them and, with a sharp report, the arbalests fired. The heavy bolts ripped through the ridiculous steel skirts that hung over the horse's chests and then ripped into the flesh. The spearmen braced their weapons against the earth, as what was left of the line crashed into them.

Klöss watched his men shift backwards, allowing the fight to move them rather than becoming locked in one position. His location afforded him a good view of the battlefield, but the chaos was just too intense for him to see what was going on with any clarity until it was too late.

The second rank of heavy lancers had been positioned far enough behind the first that almost thirty seconds had passed by the time they struck. There was simply no time to reset the arbalests, however. The heavy weapons were notoriously slow to reload. The heavy lancers drove their horses into the Bjornmen, trusting in the weight of the animals rather than their own weapons. They broke through the line before wheeling and stabbing down into the mayhem. They worked swiftly, destroying the Islanders before retreating to the relative safety of their own lines.

Klöss swore and gave the order to charge. He looked out at the battlefield to see a single Islander moving. He continued to watch, even though he knew it was a mistake. The man lay face down in the dirt, surrounded by blood and gore, crawling mindlessly towards his own lines. The lone remaining lancer sat astride his horse, calmly looking down at the Islander. For a moment, he seemed content just to watch as the man dragged himself along, grasping at the grass and dirt. The charging Bjornmen were less than a hundred feet from their companion when the lancer drove his weapon down, ramming it through the man's shoulder blades and into the blood-soaked earth. The Islander screamed then, all his energy spent in one long, agonised burst.

The lancer left his weapon there, pinning the man to the dirt, and gave the charging Bjornmen a mock salute as he wheeled his horse and trotted back to his own lines.

* * *

"Bastard!" Rhenkin raged, as the catapults devastated his archers. "Send the horse," he screamed at Kennick. He forced himself to watch as the few men who had survived ran, falling and sliding down the hillside in an attempt to escape the deadly barrage.

"Set the archers three ranks in behind the front lines, ready for when they try and close with us. I want them to use a combination of direct shots and overhead volleys for as long as is practical," Rhenkin ordered. "Let's see the bastards try and do their shield wall tricks against two lines of fire. Have small squads of the heavy lancers ready to charge the moment they drop into a tortoise, too."

They watched as the heavy lancers charged, their two ranks split far apart. Rhenkin was impassive as stone as the Bjornmen fired their crossbows. Kennick, to his credit, said nothing, though he winced visibly as the first rank of horsemen was torn apart by the heavy bolts.

The second rank struck, crashing into the unprepared Bjornmen. For the first time while fighting these people, Rhenkin felt a surge of triumph as he watched the horsemen do their grisly work.

The Bjornmen charged. It was not a probe or a feint this time. Instead, a howling mass of leather-clad savages hurled themselves forwards. There was no time to give orders and Rhenkin surveyed the scene in silence as the men crashed together, hacking and stabbing. The battle descended into pure savagery, with no room for tactics, and men slipped and fell as the ground became soaked in blood and churned into muck by heavy boots.

His remaining archers were sending a steady sheet of shafts high into the air so that they fell within the Bjornman ranks. For the first time though, Rhenkin could see the tactic was having an impact. Bjornmen positioned as far as three or four rows from the front line were being struck. It was likely some of the arrows were striking his own men too, but he forced himself to ignore that possibility. The Bjornmen began to raise their shields, robbing themselves of much of their forward momentum.

"Catapults," he ordered, sensing Kennick turn to relay the order. They hadn't found much in the way of stone but now was the time to use it. The barrage tore gaping holes in the Bjornman lines, and the attack faltered and they began to withdraw.

Rhenkin shook his head at Kennick's unasked question. The temptation to pursue and harry them was strong, but their position was too advantageous for them to consider doing anything that might risk losing it.

The day became an endless succession of attacks, with the Bjornmen coming in waves, steadily grinding away at their front line. They pushed them back twice, emerging from the cover of the hills and spilling out onto the plains, but they'd had to pull back again on both occasions. Now, as evening fell, they were retreating again as the Bjornmen sought to envelop the hills and flank them.

Rhenkin wheeled his horse and ran an eye over the formation of the front line. They'd retreated a good distance from the hills, but the stench of battle was still overpowering. The mingled stink of sweat, blood and horses was overlaid with the fetid smell of fear.

"Do you think they'll come again, Sir?" Kennick asked, glancing at the sky. "It's going to be dark before too much longer."

"I wouldn't put anything past them at this point, Kennick," Rhenkin began. "They attack then withdraw, attack then withdraw again. They ebb and flow like the waves on a beach. These Bjornmen know nothing of retreat. They are like the sea itself, pushing ever onwards, driven only by the tides and its own relentless hunger. They are unlike anyone I've ever fought before. Unforgiving, merciless and as cruel as the waves of winter."

The battle slowed as evening fell. The Bjornmen made a succession of half-hearted probes and then withdrew.

"Send the order to withdraw us further. Set sentries and fast response units," Rhenkin said, fighting a yawn as he spoke. "I want men strung out ahead of our lines. If their men take so much as a step towards us, I want us to know about it."

"Yes, Sir," Kennick replied. "I hope I'm not crossing boundaries, Sir, but you should try and get some sleep while you can."

Rhenkin gave the lieutenant a long look and then snorted in amusement. "There aren't many men that would have the balls to make that statement when they're so new to their post, Kennick. I'm impressed."

"First rule of command support, Sir," Kennick said. "Mother your commander because he's too busy to look after himself."

Rhenkin barked a short laugh. "You're right, of course. I'll try to get some sleep as soon as we're settled."

* * *

Klöss gnawed at the chicken leg in his hand. It was an extravagance to be eating fresh meat and he knew he shouldn't be doing it in front of the men. They would be on a rough stew made from dried meat that would have to cook for a good hour or more. The torches set into the ground by his tent were flaring in his eyes and he stepped around to the side of them to get into the shadows.

He could just make out the lights of the Anlan army in the distance. The name still sounded wrong to him. He'd spent too many months calling the place the Farmed Lands. He tossed the bone aside and fingered the letter tucked into his belt. It was well worn and creased, and he'd lost count of how many times he'd read it now.

Gavin's story bothered him. It was something he'd had to fight not to scoff at. It was an instant reaction. Keiju and trells, the stuff of fairy tales for children. To hear that one of them had supposedly snatched his son and carried it away was laughable, yet the man had travelled halfway around the world to find him. He'd passed through the Vorstelv just to deliver his message. That, alone, gave Klöss pause for thought.

The note he'd received from his father had mentioned none of this, saying only that Ylsriss had vanished with the child. Rhaven had never been one for long messages, but the letter seemed to be short on details, even for him.

He batted the thought away and looked towards the lights of the enemy camp. They'd pushed them hard today. Twice he'd thought they had them at the point of breaking, as his men broke ranks and worked their way in amongst the enemy lines. The tactic worked particularly well against these men from Anlan. They were so regimented that they couldn't think outside of a unit. They didn't know how to react when faced with men who were just as happy to fight alone as they were in a squad.

It had been their commander who'd made the difference, sounding a retreat to restore control even though their own men outnumbered those attacking at that point. Klöss smiled in grudging admiration of the man. A commander without vanity was a rare thing.

He glanced up at the sky. The full moon was hidden by the clouds, unlike on the past two nights when it had lit the plains almost as clear as day.

"Christoph!" he called, making his way back into the torchlight again.

A head poked out of the command tent. "Shipmaster?"

"Get me some volunteers for a reaping. A goodly-sized one." Klöss didn't wait for the response and stepped back into the darkness, his eyes on the enemy campfires again. If they found it hard to cope with men who could function outside of units, it would be interesting to see how they managed in the dark.

The man worked quickly, passing the word to gather volunteers and lining them up outside of the camp. The Bjornmen's dark leathers worked well in the night and even Klöss struggled to make them out as he worked his way past the sentries. He spotted a form that could only have been Tristan looming out of the dark and headed that way.

"How did we do?" he asked, softly.

"It's too dark for counting, but I think close to a thousand," Tristan rumbled. "Your messenger included."

"Messenger?"

"He means me," Gavin supplied, emerging from behind Tristan.

"What are you doing here?" Klöss asked.

"I wouldn't be if I had more sense, but I owe your friend here a debt." Gavin shrugged.

"You know what a reaping is?"

"Not the finer details, but it's pretty obvious it's a night attack."

"It's more than just a night attack, boy," Klöss explained. "You're on your own in this. We don't work in units and you don't owe anything to the men with you. Your only job is to get into the enemy camp and kill as many of them as you can. If you can get out alive, that's always a plus."

Gavin nodded slowly. "I understand."

Klöss gave him an appraising look and then shrugged. "It's your life. At least for now, anyway." He looked at Tristan. "Are they ready?"

Tristan nodded.

"Then let's move them out."

They jogged slowly, quiet despite their numbers. None carried shields or more than a single weapon, taking nothing with them that could make a noise and give them away.

The reaping expanded behind Klöss and Tristan as they ran, spreading over the grass like ink spilled from a bottle. Gavin just managed to keep pace with the pair. The men spread out, none any closer than ten feet from the next, moving further apart as they travelled.

The only sound the first sentry made was a gurgling moan and, by the time the third guard had screamed his last, the reaping was well within the camp. Gavin pulled his knife as he ran, keeping low and following Tristan and Klöss. The two men seemed intent on killing themselves, as they charged headlong into the enemy camp.

The attack was so uncoordinated as to be a stroke of genius. There were no units, no formations and no plan more complicated than causing damage. The men simply moved as fast as possible. No time was wasted delivering a killing blow when a serious injury could be delivered instead. Dead men can be left behind, but the injured slow and hamper a force.

Gavin darted around the back of a tent and leapt over the guy ropes in an effort to keep Tristan in sight. The sounds of steel on steel were ringing louder than any alarm could have but, from what Gavin could see, the response was more confused than anything else.

There were no attacking units for them to face, Gavin realised. Instead, a thousand tiny fights began and ended every few moments.

A man emerged from between two tents, holding his sword ready. Gavin ducked smoothly under the swing of his blow and moved up behind his attacker, dragging his knife across the man's throat and moving on. He was ten feet away by the time the body hit the ground.

He caught up with Tristan easily. The man had stuck doggedly to Klöss, fighting when he had to, but clearly acting as a guard. Klöss, on the other hand, was like a fell wind, dealing death and injury to anything that came within his reach. He left a swathe of dead and groaning behind him, moving through the enemy camp in a wide arc which would eventually bring them back out to the front line.

It was the horn that first alerted Gavin. It seemed out of place. The Anlan army used brass instruments - trumpets and cornets. This was a hunting horn. As it sounded, its note was joined by others. He whipped his head round at the noise and his eyes widened.

The skies to the west were filled with a roiling cloud bank that rushed towards them in the moonlight. It seemed almost as if the horns were sounding from within it. Men around him froze and turned as, for the moment at least, the fight was forgotten. The cloud had a strange greenish cast to it, with flashes that could have been lightning appearing from beneath its churning surface. As the horn sounded again, the cloud erupted and a mass of creatures emerged, charging down out of the skies and into the ranks of the army. Tall figures riding on horses as pale as any ghost.

Smaller figures moved through the skies, running alongside the horses, and the crash as they descended into the Anlan ranks was thunderous. Gavin moved to Klöss's side as the reaping was forgotten. Arrows flew up to meet the charge and blue fire lit the skies as they struck the creatures.

Klöss watched the creatures' descent with an unreadable expression on his face. He glanced at Tristan as the man muttered something, then gave him a curt nod before looking at Gavin as if he'd only just noticed he was there.

"This seems like a good time to get out of here."

Gavin wasn't about to argue. Tristan gave three long blasts on his horn and they ran. If the camp had been in uproar during their attack, it was in chaos now. They sped to the front line almost unimpeded, ducking around men they would have chosen to fight before. It was only as they raced back towards their own camp that it became apparent the creatures were attacking the Islander army as well.

Gavin grabbed at Klöss's arm and stopped for a second.

"Klöss, those things that are attacking..."

"Not now." His face was hard and impatient.

Gavin grabbed at him again, ignoring the man's furious look. "That's what took, Ylsriss," he said. Klöss's anger fled in the face of the shock and horror that followed.

CHAPTER TWENTY

Devin looked back, checking the packhorses that were tethered to his saddle. They were fine, which was more than could be said for the rider in front of him. The old man was swaying back and forth on the horse. They'd been on the road for weeks and Devin had quickly learned that Obair pushed himself. He wouldn't stop to take a break himself and he resisted resting the horses.

"Obair!" He stifled a laugh as the man jumped and nearly fell out of the saddle. Obair turned as Devin's horse drew level and glowered at him from under his hat, a wide-brimmed affair that seemed to use up all of its shape in maintaining the brim before giving up on the rest.

"Was that entirely necessary, Devin?" the old man asked, testily.

Devin grinned. "You were asleep again."

"I was no such thing!" Obair retorted, the very picture of righteous indignation.

"Obair," Devin sighed, suddenly not having the energy for this, "do we really need to go through this again? You ride poorly enough as it is. You can't afford to fall asleep. You'll fall off and you'll probably hurt your horse. Let's stop for a bit. The horses need a break, anyway."

"We can't afford to stop, Devin," Obair snapped, "as well you know."

"It'll take a damn sight longer to get there if the horses go lame, old man," Devin shot back, his temper finally gone.

Obair glared at him and drew in a breath to retort, before blowing it out in an explosive sigh. "You're right again," he said. "I'm sorry I snapped at you."

"I'll tell you what," Devin said, "we'll walk the horses for a few miles instead. If you can stay awake, that is?"

Obair gave him a wry smile as he clambered down from the horse. "I expect I'll manage." He glanced at the young man and raised an eyebrow. "Still?" he asked, tapping at his temple.

"Still." Devin nodded. The headache had changed over the weeks, dulled. The pain was still there but he'd found he could almost ignore it. There was a sensation hidden within it though, a whisper drowned out by the thunderclap, and he found he was pushing the headache to one side as he searched for the feeling that lurked just on the edges of his perception. It still came and went, only ever-present between new and full moons, following the cycle so important to the fae.

He surveyed the land around them. The trees that climbed out of the valleys and into the hills were mostly pines. It seemed a lonely landscape, harsh and unwelcoming.

"How long were you alone?" he asked, the question coming before he really had time to think about how personal it was.

Obair looked faintly offended for a moment. "Probably the best part of thirty years, Devin."

Devin blinked. The notion of spending the better part of a lifetime alone was alien to him, something his mind shied away from. "How did you cope?"

"Badly." Obair chuckled but then fell silent, seeing Devin's confused expression. "I lost myself in a routine. That helped a bit. The days sort of fell into a pattern. A bit like the ritual itself, you know? I'd start each day with the ritual anyway, then there were the animals and the crops to tend. It's easy enough to distract yourself, provided you can keep busy."

Devin was silent. The man's entire life had been a sacrifice of one form or another. It made it hard to talk to him.

They walked for an hour, stopping briefly to water the horses at a stream that cut close to the road.

"How far do you think we have left to go?" he asked that night as he watched the old man coax the fire into life.

"I'm not entirely sure," Obair admitted. "I can't judge distances using this map, so I'm mostly going by memory."

"You are sure you know where we're going?" Devin asked. He couldn't entirely hide the accusation in his voice and Obair's face made it clear that he'd found it despite his efforts.

"Yes, I am quite sure, thank you."

Devin looked away, feeling the heat in his cheeks. He knelt and set to work spitting the two pheasants he'd brought down earlier.

"There's something I've been meaning to ask you," he said, not looking up from the birds as he worked.

"Go ahead. As long as it doesn't involve any more insults about my memory or sense of direction."

"That night in the glade, when the fae came through, I think saw my mother." He spoke in hushed tones, as if the words were too raw to survive if spoken with any volume. "I saw the fae that took her too. She looked right at me. She spoke to me."

"What did she say?" Obair interrupted, his curiosity peaked.

"Just a single sentence. She said 'Fie, fly, flee, little manling'. It was similar to something she'd said to me years before. Before she took my mother." He coughed and swallowed down a mouthful of water from the skin.

"That's not important right now, anyway," he continued. "What I was going to ask you was how she'd grown so old? My mother, I mean. She was taken when I was a small child but she looked ancient. She looked older than you."

"Thanks," Obair said, dryly. "You're sure it was her? Not just someone that looked like her?"

"No," Devin met his gaze and held it. "No, it was her. I know it."

Obair nodded. "And how old would you have said she was when she was taken?"

"I don't know for sure," Devin shrugged. "Does any child that young know how old their mother is?"

He looked into the fire for a moment before he spoke again and, when he did, his words sounded like a confession. "I was very young and now I think that there has been a lot that I've kept buried inside, locked away in my head, until just recently. It was that night, when I saw her and the fae, that I think brought it all out again. I keep remembering things I didn't know I'd forgotten."

He shook his head and then looked around at the old man. "I suppose she must have been about thirty or so? Does that sound about right?"

Obair ignored the question. "And you say she looked older when you saw her?"

"She looked ancient, Obair. Older than anyone I've ever seen!" He set the pheasants to cook, close to the edge of the fire.

"I don't know, Devin. There's so much we don't know about the fae and their world," the old man confessed. "Are you going to put the kettle on since you're down there?"

Devin gave him a dark look and then filled the kettle with water from a skin before setting it to boil. "There are fairy tales that talk about people going into the lands of the fairies. They live there for years and years, but when they come back out into this world, hardly any time has passed at all."

"Fairy tales, Devin," Obair snorted. "Full of nonsense and foolishness."

Devin looked at him. "Are you actually telling me that there's no chance of a fairy tale holding some truth, Obair? You, of all people?" The old man looked at him and met his eyes for a full five seconds before he started to laugh.

They slept in watches, as they had done since the first night they were really alone. Devin had woken to find Obair huddled beside the fire, staring into the darkness. He'd been genuinely terrified, convinced that fae were going to charge screaming out of the night. He would only sleep through the night if it were between the new moon and full moon.

Devin sat with his bow in his lap, an iron-tipped arrow nocked but held loosely in one hand. He glanced over at the old man. For all his worries, the druid had no problems sleeping once he knew Devin was on watch, and the soft sounds of his breathing brought a smile to Devin's lips.

He looked up at the stars. His mother was out there somewhere. Did it work like that? Was the world of the fae under these same stars? Was she somewhere else? Or was she lying down in the night somewhere in the same world as he? He had a moment's guilt as he thought of Hannah and the way he'd left her at the duchess's palace.

He became aware of the noise slowly. It was so faint to begin with that he mistook it for his own breathing or a snatch of birdsong. It grew louder by degrees until at last he could place it. It was the distant sound of flutes. The rage came upon him so quickly, he was shocked by it. He could taste it, a bitter iron flavour, like blood upon his tongue.

He glanced back at Obair and snatched up the quiver full of iron-heads and the short spears as he stood. The leaves made no noise as he passed out over the iron scraps that lay strewn over the ground, encircling the camp as a final layer of defence, should they need it. With a last look at the old man, who was still sleeping in the dim glow from the coals, he disappeared into the night.

The darkness beyond the campfire was almost absolute and it took a while for Devin's eyes to adjust enough for him to be able to move with any speed. The music called him on and he felt chills as he remembered another night, when another person was called onward by the flutes.

Devin slowed and took deep, nearly silent, breaths. His heart was hammering in his ears and that would make for lousy marksmanship when he needed it to be perfect. The music was closer now. He pulled himself tight against a fir tree as the first glow of the coloured lights filtered through the trees.

He edged in towards the sound, travelling from tree to tree until he spied them. The five satyrs laughed as they danced, chattering away in a language that sounded more like music than words. Glowing balls of light floated in the air above them as they went, painting the woods in bright shades of red, violet and emerald.

Anyone with any sense would just lie silent until they'd moved on, he told himself. Anyone with any sense wouldn't be setting their arrows into the ground in front of them for greater speed. His anger was burning inside him so fiercely, he felt he might scream with pure rage. These *things*, these monsters from another world, had torn his family apart. They would pay. It didn't matter to him that the satyrs passing in front of him might have had nothing to do with Widdengate or with what had happened to Hannah and Khorin. All that mattered was that they were within range.

His first arrow flew true and he already had the second nocked, the string of the bow pulled back to touch his lips, as the night exploded with blue fire and screams. He let it fly and it took another satyr in the throat. He took his time aiming with the third, trusting to the hope that they couldn't see him in the darkness. They had turned towards him, following the path of the arrows' flight, and he glimpsed glowing eyes darting here and there as they searched for a sign of movement. Then they saw him and came charging through the trees. He fired, taking the closest beast in the thigh and dropping it to the ground. The blue fire flared, spreading through the satyr's body as if it were dry grass, as the creature screamed and writhed in the embrace of the flames.

They were close now, tearing through the bushes and trees, knives held ready. Close enough for him to hear the panting of their breath, as they bared their teeth in feral grimaces of hate and charged at him. He fired his fourth arrow when the first satyr was barely ten feet from him, and the creature fell to its knees.

The final satyr hurled itself into the air, reaching out with its knives as it flew towards him. Devin didn't hesitate. He grasped the two iron-tipped spears from the ground by his feet and drove them before him, stepping into the thrust, and then the world exploded into blue fire.

It might have been moments or hours later when he came to. He had nothing to judge the time by. It was still as dark as it had been though, so he reasoned that must mean something. He pulled himself to his feet and ran probing fingers over his body, feeling for pain or cuts. His skin felt sensitive where it was uncovered, but other than that he seemed unhurt. A grim smile crept onto his lips as he felt around for his bow and the remaining arrows. The spears were ruined, charred and useless.

The walk back to camp took longer than he expected. The calm he'd maintained throughout the fight left his body, seeping away until he shook with shock at his own actions. Five satyrs. Should he be proud of himself or appalled at his own stupidity?

He was still pondering that question as he made his way out of the undergrowth and back into camp. Obair was still snoring. Devin stepped back into the circle of scattered iron with genuine relief. Sleep would not come, though, and he lay staring into the night sky, as the stars slowly paled and were swallowed up by the approaching dawn.

* * *

The hills grew steeper with each passing day, and both the horses and the two of them were showing signs of wear. Devin knew how to care for a horse, but there were limits to what he could do while they were still on the road.

He felt an almost palpable sense of relief when Obair led them in a new direction, following the line of a dense wood.

"It's funny how you remember things," the old druid mused, glancing back over one shoulder at a black rock with a line of white quartz running through it.

"What?" Devin turned his eyes from the path to look at him.

"Well, you worry you've been going the wrong way for days and then you spot something you didn't even realise you remembered. That rock back there. I asked my master about it all those years ago. I remember the conversation as clear as day, but I haven't thought about it in years." He broke off with a chuckle, then noticed Devin's expression. "What?"

"You haven't been sure we've been going the right way for days?" Devin asked in tight, controlled tones.

"Well, you know how it is. You second-guess yourself," Obair said, weakly. Devin muttered darkly to himself as he clenched his eyes shut and shook his head.

"It worked out. That rock shows we were going the right way the whole time!" Obair protested.

Devin nudged his horse past him, ignoring the old man as he called after him.

The path wasn't even a trail, just a direction that Obair had steered them in. They trudged along at the edge of the steep hillside. It was little more than an exposed scree really, with the occasional tuft of grass or stubby bush poking out from between the stones.

The ground ahead of them sank down, as they skirted the trees, some of which came all the way up to meet the scree face. Eventually, they spotted something glinting in the sunlight. "Water!" Devin cried.

Obair nudged his horse faster, clinging to the saddle as he bounced around, and they rushed to the lake. They climbed off the horses at the edge of the water and let the animals drink their fill. The lake was large, so far across that the far bank was a just distant haze. Swifts darted in the air above the water, as they hunted the insects that flew in the late afternoon light. The place had a remote quality to it. According to the map, it was less than a week's journey from the nearest village, but it might as well have been on the other side of the world.

Devin watched Obair for a moment. He was leaning against his horse, a faraway look in his eyes, as if he was staring through the veils of a memory. His face was pinched, almost pained, and Devin wondered again at the life he must have led. Had he ever truly known happiness?

"Do you recognise it?" he asked, in a hushed voice. The sense of peace was overwhelming and he was hesitant to shatter it.

"Oh, yes." Obair gave him a small smile. "It hasn't changed all that much. We need to skirt around to the east. If I remember rightly, the cottage is about four or five miles away."

Devin refrained from making any of the numerous comments that sprang to mind about Obair's sense of direction and memory. He had led them here after all, despite keeping his fears of going the wrong way secret.

The trek around the lake was pleasant. The ground was level and even, and they opted to walk rather than ride, so that they could give the horses a break. They spoke little, however. Obair drifted out of the conversation and into a silent reverie twice, so Devin gave up.

He couldn't see the cottage when Obair stopped, but the druid's hissed intake of breath was signal enough. Devin followed Obair's gaze and ran his eyes over the bushes and trees. "What is it?" he asked, giving up his search. "Do you see it?"

Obair nodded and pointed in silence. It still took Devin a moment to make it out. The cottage was built against a massive oak tree, with the trunk forming part of the structure. Like Obair's cottage, it had a tumbledown air to it, and the timbers were covered with ivy and moss. The shadows created by the oak broke up the image and the windows were hard to pick out unless he focused.

It was quiet though, too quiet. Devin slipped his bow off his back and set an arrow to the string as they approached, earning a look from Obair but no objections.

"Hello?" Obair called out, as they approached. His voice was too loud in the silence and birds flew up from the trees, disturbed by his shout.

The body lay in the long grass, one outstretched hand jutting up from the ground like a twisted, broken stick. Gnawed, sun-bleached bones wrapped in the shredded remnants of clothes were all that really remained. Devin froze as he saw it, and Obair muttered something long and hushed in a pained whisper.

The druid raced towards the body and knelt over it in silence. His moan, when it came, was low and terrible, the agonised wail of a man who had trapped his feelings deep down within himself. They tore free of their prison, rising within his body and growing in strength, until a cry burst from his lips and banished the peace of the lake, its echoes forming a harmony of anguish as they carried through the trees.

Obair clutched the bones to his chest. They were held together by scraps of grey fabric, tiny remnants of hair and leather-like tatters of flesh. Devin turned away, unable to watch any longer, and made his way towards the cottage.

The door was closed tight and the structure seemed sound. He ran a hand over the ivy and moss that covered the walls, noting odd lumps in the surface. Picking at the moss, he revealed short stubs of iron that had been embedded in the wooden beams of the cottage and jutted out to ward away those that sought to enter.

He gave the door an experimental push but it was stuck fast, warped by rain and neglect.

"Give it a shove," Obair said. The man stood a few steps behind him, his face an emotionless mask.

Devin shoved it hard, but it only moved an inch or so before sticking again. He had to pound his shoulder into it to make it give. The interior of the cottage was dark, the windows too filthy to let much light in. Devin wiped at the glass with a cuff and the light that shone in revealed a much larger space than he was expecting. A small kitchen led into a large living area where a long desk, surrounded by bookshelves, was tucked away in a corner. A low doorway led into a dark room which Devin assumed must be sleeping quarters. He moved aside to let Obair pass him and stepped back outside into the daylight. There were small outbuildings set back behind the house in a little clearing that had been stolen from the woods, and he could make out a small barn, as well as a patch of ground which, at some point, had obviously been a vegetable plot.

A well-worn path led off into the trees and, on a whim, he followed it. Obair needed some time alone and Devin needed to be away from the pain etched on his face.

The path led to another clearing and, as he stopped at the end of it, beside an old wooden bench, he wondered what else he had been expecting. A ragged circle of stones surrounded three larger stone blocks with one laying atop the two uprights to form an arch of sorts, or a doorway.

Devin found Obair at the desk, a small book in front of him. He glanced up as the young man came in. "A diary," he said, waving the book in the air. "Her handwriting is awful, but it might tell us something."

Devin nodded. "What do we do now, though? I mean, we came hoping to find someone. Do we head back?"

Obair shook his head. "I don't think so. At least, not yet. There are a lot of books here. Who knows what they might tell us. I'll need at least a week to go through them and see if there's anything of any use there."

"There's a stone circle around the back, like the one in your glade," Devin said. "Are we going to be safe here, though? I mean, you said the Wild Hunt comes from your circle. Will something else come out of this one?"

"That's a good point," Obair said, glancing at the rear wall of the cottage. "Maybe the books will give us some answers. The cottage is studded with iron. If we clear off the moss and ivy, that should be protection enough, should we need it."

"There were an awful lot of ifs and shoulds in there, Obair," Devin noted.

Obair spread his hands. "I have nothing else to offer you, Devin. You know as much as I do at this point."

Devin sat down in a plain wooden chair. "So what do I do? You're going to have your nose in a book for a week. What should I be doing?"

"You could always help me," Obair suggested. "Or we could try something," he added, as he saw the look on Devin's face. It might come to nothing, but it can't hurt to try."

Devin gave him a confused frown. "What are you talking about?"

"Show me these stones. It will make much more sense there, anyway."

* * *

"No, not like that." Obair stopped him. "Your left leg has to sweep the ground there. It's not just a step. Watch." He performed the sequence again, slower this time. He took a slow, measured step to the right and then brought his left leg around in a long sweeping arc.

Devin sighed. "I'm not going to get this, Obair."

"Of course you are!" Obair laughed. "You're much farther along than I was on my first session. We've got three sequences down already. I didn't even get past the first one."

"Really?" Devin perked up a bit at that, but then a thought occurred to him. "Three out of how many?"

"That's not important. It's enough that you realise you really are doing very well."

"How many, Obair?" Devin demanded.

"A hundred and forty two," Obair admitted, in a small voice. "Look, just keep practising this one. I'll come and check on you in an hour or two."

Devin gave him a defeated look. "Can't I at least do it by the cottage? This place gives me the creeps."

Obair looked around, as if seeing the stones for the first time. "Really? I find it rather peaceful. And no, you need to get the sequences in the correct placement and you can't do that without the stones. It's as much about doing the sequence in the correct position as it is getting the movements right."

Devin sighed and moved back to the starting position. Obair watched in silence as the young man began again, moving slower than necessary, concentrating on his movements. He smiled to himself and then set off back down the path to the cottage.

It felt odd to sit in Lillith's chair. No, it was worse than odd. It felt like a violation and reading her diary did not make the feeling any less.

The book was more than frustrating. It had the look of a journal but it didn't appear to have been used as such. Or rather, it had been, but not in the normal sense. Lillith hadn't written a daily record of events; instead, she'd just jotted down random thoughts. At some point, she must have run out of pages and had gone back through the book, using up any spare space. The result was a tangled web of thoughts, scrawled in a cramped, untidy hand. She used a shortened form of writing that probably made perfect sense to her, but it was taking him time to tease any meaning from it.

He sighed and leant back in the chair, angling the book to catch the light from the windows.

"It remains to be seen," Lillith had written, "if the guardian can maintain the barrier with the increased pressure. Anastasia has proven to be an apt pupil, but I am loathe to divulge the vile truth of our burden too soon. She is so young. Was I ever that young? Of course I was, yet sometimes it seems as if it all happened to someone else. I am fighting the urge to send a bird to the guardian again. Anastasia is a diversion to me and her training occupies both of our minds, but she is poor company. It is hard to accept anyone else in my space after all this time. The girl questions too deeply, argues too often and trusts too much that what we do is for the good of all. If she only knew."

He set the book down and stared up at the ceiling. There were so many questions. Who was this guardian the book mentioned? Worse still, what was this mention of a burden and why would she have considered it to be evil? Obair sighed and made his way outside. They hadn't really unpacked; they'd just unloaded the packhorses next to the cottage. He rummaged around in the bags until he located the kettle and filled it from the skin. At least, with the lake close to hand, lack of water wouldn't be an issue.

Lillith's stove was covered in dust and cobwebs, but clean enough to light. He set about making the tea, his mind working as his body went through the mechanics automatically.

The books were unlikely to be of much help. He'd had a quick skim through them. They covered an eclectic range of topics, including everything from herbalism and the medical arts through to wildfowl and their migratory patterns. There was little of any use, or interest.

He left the kettle to boil and picked up the diary again, flicking through random pages.

"She is becoming a worry. Though she knows nothing of the secret, she is concerned at the burden that maintaining the Wyrde places on the guardian. More than once, she has asked why it is that we do not shoulder some of the burden ourselves. How can I explain that whilst the guardian maintains the Wyrde by keeping the source trapped and confined within, we maintain the barrier itself? The truth would horrify her. It still horrifies me."

The kettle was boiling, but he sat there ignoring it as steam belched out of the spout and the kettle itself jumped and shook from the water bubbling way inside. The book hinted at things he didn't understand. What did it mean confining the source? A sense of dread was coming over him though he couldn't say why. Frustrated he tossed the book down and stood to make the tea.

* * *

Devin slipped again and swore as he crashed to the dirt. He'd almost had it then. There was a rhythm to it, something he'd felt the edges of the last few times, but not quite managed to grasp.

He hauled himself up and pulled the iron staff upright. It ought to provide more support. If he had to move around in these ridiculous patterns, it really would make more sense to use the staff to lean on. More often than not though, he had to hold it on the wrong side of him, making him even more off balance as he strove to keep its weight off the ground. Tapping here and marking out a complex shape there, it was like using a oversized pen, in many ways.

The grass was becoming worn. "Stop falling into it then," he told himself. His laugh was too loud in the silence and he stopped himself quickly. The stones gave the clearing an uncomfortable feel. He'd always been at home in the woods and here, surrounded by trees, he ought to be at ease. He wasn't though. He felt tense, almost as if he was being watched, though it wasn't quite the same sensation.

A look at the sky told him it wasn't past noon-hour yet. Obair hadn't come as he'd said he would, but then Devin hadn't really expected him to.

"One more try and then it's time to see what there is to find in these woods," he muttered to himself, thinking of his bow and the simple pleasure of tracking a deer.

The starting position to the ritual was easy enough and he flowed easily through the first sequence. Obair had mentioned that, at some point, he'd need to do the movements in his mind at the same time, forming images that mirrored the steps of the ritual, creating channels and forcing the sensation of the headaches to flow through them.

Devin tried to picture the movements as he made them. It was easier with his eyes closed, though he had to slow himself to keep his balance. *How odd that balance depends so much on being able to see.* He caught himself as he felt his mind wandering and bore down harder, concentrating.

There was something there. He could feel the edges of it, tantalisingly close. He held the image in his mind and fancied he could feel the surge of the force, as it poured through the channels he was trying to hold in his imagination.

There was a pressure building. It didn't seem like it was coming from him though, or even from anything he was doing. It felt more like it was coming from the opposite direction, moving towards him. The feeling grew stronger, taking shape and form, as it crashed into the channels he'd formed in his mind and tore them apart.

His balance fled and he opened his eyes as he tumbled to the grass, clutching at his temples as the pain grew and then the scream exploded out of him.

The air was shaking, or so it seemed. Maybe that was just him. He tried to concentrate on a stone, pulling his eyes back into focus as his vision swam. After long moments he struggled back to his feet and turned to the central stones, pulled by sensations he couldn't understand. The air was shimmering, like the distorted air over a fire. He looked about for his bow before remembering he'd left it at the cottage. The staff! He ran for the iron staff and snatched it up, holding it before him like a shield against any fae that might emerge from the stones.

The air became almost reflective and rippled like water in the breeze. The figure that emerged from the stones and staggered forwards onto the grass was nothing like he would have imagined. It was a young man, his eyes wide with horror as he collapsed to the ground, dropping the blonde-haired woman he'd carried over one shoulder.

Devin stared as he felt his mouth fall open. They were human. At the very least, they certainly weren't fae. He dropped the staff and stepped closer. The man didn't look much older than him. He lay on the grass, curled into a fetal position, shivering so violently it almost looked like he was having a fit. As Devin drew closer, he realised the white coating on the man's clothing was frost. It covered his hair and formed a crust on his exposed skin. These two were no threat. They were barely alive.

"Kris han shellern vere?" the young man gasped, seeing Devin for the first time.

He shook his head. "I don't understand."

The young man smiled then, relief flooding his face, and he spoke again. The words were pronounced badly and with an odd accent, but they were undoubtedly Anlish. "Where are we?"

CHAPTER TWENTY-ONE

Obair pushed the rest of the books to one side and picked up the diary again. The wind was blowing through from the open window and he'd propped the door open, but the place still smelled musty. The smell of death, he thought to himself. The smell of a place with nobody moving to stir the air.

"A tomb," he whispered, then shuddered at the thought. He pushed himself away from the desk, scraping the chair over the wooden floor, and walked over to the doorway. The sun was still low over the lake and the birdsong carried on the breeze.

He was glad of the quiet. He'd sent Devin off to practise the ritual, more for a chance to have some peace so he could read than for anything else. The lad...no, that was wrong...he wasn't really a lad any longer. Young man might have been more accurate, but Devin wasn't really that, either. He'd been aged by events, by the things that had happened to him. In many ways, he was older than Obair himself.

The young man had a talent for the ritual, that much was clear. He was picking up sequences and movements far faster than Obair ever had. He'd even grasped the concept of making the movements in his mind at the same time as making the physical motions. All of this, however, was overshadowed by the question that niggled at Obair constantly. If the Wyrde was gone, and he'd felt it fail himself, then what it that Devin was feeling? It was the Wyrde itself that should be allowing him to feel the changes in the phase of the moon. If it wasn't there, what Devin was doing ought to be impossible.

He breathed in deeply, enjoying the fresh air outside the cottage. They'd tried to make the place habitable, sweeping out the worst of the leaves that had been blown in. The door must have been left open and then blown shut at some point.

There were still layers of dust in places and the spiders' webs in the highest corners were as thick as spun wool, but it would do for now.

Food wouldn't be an issue in the short-term, either. The forest was likely to be full of animals that Devin could hunt and, although the vegetable plot at the back of the cottage was overgrown with weeds, some plants still grew there. Coupled with their remaining supplies and the dried goods in the kitchen, they would be fine.

The wind caressed the grass, tossing the tattered ends of the clothes on Lillith's remains about. He'd told Devin not to move them, that they should rest where they lay. Now he regretted it.

He tapped the book against his lips, stopping in surprise. He hadn't even realised he'd brought it with him. "Why did you have to be so bloody awkward, Lillith," he muttered, as he turned the pages. The entries had no uniformity. Some were neat and concise, while others were scrawled. Some were even written at a different angle to the rest of the text. He stopped at random on a page near the front.

"I can no longer bear to write to the guardian. His task horrifies me. The very fact that he is ignorant of what it is he does makes it worse."

Again, these hints. He tried to force himself not to dwell on it. The diary was completely full, so perhaps...? He moved over to the shelves as the thought struck him and pulled a handful of books off them. He flicked through the pages of each one and then pushed it aside. The books all had notes in the margins but they were related to the text. Finally, he found what he sought.

"The girl was never suited to her task and I should have sent her away long before now. Now she has learned too much and I am forced to choose between continuing to train someone who I cannot trust with the task, or releasing a girl who knows enough to risk all."

The next page contained only the text of the book. Obair flicked through the rest of the pages, cursing under his breath, but there was nothing more to be found.

He snatched up another book and scanned the pages, tossing it onto the desk when he found only the main text. Another five followed in its wake before he found something.

"I have been a fool. I saw only what I wanted, a girl able to accept the truth and carry on my work. Instead, she was a coward, pressed into service and sullen for all these years. How have I not seen it before now?

It matters little, I suppose. I tested her and she has failed. The secret, that vile knowledge that I have kept inside myself all these long years, has been told. It is no wonder she fled. There is a part of me that envies her. The Wyrde is weakening. Obair, in his distant glade, works his ritual as well as he ever has. I can feel the source is secure, yet the Wyrde weakens. When I work the ritual, I can feel that it does not have the power it once had. Things are slipping through.

I curse those who thought this would ever work. It makes a horrible sense to keep the guardian ignorant of the soul he keeps trapped by his working of the ritual. The power of this soul is all that allows me to maintain the Wyrde itself. Yet, in forcing the keepers to pass down this knowledge, they have placed the burden on us. I do not blame Anastasia for running into the night, I envy her. I wish I had done the same all those years ago.

She is gone, fled into the moonlight. Stupid girl, has she never listened to me speak of the things that can pass through between the full and new moons? I must find her."

Obair forced himself to read the last sentence again, the book shaking in his trembling hands as the realisation of what the words meant struck him. and his words were coated in guilt as he rasped, "Stars above, what have I done?"

* * *

Devin yanked the door open, ignoring the crash it made as it slammed back against the wall.

"Obair, help!" he shouted, as he struggled to support the man with one arm while trying not to drop the blonde woman he had thrown over his shoulder.

Obair rushed to the doorway, reaching out to take the man's arm and ducking his head under it, so he could walk him to a chair, while Devin carried the woman through to the bedroom.

"What's going on? Who are these people?" he demanded, calling through the doorway.

Devin ignored him, covering the woman in the blankets as best he could. She hadn't moved once. If it wasn't for her shallow breathing, she could have been a corpse.

Obair knelt down beside the woodstove, slicing up a log with his knife and feeding the small slivers of wood into the fire. He looked up as Devin came back in. "Grab the other blanket for this fellow. He looks like he's frozen solid."

It was true. The man was slumped in the chair, his face an unhealthy blue colour and his eyes glassy.

"Who are they?" Obair asked, as Devin wrapped the blanket around the young man.

"I have no idea," Devin replied. "They came out of the stones."

Obair gaped at him, his jaw working but producing no noises that came close to a word. "They what?" he finally managed.

"They came out of something between the standing stones. It looked like they were passing through a doorway," Devin said, as he studied the stranger. He didn't look much older than he was himself. His dark hair still had chunks of white in it, where the larger bits of frost had merged together to form ice.

"What does this mean?" he asked, looking at Obair. The old man was staring at the semi-conscious figure in shock.

"I don't know but, for some reason, it gives me hope." The druid glanced into the kitchen. "Put some water on to boil. We've got to warm this one up."

They both turned as the man hissed something between lips tinged cobalt from cold.

Obair leaned closer. "Try again?"

"Safe?" the man whispered.

"Yes, you're safe here," Obair muttered, as he raised an eyebrow at Devin.

They watched the stranger in silence as they waited for the kettle to boil, then helped him to take a few sips of tea. As he warmed up, the shivers began and, before long, he was shaking so hard that if both of them hadn't held onto him, he'd have fallen out of the wooden chair.

"We'll get nothing from this one for now, Devin," Obair decided, shaking his head. "Let's get him into bed. We can try again once he's warmed up a little."

He stood at the stove, watching as Devin placed the man's arm around his shoulder and walked him into the bedroom.

"Tell me again," Obair said, sipping at the cup in his hands, when Devin came back.

Devin looked over to the small doorway that led into the bedroom. "I was working the ritual. You know, the sequences you taught me?"

Obair nodded in silence.

"I'd been doing it for a while. I was getting ready to give up, to be honest." Devin started to laugh but Obair's expression stifled it.

He cleared his throat. "Anyway, I started to feel something. It was faint but still there. It was like a surge to begin with. I'd tried to imagine the path of the sequences, drawing the movements in my head and sort of pushing the sensations of the headache through it." He stopped and looked up at the old man. "Does that make sense? This is hard to describe."

Obair nodded and waved his hand in a circle impatiently, motioning for him to continue.

"Well, I felt a sensation, like I was right on the edges of something, but then it all shifted. It wasn't so much that the force was coming from me but more that it was flowing into me, like someone was pushing it inwards. I felt a blinding pain and I remember seeing something weird in the air between the central stones. Then he stepped through and fell onto the grass."

"Did he say anything to you?" Obair pressed.

"He started to but it was in a different language. I couldn't understand him. When I told him that, he sort of smiled and then spoke in Anlish."

"What did he say?" Obair quizzed.

"He asked where he was," Devin said. "What does this mean, Obair? How did they even come through the stones? I thought they were fae to start with!"

"I don't know. I didn't think that was possible. Did they come from where the fae are? Did they come from somewhere else? I don't have any answers, my boy, I'm afraid. We'll have to wait for them to wake up before we get anything from them."

Devin sighed and looked at the books that were strewn across the desk. "How about these? Have you found anything of use?"

Obair's eyes flickered to a small book at the edge of the desk before he looked back at him. "Not really. There's a lot of it to go through. Nothing so far." His words were flat, but his eyes were haunted.

* * *

Obair raised an eyebrow as the young man made his way into the main room of the cottage. "I didn't expect to see you up so soon," he said, with a smile.

"I probably shouldn't be," he replied. His face was still drawn and he leaned heavily on the wall as he made his way to an empty chair.

"Well, I expect you might feel better with some food inside you. We haven't much, but you're welcome to some porridge, if you'd like some?" He motioned to Devin, who spooned some out into a wooden bowl in response to the man's small nod.

"I expect you have quite the tale to tell. Do you feel up to answering some questions? Your name is probably a good way to start."

The man nodded as he ate a small mouthful. "My name is Joran," he managed around the porridge.

"Joran," the druid said, testing out the word. "I'm Obair. Now, my young friend here, Devin, says that he saw you two come out from the stones. I've only ever seen fae and satyrs do that. How did you manage it?"

"We escaped," Joran said. "We were both held in the slave camps near the fae city of Tir Rhu'thin. When we escaped, we stumbled upon the ruins of a human city. There were glyphs there that Ylsriss was able to use to get us home."

Obair's eyes widened. "This might be faster if I just ask you some questions, rather than interrupting you every two minutes."

Joran smiled and nodded, taking another mouthful of porridge.

"Ylsriss? That's the name of the woman you're with?" Obair waited for the nod. "So, you escaped? Am I right in thinking you were in the world of the fae?"

"They call it the Realm of Twilight, but yes."

"And there are other humans there?"

"Hundreds, maybe thousands. More arrive every day. I never saw all of the camps and there are many more in the breeding pens."

"Breeding pens?" Devin burst out.

Obair held a hand up quickly to stop Joran's response. "No, wait. Let me ask things in order or it'll just get confused. Tell us about the other humans there," Obair asked, after a moment.

"Most are taken there as young children, some still as babies. I think the idea is that they grow up in the Realm of Twilight and never know any other life. If you don't know that there is anywhere else, why would you try to escape? Even those that weren't captured as children accept their lot, though. There's something about the fae that makes humans compliant and docile if they stay with them for too long. Ylsriss calls it the Touch," Joran shrugged. "It's as good a name as any."

Obair opened his mouth to speak and then stopped, frowning. "Hold on a moment. You said children grow up there? How long were you there?"

"I don't know for certain," Joran explained. "It's hard to tell the time, the days work differently. The sun isn't in the sky for long. I was probably about nine or ten when I was taken and I think I'm seventeen now. No older than nineteen, anyway."

"You don't know?" Devin asked, his face twisted in disbelief.

"You don't understand. I was under the Touch for a long time. Nothing matters to you when you're like that. Not the passage of time, not hunger. All you live for is to please the fae." He fell silent, staring into the empty bowl in front of him.

"I'm sorry," Devin said, in a soft voice. "I didn't understand."

Joran snorted. "You still don't. There's no way you could."

They carried on, Obair asking question after question and becoming increasingly disturbed by the answers. They listened as Joran told the tale of the fae realm, their escape and discovery of the human city, and finally the fae that had helped them to find their way out through the stones.

"This is what confuses me the most," Obair confessed, as he sipped at a cup of tea. "Why would she help you?"

"I don't know," Joran shrugged. "We'd grown close, but there was much that Aervern didn't share with me. She did make it clear that she and her kind have nothing to do with those at Tir Rhu'thin though."

"Hold on for a moment, Obair." Devin stopped him. "I think maybe the problem is we're thinking of the fae just as monsters. An evil force intent on killing us all."

"Aren't they?" Obair asked, giving him a look.

"Well, perhaps, but what if they're more. What if, in some ways, we're not that dissimilar?"

"Go on?"

"Well, look at us. Mankind. Our world. We're made up of who knows how many nations and peoples. We don't all want the same things. Who's to say the fae do either?"

"Did she say anything else? Any little thing might be important," Obair pressed.

Joran's face twisted in concentration as he tried to remember. "She did say something. She said that her people hadn't had direct contact with those that had returned yet."

"Those that had returned? Returned from where?" Devin broke in, but fell silent at a look from Obair.

"There's not much more. He's right, though." Joran nodded at Devin. "There's a lot we don't know. She mentioned something about a court. I don't know what that means."

"Factions?" Obair muttered to himself. "What about the woman with you? Will she know more?"

"Not really," Joran shrugged. "I doubt she'll want to talk to me after what I did, anyway."

"What did you do? It sounds like you saved her!" Devin said, before he could stop himself.

"I did, I suppose," Joran said, in a low voice. "At the end, though, she couldn't leave her baby. We'd agreed we would try to search for him, but then there was the city and the satyrs coming at us...I couldn't just leave here there to die, could I?"

"What did you do?"

"I hit her," Joran confessed. "She wasn't thinking straight, so I hit her, then picked her up and carried her. I dragged her through the stones to keep her safe, but I've stolen her baby from her as much as the fae ever did."

* * *

Ylsriss woke to pain. Her entire body ached, as though she'd spent a hard day in the fields. She rolled over in the bed, wrinkling her nose at the stale smell, and her eyes snapped open. This wasn't her bed or even her blanket. Where was she? She pushed herself up, trying to see through the darkness. Someone was breathing softly nearby. She wasn't alone.

"Joran." The word was a whispered curse in the darkness and, as she spoke, it all came back to her. The satyrs, the glyphs at the stone circle, and Joran sweeping her into his arms and carrying her onto the stone plate, as she screamed at him to leave her there.

The memory was bitter, bringing a foul taste to her mouth, and she clenched her fists as she thought of it. She stood, steadying herself on the edge of the bed, and looked towards the source of the breathing, as her eyes gradually adjusted to the darkness. It was him.

For a moment, she just watched him as he lay there, the fury within her growing at the sight of him sleeping in peace, guiltless. Ylsriss threw herself onto his bed, punching him scratching him and screaming at him, all at once. He grunted in pain and then grabbed at her as she punched at him, rolling with her until they crashed down onto the floor.

"Ylsriss!" he yelled, trying to get a word through her screams. "Ylsriss, stop!"

"You *took* me. I told you to leave me, you bastard!" She screeched and clawed at his face.

His hand went to his cheek and he could feel the blood. "Shit…" He reached for her wrists and pinned her to the rough floor. "Ylsriss, just calm do…" He cut off as she slammed her knee up hard, and he crashed sideways to the floor with the high-pitched whimper that only a well-placed kick between the legs can produce.

Lamplight flooded the room as a door opened, and she felt hands on her, pulling her away from him. The fight left her all at once. The anger draining away in a flood, and the void that remained was swiftly filled with the certain knowledge that she'd never see her baby again. She felt her knees give way and the strength left her. As the tears flowed, hot and bitter, she sagged down into the nameless arms that held her.

They led her through into another room and sat her down in a chair. She was vaguely aware that they had helped Joran as well, but she didn't really care about that. The tears wracked her body. It seemed like she was tearing flesh from her own throat with each retching sob.

A hand fell gently on her shoulder and then a man handed her a steaming cup. His face was old. Weary and old, but the sympathy in his eyes was real.

"Ylsriss?" Joran's voice. She didn't want to hear it. He could rot. She sniffed the cup. It was a tea of some kind.

"Ylsriss?" he called again, his voice soft but insistent. She turned her face to him, trying to muster as much hate as she could as she glared at him.

He recoiled from her expression and she felt a tiny spark of satisfaction.

"Ylsriss, I know you don't want to talk to me. It's just you can't speak their language. I just want you to know that you're okay here. We're safe."

She considered hurling the tea into his face, cup and all, but settled for sipping it. The others were babbling away in their language. She couldn't understand a word. It was faster than Islik, all Rs and Ls. She wondered how Joran could pick out enough to make sense of it.

The old man seemed to be questioning Joran intently, leaning forward on his chair. The looks he was giving her made it clear they were talking about her. The other one was a young man, around Joran's age, perhaps, although it was hard to tell. He looked on, speaking occasionally but seeming content to listen, for the most part. He looked at her suddenly, as if feeling her eyes on him. His expression was questioning but friendly enough.

On an impulse, she stood and walked over to the door, stepping out into the night. The sky was cloudy but a few pinpricks of light showed through. Stars, she realised. Stars and moonlight. The night air was cool and she revelled in it. The Realm of Twilight had never really grown cold and it felt wonderful to feel goosebumps rise.

She heard footsteps behind her and turned. The young man held the grimy blanket up, raising an eyebrow to make it a question. She nodded her thanks and let him drape it around her shoulders.

"Devin," he said, pointing at himself.

Was that his name? A request? She pointed at him. "Deh'vin?" The word felt odd, the inflections flat and nasal.

"Devin," he corrected her, with a smile.

"Ylsriss," she said, pointing at herself.

They spent time pointing out simple things and naming them. The sky, the stars, the moon. She knew she wouldn't remember half of the strange words, but it was something to occupy her mind. It felt odd not knowing what time it was. It looked like the middle of the night, but it felt like it should be morning.

Devin broke off as Joran came out to join them.

"What do you want?" she snapped.

"I thought I should fill you in on what I've learned," he said.

Try as she might, she couldn't find fault with that. "Fine," she said. "How do you know their language, anyway?"

"When I was first taken, it was the only language the others spoke in the pens." He shrugged. "It's been a long time, but I remember enough to be able to make myself understood."

Ylsriss nodded. "So?"

"We're in a place called Anlan," Joran explained. "I think it's the place you told me about. The Farmed Lands?"

"Fine." She looked at him with cold despite. "Go away."

He looked like he was going to say more, but then turned away without a word.

Ylsriss lived in a fog for the next couple of days. She ate when food was given to her and slept when it was dark, although it took days for her to become accustomed to the time again. Day still felt like night and, try as she might, she couldn't get to sleep when she should. She felt numb. No, it was more than that. It wasn't that she couldn't feel, it was just that she couldn't bring herself to care.

The others worked to expand the living space in cottage as best they could, making up extra beds in the main room. Devin and Joran hunted, while she tried to resurrect the vegetable plot, picking through the weeds in a half-hearted attempt to rescue the remaining plants.

The old man spent most of his time searching through the books in the cottage. When he wasn't reading, he peppered them both with questions, with Joran translating as best he could.

She sat on the small bench in the clearing that contained the standing stones. It was peaceful there and she felt closer to Effan when she was near the stones. The breeze was just enough to rustle the leaves above her head and she took a strange joy in seeing green, rather than the reds and golds of the Realm of Twilight.

Devin was moving about the clearing, practising the odd ritual he did, when she heard the leaves crunch behind her. She didn't need to look up to know it was Joran.

"What do you want?"

"I thought we should talk," he said, simply. "It's time, Ylsriss. We can't go on like this."

She looked round at him, genuinely confused. "Like what, Joran? This isn't some little fight. You didn't upset me somehow or lose your temper and say something that you regret. You dragged me out of one world and into another. You made it certain that I can never see Effan again."

"You'd have been killed, Ylsriss," Joran retorted. "Surely you must understand that? There was no way you could have made it past the satyrs."

"You had no right!" She bit off the words. Her temper was rising now and the bitter sting of tears pricked at her eyes.

"I couldn't just leave you there to die!" Joran insisted.

"Why not? It was my choice!" Her voice rose and Ylsriss realised she'd stood and was shrieking at him. She rubbed the tears away with the back of one hand and sat back on the bench.

"You know, now I wonder how much of it was about me." Her voice, which had been filled with anger as she screamed at him, was now cold and dispassionate.

"What do you mean?"

"You had no one to come back for," Ylsriss began. She spoke in calm, level tones that cut deeper than her frenzied screaming ever could have. "You have no home to go to, no place in this world where you belong. I doubt you even remember where your family is, if you even have one left. You weren't saving me from the satyrs, Joran, you were saving me for yourself!"

Joran's face turned ashen as he looked down at her. "Ylsriss, you must know that's not true."

"I don't know anything. I would never have believed you'd do something like this. That you'd even be capable of it."

He looked away from her, gazing blankly into the clearing where Devin worked the ritual of the Wyrde, oblivious to their argument.

"Yes, look away, Joran," she spat at him. "I can't stand to meet your eyes. I don't think you have any idea how much I despise the very sight of you!"

"Ylsriss," he said, not turning away from Devin.

"You sicken me. You know that? You say you hate the fae but then you're the first to lie down with one as soon as an opportunity affords itself." She was past hearing him, lost in an orgy of hate and vitriol. "You're as bad as the fae themselves. They creep into our world to steal children to raise for the breeding pens. You stole me and, in doing so, you stole my baby."

"Ylsriss!" he repeated, louder this time.

"What!" she snapped.

"Look at him."

"What?" The request was so outlandish that she couldn't understand the sentence.

"Devin. Look at him!" Joran pointed.

"Stop trying to change the subject. You wanted to talk about this, so let's talk about it." She stood again, clenching her fists by her side. "You can't ask me to forgive this, Joran, this is too huge. You've forced me to abandon my child!"

"Ylsriss, just shut up a second. Look at him!" Joran stepped closer, placed his hands on her face and turned her head towards Devin.

She batted his hands away. "What are you talking about? He's practising. It's like a dance or something. Some ritual that kept the fae away, or something like that."

"Look at the way he moves his feet. Look at the whole picture."

She fell silent. The urgency in Joran's voice had robbed her of her anger and she watched Devin. There was something there, right on the edge of her understanding. The movements he made were clumsy, but the pattern...

"Oh, Lords of Blood, Sea and Sky!" Her hand flew to her mouth as she gasped a breath in through her fingers.

"You see it, don't you?" Joran asked, eyes bright with excitement.

"I see it," she nodded. "Joran, this ritual, the pattern of it..."

"I know." His grin matched the wonder in his eyes.

"Joran, those are glyphs!"

About the Author

Graham began writing with children's books for his own kids. Fantasy is the genre he has always read himself though, and this is why he started The Riven Wyrde Saga, a fantasy series beginning with *Fae - The Wild Hunt*.

Visit his blog at grahamak.blogspot.co.uk where you can sign up for e-mail updates and be the first to hear about new releases.

Find Graham on Facebook at on.fb.me/1pMyWmK.
He loves to chat with readers.

Follow him on Twitter at www.Twitter.com/Grayaustin

Graham can be contacted at
GrahamAustin-King@Hotmail.co.uk or through his website:
www.GrahamAustin-King.com.

Acknowledgements

Once again I owe a debt of gratitude to the team that helped put this book together. Clare Davidson, Anya J Davis and Vin Hill you guys are great. To my wife Gillian and my kids, thanks for putting up with me while my head was in a book (I kind of did it again didn't I?) Finally a big thanks to everyone who bought *Fae – The Wild Hunt* and got in touch, or left a review. Your support is more valuable than you know.

Thank you for taking the time to read *Fae – The Realm of Twilight*. If you enjoyed it, please consider telling your friends or posting a short review. Word of mouth is an author's best friend and much appreciated.
—GRAHAM AUSTIN-KING

Lightning Source UK Ltd.
Milton Keynes UK
UKHW041834080319
338775UK00001B/76/P